WHILE YOU SLEEP

STEPHANIE MERRITT

HarperCollins*Publishers*

HarperCollins*Publishers* Ltd
1 London Bridge Street,
London SE1 9GF

www.harpercollins.co.uk

First published by HarperCollins*Publishers* 2018
1

A catalogue record for this book is available from the British Library

ISBN: 978-0-00-824820-8 (HB)
ISBN: 978-0-00-824821-5 (TPB)

Typeset in Sabon by Palimpsest Book Production Ltd, Falkirk, Stirlingshire

Printed and bound in Great Britain by CPI Group (UK) Ltd, Croydon, CR0 4YY

MIX
Paper from
responsible sources
FSC
www.fsc.org FSC™ C007454

'When those are the very things one is hoping to escape from *through* silence, it is not at all surprising that one starts to see one's longings as "works of the devil" and this sense of the demonic is itself intensified by the silence.'

Sara Maitland, *A Book of Silence*

Prologue

It begins, they say, with a woman screaming.

You can't tell at first if it's pleasure or pain, or that tricky place where the two meet; you're almost embarrassed to hear it, but if you listen closer it comes to sound more like anguish, a lament torn from the heart: like an animal cry of loss, or defiance, or fury, carried across the cove from cliff to cliff on the salt wind.

If you stand on the beach with your back to the sea, they'll tell you, looking up at the McBride house, you might catch, behind tall windows on the first floor, the fleetest shift of a shadow. All the rooms dark through glass; not even the flicker of a candle, only the shape that shivers at that same window and vanishes, quick as breath, under the broken reflections of clouds and moon. They'll say the woman's keening grows louder as the gale seeks unprotected corners of the house, swirls around the pointed gables, shakes the weathervane on the turret and rattles the attic windows in their frames. But listen again; when the wind drops, there is nothing but the wild sea, and the occasional drawn-out moans of the seals beyond the headland.

Only on certain nights, the islanders will tell incomers; when the moon is high and the air whipped up like the white-peaked waves in the bay. Be patient and you might hear her. Plenty will swear to it.

The two boys crouch by a ridge of rocks at the foot of the cliff, watching the house. It is still half a ruin; naked beams poke into the moonlit sky like the ribs of some great flayed beast. They hesitate, each waiting for the other to move. They have come this far to test the old stories, they can't lose face now. The summer night is mild and clear; too balmy for ghosts. They are girding themselves when the screaming starts. They turn to one another in astonishment; fear makes them giggle.

'Let's go,' whispers the nimble, ginger boy. He has his phone in his hand, ready to capture it on film.

But his companion has frozen to the spot, stricken, his eyes stretched wide and fixed on the house.

'Come *on*, we'll miss it.'

The heavier boy retreats a few paces, shaking his head.

The ginger one hesitates, his lip curling with scorn. 'Pussy.'

He sets off over the sand and marram grass to the half-open door, his phone held out at arm's length. Left behind on the beach, his friend watches him disappear into the shadows.

The waves break and retreat, over and over, dragging layers of shingle into the restless water. A new scream echoes across the beach, a child's cry this time. The last traces of light ebb from the sky and behind the windows of the McBride house there is nothing but solid darkness.

1

The island appeared first as an inky smudge on the horizon, beaded with pinholes of light against the greying sky. As the ferry ploughed on, carving its path through the waves, the land took form and seemed to rise out of the sea like the hump of a great creature yet to raise its head. Bright points arranged themselves into clusters, huddled into the bay at the foot of the cliff, though the intermittent sweep of the lighthouse remained separate at the furthest reach of the harbour wall.

The only passenger on the deck leaned out, gripping the rail tighter with both hands, anchored by the smooth grain of the wood beneath her fingers. Doggedly the ferry rose and fell, hurling up a cascade of spray each time it crested a wave and dropped away. Wind whipped her hair into salt strands that stung her lips; she wore a battered flying jacket and pulled up the collar against the damp as she planted her feet, swaying with the motion of the boat, determined to take it all in from here as they docked and not through the smeared window of the passenger lounge downstairs, with its fug of wet coats and stewed tea. Outside, the wind tasted of petrol and brine. She pushed her fringe out of her face and almost laughed in disbelief when the noise of the engines fell away and the men in orange waterproofs began throwing their coils of rope and shouting orders at one another as the boat nosed a furrow through oily water to bump alongside the pier. Two days of travelling and it was almost over. She tried not to think about the old saying that the journey mattered more than the arrival. She tried not to think about what she had left behind, thousands of miles away.

The ferry terminus hardly warranted the name; there was a car park and one low, pebble-dashed building, the word 'Café' flaking off a sign above the door. She edged down the gangplank, pushing her wheeled art case in front of her and yanking the large suitcase behind like two unwilling toddlers, a travel easel in its holder unwieldy under her arm. Each time it hit the rail as she turned to wrestle with one bag or other, she was grateful that now, in mid-October, the ferry was not crowded, so that at least she did not have to worry about how many of her fellow passengers she had maimed in the process of herding her luggage ashore.

At the head of the slipway she saw a man in a leather jacket, its zip straining over a comfortable paunch. He was holding a home-made cardboard sign that read 'Zoe Adams'; as soon as his eyes locked on to hers and met with recognition, he broke into a broad smile and started waving madly at her, as if he were trying to attract her attention through a crowd, though she was only yards away and the few remaining foot passengers had all dispersed. She smiled back, hesitant. He was around her own age, she thought; early forties, with thinning blond hair and a round, open face, cheeks reddened by island weather or a taste for drink, or perhaps both together. He approached her with an anxious smile.

'Mrs Adams?'

She hesitated. She could have let it go, but there would only be more questions later on.

'Uh – actually, it's *Ms.*'

'Eh?'

Zoe tilted her head in apology.

'I'm not a Mrs.'

'Oh.' He looked afraid he had offended. 'My mistake. You're no married, then?'

She made a non-committal noise and set down one of her cases so that she could stretch out a hand. 'You must be Mr Drummond?'

'Mick, please.' He beamed again, grasping her fingers and shaking them with a vigour intended to convey the sincerity of his welcome. 'I'm the one who's been sending all the emails.' He released her hand and held up the sign with a self-conscious laugh; the wind almost snatched it from his grip. 'My wife's idea. I told her, it's no as if there's going to be hundreds of them pouring off the boat, but she said it would spare you feeling lost when you first set foot here.'

Zoe smiled. If only that were all it took.

'It was very thoughtful of her.'

'Aye, she's like that. Kaye. You'll meet her. Here, let me take those.' He tucked the sign under his arm and hefted her cases into each hand, nodding across the car park to an old Land Rover, its flanks crusted with mud.

Zoe looked back at the harbour as he loaded her bags into the trunk. Through the lit windows of the ferry she could see the shapes of people cleaning, swinging plastic bags of trash, ready for the return trip, the boat garish in its brightness against the encroaching dark of sea and sky. The gulls shrieked their tireless warnings. Here, the rolling of the waves seemed louder and more insistent, as if the sea wanted to make sure you did not forget its presence. She wondered if she would grow used to that, after a while. A faint wash of reddish light stained the line of the horizon, but it was too overcast for a proper sunset like those in the photographs. Still, there would be time.

'Hop in, then.' Mick held the door open for her. For one

5

panicked moment she thought he expected her to drive, before she realised she had made the usual mistake. That perverse habit of driving on the left. Perhaps she would get used to that in time, too. The quick flurry of palpitations subsided.

'Is it far, to the house?'

'Five miles, give or take.' He glanced over his shoulder, shuffled his feet. 'Look – it's been a long journey, I know, and you'll be tired, but we wondered if you'd like to come by the pub for a wee drink before I take you up to the house?'

Zoe began a polite refusal but he cut across her.

'Thing is, we've music on tonight, local band, it's a thing we do on Thursdays, so there'll be a lot of folk out and we thought – well, it was Kaye's idea – she thought it would be nice for you to say hello while they're all in one place. Since you're staying a while, you know. Only a wee glass.' He twisted his hands together and looked at his boots before raising his eyes briefly to hers, as if he were asking for a date. 'She's dying to meet you,' he added. 'They all are.'

Zoe sucked in her cheeks. Christ. She was far from dying to meet them, whoever they were; quite the opposite. She felt grimy and dishevelled from the overnight flight, the five-hour train journey and two hours on the ferry; she probably didn't smell too fresh either, under all her layers. And the point was to be anonymous here, to slip quietly into her coastal house and be left alone. She had not come here to make friends. But it had been naïve, she now realised, to imagine that a newcomer to a small community, out of season, would not immediately become a subject of gossip and speculation. If she was going to stay here a few weeks, it would be wise not to offend the locals on day one.

'I'm not really dressed for going out,' she said, though the protest was half-hearted.

'You're grand,' Mick said, giving her a cursory glance. 'It's no as if they'll all be in dinner suits.' He clicked his seatbelt.

'Just the one. And then I'll run you up to the house, I promise. We can leave all the bags in the car.'

Zoe leaned her forehead against the window, the cold solidity of the glass reflecting her exhaustion back at her. Without make-up, the jet lag and all the sleepless nights of recent months were etched on her face, like a confession. Was that why she was so reluctant to go to the pub, she wondered – plain old vanity? Was it that she didn't want to be judged by her new neighbours until she could at least brush her hair and paint some colour into her washed-out face? Of course, it could be a scam; she would blithely go in for one drink and when she came out there would be no sign of Mick or the car, or her bags. But if she was going to think like that, the whole thing could be a scam, as Dan had repeatedly pointed out. All she had seen was a website – an amateurish one at that – and a few emails. Maybe the house didn't even exist. If that were the case, it was too late to worry about it now; she had already transferred the money.

'Sure,' she said, forcing enthusiasm. 'Why not?'

'Lovely. I wouldn't hear the last of it from Kaye if we'd no given you a proper welcome.' Zoe could hear the relief in his voice as the engine belched into life. 'You'll like it – they're a colourful crowd. I mean – it's no exactly the nightlife of New York,' he added, as if fearing he might have created false expectations, 'but then I suppose you've come here to get away from all that.'

'I'm not from New York,' Zoe said, watching the mournful lights of the café recede as he pulled away. Then, thinking she ought to offer something else, she added, 'Connecticut. You're not far off.'

'Oh, aye?' Mick turned out on to the main road. 'Never been myself. America. I'd like to, mind. When the kids are older, maybe. Kaye wants to go to Nashville. She's into all the country music and that, you know? Now me, I've a fancy for somewhere more rugged. Hiking, fishing, that sort of thing. I've always liked the idea of moving to Canada.'

'So does half my country right now,' she muttered.

'Aye, the great outdoors,' Mick continued, missing the point. 'That's where I'm at home. Can't get my girls interested yet, though they're quite into animals and all that. We get otters up here – you'll maybe see some around the bay.'

Zoe leaned against the window and let Mick fill the silence with his wilderness dreams. For as long as he was talking about himself or otters, he was not asking her questions. They passed through what she assumed was the main street of the town: a general store; a place that sold hardware, electronics and fishing supplies; a tea room; a bookshop; a few vacant shopfronts, the windows opaque with milky swirls of whitewash as if to veil their emptiness from public view. At the far end, the street broadened out into a triangular green with a war memorial in the centre, a school playground on one side and a small, plain church opposite. Mick swung the Land Rover to the right, past the church-yard, into a narrower lane. The cottages on each side lined up crookedly against one another, like bad teeth, but they looked snug, with lights glowing warmly behind drawn curtains.

'Have you always lived here?' she prompted, when he seemed in danger of running out of talk. He slid her a side-ways look and she sensed that a certain wariness had descended.

'Born and bred,' he said. She was not sure if the note in his voice was pride or resignation. 'Got away as soon as I could, mind. All the young ones do. But my mother passed away five years back and my da couldn't manage the pub on his own, he was getting on, you know? So I came home. Brought my wife and daughters with me.' He heaved a deep sigh. 'Sometimes a place is in your marrow. It pulls you back. Nothing you can do about it.'

'Uh-huh.' Zoe nodded. 'My grandmother came from this part of the world, actually.'

'Is that right?' He eyed her with greater approval. 'So you've come in search of your roots?'

'Something like that. I guess my Scottish blood's pretty diluted by now. She married an Englishman. My mother grew up in Kent. I was born there too.'

'I'd keep that quiet round here, if I were you.' He winked. 'You don't sound like you're from Kent.'

'We moved to the States when I was a kid. My dad's from Boston.' She wrapped her arms around herself; the thought of her father speared her with a sudden pang of longing. No use thinking of that now. She forced a brightness into her voice, changing the subject. 'So did the house always belong to your family? The one I'm staying in?'

Again, that slight hesitation, the flicker of a glance, as if he suspected her of trying to catch him out.

'Aye.' It looked as if this was the extent of his answer, but as they approached a turning with a painted sign at the entrance showing a white stag on the crest of a hill, he cleared his throat. 'But it didn't come to me until my father passed on last year.'

'Oh, I'm sorry,' Zoe said automatically. 'About your father.'

'Aye, well, he was eighty-seven and still working, more or less – that's no a bad run.' Mick sniffed. 'But he'd let the house go over the years. They all had. Took a lot of work to make it fit to live in. Don't get me wrong' – he turned to her with that same anxious expression – 'it's all good as new – better. I did most of the work myself – that's what I used to do, down in Glasgow, you know – restore houses. It's lovely now, though I say so myself. Well, you'll have seen the photos on the website. They're no Photoshopped or any of that,' he insisted, a touch defensive.

'It looks beautiful. You didn't want to keep it for your family home?'

9

He snapped his head round and his eyes narrowed. Then his face relaxed and he laughed, almost with relief. 'Too far out for us. We stay here, above the pub. That way we're on hand if there's any problems. And the girls can walk to school in five minutes. That's the only reason,' he added, as if someone had suggested otherwise. 'No sense in making life more complicated.' He indicated the building in front of them, a whitewashed inn of three storeys with gabled windows in the roof. The car park outside was busy, and as he switched off the engine, Zoe heard music and laughter drifting through the clear air. 'But if it's peace and quiet you're after, it'll be perfect for you.'

He was trying too hard, Zoe thought. Perhaps there was something wrong with the house after all. It had looked so idyllic on the website; eccentric, as if the original architect had thrown at it all the excesses of the Victorian Gothic and hoped for the best. From the pictures she had seen, the interior was tastefully restored and minimally furnished, but what had really hooked her was the light. The photographs had been taken in summer, but even in sunshine there was a bleakness to the island's beauty that had whispered to her, stark bars of cloud lending shadow and depth to the sky. A veranda ran around the west and south sides of the house, overlooking an empty strand of sand and shingle, marked only by coarse clumps of seagrass, tapering down to a small bay that gave on to the vast silvered expanse of the Atlantic. The house was set a little way back from the beach, built into the slope of the cliff at its shallowest point, while a ridge of rock rose up behind, as if to protect it from prying eyes. She had noticed the quality of the light with a painter's eye, and known with some instinct deeper than thought that she needed to wake under that sky, to the sound of that empty ocean and the seabirds that wheeled and screamed above it, if she was ever going to find her way back. Whether some ancestral tug in the blood had drawn her there, she could not say. She had only felt a certainty, on seeing the house, that had eluded her for months; the knowledge that it was meant for her.

'Peace and quiet is absolutely what I want,' she said, but with a smile, so as not to seem antisocial.

Mick opened his door, then turned back to her. 'The thing is, Mrs Adams – *Ms* – sorry, Zoe . . . ' He chewed his lip, unsure how to continue. 'There's a lot of history to this place. Legends, and so on. And a lot of families have been here for generations. So people have their superstitions, you know? Plenty of folk here have barely been off the island.'

Zoe nodded. 'I guess that's part of the charm.'

'Aye, but . . . ' He looked uneasy. 'It's only – if you hear people telling tall tales, as they like to do with a drop of whisky inside them, pay them no mind. Fishermen's yarns, old wives' gossip – that's all it is.'

'Oh, I love all those folk tales. My grandmother used to tell them when we were kids. Selkies and giants and what-ever.' As soon as she'd said the words, she regretted them, picturing herself trapped in a smoky corner by some ancient mariner.

'As long as you know that's all they are. Bit of fun. Tease the incomers.' Mick smiled back, but he did not look reas-sured. 'Come on then, you must be gasping for a drink.'

The warmth of the pub hit her face like a blast from a subway vent, thick and yeasty, homely smelling: woodsmoke and winter food, stews, hot pastry and mulled cider. A wave of sound broke over her at the same time, a fast and furious jig from the band, accompanied by raucous singing, foot-stamping and the banging of beer mugs, so that for an instant Zoe felt overwhelmed by the force of it, the noise and heat and smell of so many people crammed into a lounge bar designed for half their number. She stood very still, one hand to her temple as if her head were fragile as an eggshell, and closed her eyes as the weight of her jet lag settled inside her

11

skull. When she opened them, every head had swivelled to stare at her. She allowed her gaze to travel the room, taking in the questioning faces – no hostility in them, as far as she could see, most had not even missed a breath in their singing – and felt her own expression freeze into a tight little smile, fearful of offending. She cast around for Mick with a flutter of alarm, until she realised he had flipped open the bar and taken up a position of natural authority behind it. He beckoned her over and pushed a heavy crystal tumbler across the polished wood. A generous measure of Scotch glowed honey-gold, with no ice.

'Get this down you,' he said in a low voice. 'Put some colour in your cheeks.'

Zoe lifted the glass to her mouth and breathed in peat and smoke, ancient scents, the land itself. The heat slid down her throat and uncurled through her limbs. Behind her eyes the headache intensified briefly, then began to melt away. She set the glass down on the bar and Mick immediately refilled it, with a wink.

'That's my Kaye there,' he said, nodding to the makeshift stage where the band were building to a crescendo. Zoe turned to look. The singer was a buxom woman dressed younger than her age, in drapey black skirts and a black lace top, her long pink hair bright and defiant. She sang with her eyes closed, a fist wrapped around the microphone, one foot in floral Doc Martens pounding the stage to the beats of the bodhran, her voice bluesy and hard-edged, smoke and whisky. Though Zoe could not make out the words, she surmised from the ferocity of the singing that it was some kind of nationalist rebel song, and that the anger soaked through its lyrics was still keenly felt by a good many of the patrons.

The rest of the band were men; all – apart from the young fiddle player – well into middle age, with grey hair pulled back into ponytails, and grizzled beards, leather waistcoats and cowboy boots. There was an accordion, a pennywhistle and a guitar as well as the bodhran and the violin; the music sounded vaguely familiar, the kind she had heard on a loop in Irish bars in Boston and New York, but here it did not feel manufactured for tourists. The musicians played with their eyes closed, as if every note mattered.

The rebel song ended in a burst of cheering and applause, but the band did not even pause to acknowledge it; instead the woman launched into a wild and wrenching lament, accompanied only by the violin and the heavy heartbeat of the drum. The room stilled to a reverent hush as her voice soared to the blackened rafters, transformed now into a fluting, other-worldly alto, holding tremulous notes that made goosebumps prickle along Zoe's arms and the back of her neck. Though she did not understand the strange language, she could not miss the heart-cry in the music: a grief that seemed centuries old. Looking around, she saw old men with tears running down their faces, mouthing the words to themselves. The woman's voice faded out and the young fiddle player stepped forward for a solo, his lips pressed tightly together, slender fingers moving nimbly over the strings, brow furrowed behind the long fringe that fell over his face. Zoe sipped her second whisky and experienced a sudden urge to reach forward and brush it out of his eyes, the way she would with Caleb when he was bent over his iPad, absorbed in whatever animation he was making, oblivious to everything. She became aware that Mick was leaning over the bar behind her, a dishcloth pressed between his clasped hands.

'She has an incredible voice.' Zoe realised she was expected to comment.

'She's something, isn't she?' Mick said, not taking his eyes off his wife. That glimpse of tender pride caused Zoe to flinch briefly. She remembered seeing the same expression on Dan's face, at the first exhibition she had invited him to when they started dating; admiration of her talent and the thrill of being allowed to claim some share in it. She could not remember when he had last looked at her like that.

At the end of the song, the band set down their instruments and announced a break. Around the bar the hum of conversation resumed; glances once more directed openly at her, murmured observations that made no effort to disguise the fact that she was the subject. The woman with the pink hair sprang down and pressed her way across the bar, scattering smiles to left and right. She stopped breathlessly and caught Zoe's hand between both of hers.

'Zoe! We're so glad you're here. I'm Kaye Drummond. I hope he's got you a drink? Top her up there, Michael, will you? You're our guest tonight. Are you hungry?'

Zoe shook her head. If she had been hungry, the whisky had blunted all memory of it. Kaye looked up at her with anxious eyes. Though her figure was voluptuous, her face was delicate, almost elfin, the wide blue eyes rimmed with black kohl, her rosebud mouth painted the same shade of fuchsia as her hair; Zoe guessed her to be in her late thirties. She wore large silver rings on every finger, so that Zoe felt she was being clasped by armoured gauntlets.

'That was a beautiful song just now,' she said.

'Oh, aye, thanks.' Kaye beamed, her eyes shining. 'It's an old one. Everyone round here remembers their granny singing it.'

'What does it mean?'

'Och, they're all awful depressing. It's about a woman who loses her love to the sea and drowns herself of a broken heart. Most of them are, if they're not about the Clearances. People have long memories up here. Have you come to paint? I said to Mick, we could have a wee show here in the pub if you wanted. Folk might like to see them. They might even buy one, if they weren't too . . . ' she made a knowing face and rubbed her thumb and forefinger together.

14

'Oh – that's kind, but . . . ' Zoe felt herself growing flustered. 'I hadn't thought of selling. I'm a little out of practice. I'm here to find my way back to it, I suppose.'

'Well, you let us know,' Kaye said, undeterred. 'It's no like we're experts. They could be total shite, we wouldn't know any different.' She broke into peals of laughter and flicked Zoe on the arm with the back of her hand. 'I'm only messing with you. I'm sure they're no shite. You'd buy one, wouldn't you, Ed?'

She nudged the young man next to her, the fiddle player, in the ribs. He turned from the bar and gave Zoe a shy smile from under his fringe. He wore large tortoiseshell glasses that reflected the light, making it hard to see his eyes clearly.

'Buy what?'

'One of Zoe's paintings.'

'Oh. Well – ah – what are they of?'

'I haven't done any yet,' Zoe said, smiling to ease his embarrassment. 'Well – not here. But I guess I paint landscapes. Or I used to. Kind of impressionistic. Not very original,' she added, with an awkward laugh.

He shrugged. 'Everyone likes a landscape, don't they? I mean, at least you know what it is. People don't stand around in galleries arguing about what a landscape means, right?'

Oh, they do, Zoe almost said, but stopped herself; condescension would not be a good look. The boy took off his glasses and rubbed them on the hem of his shirt; his face appeared soft and exposed without them. A pint of dark beer was slopped down on the bar top in front of him. She glanced up and caught the eye of the barmaid, a thickset girl of about eighteen with heavy make-up, a top that was too tight to flatter and dyed black hair scraped into a messy topknot, pulling her small features taut under ruthlessly plucked brows. She looked at Zoe with evident disdain, even when Zoe ventured a smile.

'Cheers, Annag.' The boy, Ed, replaced his glasses, took a

sip from the top of his pint and fished in his pocket for coins with the other hand. She noticed he did not look at the girl behind the bar. Instead he cocked his head towards Zoe. 'Can I get you a drink?'

She glanced down at her glass. While her back had been turned, it had magically acquired another two fingers of Scotch. She would have to take it easy; already a gentle numbness had begun spreading up the side of her face, warm and comforting, as her head was growing lighter.

'I'm good, thanks.' She hesitated. The barmaid continued to watch her. 'I'd take one of those, though.' She nodded towards the open breast pocket of his shirt, where a pack of Marlboro Lights nosed out. As soon as she'd asked, she wondered why she'd done it. She hadn't smoked for over a decade, not since before she was pregnant with Caleb. She hadn't even been aware that she'd missed it. She had a sudden memory of the first day of college, self-consciously lighting a cigarette almost as soon as her parents had driven away, because for the first time there was no one who knew her and she was at liberty to try out a new version of herself, one less timid and constrained by expectations. Perhaps this was the same thing, twenty-five years on. Dan would be appalled. She supposed that was precisely why she had asked.

'Course.' The boy picked up his pint and patted the ciga-rettes in his pocket. 'We'll have to go out the back.'

As she turned back for her drink, Zoe saw the look of naked hostility on the barmaid's flat face and realised, too late, that she might unwittingly have stepped on someone's toes.

'I don't really smoke,' she said, by way of apology, as the boy held open a door at the side of the bar and led her through to a paved courtyard that opened on to a grassy area with picnic tables overlooking a low wall. Beyond this, some way below them, lay the vast black expanse of the sea.

'Nor do I.' He flipped open the pack and offered it to her, glancing around as he did so. 'At least, not where the children might see me.'

She looked at him, surprised. He could not be past his early twenties. People started younger in the country, she supposed. 'How many kids do you have?'

'Eleven.' He left a significant pause, grinning at her expression. 'Youngest four, oldest nearly twelve. I'm the schoolteacher here.'

'Oh.' Zoe laughed, to show that she had fallen for the joke. She regarded him with a new curiosity. 'Just you?'

'Just me. There's only one class. The older kids take the ferry to the mainland and board during the week.'

'Wow. How long have you been here?'

'Since Christmas. The previous teacher had to retire on health grounds, they needed someone quickly. I was lucky. It's my first job out of college.' He gave a diffident smile and struck a match, cupping his hands around the flame as he brought it to the tip of her cigarette. He leaned in close enough for her to see the fine dusting of freckles over the bridge of his nose. Behind his glasses, his lashes were so long they brushed the lenses, and dark, darker than his hair. He sensed her looking and raised his eyes; a gust of wind snuffed out the flame before it could make contact.

'What made you choose somewhere so remote?' she asked quietly, as he threw down the burnt match and struck another.

'I could ask you the same thing,' he said. He laughed as he said it, but she glimpsed a flash of wariness in his eyes. The match guttered out and he dropped it with a soft curse.

'Running away,' said a firm voice behind them. Zoe jumped, as if caught in a forbidden act; she whipped around to see a man seated on a bench by the door, against the wall of the pub, almost hidden by shadows. He spoke through a pipe clamped comfortably between his teeth. A black Labrador lay at his feet, half under the bench, so dark its

17

hindquarters seemed to disappear. 'Everyone who comes here is trying to escape from something,' he repeated, amusement lighting his eyes. 'And those who were born here dream of running away.' He rubbed his neat white beard and smiled, as if they were all included in a private joke. 'Here, Edward –' he held out a silver Zippo – 'you'll be there all night with this wind.'

The boy stepped forward to take the lighter. 'What are you running from then, Professor?'

The older man considered. 'History,' he said, after a pause. His gaze rested on Zoe. 'And you must be the artist from America. We've been looking forward to meeting you.' He did not speak with the local accent, but in the rich, sonorous voice of an English stage actor. A reassuring voice, Zoe thought.

She inclined her head. 'Zoe Adams.'

'Charles Joseph.' He held out a hand, though he didn't get up, obliging her to cross to him so that he could shake hers with a brisk grip. Even in the half-light she could see that his face was tanned and weathered, his eyes a sharp ice-blue. He could have been anywhere between fifty and eighty. 'And this is Horace. Named for the poet. He has a decidedly satirical glint.' The dog raised its eyebrows and thumped its tail once in acknowledgement.

'Are you a professor of history, then?' she asked, to turn the conversation away from herself.

He laughed. 'I'm afraid this young man is flattering me. Or mocking me, I'm never sure which. I have been a university teacher in my time, it's true, though I never held tenure. Never stayed anywhere long enough.'

'Everyone calls him the Professor, though,' Edward said, cracking the Zippo into life. Zoe held her cigarette to the flame, inhaled and coughed violently as her head spun. 'He's our local historian. Anything you want to know about the island, he's your man.'

18

'Well. I can't promise that, but I can usually find a book to help.' Charles Joseph puffed on his pipe and folded his arms across his chest. 'I own the second-hand bookshop on the High Street. Do drop by sometime. I make excellent coffee and it gets quiet out of season. I'm always glad of a visitor.' Pale creases fanned out from the corners of his eyes, Zoe noticed, as if he smiled so often the sun had not had a chance to reach them.

'He's being modest,' Edward said, breathing out a plume of violet smoke. 'He's the one who wrote most of the books. Get him to tell you the island's stories. He can talk the hind legs off a donkey, mind.' He grinned at Charles. Zoe sensed an unspoken affinity between these two men, despite their difference in age. Perhaps it was a matter of education; in a community like this, those who read books tended to huddle together against the corrosion of a small-town mindset. That was how it had been where she grew up, anyway.

'My price is a cinnamon bun from Maggie's,' Charles said, lifting the pipe out of his mouth. 'That's the bakery three doors down from my shop. Bring me one of those and I'll tell you all the tales you have time for.'

Zoe thought of Mick's hesitant warning in the car, about the locals and their legends, embellished to frighten incomers. She took another drag, the second easier than the first, and felt the nicotine buzz through her blood.

'How do you know so much about the place?' she asked.

'I lived here for a while, many years ago.' Charles paused to relight his pipe. After considerable effort and fierce puffing, he looked up at her through a cloud of smoke. 'After I retired, I drifted back. I think I always knew I would, deep down.' He made it sound fatalistic, the way Mick had.

'You missed it?'

'It called me back. Simple as that. I took a look around and it occurred to me that people here could do with a bookshop.'

He drew on his pipe again with a rueful smile. 'Not many of them agreed, if my accounts are anything to go by.'

'Rubbish,' Edward said. 'People love the bookshop. Your profit margins would be a lot better if you weren't always giving books away for nothing.'

'Well, that's the trouble, you see.' Charles leaned forward, pointing the stem of his pipe at Zoe as if he were imparting a confidence. 'Whenever someone comes in, I think, a-ha, I know just the thing he or she should read. But people have very fixed ideas about what they think they like – have you noticed? Sometimes I have to fairly insist they take it, and then I can hardly charge them. But I'm almost never wrong – Edward will tell you. Besides,' he sucked on the pipe and sighed out a fragrant haze, 'I hate to see books sitting alone and unloved on a shelf. I'd much rather they found a home.'

'Not the smartest way to run a business,' Edward said, with affection. Charles inclined his head.

'True. But only an idiot would open a second-hand bookshop to get rich.'

'Did you live here as a child?' Zoe asked.

Charles looked at her, his white eyebrows gently puckered, as if the question required careful deliberation.

'*There* you are!' The door banged against the wall and Kaye stood on the step, a pint glass of water in one hand, jabbing a finger towards Zoe in mock-admonishment. 'Thought we'd lost you.'

Zoe saw her take in the cigarette and felt immediately guilty, as if she were still her adolescent self and had exposed herself to the censure of the neighbours. Kaye's look changed when her gaze fell on Charles, stretched comfortably over his bench, Horace's chin resting on his boots.

'Has he been filling your head with nonsense?' She nodded towards him. She was trying to keep her voice light, but Zoe did not miss the underlying sharpness, the anxiety in Kaye's eyes.

'None that wasn't there before,' Zoe said with a smile.

'He's a great one for the stories, is our Professor,' Kaye said, fixing him with a stern eye. 'Keeps us all entertained round the fire when the nights draw in. Ed – Bernie wants to go in five. Give us a drag of that.' She took Edward's half-smoked cigarette from his hand without waiting for an invitation, throwing a guilty glance towards the upper windows of the building behind them. 'If my girls are looking out, I'm in trouble.'

She hauled in another lungful and leaned down to stub out the butt in a pot of sand by the door. Edward dug his hands into his jeans pockets and dipped his head towards Zoe. 'Nice to meet you. Hopefully we'll see you up here again, if you're around for a while.' The diffident angle of his glance, the not-quite-meeting of her eye, the studied nonchalance of his tone, all caught Zoe off guard; was he *flirting* with her?

'Sure,' she said, aiming to sound neutral. The idea seemed so unlikely that almost as soon as it had occurred she felt embarrassed by it, in case he had guessed at her presumption. He nodded, gave Charles a brief wave and disappeared back inside the pub. Kaye beamed widely and looked at the door, as if she could will her guest back inside with the force of her smile. Zoe was too foggy with tiredness to offer any resistance. She looked at the cigarette burning slowly down between her fingers as if she couldn't remember how it had come to be there. She ground it out in the sand and turned back at the door to Charles.

'I'll look out for your shop, Mr Joseph.' She did not quite have the nerve to call him 'Professor'.

'Please do,' he said, reaching down to tousle the dog between its ears. 'Horace and I are there every day, putting the world to rights with whoever drops by. We'd be delighted to see you. I promise I'll find you an interesting read.'

A brief twitch of alarm passed across Kaye's face. 'Mind you behave yourself,' she said, pointing at him. 'Mrs Adams

21

is our guest.' Once more, the jokey tone, with the undercurrent of warning. It was curious, Zoe thought; Kaye obviously liked the Professor, but she seemed keen to keep him away from her, without ever quite making it explicit. Did she fear he might tell her some local legend that would spook her so much she'd run away tomorrow and shout it all over TripAdvisor? She almost laughed, that they could think her so skittish. They had no idea; no story could be worse than the one she carried with her. Besides, she had already paid half the rent up front.

'I like history,' she said to Charles. 'And poetry.' Her tongue felt thick and woolly in her mouth as she spoke. She looked down at the glass in her hand and realised it was empty; she did not remember drinking it. She felt Kaye's solid presence at her back, ushering her firmly but gently indoors.

After the night air of the courtyard, the heat of the log fire and the press of bodies crowded in on her. The whisky churned in her empty stomach and the nicotine pulsed in her temples, dizzying her and blurring her vision. She leaned against the wall, briefly closing her eyes. Her skull seemed to squeeze tighter and she took a deep breath to quell the nausea. Though she had no interest in making friends here, she did not want to be known forever as the woman who threw up in the bar within an hour of arriving.

'You all right?' Kaye laid her metalled fingers lightly on Zoe's shoulder.

Zoe nodded. 'The bathroom?'

'Past the bar, on the right.' Kaye patted her, as you might a small child.

The bathroom was even more stifling, airless with the heat of hand-driers in a confined space. Zoe took off her flying jacket and tucked it between her knees, splashed cold water over her face and dried it with the sleeve of her shirt. She rested her forehead against the cool of the mirror and watched as her breath fogged a circle on the glass. Her reflection stared back at her with frayed outlines. Her skin looked blanched, the shadows beneath her eyes so deep they appeared bruised. She had taken her make-up off before the flight and been too tired to bother applying any more. Straight off the red-eye, Bradley to Dublin, connecting flight to Glasgow and on to a five-hour train journey to the ferry, to bring her here. When she had planned it, back home, it had seemed a good idea: get all the travelling done at once, no layovers, no breaks for sightseeing. She was not here for tourist attractions. All she wanted was to get to the sprawling old house by that deserted shore that had called to her over the Internet, and wrap its solitude around her. She had no sense of time any more; she struggled to remember when she had last eaten, or showered.

Rubbing away the condensation of her breath with a sleeve, she met her reflection's eye with as steady a gaze as she could manage. They both seemed disappointed with each other. Turning forty-three, and looking every last day of it. Did she seriously imagine that earnest, handsome boy would have been flirting with her? But it was more than jet lag, she thought, peering closely at her own face in the mirror; all the turbulence of the past year was written into her skin, a bone-deep exhaustion she could not shake off. Perhaps here she would finally be able to sleep.

She fished in her pocket and found a Chanel lipstick, one she had thrown in at the last minute, just in case. In case of what? What occasions to dress up had she imagined would present themselves on a small island off the west coast of Scotland, in winter? She barely wore lipstick even at home. Perhaps it was a defensive measure, a reaction against all the military-coloured hiking gear and shapeless sweaters she had packed. One last vestige of femininity. She opened her lips and slicked it around them, blotting the colour on a sheet of toilet paper. Not too garish; a discreet reddish-brown that she used to think suited her but now seemed to drain all the colour from the rest of her face. She wondered how soon she could reasonably ask to leave.

The door opened; Zoe glanced up and saw that another face was staring at her, unsmiling, in the mirror. The young barmaid, Annag, reached up and adjusted the pineapple of hair balanced on her crown, her eyes critically appraising Zoe all the while.

'You're the one who's taken the McBride house.' The girl's accent was broad, rough-edged. 'Brave,' she added, cocking one thinly pencilled brow with an air of challenge.

'It's Mick and Kaye's house, I thought,' Zoe said mildly. 'Aren't they Drummonds?' She did not ask why she should be considered brave, precisely because she could see that the girl was dying to tell her.

'It'll always be the McBride house round here,' Annag said, with a meaningful look. She had an oddly flat face, Zoe thought, and wide, with all the features cramped together in the middle, like a puppet of the moon she had once seen in a kids' show. Too pale for that unnatural shade of black dye, she added, in her head. This girl's attitude seemed to provoke a mean streak in her, as if they were both in high school.

'I'm afraid I can't pronounce its real name,' she said, forcing a smile.

Annag muttered a word deep in her throat that Zoe assumed was Gaelic, but sounded nothing like the way it looked on paper. 'It means "resting place",' she said.

'Oh. That's nice.'

'You think?'

Zoe looked up and saw that the girl was smirking openly. A strange chill ran through her as she understood. Clearly, the person who named the house had not stopped to consider its double meaning. Or perhaps they had.

'Give us a lend of your lippy.' A pudgy hand stretched out towards her, open; bitten fingernails painted flaking green. Zoe hesitated. Was this a normal thing to ask a stranger? She

24

had grown up without sisters, without a close group of girl-friends; as a result she was possessive about her belongings and a little fastidious, bewildered by the kind of women who presumed all feminine items should be held in common. But she couldn't think of a good reason to refuse without implying that she considered the girl unhygienic. Reluctantly, she passed the lipstick over. Annag stretched her mouth wide, drew on a red circle, smacked her lips together and pouted, apparently pleased with the result.

'Why am I brave, then?' Zoe asked, as if this small intimacy might now entitle her to answers. 'I guess it's haunted or something, right?' She tried to make it sound jokey, as if she were happy to play along, but a look of guilt slunk over Annag's moon face. The girl concentrated on the lipstick, twisting it all the way to the top and down again.

'I only meant – staying out there on your own. In the middle of nowhere. That's brave, for a woman.' She reached inside her top with one hand and twanged a stray bra strap into place. 'Not that I'm saying— I don't mean . . . ' She turned to look at the real Zoe beside her, instead of at her reflection. 'Whatever folk say about it, you didnae hear it from me, okay? Mick'll bloody kill me.'

So Mick had warned this girl about telling whatever tales clung to the house. Had everyone else in the town been given a warning too? Charles Joseph apparently had, though he didn't seem to feel inhibited by it. What could be so terrible that Kaye and Mick genuinely feared it might drive a tenant away? It will be one of those stories like the ones people used to swap at high school slumber parties, Zoe thought: like the one where the girl hears the banging on the car roof and it turns out to be her boyfriend's head. And that's what you get for coming to the ass-end of nowhere, she reminded herself: people who take that stuff seriously. But she found that, however dumb the story might be, she didn't want to hear it on her first night.

25

'But I haven't heard anything,' she said.

'Then you'll sleep soundly in your bed, won't you?' Annag flashed her a smile that seemed to contain some element of private triumph, before walking out. As the door banged behind her, Zoe realised Annag still had her lipstick in her hand. She considered going after her, asking for it back, but decided against it. There was no point making an enemy of this girl, who already seemed to resent her presence. But if she was honest, it was because Annag reminded her of the hard-faced girls who had given her hell in high school, and she despised herself for her own cowardice. She made a note to stay out of the barmaid's way as far as possible. Out of everyone's way. She caught her reflection's eye with weary contempt, and slowly wiped away the bright slash of lipstick with a tissue.

Even in the dark, the house looked imposing. Mick had installed motion-sensor security lights at the front; a white glare leapt out of the blackness like a prison searchlight as the Land Rover descended the last slope and rounded the curve of the drive, Mick raising a hand to shield his eyes and swearing under his breath. They lit up a rambling house of three storeys, tall Gothic windows along the first floor, diamond-paned glass, pointed eaves over the windows in the attic, several tall chimneys and a hexagonal turret jutting up from the roof. A warm light glowed from one of the windows on the ground floor. As Zoe swung herself down on to the gravel, she could hear the booming of waves in the darkness beyond the house.

'Kaye's left you a few bits and bobs – bread and milk and whatnot,' Mick said, lifting her suitcase down from the trunk. 'Should see you right for breakfast. She's done a wee folder too, telling you where to find everything – it's got our number on and a few others you might need. I was thinking I could come by tomorrow before lunch and show you the other stuff.

26

How the generator works, where we store the logs, all that business. Then, if you like, I'll bring you into town so you can go to the supermarket.'

Zoe murmured her thanks, only half listening. She craned her neck and stared up at the night sky. A brisk wind chivvied scraps of cloud across the face of the moon; behind them, an extravagant scattering of stars glittered across ink blue wastes. The seabirds sounded subdued here, their cries reproachful. 'Why do people call it the McBride house?'

Mick froze, for a heartbeat, in the act of setting down her art case. 'McBride was the fella who built it, back in 1860.' He sounded unusually stiff.

'Was he a relative?'

'He married my great-great-aunt. It passed to her brother, my great-great-grandfather. Been in my family ever since. But the name stuck. Now,' he said, forcibly cheery, 'let's get this lot inside and you can settle in.'

He carried her cases into the wide entrance hall, set them down at the foot of the stairs and immediately flicked on all the lights he could find. Inside, the house smelled of new paint, furniture polish and the heavy floral scent from an extravagant vase of lilies that stood on a wooden chest opposite the front door.

'Beautiful flowers,' Zoe remarked, to fill the silence.

'Oh, aye. Kaye did those.' Mick seemed distracted, his eyes flitting around the hallway as if he half expected to see someone appear from one of the doors leading off it.

'That was such a kind thought – will you thank her?' It was gone eleven, by the grandfather clock in the hall; Zoe had lost all track of what time her own body thought it was, but the whisky sat heavy in her stomach and she was struggling to keep her eyes open. She wished he would hurry up and leave.

'I will. Well, then. There are your keys. Those are the front door. The ones for the back are on a hook in the kitchen.'

27

Mick dropped a weighty keyring into her palm, dug his hands into the pockets of his leather jacket, then took them out again as if unsure what to do with them, glancing back at the front door. He seemed reluctant to go, but at a loss as to how to prolong his visit. For one awful moment, Zoe wondered if he was hovering for a tip, but it didn't seem likely. 'Shall I take these up for you?' he asked, his gaze alighting on the cases.

'Oh, no, I can manage,' she began, but he was halfway up the stairs, telling her it was no trouble.

'Well, then,' he said, when he returned. 'I suppose I should let you get on. The water from the tap's fine to drink, by the way. And you remember there's no broadband? I mentioned that in the email.'

'It's fine. It'll be good for me to get offline.' She forced a smile.

'They haven't got the cables out to this side of the island,' Mick explained, keen to make clear it was no failing on his part. 'In the next year or so, they reckon, not that that's much help to you. You can come and use ours up at the pub if you want to send emails and whatnot.' He hesitated once more, running a hand over his thinning hair. 'Like I said, our number's there in the folder. Call us if you need anything, anytime. We're only five miles away, I can be here in a jiffy if there's a problem.'

'I'll try not to disturb you if I can possibly help it. I'm pretty self-sufficient.' She was not sure if this was actually true. It was a long time since she had put it to the test, but it was important that Mick should believe it. All she wanted now was to find the bed and fall face down on it.

'Aye, well, that's good. But we're here if you need us. I mean it – anytime at all. Day or night.' He said it more emphatically this time, and his gaze darted away to the top of the stairs. At the front door he turned back, holding it half open so that moths hurled themselves towards the light, wings whirring. 'I'll be back tomorrow at noon. I hope you have a comfortable night.'

'I'm sure I will.' She almost had to push him physically out of the door. She stood on the threshold, a narrow fan of light spilling through on to the step in front of her, determinedly waving him off so she could be sure he was finally gone. He raised his hand as he reversed the Land Rover with a scattering of gravel, but in the white cone of the security light his expression was anxious, just as it had been in the hallway.

When the sound of the engine had died away, Zoe leaned her back against the inside of the front door and allowed herself to slump to the floor.

He's a new landlord, she told herself; he's bound to be nervous the day his first tenant arrives. It was sweet, she supposed, how concerned he and Kaye were about her well-being, their little thoughtful touches. She hoped they would ease up once she'd settled in, though; she was troubled by the way they kept referring to her as their 'guest' rather than their tenant. She hoped they wouldn't feel compelled to take her under their wing while she was here, save her from being lonely. Sometimes it was hard to make people understand how much you desired solitude. Or deserved it.

There was a telephone on a console table at the side of the entrance hall. She briefly considered calling home, but decided she was too tired, too fuzzy with whisky to deal with the conversation. She had texted Dan from the airport to say she had landed safely; she would call tomorrow. Instead she pulled herself to her feet, switched off the downstairs lights and climbed the stairs. On the first landing, to the right, she found her cases propping open the door to a lit room; inside, a master bedroom furnished neatly in crisp white, slate grey and duck-egg blue, with a small en suite leading off it. She threw her jacket over a chair, pulled off her biker boots in the bathroom doorway, bent her mouth to the tap and gulped down cold water, then collapsed on to the bed, where she fell asleep, fully clothed. Outside, the security lights snapped off and the McBride house was folded into the darkness once more.

2

That night, Zoe dreamed.

She was stripped naked and laid across a low couch in the long gallery that ran the length of the house on the west side, facing the sea. Both arms were stretched above her head and pinioned so that she could not move them. Around her the room lay steeped in shadow, save for the pale shaft of moonlight that filtered through the tall windows, silvering the bare boards of the floor. Though she could not see them, she sensed someone else in the room, moving closer. Two hands, reaching out of the darkness, expertly began to trace slow patterns across her skin. Hot breath on her neck, whispering down across her shoulder. Her muscles tensed; her nipples stiffened and her hips rose as she felt herself swell and open. Despite the apparent helplessness of her position, she was not afraid; instead she felt an unfamiliar boldness, a pleasure and pride in her own body that made her want to arch her back, display herself for him. Somehow he knew her, this unknown lover; he understood how she needed to be touched, and she trusted him, the certainty of his hands, his mouth, anticipating her want and need. His breath brushed her cheek and she parted her lips for him but he had moved away without a kiss and she was powerless to pull him back. She could only

31

wait for him to continue moving around her, over her, the ghost of lips on her breasts, the hands now clasped firmly around her waist with a sense of ownership. As his tongue finally made contact with her nipple she tried to cry out, the jolt of it so sweet and sudden, as if she had been wired to an electrode, a shockwave that juddered the length of her body and shot through her groin, but – as always in dreams – she could make no sound. His mouth closed over her breast and his teeth tightened and tugged, gently at first, but sharply enough to remind her that he could, if he chose, bring her pain as well as pleasure. She pushed her hips out towards him and one hand slid down over the curve of her buttock and between her legs as his mouth moved across the softness of her belly. *Good,* he whispered, inside her mind.

Zoe was aware of a level of lucidity within the dream, of existing in some liminal state between sleep and waking. But though she could direct the movements of her own body, as far as the restraints around her wrists allowed, she could not influence the shadowy lover who was deliberately withholding from her what he knew she wanted; slowly, softly, he skirted between her legs with his tongue, drawing out the torment. In one instant she would feel the heat of his breath right where she needed him, at the sharp pinpoint of her pleasure, before he moved away, licking the inside of her thigh or the smooth skin above her pubic bone, gently biting the jut of her pelvis or the soft curve of her waist while she tried pleading with him, begging him, though her words emerged soundless as she strained against the restraints binding her hands. When, finally, his tongue made stealthy contact with her most sensitive point and he slipped two fingers inside her, it felt like a concession, or a reward; her whole body was illuminated, shocked into vivid colour. One hand held her hips steady as the rhythm of his flickering tongue quickened and his fingers drove deep into her; bucking and grinding against him, she heard herself screaming, a wild, animal cry, as she felt the first spasm of muscle and the sudden hurtling, as if over the edge of a waterfall, the exquisite frustration of the desire to pull him into her and her inability to touch him at all. As the ripples of her orgasm rose over and over, she could already feel him slipping away, melting back into the shadows, and she cried out again to make him stay but her voice was stifled, stopped in her throat; her mouth worked noiselessly and she could not move her hands to reach him or claw him back.

She woke at her own mewling sounds, feeling disorientated and raw, blinking into the dark to find that she was indeed lying on a couch in the long gallery, her arms stretched above her head and crossed at the wrists. A draught from the curtain-less windows stirred goosebumps over her naked skin and it took her a few moments to locate herself, to understand that she was no longer dreaming. How had she ended up here? She lowered her arms gingerly, as if afraid she might meet with some resistance; her shoulders ached and her fingers had grown numb from being held aloft. She had no recollection of leaving her bed, or having undressed herself, but the memory of the dream remained vivid, the imprint of him on her most tender parts. She looked down at herself, bewildered, as if her body was strange to her, no longer recognisable, feeling the heat of her desire sticky on the insides of her thigh. She slid a tentative finger between her legs and flinched at the coldness of her own touch; she was still engorged, still aroused. She pressed her finger harder and began to circle it; within moments she was rising to a crescendo and a ragged, gasping climax that was fierce and necessary but lacked all the wonder, the other-worldly magic of the dream lover's caress. She stood in the room's silent shadows, feeling flayed, exposed to the elements. And yet, how stunning! It had been as if something had possessed her, as if her desire were a slumbering beast buried so deep for so long that she had forgotten to notice its absence until it was awakened. He was no one she recognised from her waking life, of that she was certain. A figment of her imagination, then, an ideal lover who had touched and manipulated her with such authority, such intimate knowledge.

The moon slipped out from between two banks of cloud, spilling pearly light across the floor. Outside, she could hear the low, insistent roar of the sea. She shivered, and was on the point of turning to leave the room, when a shadow shifted at the edge of her vision: the faintest hint of a movement. She stepped towards the windows, peering out at the black water. Immediately she flinched back. There was someone on the beach, huddled into the overhang of rock at the southerly curve, looking up at the house. Or, at least, she thought she saw a figure; panicked, she stifled a cry and grabbed a blanket from the back of the couch, wrapping it around herself before she dared approach the window again. A cloud moved across the face of the moon and the pale rim of sand was lost in darkness; when it reappeared, there were only the rocks and the steady, breaking waves. Zoe breathed out, feeling her pulse hammering in her throat, and almost laughed with relief. She needed to sleep, she told herself; her brain was wired and exhausted, that was all. She rested the tips of her fingers against the glass and took a last look at the beach, to reassure herself that there was no one there; a seabird, perhaps, or even a seal, or the movement of a cloud casting shadows. The beach remained empty. She sighed, letting her breath mist the pane.

Slowly, she became aware of a sound behind her. Barely audible, a faint scratching of nails on wood. Drawn-out, unnerving; her neck prickled and a sick chill flooded through her. Someone was trying to get in. Though the sound had stopped, the stillness that followed was the silence of held breath. She could feel it, unmistakably: a presence on the other side of the door. She did not dare turn around; instead she stood, frozen rigid, her head bowed as if waiting to receive a blow, naked shoulders stippled with cold and fear. The scratching came again, a slow raking against the wood. Zoe heard herself whimper, biting the flesh of her thumb; the sound stopped, abruptly. Whatever was out there knew she was here. Setting her jaw, squeezing her fists so tight she felt her nails cut the skin of her palms, she straightened, crossed to the door, grasped the handle, and in one movement, before the fear could undo her, she wrenched it open—

The landing outside was empty. She slumped, pent breath tumbling out in a gulp that was half-sob, half-laughter, relief turning her limbs to water. She would have to tell Mick Drummond in the morning that, for all his painstaking restoration work, he still had mice in his walls.

She returned to her room, wrapped in the blanket, and was puzzled to see her clothes neatly folded on the armchair beneath the window. When had she done this? She squinted at the clothes, trying to summon some recollection of folding them, placing them, but a great weight of tiredness had descended on her; she could not, at that moment, bring herself to care. There were pyjamas somewhere in her case, but it was padlocked shut and she could not be bothered to rummage for the key. She slipped under the duvet, still wrapped in the blanket from the couch, drained and exhausted, her body sinking into the sheets. Sleep had almost reclaimed her, when the singing began.

It was the song Kaye had sung that evening, the lament that had made the old men cry and stirred such unexpected emotion in her, though she had not understood the words. The song Kaye had told her was a woman grieving for the one she loved, lost to the sea. And now a woman was singing it, somewhere in the house, though with none of the beauty or passion Kaye had brought to the melody. This voice was thin and sickly, scored through with desolation and loss. Zoe's eyes snapped open; as she lay there listening, it seemed that the singer was in danger of being overwhelmed by the force of her grief; at times the voice would tail off, choked, and Zoe held her breath, waiting, until it resumed, the same refrain, quavering and hoarse. Though she knew it was only the echoes of her memory, another trick of her tired mind brought on by the emotional intensity of her disturbed night, she could not stand to listen to it any longer; she threw off the cover, pulled the blanket tight around her and opened the door to the landing, tensing on the threshold with her head on one side. The song was drifting from the floor above. She groped about on the wall at the foot of the stairs, but could not locate the light switch.

The stairs creaked as she ascended, one step at a time, pausing to listen. Again she felt that creeping cold at the back of her neck, a clenching in her bowel. Perhaps she had not been mistaken; perhaps someone had found a way into the house. She had locked the front door behind Mick, but there must be other doors and windows in a place this size; she had not checked them all before she fell asleep. But why would an intruder advertise her presence by singing? Zoe advanced as far as the landing, wishing she had thought to bring some makeshift weapon – a poker, or even an umbrella. If someone had broken in, they could be unhinged, and potentially dangerous. She glanced over the banister into the pool of darkness below, thinking of the telephone on its table in the hall; briefly she considered running back down, calling Mick and Kaye. How long would it take Mick to drive here – fifteen minutes, perhaps, twenty at the most? She stopped, took a breath, registered her own choice of words. *If* someone was there. She had somehow undressed herself and sleepwalked naked into the gallery; who was to say she was not still half-asleep, imagining the singing, the presence, the scratching? She could not call Mick and Kaye in the middle of the night, on her first night here, because she was hearing things and it turned out she was not as brave or self-reliant as she wanted to believe. Gripping the banister, she walked the length of the second-floor landing with a purposeful stride, her mouth set firm. The singing continued, its volume unvarying, as if the singer was oblivious to Zoe's footsteps or the creak of the stairs. It seemed to be coming from behind a closed door at the far end. Zoe stood in front of it, hesitated, then tried the brass knob. The door was locked.

She turned it in both directions, rattled it hard, but the door refused to give, and the singing continued, unperturbed; if anything, the bleak emotion in the singer's voice intensified. Zoe found herself arrested by the sheer force of the woman's grief; it infected the atmosphere of the entire house, soaking through Zoe's skin until she felt saturated with it, until she feared her heart might crack open with the weight of such fathomless loss. She mastered herself, tried the door once more. When it remained stubbornly locked, she knocked on it, hard, with her knuckles.

'Who's there?' she called, tentatively at first, then bolder. 'Who are you? Come out.'

No one answered, though she thought the voice seemed to grow a little fainter. She knocked again, shook the doorknob, and the next time she called, the song faded gradually away, like a track on an old record, leaving only an expectant silence. The landing settled into stillness. Zoe pulled the blanket tighter around her and leaned against the door, felled by exhaustion. There was no one here; she felt unaccountably angry with herself for her own weakness. As she turned towards the stairs, she sensed a draught on the back of her neck and, in her ear, a breathy sound that might have been laughter, or a sob.

When she woke, it was past eleven and sunlight streamed through a gap in the curtains. She was lying in bed, naked, the woollen blanket she had pulled from the couch in the gallery bundled under the cover beside her. So she had not dreamed that part, at least. She sat up, hugging her knees to her chest, squinting into the light. After the whisky, the jet lag and the disturbed night, she had expected a jagged-edged hangover, but as she uncurled her fingers and stretched her arms out, rolling her shoulders, she could detect no trace of a headache. Instead she felt unusually light and invigorated. She swung her legs over the bed and the sight of them – long, lean, pale – brought back a flash of images from the night before. That dream – she flushed at the memory of it, squeezing her thighs together. She used to have intensely vivid sex dreams when she was younger, but they had retreated into the background somewhere along the way, like the rest of her sex life. Back then, though, the lovers who featured in her dreams were variations on men she knew, often men she had never knowingly entertained any such feelings towards in her waking life. But this dream lover was different; he was unreal, perfect, formed from her own unarticulated longings. If she could, she would have fallen back on to the bed and invited the vision back, but she knew that would never happen. It was fleeting, delicious, gone. And everything that had followed – the fear, the scratching, the singing – seemed easy to explain away now: fevered imaginings of a mind torn abruptly from sleep and confused by dreams. Thank God she had not called Mick and Kaye with her wild night-terrors; how ridiculous she would have looked. She curled with shame at the thought.

Zoe unlocked her suitcase, dug out a pair of track pants, a tank and an old cashmere jumper of Dan's, and padded down to find the kitchen. It was a large, wide room at the back of the house, facing the shore, with a door that led out to the veranda; a proper old farmhouse kitchen, tastefully modernised, with a stone floor and walls painted in a muted slate-blue and cream. She opened and closed a few wooden cupboards. All the appliances and cookware were branded, the kind of names that would meet with the approval of the well-heeled guests they obviously hoped to attract. Zoe filled the kettle, found a cafetière and an unopened packet of filter coffee and considered again, while it was brewing, how strange it was that Mick and Kaye should have gone to so much trouble and expense to restore this house so beautifully and leave it to strangers, while they went on living above the pub. A five-mile drive to work would be nothing, for the joy of waking up to this view every morning. Perhaps they were counting on the income as an investment; she supposed the pub trade must suffer out of season. Perhaps – and she pushed this thought to a corner of her mind – they did not want to risk being cut off in winter.

The kitchen door was firmly locked and bolted from the inside, the keys hanging on a hook behind it, as Mick had said. All the windows were closed and secured, she noticed, with window locks; there was no chance that anyone could really have entered the house last night. Tired brain, she reproached herself, sliding back the bolts. She poured her coffee into a large pottery mug and stepped outside with it into a warm wash of golden, late-autumn sunshine. The boards of the veranda felt damp under her bare feet and though the air carried the sharp, clean edge of October, the light was gentle, caressing her face. She wrapped her hands around the steaming mug and took in her new home for the first time.

The sea had retreated, leaving a corrugated expanse of tawny sand, scattered with pebbles and ribbons of kelp. The wind of the previous night had dropped and in the curve of her little bay the water shone like mercury under the light, calm now and docile, lapping in slow rhythmic waves at the shore. Above it, scalloped rows of white clouds drifted across an expanse of blue, rinsed clean and bright. Seabirds wheeled overhead, banking sharply or floating on invisible streams, complaining to one another. Zoe walked to the end of the veranda, to the corner where it joined the north side of the house, and tilted her face to the sun, breathing in salt, damp earth, fresh coffee as she absorbed the colours of the bay – violet and gold, azure, emerald and indigo – picturing how she would mix those colours in her palette, how thickly they could be layered to recreate the textures of sea, rock, cloud. She sensed the old quickening in her gut at the prospect of creating something from nothing, the days stretching ahead, blank canvases, no demands on her except the paintings themselves, their own forms. Was this freedom, then? Was this it – the freedom she had secretly craved over the past decade: no husband, no child, only herself alone with an empty canvas and a view of the wild sea? She allowed her gaze to sweep around the deserted beach. The answer, of course, was no. This was not true freedom, not the freedom of her youth, because implicit in their absence was her own dereliction – of her responsibilities, of the ties that should have anchored her. There could be no freedom now that was not tainted with guilt.

'I hope you find what you're looking for.' The last words Dan had said to her before she left, in a voice tight with anger, making clear that nothing she might gain from this decision would ever outweigh the price she was asking everyone else to pay. Leaning against the wall in the hallway, arms folded across his chest, as the cab driver rang the buzzer. Watching as she tried to wrestle her cases down the stairs, not offering to help, in case she should mistake that for approval or acquiescence; determined to the very end that she should not imagine, even for a second, that she had his blessing.

'The *fuck*?' he had said, the night she had announced her project over dinner. So she had repeated it, clearly, patiently, but he had continued to stare at her, knife and fork poised in mid-air.

'So you went ahead and planned all this without even asking me?' he said, when he had eventually processed it.

'Like you went ahead and decided to quit your job without discussing it,' she replied, evenly.

'What – you can't even compare—' He put the cutlery down, ran both hands through his hair, clutching at clumps of it. 'There was nothing to discuss – it was a good offer.

Better than I expected. Architects are the first to suffer in a downturn, you know that. The whole construction industry's feeling it. Guys are being laid off all over. I had to take that deal before I was left with no choice. I did it so I could be around for you more. It was the opposite of fucking *running away*.'

Zoe said nothing; it was easier to let Dan go on believing himself to be right. How could she explain it to him? The last decade had not diminished him, as it had her. He had not had to give up his place in the world since becoming a parent; he still put on a good suit and set out to work every day, solved problems, engaged his intellect, kept his skills sharp. He spent several evenings a week dining with clients and associates, occasionally taking her along when they could find a sitter, but mostly not; he continued to travel frequently for contracts and conferences, sometimes to Europe, more often across the country to consult on projects with the Seattle office. She had not failed to notice that meetings were often arranged there for Monday mornings, obliging him to stay the weekend; she had noticed too that his first point of contact in Seattle was a colleague called Lauren Carrera, a woman who appeared to have no concept of time zones and would call him on his cell with supposedly urgent queries long past midnight, calls he would retreat downstairs to take in his office, his voice soft and light, full of easy laughter, the way she had not heard it in a long time. Lauren Carrera was in her early thirties and too exhibitionist to set her Facebook photos to private; in all of them she was skiing or surfing or running half-marathons for charity, or raising tequila shots with a vast and diverse group of friends. Zoe had never asked Dan outright if he had slept with Lauren Carrera, because he was no good at lying and she didn't want to have to watch him try.

Dan's life was compartmentalised, in the way that was permitted to men; home, fatherhood, was only a part of it.

It had always been assumed that she would stay home once Caleb was born, and she had felt in no position to argue; it was not as if she earned enough from her paintings to support a family – though one day she might have done, if she had been allowed to try. She would never know now, what her early promise might have flowered into. 'You can always paint while the baby's asleep,' Dan had said cheerfully, knotting his tie in the mirror after five brief days of paternity leave, unwittingly revealing with those few words how he regarded her work. A small chip of ice had embedded itself in the heart of their marriage, though as usual she had said nothing. For the best part of a decade she had been disappearing, her life shrunk to a cycle of bake sales and swim team practice, as the ice spread slowly outwards from the centre. In recent years she had found herself growing panicky, all her thoughts swarming relentlessly back to the same, unanswered question: *Is this it?* In her darkest moments, she sometimes wondered if she was now being punished for her ingratitude, her inability to be content.

'How will this help?' Dan had persisted, the night she had told him about the island. 'I've said over and over we should go back to counselling, but you just want to run away from everything, like some adolescent?'

'We tried counselling. It didn't work.'

'It's not fucking *magic*.' He pulled at his hair. 'You have to stick at it. Jesus, Zo . . . ' The anger subsided into weary despair: 'We can't go on like this. You know that.'

'I need some time by myself.'

'That's not how marriage works. You don't get to take a break for a bit when it gets difficult – you do it together. That's what I always believed, anyway. What does Dr Schlesinger have to say about your big plan, huh?'

She didn't tell him that she had stopped seeing Dr Schlesinger weeks ago; the suggestion that she was expected to seek permission for her decisions needled her.

'It's only a month,' she had replied instead, surprised by how calm she sounded. 'I'll be back before Thanksgiving.' It was easier to let him believe that too.

He changed tack. 'How are you paying for this?'

'I saved.'

'Oh, you *saved*?' He cocked an eyebrow. She didn't respond. All the implications contained in that question that was not a question at all but an accusation. What's mine is yours, and what's yours is yours, is that it? But her income, such as it was – from two days a week teaching art at a Catholic girls' middle school – was always supposed to be for her alone, that was what they had agreed, for the little luxuries that she would not have dreamed of taking from the household budget. Clothes, perfume, occasional nights out with her girlfriends. But she had had no social life for the best part of a year, much less bought new clothes. Unsurprisingly, Dan had failed to notice that.

'And what about *us*?' he had asked quietly. 'What about . . . ?' and pointed up at the ceiling, meaning Caleb's room, saving the lowest blow for last.

At that point she had raised her hand, *enough*, and stood up from the table, walked out of the house.

Now, with this unfamiliar sea stretching before her, she smiled into the sunlight, forcing herself to shake off her guilt. It had been Dan's choice to take voluntary redundancy, a choice he had not thought to discuss with her before presenting it as a *fait accompli*, but in it she found an opportunity; she could not have imagined herself leaving otherwise. It would be good for him to spend some time at home, to think of Caleb first for once. They could not have continued as they were; on that, at least, they agreed. Draining the last of her coffee, she set the mug on the veranda and padded down the wooden stairs – eight of them – on to the beach. The chill of the sand between her toes made her gasp; she had to step gingerly over the bands of shingle, until she reached the lacy patterns of foam where the waves petered out and receded. The water touched her feet, cold as a blade.

She walked along the shore as far as the outcrop of rocks at the south end of the bay's crescent and looked back at the house, squinting into the sun, shielding her eyes to take in its silhouette. In the morning light it looked benign, its crooked gables, ecclesiastical windows and roof turret charming and eccentric. Where she was standing now – this was where she had thought she glimpsed a figure on the beach, after she woke from her unexpected dream and her sleepwalking. The sand was smooth and undisturbed in this sheltered corner, where the sea did not reach. Not a trace of a footprint that wasn't her own, except the pointed tracks of the gulls. Of course there wasn't.

It was only later, when she showered, hot water needling her newly sensitised skin, that she happened to glance down and notice a small reddish-purple bruise on the side of her left breast, by her armpit. Probably where the strap of her bag had rubbed in all the hefting of luggage yesterday, she thought. But when she examined the bruise more closely in the mirror, it looked almost as if it bore the faint impression of teethmarks.

3

Zoe had installed herself outside on the veranda, leaning back on the bench with her legs stretched out, bare feet braced against the wooden balustrade and a sketchbook in her lap, when Mick arrived at noon. She heard the growl of the Land Rover and the scattering of gravel in the drive. After a few moments, he made his way around the side of the house, calling brightly so as not to alarm her, and approached the veranda from the beach. His expression was hesitant at first, anxious even, but it softened into relief to see her so apparently at ease.

'I see you're straight to work.' He shielded his eyes to look up at her as he climbed the steps.

'Couldn't miss this light.' She waved her sketchbook and grinned, surprised by her own jauntiness. The sensuality of the previous night's dream seemed to have left her lit up, more awake, more aware of her own body and her physical presence: the damp wood against the soles of her feet, the play of the wind on her face, the pencil's precise weight and balance between her fingers. She felt unusually vivid.

'And you slept all right?' Mick seemed caught off guard by her good humour, as if it was not what he had expected to find and was not quite convinced by it.

'Like a log, thanks.' She felt the colour flare up in her cheeks.

He looked at her, pulling on his earlobe as if he was on the point of asking another question, but after a hesitation he smiled and breathed out. 'Well, that's great. It's nice and quiet, at least – apart from the wind.'

'And the sea,' she said, laughing. 'And the gulls, and the seals.' She stopped, abruptly. She had almost said, 'and the singing.'

'True. But you'll get used to those in time, I hope. Can I interrupt you for a quick tour of the boring stuff?'

He showed her how to change the timer for the heating and hot water, the outbuilding at the front of the house where he had stacked chopped wood for the kitchen range, the fuse box under the stairs and the cellar with the generator that would, in theory, run the electricity in the event of a power cut. She wasn't wholly paying attention to the instructions; the cellar had a dank, forbidding atmosphere and a musty smell that made her want to get out as quickly as possible, and she was alarmed by the thought of being stuck out here with no power.

'You'll be fine, don't worry,' Mick said, catching her expression as he demonstrated how to light the hurricane lamps. 'It's just that it's all very new out here – there was no mains electricity or running water when we started doing up the house, it all had to be put in from scratch. The pipes make a bit of a racket too, I'm afraid, you probably noticed – banging and what have you. Everything's settling in and we don't know how it will fare in the winter storms.'

'So I could be stuck here with no lights?' She heard the catch in her voice as she pictured herself alone in the house with only a candle. A sharp memory of that pale singing jolted through her and she shivered, despite the sun.

'No, no – that's why we've put in the generator. Don't fret – you won't be left sitting out here in the dark.' He laughed, a touch too loudly. 'Well, then. If you're ready, I can drop you into town for the shops and bring you back before I have to get to the pub.'

'Oh – what about that door that's locked upstairs?' Zoe asked, as they returned to the kitchen.

Mick frowned. 'What door?'

'On the top landing. Right at the end.'

'The turret room, you mean? Have you no had a look up there? Lovely views all across the headland. On a clear day, you can see right across to—'

'But I don't have the key.'

'There is no key.' The crease in his brow deepened. 'None of the rooms are locked.' He looked at her as if trying to work out whether she was having him on. 'Maybe the handle's stiff. Shall I take a wee look?'

'Don't worry if it's—' she began, but he was already in the hall, bounding towards the stairs, telling her it was no trouble. She followed him up two flights, conscious of a flutter of apprehension in her stomach as they approached the closed door at the end of the second-floor landing.

'This one here?' Mick grasped the doorknob; it turned easily and the door swung inwards on smooth hinges, with barely a creak. Behind it was what looked like a large cupboard containing a wooden spiral staircase. He glanced back and beamed at her.

'I was probably turning it the wrong way,' Zoe mumbled, feeling the colour rising.

'Well, you'll know for next time. Go on up, if you like.' He held the door open and nodded towards the stairs.

The staircase smelled of wood polish and new paint. Light washed down the white walls from above. The air was colder here; as she climbed the short flight, she noticed goosebumps standing up on her arm and realised that she was holding her breath. At the end of the final curve, the stairs opened up into a bright hexagonal room with windows on all sides, wide enough for two people to stand with their arms outstretched. From here, two floors up, you could see across the headland to the north and out over the shining sea to three crooked rock stacks standing sentinel in the water off the coast, lined up like the remaining pillars of a giant ruined pier. On the other side, the view stretched as far as the moorland and the low purple mountains that formed a ridge along the centre of the island. There was no furniture in the room except a high wooden stool and a ledge that ran all the way around under the windows, wide enough to use as a writing desk. It must have been intended as some kind of observatory. No one could approach by water unannounced.

'It's quite something, eh? I'd have liked to put a telescope in there.' Mick's voice floated up from the foot of the stairs, with that same note of pride and affection that betrayed how much the house had been a labour of love for him. She had heard the pang in his voice as he had shown her around, pointing out examples of local craftsmanship or areas where the restoration had been particularly tricky. He envied her the chance to live in it, that much was plain. Perhaps it had been Kaye's choice, not to move the children. But what child would not want to live here, with a beach and seals on their doorstep?

'This view is amazing.' She glanced around the empty room. The singing had sounded so definite, in the depths of the night, the woman's pain so stark from behind the door. Strange, she thought, the tricks a fraught mind can play. She looked back out at the sea and, for the space of a heartbeat, she felt someone looking over her shoulder, a cold breath on her neck, so that she snapped around, thinking Mick had come up the stairs silently behind her. The room was empty. Downstairs, Mick gave a little cough, a hint that he wanted to get going.

He closed the door to the turret room behind her and immediately reopened it, turning the handle both ways to prove how easily it worked.

'There. Definitely not locked.'

'No. My mistake. Sorry.' She had the sudden, absurd thought that someone must have been holding the handle from the other side, though she dismissed it straight away.

Mick dropped her in the main street of the village by the parade of shops she had seen the night before.

'Half an hour do you? You've the wee supermarket across the way there and a chemist further down, and there's – well, you'll see. Have a wander. I'll meet you back here.'

Zoe thanked him and was about to cross the street when he called her back, leaning out of the driver's window.

'Uh – Mrs Adams?'

'Zoe,' she said patiently.

'I was wondering – had you any thoughts about what you would do for transport?' He looked embarrassed, as if he should not have to be the one raising this subject.

'Transport?' She looked at him, not quite understanding the question.

'It's only – you're a long way from civilisation out there. I mean, I'm happy to give you a lift now and then for the shopping, but there might be other times you run out of stuff or you just, you know, need to get out of there.' He stopped, his face confused, as if he realised he had slipped up. 'I mean, you might fancy a trip into town or, I don't know. And, like I say, Kaye and I will do whatever we can to help, but if we're not free . . . '

'Oh, God, no – I wasn't expecting you to drive me around the whole time.' Zoe heard her voice come out unexpectedly shrill. Now she was embarrassed too; it was true that in her impulsive enthusiasm for the beautiful light over the sea she had not given much thought to the fact that she would need food and basic supplies in her splendid isolation. She supposed there had been a vague notion of cabs in the back of her mind. Now that she was here, she realised how foolish that had been. 'I was thinking maybe I could rent a bike?'

49

'It's a thought,' Mick said carefully, in a voice that implied it was a stupid one. 'There's a bike shop right at the end of the High Street, before you get to the school.'

A quicksilver flicker of interest in her belly at the mention of the school. She thought of the young teacher, his fringe falling in his eyes, his shy smile and his Andy Warhol glasses, and with the thought came that prickling awareness of her own body, alive and responsive, the way she had felt after the previous night's dream. She had to look away from Mick in case he noticed the colour in her face.

'But, listen – when the weather sets in, you won't be wanting to cycle on those roads,' he was saying, oblivious. He cleared his throat. 'I only mention it because my pal Dougie Reid up at the golf course has a car he could rent you while you're here. Very reasonable. Nothing fancy, but—'

'That's kind. Maybe . . . ' Her throat closed around the words. He was right; she had realised during the drive across grandly bleak sweeps of rust-coloured moorland that she would not manage here without her own car. It was six months since she had been behind a wheel. Each time she had tried, the panic rose up through her chest and engulfed her, so that she felt choked by it: the shakes and pounding heart, the numbness in her limbs, the sweat and the fast, shallow breathing. Perhaps here, in a different landscape, she might be able to face that down. There was a different anxiety in Mick's expression, though, that she could not quite identify, one that had nothing to do with the worry that he would end up ferrying her around. He wants me to be able to escape, she thought, as if by sudden intuition. *You might need to get out of there,* he had said, then tried to correct himself. Did even Mick – stoical, pragmatic Mick Drummond, scoffer at old wives' tales – fear there was something she might need to flee at the house?

'Great stuff – let's find a time to go up there and take a look at it, at least.' Mick seemed relieved. He glanced at his

50

watch. 'Half an hour, then. Shouldn't take you more than that.'

He pulled away with a cheerful toot of his horn and Zoe crossed the street towards the grocery store. The food would be basic here, she suspected, none of the fancy stuff she liked from Whole Foods or the Thai grocer, but that was OK. She had little interest these days in cooking. There had been a time, when she and Dan had first moved in together and the idea of their first home was new and felt like a game, when she had liked to experiment with food. Dan was an enthusiastic cook; they had learned together. But lately, the business of making a family meal had come to feel like a thankless chore, an increasingly hollow pretence at normality, the time and effort expended so disproportionate to the end result, which was only ever bolted down so that everyone could return as quickly as possible to their separate rooms. Here she planned to live simply, to eat only things that required minimal effort. Cold meat, cheese, salad, bread, breakfast cereals. Coffee, maybe even cigarettes. The way she'd lived when she was at art school, and was so driven by her work that it was too important to interrupt for anything as trivial as eating. She wanted to recapture that kind of absorption, see if she was still capable of losing herself like that in the work. That's why it was good there was no phone signal and no Wi-Fi at the house, she thought. No Twitter, no Facebook, no Instagram. No distractions. Not that she had felt like sharing much in recent months anyway. She couldn't bear to look at the news, and she only ever looked at her friends' lives now with a twist of envy below her ribs and a feeling of exclusion, occasionally an unforgivable wish – there and gone in an instant – that some misfortune would slam into their apparently perfect lives. These thoughts quickly warped into self-loathing; she did not wish harm to her friends, how could she? And yet she could not help resenting them either, for their insularity, their self-satisfaction. For some time she

51

had felt it might be easier to disengage entirely. In a flash of what had seemed at the time like boldness, she had deleted her Facebook and Instagram accounts before she left. She wanted to concentrate on *being* here, not clinging on remotely to the shreds of a life back home or worrying about how to curate her experience for other people's approval. She was already starting to regret the decision.

A warm gust of air caught her as she walked past an open shop door, a scent of bread and vanilla, and she realised with a twinge that she had not eaten breakfast. In the window beside her, rustic loaves fanned out in baskets and pastries glistened wantonly on silver tiered cake-stands. A painted sign swung above the door, proclaiming *Maggie's Granary* in curlicued script. A cinnamon bun from Maggie's, Charles Joseph had said: the price of his stories. She hesitated on the threshold. If anyone in this place was likely to tell her the truth about the house, it would be the Professor.

4

The door of C. Joseph, Rare & Second-hand Books produced a sonorous chime as she pushed it open to enter an atmosphere of rarefied, eccentric chaos. The interior was done up like a gentleman's library from the last century, or the bar at a fancy country club, without trying so hard: all mahogany panelling and scuffed wine-dark leather winged chairs, books stacked floor to ceiling along every wall and piled in precarious towers in corners. It smelled reassuringly of tobacco and old paper.

'Give me a minute,' called a voice from somewhere at the back of the shop. Zoe peered around a bookcase to see the old Labrador padding towards her, nose quivering towards the paper bag in her hand.

'Hey, Horace,' she said, reaching down to scratch him behind the ears. When she looked up, Charles Joseph was standing in front of her, hands clasped together.

'She remembered the buns, Horace,' he remarked to the dog, with solemn pleasure. 'I told you she would. Your timing is impeccable, Ms Adams – I've just put a fresh pot of coffee on. Come through to the back.'

He led her past a wooden desk with a cash register and through an arched doorway into a smaller room. This, too, was lined with bookshelves along the walls, but the central space had been left for a couple of shabby armchairs and a wide desk that looked like an antique. In one corner a jumble of coloured beanbags and cushions sprawled across the floor.

'I call this the Reading Room,' he said, with a sweeping gesture. 'Rather grand, I know. But sometimes people like to have a quiet place to sit down with a book while they're in town. Some of the youngsters come here to study at the weekends, if they can't get any peace at home. People drop by in their lunch hour and the children like to stop off on their way home from school. I'm always pleased to have company.' He waved towards the coloured cushions.

'You're better than a public library,' Zoe said, smiling. The old man's face grew serious.

'I'm afraid that's more or less true. They closed our library down a couple of years ago. Someone on the mainland decided it wasn't financially viable. I'm all the islanders have now.' He lifted his hands in a gesture of helplessness. 'That's why I give away so many books, though our young friend Edward despairs at my business sense.'

'And you don't . . . ' she hesitated, searching for the right way to phrase it ' . . . worry about the money?'

Charles gave an indulgent chuckle. 'My dear girl, I worry about it all the time. But I've been fortunate. I wrote a number of books when I was younger that enjoyed some success. I invested wisely, and that's given me an income over the years. And I dabble in rare books – now and then I come across an item of more than average value, and that keeps us afloat, with what I make from the maps and walking guides. So I can more or less afford to allow my charitable instincts to get the better of my commercial ones.'

'What kind of books did you write?'

'Oh, studies of myths. That was my field. There's bound to be one around somewhere.' He poked about on a nearby shelf, running his finger along dusty spines until he pulled out a fat volume in a transparent plastic cover and handed it to

Zoe. *The Myths That Make Us* by Dr Charles M. Joseph. The dust-jacket featured a reproduction of Rubens' *Saturn Devouring His Son*.

'Is it history?' she asked, turning the book over to look at the back cover.

He tilted his head. 'Partly. History, anthropology, psychology, literature, art, travel – there's a bit of everything in mythography. This one found its way on to various university syllabuses over the years – that's why it's still in print.'

The inside cover showed a black-and-white photograph of the author in a tweed jacket much like the one he was currently wearing, his eyes crinkled at the edges as he smiled into the camera. He didn't look a whole lot younger than he did now, Zoe thought, yet this book was clearly published in the last century. She turned to the inside flyleaf to find that it was dated 1975. Charles caught her looking at him and smiled.

'I was born middle-aged,' he said. 'Now then – take a seat while I find a plate for those buns. Milk and sugar?' He disappeared into a small kitchen through the back. Zoe could hear the chinking of crockery and the hiss of steam.

'Neither, thanks.' She sank back into one of the armchairs, the book in her lap, and flicked through a few pages, her eyes lingering over the lavish illustrated plates – reproductions of paintings, sculptures and maps.

'Take it home if you like,' Charles said, setting down a mug of coffee on a table he pulled up between them. She handed him the paper bag and he settled into the other armchair, elbows jutting out and hands folded together, watching her. 'What did you want to ask me, then?'

'Oh.' She looked up, startled. 'I was interested in finding out a bit more about the local history. Since I'm going to be living here for a bit.'

He continued to look at her. 'Naturally. But I think you wanted to ask something in particular?'

'What's the story with the house?' she blurted. 'The one Mick and Kaye don't want me to hear?'

'Ah.' He picked up his bun and took a large bite, leaving the question hanging while he chewed it, nodding several times in appreciation. Zoe wondered if he would make her wait until he had finished the entire thing, but when his mouth was empty he glanced towards the doorway. 'Mick's put a great deal of time and money into doing up that old place. Love, too, in a sense. It was important to him to redeem it. The house had been left to ruin when his father died – perhaps when you're more settled you can get him to show you the photos. What he's done there is extraordinary.'

'Redeem it from what?'

'From its history. You're their first tenant, you know. They'd only had the website live two days when you emailed him, he said, and he was fretting that he might not find anyone at all over the winter. So you were a bit of a godsend – you can understand why they don't want the locals putting you off the place with lurid tales. Especially a woman on her own.'

Zoe gave him a stern look. 'I'm interested in the tales. I think I'm old enough to tell fact from fiction.'

He met this with an enigmatic smile. 'Well. I wonder if any of us can really claim to know that.'

There was an odd pause while Zoe tried to judge whether or not he was serious. 'So – it's supposed to be haunted, right?' She made the question sound deliberately sarcastic, but as she spoke she recalled the chill she had felt on the stairs, the plaintive tone of the woman singing. But that had been the whisky and jet lag. No point in telling him about that.

Charles picked up his coffee and leaned forward. 'Are you sure you want to hear this story? Only, one can't *un*know things, you see, and there's a world of difference between hearing it here, all cosy over buns, and remembering it later, after dark, alone in that big house.'

'You're doing it too, now. I'm not a child, Dr Joseph.'

'I apologise.' He nodded, smiling, but there was a trace of resignation in his tone, as if what she was demanding were an unpleasant but necessary cure.

'Well, then.' He set his cup down and eased back in his chair, steepling his fingers. 'Tamhas McBride owned this island in the mid nineteenth century, though he never lived here until he married Ailsa Drummond in 1861. She was the eldest child and only daughter of the Reverend Teàrlach Drummond, great-great-*great*-grandfather to our Mick, who was then minister of the island's kirk. The reverend was widowed and Ailsa refused to abandon him on the island after her marriage, so her new husband had a grand house built overlooking the bay on the northern coast. To say the McBrides were not liked here would be an understatement. Tamhas's father had been a Glasgow industrialist who bought the island in the 1830s when the laird went bankrupt – it happened all over this part of Scotland. His first act as landlord was to send sixty of the inhabitants to Nova Scotia.'

'Jesus. What, like a punishment?'

'He claimed the island was over-populated. "Assisted voluntary emigration", they called it. Nothing voluntary about it, of course – it was eviction by another name, and the rest were supposed to be grateful they were allowed to stay. Some islands were cleared altogether.' He paused to shake his head. 'So the McBrides were not well-loved, as you can imagine, though Tamhas was less interfering as a landlord than his father. He was getting on for fifty by the time he married Ailsa – his first wife had died in childbirth, along with the baby. Ailsa was thirty-four – her family had given up any hope of her marrying, so to find such a prestigious husband was seen as a blessing, despite his name. The islanders must have hoped Ailsa would be their advocate.' He paused for a longing look at his bun. Zoe grinned and nodded her permission. Now that he had agreed to talk, she was willing to indulge him.

'Tamhas McBride travelled a lot on business, leaving his wife at home,' Charles continued with his mouth full, brushing sugar from his beard. 'But she seemed contented enough out there in her big house, according to the letters she sent her younger brother.'

'That would be Mick's great-great . . . ' she paused, trying to calculate.

'Great-*great*-grandfather, that's right. William Drummond. He was ten years younger than his sister and studying theology in Edinburgh – he was intended for the kirk, like his father. William and Ailsa corresponded regularly. Everyone assumed there would soon be a McBride heir and that would keep Ailsa occupied. But they had been married less than a year when Tamhas was drowned. He was on board a ship that went down during a storm in the Atlantic, all hands lost. On his way back from America, as it happens.' He added this with an encouraging nod, as if it would give her some sense of participation in the story.

'And he haunts the place?' She tried to sound light, but it came out nervous and over-excited. Charles chuckled, as you might humour a child.

'I've never heard of Tamhas giving anyone any trouble from beyond the grave.'

'Then . . . ?' Zoe found she was gripping her mug tighter.

He uncrossed his legs, leaned back in his chair and recrossed them the other way around.

'Tamhas McBride's death was only the beginning. After she was widowed, Ailsa became reclusive. She dismissed all the staff except one maid for housework and laundry, and a woman from the village who came in once a day to cook – despite the fact that Tamhas had left her a rich woman.'

'She stayed in the house?'

'Apparently she would walk every day along the cliffs, or sit on the beach drawing – the same scenes over and over, the sky and the sea.'

58

Zoe felt an odd chill.

'How do you know all this?'

'Mick Drummond inherited a remarkable trove of letters and photographs when his father died last year,' Charles said, running a moistened finger around the edge of his plate to mop up any stray crumbs. 'Passed down through the generations, though his father had kept them hidden away. There was an unspoken agreement in the family to leave the story buried, though God knows I did my best over the years to persuade old Mr Drummond to part with those papers, without success. Mick offered them to me, knowing my interest, on condition I didn't publish anything without his permission. He said he had no time for poking through the past.'

'Does Mick's family still own the island?'

'No – I'm afraid the Drummonds have rather fallen from their former glory. The land has all been sold off piecemeal over the decades – most of the centre is National Trust Scotland now, thank goodness, so it's protected. But he owns the cove where your house is. The McBride land, as it's known. He either can't or won't get rid of that.'

'So did you find anything good in the letters?'

'Oh, a great deal. Plenty relating to the McBride case, which has taken on all the colour of a melodrama over the years. I plan to write a book based on the letters one day, but Mick was adamant he didn't want anything made public yet. I'm hoping he'll change his mind, of course, but once he'd decided to do up the house, he was afraid any kind of publicity about the case would frighten people away.' He took a gulp of coffee. 'Or, worse, attract them. The wrong people. Haunted-house nuts, psychic researchers, amateur detectives – you know the kind.'

'So it *is* haunted?' She pointed at him, triumphant, as if she had tricked him into admission. Charles merely gave her his quiet smile.

'I'm coming to that. Most of what I'm telling you I've gleaned from William Drummond's letters.'

'Ailsa's brother.'

'Yes. Young William was a prolific correspondent, it seems – first with his father and sister, and later, after the reverend died, with the solicitor who took over the McBride estate. One of the chief subjects of his letters is his sister's welfare.'

'So what happened to Ailsa?'

'Well, at first she kept to herself. Stayed away from the village, turned down all social invitations. Of course, she had become an intriguing prospect, as you may imagine – a wealthy widow living alone in a large house, relatively young, certainly young enough to remarry. As soon as a decent interval had passed, the suitors began paying court. She spurned every advance, according to the maid. Burned letters unopened.'

'Perhaps she was still grieving her husband,' Zoe murmured.

'Perhaps,' Charles said evenly. 'She saw her father occasionally, but much less than she used to, and not at all once he became too ill to make the journey out to her. Eight months after Tamhas was drowned, the Reverend Drummond also passed away, from pneumonia. Ailsa McBride finally emerged for his funeral – the first time she'd been seen in the village since they buried her husband – and shocked everyone by turning up in an advanced stage of pregnancy.'

'Wow.' She stared at him, eyes wide, the mug halfway to her lips. 'Was it her husband's?'

'Naturally, that's what everyone wanted to know. But no one quite dared to ask her directly and she never offered an explanation. She wrote to her brother of her "poor fatherless child", but in the same letter she says "his father will always be watching over him", which sounds like a sentimental reference to her dead husband. But here's the bombshell.' He paused for effect, raising an eyebrow over the top of his cup. 'Ailsa McBride gave birth to a son nearly eleven months after her husband was buried.'

'Whoa.' Zoe sat back. 'Naughty Ailsa. Unless they miscounted?'

'The dates are there in the church records. Ten and a half months after the burial. And Tamhas had been away for the best part of two months before he died. You can imagine, in a village like this, the gift that would have been to the gossip mill. But that was the point at which she truly became an outcast.'

'She doesn't sound like someone who would have cared too much about that,' Zoe said.

'Apparently not. She kept to the house after her son was born. Dismissed the maid, saying she intended to care for the child herself, which of course was unheard of for a woman of means at the time. The maid was less than delighted – there was little work available on the island. It's my view that much of what was passed down had its roots in malicious rumours put about by the maid in anger at losing her position.'

'Like what?' Zoe sat forward, intrigued.

'Oh, that there was something wrong with the child. Ailsa didn't send for a midwife – only the maid was present in the house when the child was delivered, and she swore it was stillborn. Ailsa never had the boy baptised either – you can imagine the scandal of that. The cook continued to visit every day but she said she never once heard the child crying, nor ever saw him, though Ailsa was always sewing clothes for him. This went on for a couple of years. This cook said Ailsa McBride was growing stranger and stranger – more remote, as if she was in another world most of the time.'

'Losing her mind, you mean?'

'That's what the new reverend implied in his letter to William Drummond. Though you must remember how quick people were to diagnose madness in women in those days. But even that was principally among educated people. Rough-hewn island folk jumped to other conclusions first.' He raised a finger, as if he were giving a lecture. 'Consider it. A woman

61

living alone, who shuns church and refuses to answer the door to the minister, with an unbaptised child no one ever sees?'

'They said she was a witch, I guess?' Zoe felt the goose-bumps rise on her arms and the back of her neck. 'Did the rumours never imply who the father was?'

'Oh yes.' He gave a mirthless smile. 'They said it was the Devil himself. There was even a rumour that she had murdered the child at birth in some kind of blood sacrifice, which was why no one ever saw him.' Charles's face tightened in anger, as if he took such ignorance and prejudice personally. 'But that *is* a real mystery – with all the gossip flying, there was never a finger pointed at any of the island men. Not even the disgruntled maid could confect any plausible evidence of male visitors in the year after Ailsa was widowed. Even the minister didn't cross the threshold.'

'Wow. She really knew how to keep a secret.' Zoe felt a growing admiration for Ailsa McBride and her disregard for convention.

'So it seems. But after the child was born, Ailsa left the management of her financial affairs to the one solicitor in the village, a Mr Richard Bonar,' he continued. 'Bonar would go out to the house once a month to discuss the estate. His letters to William Drummond are fascinating.' He leaned forward, eyes bright. 'He says despite the talk, he's never found Ailsa anything less than entirely lucid. She is always impeccably dressed, the house clean, and she displays a sound under-standing of her accounts and investments together with an impressive grasp of arithmetic for a woman.'

'Big of him,' Zoe remarked.

Charles laughed. 'Yes. Though it's curious – I can't help but wonder about the effect of those letters. What might have happened if Bonar had been less pragmatic, if he had encour-aged William to come back and see his sister. But William was evidently reassured by Bonar's words. Especially when, a couple of years later, the solicitor said he'd seen the child.'

'So the son was alive?'

'Most definitely. A frail boy, Bonar says, very pale, but to all appearances well cared-for, though he suspected he might be mute. So William saw no need to get involved. He was engaged to be married by then, to a girl from an Edinburgh clergy family of some standing – he was moving up in the world and had no wish to be burdened with the care of a widowed sister and sickly nephew on a remote island, particularly when that sister had more than enough money to look after herself and there was a rumour of illegitimacy hanging over the boy. He writes encouraging Ailsa to sell the land and move to Edinburgh so they can see more of each other, but he doesn't make much effort to persuade her.' He stopped for another gulp of coffee and shook his head. 'Perhaps if he had taken more trouble with her, the story might have had a different ending.'

Zoe watched him with a frisson of excitement, waiting for the reveal.

'Would you like to see her?' Before she could answer, he crossed the room to a vast walnut cabinet against the back wall, crouched to unlock the top drawer and drew out a leather folder crammed with documents. After some riffling through papers he held out a yellowed photograph, curling at the edges. She reached out for it, aware of a strange tightness in her throat.

'I'll put another pot of coffee on,' Charles said, setting the folder down on the desk and leaving her with the picture.

Zoe looked down. The photo in her hand was a formal portrait, the woman sitting stiff-backed in her black dress with its high lace collar and wide skirts, hair severely parted and pulled back into a bun. The face was stern, not beautiful but strong-featured, with fierce dark eyes that stared into the lens as if issuing a challenge. No wonder the locals left her alone, Zoe thought; the force of that gaze would make anyone

63

step back and apologise. Around her neck, Ailsa wore a silver Celtic cross patterned with ornate tracery.

'Formidable woman, isn't she?' Charles's voice over her shoulder made her jump. 'Shall I get you a refill?' He leaned over for her empty mug. 'You wouldn't want to be on the wrong side of her, to judge by that expression. You can see why she made the villagers nervous.'

'So what did happen to her?' Zoe called, as he pottered back to the kitchen.

'I'm about to tell you,' he said. At the same time, the bell above the shop door chimed. Charles emerged from the kitchen, wiping his hands on a tea towel, as Mick appeared in the archway to the main shop. His gaze alighted on Zoe with the photograph in her lap and she watched his face working to suppress a reaction. Again, Zoe felt she had incurred his disapproval; guilty, she glanced at her watch.

'Thought I might find you here.' Mick pressed his lips together, but his reproving look was directed at Charles.

'I'm so sorry,' Zoe said, half rising. 'I didn't realise how quickly the time had gone.'

'It's my fault entirely,' Charles said, with his charming smile, flipping the cloth over his shoulder. 'I persuaded her to stay for coffee, I'm afraid.'

'And a wee history lesson, I see.' Mick nodded to the picture in Zoe's hand.

'I asked him to tell me,' she said, looking at Mick. She did not want to be the cause of ill feeling between the two men, but she found Mick's efforts to hide the stories from her both irritating and a little ridiculous. Perhaps he was ashamed of having a family history that included witchcraft, or madness. That sort of thing still mattered in a place like this. 'The island is so fascinating. I thought it might be inspiring for my painting.'

Mick's face clouded further. 'I don't think—' he began, but changed his mind. 'I need to get back up the pub in a minute.

If you do a quick dash round the shop now, I can run you home, but we'll need to get a shift on.'

Zoe stood. 'Look, I don't want to put you to any trouble. Couldn't I get a cab? That way I can take my time and explore a bit more.'

Mick laughed. 'A cab, she says. Good luck with that.' He folded his arms and appeared to relent. 'Nae bother. You've my mobile number – if you can't get a lift, I'll be free again after about four, you can try me then.' His eyes darted back to the photograph. 'And don't believe anything *he* tells you.' He turned and stalked briskly out of the shop, leaving the bell jangling as the door banged behind him.

Zoe caught Charles's eye and he grimaced.

'We're in the doghouse,' she said, handing back the photo, avoiding a last look at the woman's stare. 'I shouldn't have kept him waiting, when he was going out of his way to help me.'

'It's me he's angry with,' Charles said, though he didn't sound as if this troubled him unduly. He picked up the document case and tapped it with a tobacco-stained forefinger. 'But I only ever promised not to write publicly about the story without his blessing. I certainly never agreed not to discuss it. And as a publican, he should have a better grasp of human nature. The more he tries to stop you hearing, the more curious you're bound to be.' He took a long look at Ailsa McBride before slipping the picture back among the other papers. 'How was your first night in the house, by the way?'

Zoe hesitated. For one reckless moment she considered telling him about the singing and the locked door, the figure on the beach. It would be a relief to voice the strangeness of it aloud, to have someone as unflappable as Charles reassure her that she had imagined it. But in the same instant she recalled the dream that had preceded it, her own nakedness and fierce desire, and felt unaccountably ashamed, as if he would be able to read traces of that dream in her face. Besides, he had seen

65

her at the pub; he must have noticed how quickly the whisky had gone to her head. He would be too polite to tell her it was the drink, but she could hardly expect to be taken seriously. She shrugged and smiled.

'Fine. I needed the sleep.'

He raised his head, eyebrows cocked in a question. 'You didn't find the silence unnerving? People often do.'

'I'm OK with silence,' she said, still smiling, though her face had begun to feel rigid.

'That's good. Few people really know how to be comfortable with it, I find.'

'Will you tell me the rest of the story?'

Charles appeared to be on the point of answering when the shop bell rang again and a wavering voice called out as the door banged shut.

'Anyone there?'

Horace lumbered up from under his chair to greet the newcomer. An elderly woman in a clear plastic rain hood picked her way through the piles of books, nosing the air like a woodland creature.

'There you are!' Her watery eyes alighted on Zoe. 'Oh, but I don't want to trouble you if you're busy, Professor.'

'No trouble at all, Betsy. It's always a pleasure to see you.' He pushed his chair back, turning to wink at Zoe over the woman's head. 'Do help yourself to more coffee, Ms Adams, and a book, if you like.'

But Zoe sensed the earlier intimacy had been broken; Mick's appearance had cast a shadow of guilt over their conversation. She picked up her jacket and tucked *The Myths That Make Us* inside it.

'Thank you – I should get on with my shopping. I've taken up enough of your time.'

'Not at all.' He waved a hand. 'I've left you on a cliffhanger so you'll have to come back and see us.'

The old dog followed her to the door, sniffing at her legs.

She scratched his head between his ears on her way out and he made a low, throat-clearing noise of appreciation, sitting down solidly in the doorway. Zoe turned to see the elderly woman watching her through the glass as she walked away.

5

She spotted the young teacher as he jogged across the empty playground, clutching the hood of a waterproof hiking jacket around his face against the downpour, while she cowered under the brick archway of the bike shop yard, peering out at the sky, bewildered by its sudden betrayal. She took a bold step forward into his line of sight, one hand protectively clamping the saddle of her new bicycle, pretending she hadn't noticed him. The plastic carrier bag from the supermarket knocked against her leg as it swung from the handlebars.

'Oh. Hello again.' Edward's face lit up as he approached; rain had spattered his glasses and he had to take them off and wipe them with a tissue. 'You picked the wrong day for a bike ride.'

'I know, right?' Zoe pushed a wet strand of hair out of her face and grinned. 'What's going on? It was fine when I came out.' She patted the bike. 'And I just paid the guy to take this for a month. He didn't tell me it was monsoon season. Reckon I could get a refund?'

'If he gave money back for every day it rained here he'd have gone bust long ago.' Edward smiled. He seemed nervous. 'Seriously, though. You can't ride all the way back in this.

You should wait it out – the weather changes from one hour to the next.'

'I see that.' She pulled her scarf tighter. 'I was going to take my groceries home. You guys are not big on cabs around here, I understand.'

He laughed. 'Uh, no.'

'I guess it's back to the bookshop till this clears up.' She glanced along the street. 'Your Professor will think I'm hitting on him. Though I'm not sure I can afford to pay my way in buns.'

'You can wait at mine if you like.' The way he said it; too quickly, trying to make it sound casual. 'I'm across the green there, in the School House.' He indicated through the billowing curtains of rain.

She frowned. 'But you were on your way somewhere.'

'Nothing urgent. I've got biscuits, and coffee,' he added, as if to persuade her. Zoe wondered if he had seen her from the window; if he had come out specifically to bump into her. The possibility fired a small, bright buzz in her chest.

'Well – that's really kind. If you're sure I won't be in the way?'

'Of course not. Charles will be closing up soon anyway, you might as well. Here, let me take that.' He reached out for the bike; she unhooked the bag and let him steer. Together they scurried across the green, heads down into the rain as it drove harder all around them, bouncing up from the road and sluicing along the gutters in a brown stream.

She stole a glance at his profile as he fumbled to unlock the gate at the side of the School House, the bike balanced against his hip. Neat, regular features, glazed with the uncomplicated smoothness of youth, save for that fine crease between his brows that hinted at deep preoccupations, a serious involvement with the world. A brief shiver of unease rippled through her; an absurd sense that she should not step across the threshold into his life, that to do so would be to invite a

69

curse, as in a fairy tale. She shook the rain from her hair briskly and smiled as he held the front door open.

The School House was built in the nineteenth century from the same hard grey stone as the school it served. Inside it had been furnished sparely, the floral curtains and plain upholstery faded, the carpet's pattern worn indistinct by the feet of previous tenants. Edward had imposed little of himself on his home, Zoe thought, as he showed her into the cramped living room. A curved silver wireless speaker on the walnut dresser; a black-and-white photograph of dreaming spires in dawn mist; a music stand under one narrow window, his violin case leaning beside it. Scanning the room, she had the impression that he had barely unpacked, and did not intend to stay long. Only the bookshelves offered any glimpse of him. They had been carefully arranged, poetry and classics together, literary novels and the kind of non-fiction she saw extracted in the *New Yorker* and always intended to read one day. Browsing the spines, she began to feel intimidated by him: his obvious intelligence, his earnest intensity.

'Tea? Coffee?' He took off his glasses and wiped them on the tail of his shirt. That English diffidence as he looked at her from under his fringe, fearful of being refused. Funny to think she and her friends would have looked straight past a boy like this in college. Now she was the one who feared being invisible.

'Tea, thanks. If I have any more coffee I'll shoot through the ceiling. No milk.'

'So you've been to see Charles already?' he called through the open door of the kitchen, over the sound of running water. 'Has he been filling your head with lurid legends?'

'I wanted him to tell me about the house.' A wooden staircase led up from the main room, almost opposite the door. Zoe wandered over to the shelves beneath it and began lifting paperbacks from a stack.

'In defiance of Mick's Official Secrets Act?'

'Yeah – what's with that?' She picked up a hardback volume of Rilke in a plastic dust-jacket and flicked through the pages. Some had been folded down at the corners and here and there she glimpsed pencil notes in the margin. One of his college books, she guessed, and felt an odd pang of tenderness, to think of him so newly out in the world. 'Did Mick give everyone orders not to tell me?'

'More or less.' Edward came to stand in the doorway, a kettle in his hand. 'He was afraid it would scare you off. He doesn't like anyone talking about his family history at the best of times, but especially not in front of paying customers.'

'It's a little paranoid. Every old place has its stories. I wouldn't have chosen to live in a house like that if I was easily spooked.'

'Even so,' he said, in a tone that suggested he was struggling to be fair, 'it would be a big deal for some people, to find out you're living in a house where a woman killed her child. And then after what happened last year – I can see his point.'

Zoe snapped her head up from the book to stare at him. 'She killed her child? What did happen last year?'

He froze, guilt slinking over his face. 'Shit. I thought Charles had told you?'

'He didn't get to that part. Oh, come *on*,' she said, when it appeared he was turning away, 'you can't throw that out and not explain it. Who killed her child – Ailsa McBride?'

Edward sighed, flicking at the kettle lid with his fingernail. 'I've put my foot in it. At least wait till I've got the tea on, OK?'

Zoe scuffed impatiently as he clattered about in the kitchen. Over the chink of china and the wheeze of the kettle boiling, she heard him determinedly humming a tune that sounded familiar. She turned over the flyleaf of the Rilke book to find an inscription dated the previous summer in a rounded, girlish

71

hand: *My darling Ed – we'll always have Prague! Here's to all the summers to come, all my love, L xxxx.*

She darted a furtive glance towards the kitchen, where Edward was pouring hissing water into a teapot. Who was L? Nothing about this sparse cottage suggested the existence of a girlfriend. Where was L now, she wondered. What had happened to all the summers to come?

He came in bearing the mugs before him like votive offerings, steam fogging up his glasses. Zoe quickly thrust the book back on the pile, but if he noticed, he said nothing. He set one of the mugs down on another stack of books beside the sofa and gestured for Zoe to sit, then flopped on the opposite end, pressed up against the armrest – there were no other chairs in the room – and tucked one leg under him like a child, both hands wrapped around his mug while he watched her over the rim.

'Look, Charles is really the person to ask about this,' he began, half-apologetic, half-defensive. 'I only know what he's told me, and the general gossip.'

Zoe smiled encouragement. 'Tell me the gossip, then. Ailsa McBride killed her kid, is that it?'

He sighed and looked down into his tea, as if he might find a prompt sheet there. 'Supposedly she went mad, or she was possessed, or something along those lines. She's meant to have killed her son and then herself. But they never found the boy.'

'Then how do they know she killed him?'

'They found some of his clothes washed up on the rocks.' He bit his lip. 'I shouldn't be telling you this.'

'Screw Mick,' Zoe said, feeling bolder.

'It's not about Mick. I was thinking of you having to go back there on your own.'

'Couldn't they both have been murdered?'

Edward tilted his head, considering. 'I've never heard that as a theory, I don't know why.'

72

'Because the whole island had it in for Ailsa, clearly. A woman of independent means, raising her child with no need of a man? Must be crazy. They both get killed – the crazy witch lady must have done it. Case closed.'

'It *is* a bit *Wicker Man*, isn't it?' Edward caught her eye and they both grinned; in that instant, Zoe felt the unexpected click of connection and knew, with a pang of relief, that she was no longer alone here. She had an ally.

'What happened to Ailsa?' she asked, when she realised they had been holding one another's gaze a beat too long to be comfortable.

'Her body washed up further round the coast a few days later, fully clothed, no wounds on her. So they concluded she'd drowned herself after killing the boy.'

'But if the kid was never found, they can't even be certain he was killed, surely? Maybe he ran away.'

Edward shrugged. 'I suppose. But he'd have turned up sooner or later, wouldn't he, on a small island? People seem to have accepted the Ailsa version as fact, though. There's a lot of whispering about how the land is bad in that corner of the island.'

'Bad how?'

'Cursed. McBride apparently tore down the remains of a ruined chapel and used the stones to build over its foundations, and the chapel had been built on an ancient pagan site to sanctify it, so he was asking for trouble.' He grinned and shifted position, stretched out the leg that had been folded and tucked the other under.

'Great. So I'm staying in a house with an ancient curse, haunted by a child-killing witch.'

Edward laughed. 'Yup. Enjoy your holiday.'

Zoe leaned her head back against the sofa cushion and laughed along. Rain gusted against the window panes like gravel flung with malice, and the wind boomed down the chimney, shaking the doorframe. The room had grown darker around them as the last light leached from the sky; shadows stole out from the corners, settling over the hollows and angles of their faces. Edward reached behind him and clicked the switch on a standing lamp, warming their corner of the room with a soft amber glow. A silence unfolded, unhurried and companionable. She held the mug to her lips, breathing in its warmth, and found she had no desire to leave. For a while, she could almost forget herself.

'I don't know why Mick wants to keep all this hushed up,' she remarked eventually. 'Plenty of people would pay a fortune to stay in a place with that kind of history.'

'Exactly – ghouls. Unsolved-murder fetishists. Those weirdos who think you can measure paranormal activity with radio waves.' He picked at a loose thread on the cushion cover. 'There was a lot of resentment in the village when he inherited the house and started to do it up. There'd been a kind of unspoken agreement between the Drummonds and the islanders that the McBride house would be left to fall into ruin and the story allowed to die with it.' He arched his back and folded his hands together behind his head. As he moved, his knee brushed briefly against Zoe's leg and she felt a small shock jolt through her like static. 'It's seen as a taint on the island's reputation – they take all that Gothic stuff quite seriously and they don't want to be famous for it. It took Mick a long time to persuade the locals that he wouldn't use the family history as a selling point.'

Outside, a gull's mournful cry echoed across the empty schoolyard like a reprimand.

'So everyone is sworn to secrecy,' Zoe said, sitting up and wrapping her hands around her mug. 'Did Mick tell you all this?'

Edward shook his head. 'He doesn't like to talk about it. This all happened before I got here. Charles told me most of it – and Annag Logan, the barmaid at the Stag.'

Zoe thought of her lipstick with a stab of resentment. 'Are

74

you and she . . . ?' She made a vague motion with her hand that implied conjunction.

Edward's look of confusion shaded to outrage as he understood her meaning. '*Christ*, no. Would you seriously think . . . ?' He straightened up, pushing a hand through his hair. 'Not exactly my type. Apart from anything else, she's only sixteen.'

'Is she really?' Zoe nodded in mild surprise. 'I'd have said older. I didn't mean to offend,' she added quickly. 'Only – there can't be many young women out here.'

'I didn't really come here to meet women.' A corner of his mouth twisted; there was a darker note in his voice which piqued her interest. 'Quite the opposite, in fact.'

'You came here to meet men?'

It took him a moment to spot the glint in her eye; he threw a cushion at her, laughing as she tried to duck. 'That's right – big fishermen and rig workers. I love an oilskin, me.'

'And how's that working out for you?'

He made a face. 'I'm sick of the smell of herring, truth be told. And they're away so much. I'm a herring widow.'

Zoe laughed and chucked the cushion back; he jerked his mug out of the firing line, too late, as tea sloshed over the upholstery. 'Hey, watch the sofa! It's a priceless heirloom.'

'It's definitely historic.' Zoe rubbed the cheap brown fabric with a finger where the arms were worn shiny with use. Wind snarled down the chimney and worried the window frames; she thought she caught the bass note of distant thunder.

'Should I light a fire?' Edward glanced at her for approval; when she shrugged, to say she didn't mind either way, he sprang to his feet and knelt in front of the hearth. 'I usually sweep it out and leave it ready in the mornings, now the nights are getting colder,' he remarked, over his shoulder, as he reached for logs from a basket to one side.

It was the sort of thing her grandmother might have said. Zoe watched his careful, methodical movements and found it suddenly unbearably touching – the thought of him waking here alone, dutifully sweeping out the night's cold ashes before the children piled shrieking into school, laying his little fire for the long dark evening with his music and his poetry. She wondered how he could stand it, the loneliness. The room seemed shrunken in the half-light, the walls and ceiling pressing in. The McBride house was lonely too, but at least there was a grandeur to its solitude; its proud aspect, facing out to the open sea, lent an aloofness to the isolation. This cottage was merely dingy and sad; it smelled faintly of damp and spinsterhood. She watched Edward as he leaned forward, tucking old newspaper around the kindling. The movement caused his shirt to ride up, revealing a hand's breadth of bare skin above the waistband of his underwear, dusted with blond hairs; fine, taut muscles either side of his spine, not a spare inch of flesh. Zoe felt a stirring deep between her legs, a vestige of that restless energy that had not quite dissipated after the night's unruly dreams. A hot, strong throb of desire pulsed through her; for the space of a blink, she thought she recalled the elusive face of her dream lover, but when she tried to focus it had dissolved into shadow. She squeezed her thighs together and clutched the mug tighter.

'Why *did* you come here?' she asked him, fighting to keep her voice level. She pressed one hand to her cheek and felt it blazing.

He rocked back on his heels and turned to look at her, a box of matches poised in his hand, his face frank and open and impossibly young. 'I broke up with someone. I was planning to stay in Oxford for another couple of years while she finished her PhD, but . . . well. She met someone else. That's what happened.' He dropped his gaze to the matchbox, turning it between his fingers. 'So I wanted to get as far away as I could. I saw this job advertised. I didn't think they'd take me – I'd only just graduated. But it was halfway through the year and I guess they weren't overwhelmed with applicants. A place like this isn't for everyone, I suppose.'

'Is it for you?'

He paused.

'It'll do, for now. I wouldn't want to settle.' He stared into the fireplace, letting out a long sigh and covering it with the hiss and flare of a match sparking. The room fell silent; only the crack and spit of the fire as he coaxed it to life. A dark scent of woodsmoke drifted up from the hearth. When he was satisfied, he sat back, cross-legged, and turned his gaze on her. 'How about you?'

'What about me?' It came out sharp-edged; she had not meant to sound so defensive. He blinked, his expression mild behind his glasses.

'Why did you come here?'

She hesitated, watching him. How much should she say? Could she tell him everything that had happened with Dan this past year; could she unspool the brittle thread of events that had led her to this place? How much of that could he hope to understand, this dark-eyed, earnest boy, whose first serious break-up had sent him fleeing to the other end of the country? The urge to unburden herself rose up through her, fierce and strong; she caught her breath and pulled back from the edge in time.

'I wanted some quiet.' She ran a finger around the rim of her mug. 'A place to paint.'

'Long way to come for it.' Edward hugged his knees. His tone offered no judgement, though it was half a question. Zoe made a small movement with her shoulders to acknowledge the truth of this. 'So, do you have a partner?' he asked, in the same light tone, when it became clear that she was giving nothing without a prompt.

Firelight sparked in bright reflections from his glasses; behind them, she could not see his eyes clearly. She left a long pause, not because she wanted to guard her privacy, but because she was no longer even sure of the answer herself.

'I did,' she murmured, after a while. Her eyes flicked away to the lurching shadows thrown by the flames. Edward nodded, as if he understood. When he didn't say any more, she let her shoulders unclench and thanked him silently for having the grace not to force it.

'The Professor was right, then,' he said, as he levered himself to his feet and brushed down his trousers. 'We are all running away.'

Zoe looked up at him briefly with a closed little smile. She wrapped her arms around her chest and drew her knees up, turning back to the fire. Edward bent to pick up her mug.

'Do you want more tea? Or . . . ' His eyes darted away from hers and he dipped his chin. 'I have a bottle of wine somewhere, if you'd rather?'

He was looking at her from under his lashes, shoulders hunched, his torso twisting with awkwardness. Zoe shifted, wincing as the sofa's defeated springs dug into her leg. Again she felt wrong-footed by the difficulty of recognising his motives. If a man her age had offered the same, she might have presumed he was making a move, but she had no way of knowing how Edward regarded her. Perhaps he was being friendly to a stranger because he had been raised well; perhaps he simply wanted someone to talk to, and would be appalled to think she might have taken it any other way – a woman nearer his mother's age than his. She glanced away to the window; the sky had turned the colour of wet slate and rain drove at the panes with determination. There was no way she could ride the bike back now, whether she had a drink or not. Part of her wanted nothing more than to stay, to feel that first thick heat of the alcohol sliding through her, gently teasing out the snarls and tangles of her mind; to sit here and listen to this beautiful boy, so pristine in all the blithe self-assurance and anxious uncertainty of youth. She would have liked to pretend, for one night, that she was his age again; to drink wine, play music, sit on the floor into the small hours until he suggested that she stay over. Just for the company, the warmth of another body, the knowledge that she was still desirable. She closed her eyes, pinching the bridge of her nose between her finger and thumb. This was exactly the kind of situation she had resolved to avoid. If she relaxed now, she would find herself talking. It would all come out: everything she had worked so hard to tamp down, out of sight. A patient listener would undo her. And she could tell he would listen well; there was a stillness about him, an attentiveness to others rare in a boy his age. The children must adore him, she thought. Caleb would. She swiped that thought away before it could settle. Besides, she had begun to feel a strange compulsion to return to the house, a chafe of anxiety behind her sternum, as if it were calling her back.

'You won't be cycling out there now, in any case,' he said, nodding to the window as if he had heard her thoughts. 'I can drop you home later if you like, though you'd have to leave the bike here. If I only have one glass.'

'*No!*' The word cracked out of her, hard and fast as a shot, ricocheting off the walls. Edward stared at her, alarmed. She breathed in and out, tightened her hand around the arm of the sofa. She was shocked at herself; she had not meant to sound so fierce.

'I meant – you shouldn't drink at all, if you're going to drive,' she said, not looking at him, shaping each word clearly and precisely so as to keep her voice steady, though she could feel the colour rising up her neck. 'You never know—' She broke off, aware that she sounded like a parent. Well, let him think that.

Edward shuffled, chastened.

'No, you're right. I wouldn't usually, but you don't get pulled over here. More tea, then?' When she hesitated, he

79

said, as bait, 'I haven't told you yet what happened last year.'

Her scalp tightened. She was no longer sure she wanted to hear any more of these stories. Charles was right; they would take on a different shape once she was back in the house, alone, with the darkness pressing in. Whatever Edward was about to tell her, she could not unknow. But she merely nodded, watching him as he padded softly in his socks back to the kitchen to fill the kettle.

'A child disappeared at the McBride house,' he announced when he returned, holding out her mug. He settled himself on the floor near the fire with his back against the sofa. His head was close enough to her knees for Zoe to reach out and stroke his hair. She wondered briefly how he would react if she did, and clamped her free hand firmly under her thigh, because she did not entirely trust herself.

'Disappeared?' Her voice sounded high and strange. 'How?'

'They don't really know.' He stretched his legs out and crossed his feet at the ankles. 'It was last August, just over a year ago. Mick was a few months into the work and the place was a building site, but the business had stirred up a lot of talk in the town, about the house's history. Two of the village boys picked up on it and dared each other to spend a night out there, ghost-hunting, for a laugh. One of them didn't come back.'

The fine hairs prickled along her arm. 'Jesus. What happened?'

'The boy who survived, Robbie Logan – that's Annag's brother – thought his friend saw something in the ruined house. They'd hidden on the beach at first, but Robbie said when he got there, he lost his nerve and refused to go in. He stayed down by the rocks. Iain Finlay, the other boy, went alone.' He paused to sip his tea, snatching glances at her from the tail of his eye. 'Robbie says he heard Iain scream, and saw him running away, up on to the cliffs, but he couldn't be sure because it was dark and he was terrified, so he hunkered down out of sight.'

Zoe let out a soft whistle. 'Did he fall, then – Iain?'

'So they reckon. If he ran up on to the headland, away from the house, he could have missed his footing in the dark and gone over the cliff. It's a sixty-foot drop there and the water covers the rocks at the foot when the tide's high. By the time the police were called, it had already been in and out. They concluded the body must have been washed away without a trace.'

'And the other boy, Robbie – he really saw nothing?'

Edward shook his head. 'Apparently not. Although . . . ' he hesitated, rubbing his thumb along his chin, 'there was a lot of talk about that, too. How much Robbie knew.'

'Shit. I'll bet.'

'The police had trouble getting anything out of him. There was a social worker assigned to the family – she told me all this when I started at the school. Robbie didn't go home till the next morning – he'd been wandering all night, out on the moorland, he said. He hardly spoke, except to give them that version. The social worker seemed to think he'd been trau-matised, but . . . ' He held out his hands, empty.

'Not everyone believed it, huh?'

'He was only ten at the time, but he's a big lad and he had a reputation as a bully. The younger kids are scared of him, though he mostly keeps to himself now. I think people didn't buy the idea of him cowering down on the beach. Iain was always the weaker character, they said – he did what Robbie told him.'

'Why didn't the parents raise the alarm?' Zoe sat upright, indignant. 'How did they not notice their kids were out all night?'

'The boys snuck out after everyone was in bed, apparently. Though in Robbie's case, I'm not surprised no one noticed.

81

His mother's dead and his dad's a lorry driver, he was away working on the mainland. Robbie was at home with his sister. She says she had no idea he'd left the house until the next morning.'

'So people secretly think he pushed his friend over the cliff?'

'Not so secretly, in a lot of cases. It seemed the police did too, for a while, but there was no evidence. Iain's family moved away soon after, though, and a couple of other families moved their children out of the village school. Reading between the lines, I think that's what did for the old teacher – the one I replaced. She couldn't cope with the thought that one of her pupils might be a murderer and no one would ever be certain.' He leaned forward and poked the fire; a flurry of sparks erupted and vanished. 'But I think there's just as many in the village really believe it was the curse of the McBride house. Another vanished boy, on the site of a famous child murder. It got a lot of attention in the Scottish papers and of course they dug up the old story – exactly what the islanders didn't want.'

'God. No wonder Mick's so touchy.' She fell silent, wrapped in her own thoughts.

'He was so pleased you hadn't heard about it. He wanted to keep it that way. I'm sorry – it's a horrible story,' Edward said. Zoe kept her eyes fixed on the floor. She knew he had seen her flinch. 'I shouldn't have told you. Even if you don't believe in all that, it's still . . . ' He tailed off, uncertain.

'All what?'

'Well. Ghosts. Curses.'

She laughed, to show her disdain, but it sounded too loud in the small room. 'I don't mind a ghost story. It's the living you have to be afraid of.' She stopped, seeing his expression, hoping she didn't sound paranoid. 'I mean – when you look at the news, right? The stuff that goes on.'

He nodded. 'True. There's enough evil in the world without inventing it. I hope it won't frighten you away, though,' he added, glancing up shyly, a half-question in his eyes.

She looked at him, disconcerted; once more her awareness of the age gap that separated them was scrambling the signals. She felt herself flush with confusion. How mortifying it would be to respond as if she were flattered, only to find his concern was whether he would upset Mick; the embarrassment that would persist between them for the rest of her stay would be unbearable. In a place this size she could not risk having to avoid someone. Nor would it be smart to make herself a bigger target for village gossip: the American cougar. Even if he were flirting, what could come of it? She was still technically married, though she doubted that was weighing on Dan's conscience much, back home. And really, who could blame him, the way she had been this past year?

'It would take something genuinely terrifying to drive me away,' she said firmly. 'Like blocked drains.'

He laughed, but she could not help noticing the way he dropped his gaze back to his mug, as if unsure whether he had been rebuffed. They sat in silence, listening to the whispering of the fire. The conversation seemed to have petered out now they had exhausted the subject of the McBride house. She wanted to ask him more about himself, this curious life he had chosen, but was afraid it would look like she was prying; beyond that, she thought, what did they have in common, she and this boy, besides the fact that they were outsiders here, both running away – the very thing neither wished to talk about?

The rain had eased its assault on the window and through the narrow pane to her left she made out streaks of brightness struggling to break through the heaving clouds, though dusk was approaching. She shifted in her seat as a prelude to leaving, when her eye fell on the violin case in the corner.

'That song you played last night,' she said. 'The haunting one – what was it called?'

'They're all haunting,' he said, twisting to look at her with a smile, seeming grateful that the silence had been broken. 'It's the local speciality. Any more clues?'

'It was right before you took your break. Before we went out for a smoke.'

'Oh, you mean "*Ailein Duinn*"?' He hummed a few bars and she nodded, hard. 'Yes, that one always gets to people. Especially the way Kaye sings it. It's a lament for a sea captain who was drowned, supposedly composed by his fiancée. She went mad with grief and drowned herself too, a few months later. So the legend goes. The lyrics are a bit grisly, though.' He hesitated, as if he wanted to protect her from any more unpleasantness.

'Tell me.'

'She sings of how she wants to go to him in the sea. It ends by saying she wants to drink his heart's blood after he's drowned.'

Zoe tried to recall how it was to feel that kind of desperate passion for someone, the kind that draws you willingly to your destruction after them. She had been wildly in love with Dan at the beginning, or thought she had, which perhaps amounted to the same thing, but when she tried to remember the sensation it was as if she were remembering a movie she had seen long ago, or a second-hand anecdote. Now there was only Caleb. 'Eat you up, I love you so,' she used to whisper into his neck when he was smaller, clean and powdery after his bath, his hair damp; she would nuzzle closer, pretending to chomp his soft, soft skin, until he squealed with delight and wriggled away. Sometimes she felt the breath crushed out of her by that desire to enfold him, take him back into the protection of her body where she could keep him safe. But he had grown too big for that game; he had learned to push her away.

'The older folk get very emotional about that song,' Edward continued. 'We have to play it every time. I suppose it's not so long since every family on the island knew what it was to lose someone to the sea.'

It sounded like the story of Ailsa McBride. Had she too gone mad with grief for her drowned husband, and walked into the sea to join him, first killing her son, perhaps out of some deranged maternal instinct not to leave him alone? But nothing in Charles's account so far had suggested that Ailsa's 'madness' was any more than malicious gossip about a woman who refused to surrender her independence to other people's expectations. Once more Zoe found herself wondering what had really happened to Ailsa and her son.

'Will you play it for me?'

He looked surprised. 'Now?'

She shrugged, gesturing to the sky. 'Before I go.'

'I can't sing it,' he said, with a hint of alarm. 'It's not really the same without Kaye.'

'I'd like to hear the music.' She smiled encouragement and, after a brief hesitation, he sprang up from the floor in one easy bound.

She watched him tuning the violin, plucking each string with his head cocked, as if listening for invisible echoes only he could hear. In the corners, the shadows lengthened. If that song had been stuck in her head last night, to the point where she had imagined hearing it in the house, there was no sense in reminding herself of it, only to have it turning round and round once more as she tried to sleep. But she figured that perhaps hearing him play it in that drab but oddly cosy little room might rid it of any associations with last night's strange dreams and sleeplessness; a kind of aversion therapy. If it came to her again in the night she could think of the music without the words, and picture the intensity of Edward's expression as he played with his eyes closed, lashes resting on his cheeks, lips pressed firm in concentration.

As soon as he struck up the first bars, she realised that she had made a mistake. Dusk fell as if suddenly across the room;

85

the last hopeful streaks of light in the sky obscured by fast-moving clouds. The violin's mournful notes trembled on the air. Strangely, she found that she knew the words; she had the curious sense that she could hear them quite clearly, though silently, inside her head, as if it were an old familiar tune echoing in her memory – but how could she hear the words so intimately when she had no knowledge of that ancient, guttural language? She wanted to ask him to stop, but the song filled her mind so entirely that there was no room left for other words; she could not form the sounds. Behind her breastbone she felt a pressure building, tightening her throat, a great wave of grief rising up; all the grief she had ever known and buried, gathering force like a wall of black water called into flood tide by the song, threatening to overwhelm her while he went on playing, his eyes shut, oblivious to the danger; she must escape the music or the weight of it would burst her defences and drown her—

With one mighty effort of will, she wrenched herself up from the sofa and ran from the room, snatching up her jacket on the way out, wrestling with the bike in the passageway, trying to ram it backwards through the door as he followed, bow in hand, his face taut with alarm.

'What is it? What's wrong?'

But she could only shake her head, teeth clenched; she could still hear the song, yearning and wistful, and her only thought was to get away, as if it were not in her mind now but somewhere in the cottage, so that she might be able to outrun it. He tried to take hold of the handlebars, protesting about the weather and the dark, but she did not hear it, she knew only that she had to get out before she lost control in front of him; yanking the bike from his grasp, she blundered through the schoolyard to the gate, swung herself on to the saddle and rode away down the green without looking back, her plastic bag of shopping smacking hard against her shin, hair whipping in her eyes, her open jacket snapping in the wind.

A mile or so out of the village she found herself slowing as the road began to climb an incline; the street lamps had ended and dusk was closing in fast over the moorland, the daylight all but dissolved, though it could not be much past four. She brought the bike to a stop, aware, as she returned to herself, of the ragged breath tearing at her chest, the blood pounding in her temples. She zipped her jacket up to the neck – cursing at leaving her scarf behind in her haste – and cast a glance around her. The horizon had dwindled to a pale streak above the dark spine of hills. She could hardly make out the line of the road as it rose. The bike was fitted with lights but she had been in such a hurry to leave the shop that she had not waited to check the batteries; now she flicked the switch on the headlight to reveal a wavering beam that did little to cut through the shadows ahead. At least the song in her head had stopped. Rain spiked her face as she strained to listen, relieved to find she could hear nothing now but the cries of seabirds and the low moan of the wind through heather.

Perhaps she should call Mick and ask him to come out and find her in the Land Rover. It would be folly to try and continue along an unfamiliar road through moorland in the falling dark on a bike with poor lights, even if another down-pour held off. Common sense told her so unequivocally; weighed against it was her pride, and the embarrassment of her emotional outburst, the way she had fled from the School House like someone in the throes of a breakdown. What must he think of her, the young teacher? Neurotic middle-aged woman, she supposed; it would be the last time she was likely to be invited there for a bottle of wine, anyway, which was probably for the best.

She peered up at the sky. She had come here to learn how to be alone, not to rely on men for company or to ferry her around; she must not crumble at the first hint of difficulty. That was what Dan expected her to do, and so she must prove him wrong. The house was not even five miles away, and a faint light clung to the horizon; from what she could recall, the road ran straight across the moors to the cove. Setting her face into the drizzle, she pointed the bike up the hill, stood on the pedals and picked up her pace, this time feeling every twinge in her muscles without the spike of adrenaline that fear had lent her. Fear of what, though? Nothing she could quite name. Fear of betraying herself, was the closest she could come to defining the panic that had driven her from Edward's room.

A brief sense of triumph washed through her as she crested the hill, only to ebb away at the sight of a fork in the road up ahead. She did not remember this parting of the ways from her drive earlier with Mick, and neither branch had a signpost. The road that veered away to the left was narrower, less frequented, and since she could not recall a turning, she made the decision to take the right-hand fork, which seemed a continuation of the main road. There was no sign of any traffic. Long needles of rain fell harder across the cone of light from her headlamp; the wind bit colder out here and her fingers numbed around the slick rubber grips of the handlebars. Fifteen minutes of unchanging scenery passed: undulating hills, dark heather, a pale ribbon of road unspooling ahead, edged by occasional boulders. Her legs began to ache and the earlier alarm flickered in her chest. Finally, defeated, she planted her feet and reached inside her jacket for her phone to call Mick, but when she swiped the screen, shielding it from raindrops, she saw that there was no signal. She should have guessed, out here. No choice, then, but to press on.

But as she stood reluctantly on the pedals, she caught sight of a figure up ahead in the distance, walking with a purposeful stride along the left-hand verge at the side of the road, away from her. For an instant, her heart clutched in fear – there was no one else around for miles – but as she peered harder, she felt certain it was a woman, wrapped in a long all-weather coat. One of these hardy crofters who barely noticed the rain, she supposed; out gathering peat or whatever people did up here.

'Hello!' she called, but she was too far away and the wind too loud for the woman to hear. Zoe paused to re-tie her wet hair back from her face and redoubled her efforts to catch up, rising out of the saddle, crouching forward, the bottle of wine in the shopping bag bruising her legs with each movement as she pumped towards the brow of the next incline. She tried shouting again but the figure did not turn around before disappearing over the hill and Zoe was too short of breath to put more effort into it. She would overtake her on the downward slope, she thought, pushing onwards, though it seemed the woman must be walking unusually fast. Zoe breasted the hill and eased up on the pedals, coasting a little as gravity took over, straining her eyes to see the woman, expecting to draw level with her at any moment. But the road was empty; there was only the black ridge of more hills ahead.

She called out a third time, but heard no answer. Blinking hard, she wiped the rain from her eyes with the heel of her hand. She had not imagined it; that was impossible. She had seen her, a person walking up ahead, perhaps fifty, sixty yards away. The woman could not have vanished – unless she had left the road and taken a path across the moor, but surely she would have heard Zoe shout. It made no sense.

The rain fell harder; a heavy, vegetable smell of wet earth rose from the moorland to either side. Zoe pressed the inside of her wrist against her forehead, trying to think – the worst she could do would be to waste time here, indecisive and exposed. If Dan could see her now, he would feel entirely vindicated. Before she had left, when he still thought there was a chance he could change her mind, he had insisted, over and over, that she would not be able to cope on her own, but she understood now that this was part of his strategy, one of the ways he had subtly undermined her independence over the years. When she now understood that it was he who could not cope with her finding the determination to make her own decisions, to steer her life without deferring to his judgement and his choices. If it weren't for Caleb, she would have broken away much sooner, she told herself, and the thought made her immediately uncomfortable. She had been repeating this for months, but it had taken on the shape of a comforting reassurance that she knew, deep down, to be false. She was not even sure that she had left him this time. For now they were both playing along with the idea that this was a temporary departure, a rebellion she had to get out of her system.

The bike's front light flickered and died. Hot tears of self-pity pricked the corners of her eyes; she knuckled them away and squinted into the dark. Rainwater invaded the collar of her jacket in rivulets; she could no longer feel her fingers or feet. But the faint line of the road continued to spool out ahead. The only thing was to keep going. That woman must have been on her way somewhere; if Zoe followed the road, she would surely find a cottage or croft. She mounted the saddle and pushed forward a few shaky yards, riding almost blind, when she heard the sound of a car engine in the distance and turned to see two watery discs of light approaching through the downpour.

The Land Rover pulled up alongside her with the window open, Mick leaning across.

'There you are. God Almighty.' He jumped out with the engine running and flung open the back doors. 'Give me the bike. Get in out of the rain.' His tone was brusque.

She took the bag, bending her freezing fingers around the handles, and allowed him to lift the bike into the back while she slumped like a sodden towel into the passenger seat, almost crying with relief and shame.

'What were you thinking?' Mick said, slamming his door.

The wipers beat a frantic rhythm but the windscreen remained a sheet of water. 'You don't know the road and you've no lights – you'll break your neck out here. Or get pneumonia, one or the other. Why didn't you call me?'

'I didn't want to bother you.'

'It's no bother, I told you. Better that than have you lying in a ditch all night with a broken neck.' He breathed hard, trying to compose himself. 'It's damned lucky Ed called me. He said you'd gone haring off on your own.' He hesitated. 'He thought you might be a bit distressed.'

'I'm fine. I was just in a hurry to get home.' Zoe bristled. He was speaking angrily because he was relieved that no harm had come to her, the way she had screamed at Caleb more than once when he had run off out of sight at a park or a mall; rationally she knew this, but she could not quell the resentment knotting at the base of her throat, the same resentment she had been directing towards Dan a few minutes ago. She had crossed the Atlantic, and still she was surrounded by men who thought it was their job to supervise her. She wanted to tell Mick, slowly and clearly, that she was an adult; he was responsible for the house, no more than that, certainly not for her choices. And Edward was no better, sending Mick after her. He said he had a car; if he was so worried, why hadn't he come himself? But she already knew the answer to that: he was afraid he had upset her, and would not have understood why.

She wiped the drops from her lashes. 'I didn't think it would be dark so quickly.'

'Aye, well.' Mick gripped the steering wheel with both hands, steadying himself. 'Most city folk aren't used to that. You think you know what night looks like, but it's nothing like you get out here. No light pollution, see. And the weather – it'll ambush you in a matter of minutes.'

'I see that. I thought I'd have time to get back before it got too bad.'

He gave a half-laugh and gestured through the windscreen to the indistinct dark beyond. 'I hate to tell you, but you're on the wrong road, for a start. You needed to take the turning back there, otherwise you'll have to double back along the coast road, and I wouldn't recommend that in the dark.'

'Shit. I'm an idiot.' She pressed her hand to her forehead. 'I'm so sorry, Mick, really. How long till I'd have reached civilisation, if I'd kept going?'

'There's no houses along this road till the other side of the island. It's lucky I found you. You'd have frozen,' he said, grudgingly mollified.

'But I saw a woman out here walking. I thought there must be a cottage or something.'

He swivelled to look her square in the face. 'A woman? Out here?'

'I lost sight of her – I guess she went off the road. I called but she didn't hear me.'

Mick continued to stare at her, puzzled. 'I can't think who that would be. There's sheep up in the hills and a couple of old bothies but they're no really used – you might have seen one of the shepherds, I suppose.'

'Maybe that was it. She had a long coat on, with a hood. Or he.' Now that she thought about it, she could not say why she had been so sure it was a woman; she had only seen the figure at a distance.

'Best get you home then,' Mick said, releasing the hand-brake, as if it was time to change the subject.

Once again she gently but firmly declined his offers to lay a fire for her, get the range going, make her a cup of tea. 'Well, if you're sure you'll be all right,' he repeated, hovering in the doorway and twisting his hands together, until she almost had to shut the door in his face, only persuading him to leave with the promise that tomorrow she would see his friend at the golf club about renting his car.

92

She didn't bother to switch on the light in the hallway; with water running from her clothes and pooling on the tiles at her feet, she picked up the phone from the table and called home. Twice she got the international code wrong; twice she redialled, her fingers so frozen she could barely punch the numbers. Then the unfamiliar tone, thousands of miles away. Drops scattered from her hair as she pushed it back; she pictured the phone ringing in the kitchen at home and realised, with curious detachment, that hot tears were sliding down her nose. The shock of Dan's voice, so close, cheery and familiar in her ear: 'We're not in right now, leave a message, thanks!' She waited for the beep and put the phone down. She could try his cell but she knew she could expect the same result, and she couldn't think what message to leave. There was too much to say, or nothing at all.

She stood in the dark hallway, fingertips resting on the receiver in its cradle, in case he had just missed her and tried to call back. As she waited, the silence grew thicker until she became horribly aware that she was not alone. The same presence she had felt the night before: watchful, intent, not benign. Her skin prickled into goosebumps; she tensed, dreading a repeat of the scratching noise, but there was no sound except her own breathing, the ticking of the clock and the steady drip of water from her jacket. But someone was there, all the same; she could sense their breath moving in and out, matching the shallow rhythm of her own. Her limbs felt brittle, likely to snap if she tried to move them. She dared not turn her head and yet she knew she must; a charge of pure terror flashed through her, the heart-racing rush that comes with the sudden certainty that horror is imminent and unstoppable, the way she had felt in the instant she saw the truck. Mustering all her will, she wrenched her foot forward and lunged for the light switch; as she did so, she thought she heard that same half-laugh, half-sob, close to the back of her neck. Light flooded the hall; she whipped around, started and cried out at the sight of movement, a pale face in the window, half a second before her brain caught up and told her it was her own reflection. The house was as empty as she had left it. She double-checked that the front door was locked behind her, to make sure.

6

Zoe huddled at the kitchen table with her back to the wood-burning stove, dressed in warm sweatpants, a hoodie and a fleece, with a towel turbaned over her wet hair and her hands wrapped around a mug of tea. She had dumped her soaking clothes in a pile on the floor of the laundry room off the kitchen and made herself a tuna sandwich while she left the bathtub upstairs filling with hot water and lemon-scented steam. The food and sweet tea had steadied her a little; she'd been pleasantly surprised to find how efficiently the heating worked, and with the kitchen blinds pulled down the house had begun to seem cosy, the rhythmic booming of the sea outside and occasional burst of rain against the window almost reassuring. The silence in the rooms still unnerved her, though that at least she could remedy. She had brought her laptop down to the kitchen; she flipped it open now and searched for music, some cheerful sunshiny pop that would help her shake off the residual fear that had followed her in from the moors, clinging to her like the smell of fog. She clicked on a favourite song, exhaling slowly as West Coast harmonies and guitar jingles filled the room. She left the music playing while she ran up to check on the bath.

Brushing aside a spume of bubbles, she turned off the tap

and perched on the edge of the tub, waggling her fingers below the surface, feeling the heat slide over her skin. Without the sound of running water, she caught snatches of the music floating up from the kitchen, but an odd shift in the cadences made her stop and strain to listen. Again she felt that cold prickling on the back of her neck. The song she could hear was not the one she had left playing; instead it was that old, heartsore ballad from the night before, the lament of the woman who had drowned herself to be with her dead fiancé. It drifted through the house in the same thin, desolate voice she had imagined coming from the turret room in her sleepless hours. Zoe breathed in and out deliberately, forcing herself to note the cold enamel of the bath under her thigh, the sensation of her hand in the water. *Overwrought*, was the word that came to mind. That's what Dr Schlesinger would call it. She made herself walk out to the landing. All the lights were lit. She was fully awake, and yet the singer continued to pour out grief in her strange guttural language, and this time the song was coming unmistakably not from the turret above but from the kitchen, where she had left her laptop playing her own music.

She moved down the stairs towards it, counting each step, her skin cold despite the heating. The singing stopped abruptly as she entered the kitchen, to be replaced by a pregnant silence, as if the room were holding its breath. From beyond the window, the sea continued its steady rhythm: distant, implacable. The laptop screen had fallen dark; when she touched the keyboard it flashed into life to show that the track she had chosen had played and finished. It was her own fault, she thought; she had asked Edward to play that song and now it was stuck in her head, she was hearing it everywhere, imagining it in every piece of music.

She tipped the tea down the sink and instead opened the bottle of red that had battered her shin on the ride back from town, an effort that seemed worthwhile now that she could pour herself a large glass to take up to the bath. She would relax, warm up, have an early night. Tomorrow she would speak to Dan, or leave him a calm message telling him everything was fine. She would have liked to hear Caleb's voice, but she could not be selfish about that; it would be easier for him – for both of them – to get used to the idea of her absence if she left it a couple of days. Easier for Dan, too.

Tomorrow, she decided, she would hike along the cliffs and start work, make some preliminary sketches, give herself a project to concentrate on – a small canvas, to begin with, nothing too ambitious. Once she was rested and focused, these wild dreams and irrational imaginings would stop. It would take time to adapt to the silence, to re-learn how to be alone; she had known that. She reminded herself that she had chosen this; she had fought for her right to be here, and at a cost. Everything would be fine, once she could sleep.

He came to her again that night. In the dream she opened her eyes to see him standing by her bed, holding out a hand, inviting her. She reached out and allowed him to lead her, down the dark landing towards the open door of the gallery from which spilled a dim, flickering light, as of a fire or a bank of candles. As before, she felt the sensation of being awake within the dream, conscious of what was happening to her, powerless to control it. Still she could not see his face, but she knew with terrible certainty that he was unbearably beautiful, that if he were to turn and meet her eye, it would make her heart stop. Her skin prickled with anticipation, every nerve vivid, as he pushed the door open.

The light wavered up the walls, though she could see no source of it, illuminating the figure of a woman in the centre of the room, her arms stretched above her head and fastened by thin manacles to a chain suspended from the ceiling. The woman was naked, light and shadow playing in patterns over her bone-white skin. She wore a black hood over her head, obscuring her face. Zoe quickened, drawing breath; the dream lover, the shadow, gently opened her hand and placed in it a thin birch cane, folding her fingers around it. She understood; lifting the stick, she sliced it through the air until it whipped across the girl's naked haunches, leaving a scarlet welt. The girl twisted silently at the end of the chain, her thin body flinching away from the contact. A furious surge of arousal coursed through Zoe; she raised her arm a second time and brought the cane down sharply on the back of the girl's thighs, feeling the heat and wetness rising between her own legs as she lashed out, surprised by the force of her desire to hurt. *Give in*, he said, though she heard his voice as before, as thought rather than sound. Again she sliced the cane across the girl's skin, harder, and again, until she saw she had raised drops of blood in a thin line. Each time the girl writhed under the stroke without a sound, her nipples hard and pointed. Zoe lifted the cane for another blow but felt his hand around her wrist, restraining her, guiding her to slide the length of it between the girl's legs. At this, the tethered figure made a mewling sound, rocking her body against the movement, though whether in pleasure or pain was impossible to tell with her face hidden. Zoe felt her own arousal mounting as she increased the pressure, pushing the cane harder against the girl's skin, but as she felt her crescendo approaching, he folded his hand around hers and drew her arm back. He moved between them, his back to Zoe, and lifted the hood. The girl's head hung down limply, her chin to her chest, long hanks of reddish-brown hair covering her face. He beckoned to Zoe to come closer; she felt an obscure stirring of fear, but her dream-self could not resist, so she took one, two steps towards the limp figure and watched with appalled fascination as he lifted the girl's head by the hair and she recognised, unmistakably, her own face, though gaunt and wasted, her eyes half-open, glassy, unfocused. A sick coldness spread

98

through her; as if by compulsion, she turned away from the sight towards the black window to see her own reflection. Staring back at her was the stony face of Ailsa McBride, exactly as she had looked in the photograph, in her high-necked black dress, the silver cross pendant hanging from her neck, glinting eyes dark with hate. Zoe opened her mouth to scream, the face of Ailsa also opened its mouth, and in the heartbeat before the sound woke her, she glimpsed him in the reflection, standing behind her by the suspended body of the girl, there and gone in an instant. She had only the fleeting impression that he was as dreadfully beautiful as she had supposed, and that there was nothing good in his smile.

She screamed herself into a frantic consciousness and found that she was standing once more in darkness in the long gallery in front of the windows, naked and trembling, her hands bunched into fists so hard her nails dug into the flesh. Gradually she became aware of how cold she was, her bare skin icy to the touch; she sensed again that same shallow breathing, rising and falling in time with her own, coming from beyond the closed door. Slowly, she turned to face it and thought she heard a low murmuring on the other side, monotonous and indistinct. Her breath jammed in her throat; she strained to listen harder and caught it again, too faint to make out the shapes of words, only the tone of suppressed rage and the odd guttural sound that made her think the voice was speaking in the old language, the language of the song. She gathered her breath, opened her mouth to call 'Who's there?', but the words clotted on her tongue; she realised she did not want to know the answer. 'No!' was all she managed to croak, but it seemed enough; the murmuring stopped, though the presence behind it was still there, she was sure. She listened, but heard only the creaking of timber and the distant thunder of the sea. The room was barely lit, a shred of moon visible through the windows behind scudding clouds, but as she stood shaking, she glanced down and became aware of dark stains on the wooden floor. She pressed the heel of her hand to her eye, uncertain whether she was hallucinating or dreaming. Moving with the steady precision of a high-wire walker, never taking her eyes off the door, she bent and touched her fingertip to one. It came away crimson and sticky. She cried out and jumped back; the blood was fresh. Bloodstains led in a trail to the door; she gulped back a sob, terrified now that she was trapped inside the dream and would never wake, until she looked down at her own body and saw the ribbon of blood running down the inside of her leg.

Weak with relief, she slumped against the wall, knees bent, the cold plaster solid against her back. She had not known it was coming; it had been six months since she had last had her period. Stress and weight loss can do that, the doctor had said, when she had finally gone to make sure she wasn't pregnant, even though she knew in her heart it was impossible, she and Dan had not been near one another since before the accident. After that she had almost forgotten them; the absence of blood seemed in keeping with the loss of everything else that had made her feel like a woman.

She had thought her body had given up; now this seemed to explain everything. Her strange, febrile moods of the past few days; the sudden surge of sexual hunger, after months of nothing; the dreams, the hallucinations; all of it could be attributed to a flood of hormones. She should have realised. In the worst days of her depression after Caleb was born, there had been times when she'd thought she was going mad: she had heard voices and grown convinced that someone was in the house, come to kill them. Sometimes she had had to shut herself in the closet because she feared *she* was the danger, to herself and the baby. She had not told Dan the half of it, out of a terror that if people knew how tenuous her grip on herself had become they would declare her unfit to be a mother and take Caleb away. That was when Dan had first taken her to Dr Schlesinger, after he'd come home to find that she had

100

spent the day locked in the bathroom with the baby to protect them from an imaginary intruder. She had never told anyone, not even the shrink, about the waking dreams she had in those days: how vivid they seemed, how often she dreamed of violent death. But that had been ten years ago; they had prescribed medication, she had got better. More common than you might think, Dr Schlesinger had said. Some women are extremely sensitive to hormonal disruption. And was it starting again, now? Was this what she had to look forward to, at her age? She did not want to dwell on that. Although better hormones than ghosts, she thought, and forced herself to laugh; it sounded too loud in the empty room, and seemed to echo back at her from beyond the door.

She tipped her head against the wall and closed her eyes. The house held its breath around her. A hand pushed hard between her legs and she no longer knew if it was her own hand; all she could do was squeeze her eyes tight shut and rock herself against the pressure, feeling the warm wetness welling up to meet it, left palm pressed against the cold wall at her back, until she felt herself rising to a swift, brusque climax and cascading down the other side. Her knees buckled; she allowed her limbs to fold, sinking to the floor to catch her breath, blood trickling along her thigh. In the silence that followed, she heard a scratching at the door, fingernails on wood, slow and deliberate. Someone wanting to be let in.

Bending every last shred of will, she forced herself to her feet and lunged at the door, scrabbling at the handle with bloodied fingers. From the other side she heard a snatched laugh, followed by the skittering of footsteps down the landing and away up the stairs towards the other end of the house and the turret room; light, quick steps, like a child's. She flung open the door and switched on the light. The landing was empty. She paused, but the house had resumed its tight-lipped silence; there was only the ticking of the clock and the waves outside.

101

In her room, she cleaned herself up and pulled on sweat-pants and a jumper. Not anticipating her period she had not come prepared; she would have to stuff her underwear with toilet paper until she could go back into town tomorrow and buy some supplies. She glanced at the clock. Ten after three; too much of the night left, but she was afraid to sleep. Flicking on all the lights, she made her way downstairs to the kitchen and put the kettle on. Her laptop was open on the table where she had left it, the screen dark. She recoiled from it, recalling the song, but to prove that she would not be shaken, she pulled it towards her and stirred it into life, then shut down iTunes to make certain that could not happen again. She was about to close the lid when she noticed that the Wi-Fi icon was showing a full signal.

Her first thought, with a prickle of anger, was that Mick had lied to her about the Internet; he had set it up after all, but maybe it was for his own private use and he didn't want the expense of her using it. Then she thought that made no sense; he was never here, and she was paying enough that it wouldn't kill him to throw in a basic connection. And if that was his idea, he should have switched it off so that she couldn't see it.

She clicked on the icon. Only one network was showing, and it was called 'McBride'. Zoe frowned. Knowing Mick's aversion to the house's history, it seemed a sick kind of joke to call its Internet the one name he wanted everyone to forget. It was a private network, clearly showing the padlock symbol, and yet it appeared to have connected her without asking for a password. She tried clicking on her email, but the page wouldn't load, and nor would any of the sites she tried. She pushed the laptop away in frustration, relenting a little towards Mick; perhaps he had not mentioned it because he knew the connection was poor and wouldn't work. The kettle boiled; she scraped her chair back and crossed to make a cup of tea, unreasonably angry. She had thought she wanted to be cut off here, if only for a while; now that she had seen the prospect of connection dangled before her, she felt bereft.

She was pouring water into one of the pottery mugs when she heard the alert of a Skype call. Startled, she scrambled across to the laptop and spun it around to see Caleb's face, pale and wide-eyed, blinking out at her. The image was faint and badly pixelated, so that his movements appeared jerky and delayed. She couldn't see where he was – the background behind him was dark and even his face was indistinct – but it was gone ten at night back home, so she figured he must have been hiding somewhere with his iPad so his father wouldn't hear him. She clicked frantically to accept the call, but in the instant she heard his voice whisper, 'Mommy?' the connection stuttered and froze; his face hung there, distorted, before the screen went black. Fucking battery must have died; she raced up the stairs, rummaged through her luggage for the cable, slipped and almost turned her ankle in her haste to get back down to the kitchen, but by the time she had plugged the laptop in and restarted it, there was no sign of the Wi-Fi signal. She refreshed the search over and over, but it only told her no network detected. The McBride connection had vanished.

Overcome by a sudden desperation to speak to her son, she rushed back to the entrance hall and dialled home; she would get Caleb into trouble if he was up and maybe that would put an end to any chance of him trying to Skype her again in secret, but she couldn't bear to think of him so far away, unable to reach her. The phone clicked through to voicemail; this time she steeled herself, took a deep breath, tried to sound normal.

'Hi, it's me. Tell Caleb – tell Caleb I love him.'

After she had hung up, she thought that perhaps she should have told Dan too, but the words no longer came naturally. She was too jittery now to sleep; she sat at the kitchen table with her mug of tea, staring at the wall. The clock ticked steadily; outside, the waves advanced and receded. She lost track of how much time passed. After a while, she reached for the sketchbook and pencil she had left on the table. Turning to a blank page, she scratched the date. She ought to keep a record of everything that had happened these past nights, in case – though in case of what, she could not say. Beneath the date she wrote:

He came to me again tonight.

7

Squinting into the sun's glare, Zoe gripped the wheel with
both hands, sweat gumming her palms, heart speeding
against her ribs. She had not driven a car for six months,
had thought she might never be able to get behind the wheel
again, and on top of that it was at least fifteen years since
she had used a stick shift and she had never driven on the
wrong side of the road, using the wrong hands. This first
effort might have been easier if they had not both been
standing there watching her grinding the gears and stalling,
unable even to put the thing into first, looking at her with
that weary, secretly pleased expression men assume to let
you know you are proving all their theories about women
and machines.

'There's a wee knack with the clutch there,' Dougie Reid
said, leaning casually in the window and dropping ash on her
jeans. She had taken against Mick's friend on sight; a wiry
man with a sharp, knowing face and the stippled skin of a
committed chain-smoker, who spoke through a skinny roll-up
glued permanently with spit to his lower lip, the sort of man
who referred to cars as 'she' and had looked Zoe up and
down with frank appraisal when she arrived as if valuing her
bodywork. 'Let it half out before you try putting her in first.

She just needs a wee bit of warming up to get her going, like all you ladies.'

Ignoring his throaty chuckle, Zoe followed the instructions, her damp hand slipping off the gear stick in panic. Once more the car stalled. She began to suspect the fault lay as much with the engine as with her; the Golf was at least ten years old, with rust patches blooming on the fenders and worn tyres that looked as if they would skim off the road at the first hint of rain, but it was her only option short of looking for a more reputable rental firm on the mainland, which would likely cost her a thousand a month, Mick had said. She had not bothered to explain that a reputable rental company would not give her the time of day once they checked on her licence. So she was left with Dougie and this heap of junk, for which she had handed over three hundred pounds in cash taken from the village's one ATM that morning while trying not to think about her dwindling savings.

'Am I insured for it?' she asked, pressing herself back into the seat while Dougie leaned in and turned the ignition for her, the back of his hand brushing her breast unnecessarily. Moisture beaded between her shoulder blades; as if to disconcert her further the weather had performed a sudden volte-face overnight and she had stepped outside that morning into a day that belonged to late summer: clear pastel sky, sparkling water, a golden wash of sunshine. She had come out in only a sweater and still she was too warm.

'Dinnae fret about that,' he said, as the engine wheezed into life, with a gesture that suggested the small print would take care of itself. His groundsman's overalls smelled of sweat and oil. She wondered whether the car was even legal.

'I mean . . . ' she hesitated to say the words for fear of tempting fate ' . . . if I had an accident?'

'Ach, you'll be fine,' he said airily, which could have meant anything. Zoe glanced at Mick and saw him give a tacit nod seemingly meant to reassure her that all was above board.

Mick had been solicitous as usual when he picked her up that morning, asking how she was finding the house, how she was sleeping, the tenor of his questions once again making her think he was leaving something vital unsaid. Perhaps the events of the night were written too plainly on her face. She had woken in her own bed, a clear early sun seeping in at the edges of the blinds, so she supposed she must have slept eventually. Showered and dressed, with a cup of coffee in her hand, she had stood in the first-floor gallery for a long time, taking in every corner, every beam of the ceiling and piece of furniture, allowing the firm light reflected from sky and sea to scour her memory and return her to reason. There was nothing sinister about that room, nor the rest of the house. She had washed the bloodstains from the floorboards, eaten some toast and felt better, but when she had caught a glimpse of her reflection in the window she had jumped back, startled by the gauntness of her face, the shadows beneath her eyes and in the hollows of her cheeks. When she had asked Mick about the Wi-Fi connection she had briefly found, he had only looked puzzled and said he didn't know of any in the area, maybe she had somehow picked up a private network in passing, but there was definitely none at the house. She had shrugged it away then, said she must have been mistaken. She didn't tell him it was called 'McBride'; he would have thought she was mocking him.

After a couple more false starts, she managed to kangaroo the Golf across the car park in a series of alarming lurches and do the same in reverse, forcing a smile while her stomach turned over and Mick and Dougie cheered her as if she were a child on her first bike. Once the transaction was completed – cash in hand, no paperwork, adding further to her apprehension – they stood together, arms folded, and watched her as she pulled out of the golf course. Zoe wished she had not been in such a hurry to get away from their scrutiny that she had forgotten to ask how to put on the headlights or the windshield wipers. She would have to work those out for herself, before she needed them. Buttocks clenched tight, she jolted along the single track road down the hill towards the village at twenty miles an hour, so preoccupied with remembering what her hands and feet were supposed to be doing that for minutes at a stretch she forgot to think about the last time she had driven: the horn blaring at the intersection, the delayed shock of the impact, the airbag blinding her, blocking her mouth and nose.

She must not dwell on that now. Instead she leaned forward, concentrating every sinew on the road ahead, precariously lifting a hand at intervals to shield her eyes from the low sun, until she found herself crawling up one side of the triangular village green. Rather than attempt the parking spaces in front of the shops with people watching, she pulled the car up on the verge opposite the school and only realised when she switched off the engine how badly she was trembling. Sun silvered the windows of the School House, so that she could not see whether the curtains were drawn. She sat in the car for a few minutes, casting furtive glances, considering whether to knock on the door and ask for her scarf back, offer an apology, but the shame of the night before burned in her face and she was too shaken by the drive to explain herself adequately. Besides, she could not relax until she had found the chemist and bought tampons; the wad of tissue in her underpants might betray her at any moment.

The bookshop was busy, with at least five customers browsing in the front. Zoe fumbled through dates in her head, cursing softly as she realised it must be Saturday; she had hoped they would have the place to themselves. She stuck her head around the archway to the back room and found Charles Joseph seated behind his desk, glasses perched on the end of his nose, turning the pages of a large and ancient-looking volume. He glanced up and acknowledged her with a warm smile, as if he had been expecting her.

'Look at this beauty. Atlas of nineteenth-century nautical charts. Extensive water damage, sadly, or it would have been a prize to collectors. Terrible shame.'

'I guess you have to expect nautical charts to get wet.'

His eyes crinkled behind his lenses. 'A very sensible argument. Is that what I think it is in your hand?'

She dumped the bag of pastries on the desk, away from the books.

'You owe me the next episode. At least as far as the murder.'

'Ah. I see you've had a spoiler.' Charles arched his brow; he seemed amused rather than put out.

A sudden movement in the corner made her turn; a fat kid with a crew cut and a flat, sullen face was sitting cross-legged on one of the beanbags behind her. She had not noticed him at first, but he had jerked upright at their conversation and was staring at her with close-set eyes. Charles leaned across the desk and spoke kindly.

'Robbie, would you like to take that book home?'

The boy snapped it shut immediately. 'No, you're all right.' Zoe glanced at the cover and saw a photo of the Space Shuttle.

'Call it a loan. You can bring it back to me when you've finished.' Charles's voice had grown very gentle.

The boy reluctantly heaved himself to his feet, the beanbag squeaking under him. 'Nae room for it at home.' He held it out to Charles, who shook his head.

'Well, then – how about you go and read in my little kitchen? While I have a chat with Ms Adams. You might find a packet of biscuits in the cupboard.'

'Listen – I can come back,' Zoe said, though she didn't want to leave either. Charles waved a hand.

'What murder?' The child was looking directly at her, his small hard eyes accusing.

'It's a book I was telling her about,' Charles said smoothly. 'A detective story.'

An expression flickered across the boy's face; Zoe thought it might have been relief. He gave her a last wary glance before slouching his way through to the kitchen at the back.

'Poor lad,' Charles murmured, watching him. 'I get the sense someone doesn't like him bringing books home. Imagine feeling threatened by a child reading. But it still goes on. There's only so much you can do.'

If it was her shop, Zoe thought, she wouldn't leave that kid unsupervised; he looked like the kind you wouldn't want anywhere near a cash register, or your purse, or even your cookies. She disliked herself for thinking it, and surmised that Charles must be a better person than she was. Not that this could be counted much of an achievement.

'So I presume our young friend Edward Sinclair has stolen my narrative thunder?' Charles pushed his chair back and followed the boy to the kitchen. 'Out to impress a lady with Gothic tales, no doubt. And there I was, trying to build suspense. Wait here.' He returned a couple of minutes later with two mugs of coffee. 'I made this before you came. So. Where were we?'

She noticed that he had lowered his voice, and closed the kitchen door behind him. They had the back room to themselves.

'Ailsa living alone in the house with her mute child and everyone saying she was a witch.' Zoe spoke quietly to match him.

'Ah, yes. Ironic, of course, when it was her husband who was the occultist.'

She felt her eyes widen. 'Seriously? What, like Devil worship, that kind of thing?'

'Not quite.' Charles smiled. He closed the nautical atlas, laid it aside and sat back in his chair, his hands folded. 'More in the sense of esoteric philosophy. Spiritualism, mesmerism, ancient magic, Kabbala, that sort of thing.'

'Like Madonna?'

He looked politely baffled. 'Sorry?'

'Never mind. Go on.'

'Well. Tamhas McBride was a remarkable man in many ways. One of those Victorian gentlemen amateurs who wished to add to the sum of human knowledge, and had the means to indulge his curiosities. He was extremely well-travelled, spoke several languages, was a keen scientist—'

'A scientist who believed in magic?' She raised a sceptical eyebrow. He pointed a finger, mock-stern.

'May I remind you, there's an honourable tradition of it, going back to Newton and beyond. Modern science has its origins in what used to be called "natural magic". Tamhas was a utopian. He believed in the perfectibility of human nature.'

'Good luck with that,' Zoe muttered. Charles didn't laugh; he merely watched her with interest, before continuing:

'He believed, as many did in the nineteenth century, that scientific progress could go hand in hand with spiritual enlightenment. He was heavily influenced by European occultists who argued for the revival of the Renaissance scholar magus.'

She shook her head. 'You'll have to explain.'

'The magus . . . let me see.' He leaned forward, hands clasped as if he were praying. 'The medieval and Renaissance idea of the magus was a man so steeped in secret knowledge that it allowed him to exert power over the forces of the natural world. Think of Prospero in *The Tempest*.'

Zoe could only dimly recall a terrible high school production. 'You're saying he was a magician?'

Charles laughed. 'Depends on your perspective. That's certainly how he and his peers saw themselves. Tamhas practised ritual magic, we know that. Whether there was anything in it is lost to history, I'm afraid.'

'I'm amazed the islanders didn't burn him at the stake.'

'You can be sure he kept this part of his life under wraps.'

111

'So how do you know about it?' Zoe leaned in, interested despite her misgivings, her coffee cooling between her hands.

'Digging.' He offered a complicit smile and gestured towards the cabinet at the back of the room, where he kept the folder and the photograph of Ailsa McBride. 'A while ago, I had a tremendous stroke of luck. Tamhas belonged to a number of Spiritualist societies. It was surprisingly popular among the intelligentsia at the time – well, think of Conan Doyle, of course. In 1854, when he was forty, Tamhas went to London to hear a talk by a French occultist called Eliphas Lévi – probably the most significant esoteric writer of the nineteenth century. A great influence on Aleister Crowley, you know.'

He said this as if he expected recognition. She nodded, impatient.

'Tamhas and Lévi corresponded for the best part of the next fifteen years, right up until Tamhas left for his final voyage. Only a few of Lévi's letters survived in the Drummond family, sadly – I suspect the rest were destroyed somewhere along the way, for fear they were too compromising. Awful shame.' He paused to consider the loss. 'But a few years ago, I tracked down a cache of Lévi's papers to the archive of an almost-extinct Rosicrucian society in Paris. Two old keepers of the flame left, both in their eighties. Fierce hagglers, the two of them, but it was worth the price. Nearly all Tamhas McBride's letters to Lévi are there. The best part of a decade. It's an extraordinary find, at least for those of us interested in the history of occult thought.'

'Does Mick know?'

'Ah. Well. Bit of a sticky point.' He pressed his lips together until they disappeared behind his moustache. 'He knows I bought them, but not what's in them. Doesn't want to know, he says. Of course, if I decide to write a book, I'd rather do it with his blessing, but I can't force him . . . ' He shrugged, took a sip of coffee. 'The story is bigger than family history, that's the point.'

'But do these letters have anything to do with the murders?'

Charles set his mug down carefully and fixed her with a level stare. 'That all depends.'

'On what?'

'Whether you believe there is more to the world than is visible to the eye.'

A chill needled up the back of her neck. 'Spirits, you mean? Magic?' She had meant to sound sarcastic but instead it came out defensive.

He spread his hands, palms open. 'If that's what you want to call it. That which cannot be reasoned away or explained by rational means.'

'Do you?'

He paused, weighing his words. 'There are more things in heaven and earth, as Hamlet says. Until a theory is conclusively disproved, I'm prepared to allow the possibility of it.'

'So you believe in ghosts?' She made it sound like an accusation, but all the time she was thinking of the woman singing, the scratching at the door, the fleeting laughter, the skittering footsteps. She realised her hands were freezing.

'*Ghosts*, she says.' He smiled. 'For an artist, you're very literal-minded. Let us rather say I believe time is not necessarily linear. In certain places, I think, it can exist in layers, with past and present superimposed on one another, and perhaps there are moments when we catch echoes or fragments from another time that seem familiar, though we can't comprehend them with our senses as we do our present reality. And people have come to use the word "ghosts" because it's the only crude means we have to express our experience of those moments. But the phenomenon recurs across cultures and ages. Does that make sense?'

'That sounds batshit,' Zoe said, and forced herself to laugh, because his expression had grown so earnest and still while he was speaking that she almost believed him, and the idea was horrifying. Charles didn't laugh.

113

'You've never known anything of that kind?' It seemed to Zoe he was watching her intently, though his tone was merely curious.

'No,' she said, and felt the hairs stand up along her arm. 'Tell me about Ailsa and the murders.'

He sat back and crossed his legs. 'Why do you speak of murders, in the plural?'

'Edward said she's supposed to have killed her son and then herself, but . . . ' She curled her lip.

'But you've decided she was a victim too?' He spoke softly. 'Why? Because she's a mother?'

'Well – yes.' Zoe straightened, aggrieved. 'I mean, what's more likely? This rich woman living alone, miles from anywhere, hated by all the villagers, called a witch but supposedly quite sane and intelligent – she suddenly loses it and kills her child and herself? Or someone murders them both and covers it up with a story the whole island's glad to jump on because of course she must be a witch so what else would you expect?' When he did not immediately reply, she pulled her chair closer and slapped her palm down on the desk. 'If you're going to write about this, you must have considered it. Someone got away with murder that night, because this whole society believed a woman who doesn't obey the rules has to be punished.'

'You don't think it's possible that a mother could harm her child?'

There was a long silence. Zoe struggled to swallow.

'I know it happens,' she said eventually. 'I'm just saying I don't think it's the most obvious explanation in this instance.'

'There are plenty of documented cases where mothers have killed their children out of a misguided desire to protect them,' Charles said gently. 'Perhaps if the child is abnormal in some way. She may feel she's sparing him a life of suffering.'

She looked down, plucked at her sleeve; his stillness and his steady, searching gaze unsettled her.

'OK, but usually if the woman's disturbed, right? And I thought you didn't believe that.'

'Well, unfortunately, unless Ailsa's journal ever comes to light, we can't know her state of mind at the end.'

'How do you know she kept a journal?'

'William Drummond refers to it in a letter to Richard Bonar, the solicitor, after Ailsa's death, when he's dealing with her estate. William didn't come back for the funeral, you know – he couldn't face the islanders and their accusations about his family. But he implores Bonar that if he should find this journal anywhere in the house, he must destroy it by fire without reading it or allowing it to be read, "lest the poison in her mind corrupt the souls of others".' He made quote marks in the air with his fingers to illustrate William's words.

'So even her brother thought she was crazy.'

'Possibly,' Charles said evenly. Zoe looked at him. A new silence unfolded around them.

'Or what? *Possessed*, you mean?' She was openly sneering now, but she could hear the waver in her voice, and her skin was prickling.

'Bear in mind that William was a churchman, and an islander at heart. He made sense of the world according to the principles he knew. And this is 1869 – long before Freud published anything. People didn't talk about neuroses then. Not people like William, anyway. They talked about madness and possession.'

An image jolted into her mind from her dream the night before; that half-turn to see Ailsa McBride's reflection staring back from the window instead of her own, the shock of those hard black eyes, the malice in them, and the way she had sensed it directed at her, at the same time as she had also seemed to be seeing through Ailsa's eyes. If you were a simple crofter in 1869 who'd never been off the island and a woman looked at you with that stare, you might well imagine evil had taken hold of her.

115

'What did you mean about Tamhas's letters being connected with the murders, depending on your view of magic?' she asked, lowering her voice as if someone might be eavesdropping.

Charles hesitated. 'Are you sure you want to hear this?'

'Don't you dare, Dr Joseph.' She pointed her finger towards him in imitation of his schoolmaster gesture, only half-joking. 'Don't drop your ominous hints and then tell me it's too scary for little me. I want the whole story.'

She succeeded in staring him down. One corner of his mouth twitched; amused, she supposed, by her stubbornness.

'Dr Joseph?' A woman with a grey tea-cosy of hair stuck her head around the archway from the front of the shop and waved a book at Charles. 'Don't want to interrupt you, but could I pay for this?'

'Of course, Mrs McDaid, I'll be right there. Have you met Zoe Adams? She's the new tenant out at Mick and Kaye's place.'

'Aye, we've heard. The American. How do you like the house?' Mrs McDaid seemed to come with her lips ready-pursed, as if to save time by disapproving in advance.

'Oh, it's beautiful.' Zoe beamed at the woman. Damned if she was going to have any of these harpies thinking she was anything other than happy as Larry in her cursed house. 'So peaceful. And I love the island. Everyone's been so friendly.'

Mrs McDaid appeared wrong-footed. 'Aye, well, it's that sort of place. Everyone knows everyone here. We keep an eye on each other.' She made this sound far from benign.

'Help yourself to more coffee,' Charles said, pushing his chair back. 'You might check on our young friend while you're there.' He nodded towards the kitchen.

She found the boy slumped on a high stool by the window, almost filling the narrow space between the Formica units and the opposite wall. He held the rocket book open loosely

116

on his lap. Beside him, the counter was strewn with crumbs and an empty cookie wrapper. He jerked his head up as she opened the door, his face automatically guilty, and stared at her with that same naked suspicion.

'Hi,' she said brightly, lifting the coffee pot from its hotplate. 'Good book?' She almost added that her son loved space travel too, but checked herself in time. No discussion of her family with anyone while she was here: that was her self-imposed rule.

'S'all right.' The boy looked down as if he had forgotten he was holding it. Since they seemed to have reached a conversational dead-end, Zoe smiled and turned her attention to pouring.

'You stay at the McBride house,' the boy blurted, so suddenly that she started, jolting the jug and splashing scalding coffee over her fingers. She cursed quietly and moved to run her hand under the tap.

'That's right.' She flinched at the sting of cold water. 'Do you know it?'

The boy's unhealthy pallor blanched a shade whiter; his mouth worked as if gasping for words, but no sound emerged. Too late, Zoe realised that Charles had called him Robbie, and that Edward had mentioned a Robbie, the surviving boy whose friend had disappeared last summer near the house. Was this the same child – the one who now lived under the suspicion of murder? He looked so stricken at the mention of it that she guessed it must be.

'Sorry,' she muttered, glancing down, 'none of my business.'

'Do you—' he stopped, as if he did not know how to continue. Zoe gave him an encouraging nod. 'Do you like it out there?'

'Sure,' she said, making herself meet his eye. And then, firmly: 'I *really* like it.'

He went on staring at her, his unexpressive features clenched as if words were effortfully gathering force behind them.

117

'You havenae—' he began. The inflection told her it was the beginning of a question.

'Haven't what?' she prompted gently.

'You havenae heard—' As he broke off she saw his eyes flicker sideways, past her shoulder. She turned to see Charles leaning in the doorway.

'Everything all right, Robbie?'

'Aye. I have to go.' The boy slid down from his stool, scattering crumbs, and thrust the book at Charles before bolting from the room as if from the scene of a crime.

'Something I said?' Zoe looked towards the door where Robbie had vanished.

'It's not you. Skittish around adults, that one. Doesn't like being asked questions.'

'He was the one asking me questions. About the house.'

'Ah.' Charles nodded, as if this made sense, but didn't say any more.

'That's the kid whose friend disappeared up there, right?'

He gave her a long look, a faint crease appearing between his brows. 'I see you're acquainting yourself with all the local stories. Edward's doing, I suppose. Yes, that's a very troubled boy you met there. And I don't know how to help him, except by trying to win his trust, little by little. Edward's terribly worried about him, I expect he told you.'

'He said some people think Robbie killed the other boy.'

Charles looked away towards the window, but she caught the small, disapproving twist of his mouth. When he spoke, it was quietly, as if musing aloud. 'That child is paralysed by fear. It ought to be obvious to anyone. But what's frightening him will remain a mystery, unless he can be persuaded to confide in someone. And at present, it's clear that his terror of the consequences is greater than his desire for help. No one is going to force the truth out of him.' He spoke with stern finality and Zoe felt implicitly chided for speculating on local gossip, though she sensed that his irritation was directed

118

not at her but at the whole community, for their lack of compassion. But what if the boy *had* pushed his friend to his death, she wanted to ask?

'You were talking about Tamhas McBride's letters,' she said instead. 'The connection with the murders.' But she could see that Charles was distracted, his eyes fixed on the door and a thumbnail worrying at his lower lip.

'Hm? Oh, the letters.' He pulled his attention back to her. 'Well, they suggest that Ailsa was involved in her husband's experiments. Whether that counts as a connection very much depends, as I say, on whether you believe there was anything to them.'

'*Experiments?*' She dropped her voice to an outraged whisper, though the back room was empty.

'In common with many people at the time, Tamhas and Lévi were concerned with trying to summon spirits.'

'Like a séance, you mean?'

'Similar. But not dead relatives from the beyond – they were more ambitious than that. They rather looked down on traditional Spiritualists as dabbling in the shallows.'

'What, then?' She found her skin had grown cold again, despite the sun slanting through the window.

Charles leaned against the doorframe, tucking the rocket book under his arm. 'They were interested in ancient religions. The Egyptians, Persians, Sumerians, Chaldeans, Manicheans.' He stopped at her blank expression. 'The philosopher-magicians of the Renaissance believed that adepts of these ancient cults communicated with immortal beings and were able to channel certain powers as a result. Lévi saw himself as continuing this tradition. It appears from the letters that he and Tamhas McBride were attempting to conjure these spirits and reporting their progress to one another. Shortly before his final voyage, Tamhas writes to Lévi of "success in our Great Work". He couches it in careful terms, of course, but he begs Lévi to visit him here on the island when he

119

returns from America. Of course, Tamhas never did return, and none of his own writings on his experiments have survived, so we can only surmise from the letters what he thought he'd achieved.' He shook his head sadly and crossed the room to his desk, where he opened the nautical atlas as if the story were over. Zoe stood over him.

'But what about Ailsa? Was she summoning spirits with him?'

'That I don't know.' He laid a hand flat on the book and looked at her. 'But in that final letter, where he writes of his success, he goes on to say something rather enigmatic.' He cleared his throat to announce Tamhas McBride's words:

'The effect upon my wife has been transformative – such that I am almost loath to leave her alone in the house. I would that you might see the results for yourself. Yet much may come of it to ensure our legacy – you know whereof I speak – provided she remains obedient and keeps herself apart from the censure of the narrow-minded and puritanical, that is to say, all of Society. Though in this place I fear that is no simple task.'

'Jesus.' Zoe stared at him. 'It sounds like he was experimenting on *her.*'

'That's one way to read it. I suppose it depends how suggestible Ailsa was, and how much in thrall to her husband. Her letters give the impression of a practical, level-headed woman, but Tamhas was clearly a forceful personality. He may have persuaded her that she was susceptible to certain influences.'

'Hypnotised her, you mean?'

'Needn't be so overt as that. If you keep someone socially isolated and repeatedly tell them certain things about their behaviour or their situation, it's not surprising if they come to accept your version of reality. Happens all the time, even

120

now – most frequently, I'm sorry to say, between husbands and wives. It's a form of control.'

'But Ailsa wouldn't have let herself be bullied like that.' Zoe realised as she spoke that she was basing this defence on nothing but the picture of Ailsa she had formed in her own mind. Yet the memory of those eyes in the photograph, and the strength of will she had sensed in her dream, convinced her that she was right: Ailsa McBride had been a fierce woman, unforgiving, implacable. Zoe admired and feared her in equal measure, though she could not have explained how she felt she knew Ailsa so intimately.

Charles looked at her curiously. 'Ah, well. I suppose we'll never know. Ailsa's voice has been lost to us.'

It seemed that he was about to speak again, but a middle-aged couple in hiking gear appeared through the archway, asking for maps. He excused himself and Zoe sensed that he was relieved to abandon the McBride story for the present; Robbie's sudden departure seemed to have troubled him. But as she slipped past him towards the door, raising a hand in farewell, he called out an invitation to dinner the following night, saying he would be in touch. Surprised and pleased, she nodded her agreement and opened the door into a riot of unseasonal sunshine and a salt breeze. It was hard to feel too unsettled by tales of séances and possession with this warm light on her skin and her own beach calling to her across the island.

8

The road over the moor rolled out clear and unmistakable in the blazing sunshine; it seemed absurd to Zoe now that she could have lost her bearings the day before. With each mile, she grew more familiar with the hiccupping Golf and its character flaws – the odd jerking of the brake pedal, the place where the gear shift stuck between third and fourth – so that her confidence tentatively returned, and from time to time she allowed herself to stop holding her breath and venture above 20 mph. The road lay empty in both directions, silvered with a wash of light where the sun's glare met pools of water from the previous day's rain. At the horizon, a row of hills rose up in a haze of purple, their spines curved gently against the blue sky, a world away from the looming shadows of the previous night. Almost for the first time since she had arrived on the island, Zoe felt a lifting of her spirits, a brief charge of possibility.

She parked in the drive, dropped her bags of shopping in the kitchen and let herself out of the back door, racing along the veranda and down the steps to the beach, nearly tripping in her haste to pull off her boots and socks as she ran. It must have been seventy degrees at least, summer weather; the dry sand curled warm between her toes as she ran over the strand towards the water's edge. The tide was on the retreat, strewing the beach with rags of kelp and bladder-wrack. Zoe turned to face the house, jogging backwards, shielding her eyes against the glare. Long shadows stretched across the dunes and the empty beach; the cliffs behind the house shielded her from view. She glanced back at the sea. Small, white-edged waves licked at the sand; further out, patterns of light strobed and flickered across dark-blue water. Seized by a sudden impulse, she stripped off her sweater, jeans and underwear and let out a wild cry as she hurled herself the rest of the way towards the sea, feet pounding the sand, legs pistoning under her, all her senses vividly awake, until the slap of icy water shocked her into silence. She pressed on, determined, until she was immersed and the numbness that spread through her skin gave way to new sensation; she struck out into the waves with broad strokes, skin tingling, laughing aloud as the water buoyed her up and she swam out towards the curve of the cliffs at the southern end of the cove. The tide propelled her forward; her muscles were warming up now, her arms cut through the rising waves and with every stroke she felt powerfully alive. Pausing, she trod water to look back at the shore, surprised to see that it was further away than she had anticipated. A movement in the distance registered at the edge of her vision; she squinted into the reflected light and felt her heart lurch. Someone was standing on the beach, up by the house, watching her. She squeezed her eyes tight, brushing salt drops from her lashes, and peered harder; the figure was still there, motionless against the backdrop of the cliffs. She remembered her first night, the dream and its aftermath, the silhouette she would swear she saw out on the sand through the window of the gallery, there and gone in a blink. Her pulse quickened; she hung in the water, unsure whether to go back or forward. The waves had grown choppier out here, the water colder, and she could feel the pull of the undertow. She knew she needed to swim

123

back towards the beach before the tide carried her any further. Stretching down with her toe, her foot scrabbled hopelessly for solid ground; panic jabbed her under the ribs as she realised she had swum out of her depth. She struck out blindly, lashing at the water as hard as she could, but the swell seemed to have grown stronger. Brine and liquid light stung her eyes as another wave crashed over her. Sticking her head forward, she ploughed on, straining her arms as if she could shovel water out of the way with brute strength, but when she looked up, she seemed no closer to the beach; her heart juddered with fear and her limbs grew slack and heavy. The next time she raised her head, the figure on the shore appeared to be moving closer towards her. She was shivering violently now, chilled through, hands and feet numb; she flailed an arm, though she did not know whether she meant to call for help or ward him away. Gathering her forces for a final push, she struck out and, as she did so, a cold grip curled around her ankle, anchoring her.

Zoe struggled, fighting to keep her face above the waves; bright patterns blinded her as she kicked hard, but it was dragging her down with surprising force. A large wave rose up behind and broke over her head, submerging her, so that when she opened her eyes there was only blurry greenish light and a frenzy of bubbles. Her lungs began to burn. Whatever was wrapped around her leg seemed to pull harder as she tried to resist, and it felt not so much like seaweed now as a hand, fingers tightly coiled, pressing into her flesh. She pushed her face up to the light, but her nostrils filled with water, just as she felt another hand grip her upper arm, lifting her firmly. The tendrils holding her ankle fell away and she allowed herself to be carried to the surface, where she sucked in painful gasps of air, coughing salt water while the strong hands that had plucked her from the sea now bore her forward until her toes scraped over sand underfoot. At last she stood doubtfully on weak legs, jagged breaths heaving in her chest, pushing the wet hair from her face as she blinked into the sun. In the same instant she remembered that she was naked.

'Are you OK?' her rescuer asked, his voice shaky.

Zoe crouched low in the waves, shivering, one arm wrapped across her chest as if that might hide her, like Eve being expelled from Eden. Of all people, it had to be Edward. Now that she was standing on firm ground and could catch her breath, she burned with shame at her idiocy. She could not even lift her head to look at him. She would never be able to face him again.

'I – uh – I only came to bring your scarf back. I thought you were drowning,' he said sheepishly. He was shivering too, his teeth chattering so badly it was making him stutter. She managed to lift her eyes as far as his legs, bare and white and goosebumped, with the surf swirling around them. He must have torn his jeans off to dive in after her. If he hadn't appeared – what then? The memory of that weed, wrapped around her ankle like fingers, sent another shudder rattling through her.

'There are rip currents in the bay here, they can catch you out if you don't know to watch for them.' He was determinedly looking back to the house, away from her; she sensed he was talking to cover the awkwardness. 'We should probably get out of the water,' he said eventually, a sensible teacherly note to his voice. His wet T-shirt and underwear clung to the ridges of his body.

'Could you, maybe . . . ' She pointed in the direction of the beach. 'While I get my clothes?'

'Oh God, sorry, yes.' He sounded terribly English, as he scurried towards the house, still apologising, water streaming from his limbs, his gaze fixed obediently on the horizon. She hobbled after him, arms crooked across herself in case he should turn around, and grabbed up her gleefully discarded clothes, ramming her legs into her jeans and yanking her sweater on as fast as possible, ignoring the scrape of sand

and salt on her wet skin. Her lungs rasped with each unsteady breath, her raw throat stung.

A veil of cloud had drifted across the face of the sun, casting the beach into shadow, the bright summer cheer all vanished. Zoe could hear her teeth rattling like maracas. Ahead, Edward walked slowly towards the house, carrying his shoes in one hand and his dry jeans over his arm.

'I'll get the stove on,' she said, not quite catching up. She still could not bring herself to look at him. Her memory tried to piece together what had happened out there: the current, her leg caught in the weed, and then his hands around her arms, bearing her up. She had been so panicked by then that what followed was unclear; had he held her, swum with her? While she was naked? Jesus; if she'd behaved like a crazy woman last night, what must he be thinking now? And yet he had driven out here – to bring her scarf back, he said, though that sounded like an excuse, even to her. He must have wanted to see her. Well, he had seen more than he bargained for.

The kitchen felt cold without the sunlight. Zoe pulled the basket of logs over to the stove, but Edward laid a trembling hand on her arm.

'I can do that, if you wouldn't mind finding me a towel?' He sounded so impeccably polite, as if he were speaking to a friend of his parents. Water dripped from his boxers, pooling on the tiles. She mumbled a reply and scuttled up the stairs to the bathroom. When she returned, he was stoking the fire in the stove; she thrust a towel at him and wrapped one around her own hair, not quite meeting his eye. With a nod of acknowledgement, he disappeared into the small laundry room off the kitchen. She heard the slap of his wet clothes falling to the stone floor and busied herself with filling the kettle as a distraction from the thought of him standing naked out there, beyond her eyeline.

He padded softly back into the room as she was setting

the kettle on the stove and they looked at each other frankly for the first time since they had emerged from the water. His hair stuck up in tufts where he had rubbed it with the towel, now draped around his bare shoulders like a shawl. He wore only his jeans; they sat low on his narrow hips, below the jut of his pelvis, and Zoe could see the faint line of dark fuzz leading down from his belly button. The skin of his chest was smooth, almost hairless, like a boy's, lean and subtly muscled. Zoe dropped her gaze to the floor, conscious that she was staring.

'I'll make some coffee when that's boiled,' she said, for something to say, as she edged closer to the stove for warmth.

'I wouldn't mind a slug of brandy in it, if you have some,' Edward said, huddling himself into the towel. 'And, uh – I don't suppose you have a jumper I could borrow?'

She looked at him doubtfully, this time with permission to appraise him for size. He was slim, fine-boned, but his limbs were long and his shoulders broader than hers. Nothing of hers would fit – then she remembered.

'Wait here, I might.'

She scrambled up the stairs to her room and rooted through the wardrobe drawers until she found what she was looking for: that old cashmere sweater of Dan's; heathery blue, soft as a baby's blanket. She held it briefly against her cheek, recalling, as she descended the stairs, how she had given it to him the first Christmas they were married. He'd worn it all the time that winter, but of course he'd failed to put it away inside the zip-up bag like she'd told him and so eventually the moths had attacked; a constellation of chewed-out holes had appeared on the back of the left shoulder. Dan had seemed irritated when she'd pointed them out, as if he were being criticised unfairly. 'I can keep it for around the house,' he'd said, and she had been obscurely hurt by this. Somehow she felt it reflected on her; that she too, in time, might become something he kept for around the house, comfortable, familiar, not presentable enough for his wider world. But she had snatched up this sweater from the back of the closet at the last minute when she was packing to leave, like a comfort blanket, a way of anchoring her to home while she was away, should she need that. His smell was sunk deep in its fibres; soap and Guerlain aftershave. If Dan missed it, he would think she had thrown it out. He would not suppose that it was being worn by a beautiful boy who had saved his wife from drowning.

She handed the sweater to Edward and watched him pull it over his head, marvelling at how smoothly the skin of his stomach slid over his muscles as he shrugged his arms in.

He pushed his hair out of his face, settled his glasses on his nose and offered a tentative smile. 'Is it your husband's?'

Her face coloured. 'I've had it years,' she said, turning her back and searching for the coffee pot. It wasn't an answer, but he didn't press her further.

There was no brandy, but she had bought a bottle of the local whisky in town. She dug it out of the shopping bags and poured a generous measure into two mugs.

'Well, I wasn't expecting quite so much drama,' Edward said, with an artificial laugh, leaning his elbow on the counter and gulping the whisky down without waiting for the coffee. 'I was afraid I might have upset you yesterday with those stories.' He was speaking fast, as if he had prepared his speech and needed to speed through it all at once, before he lost his nerve. 'I thought I'd bring your scarf back and see if everything was all right. Lucky I did.'

Zoe took a sip of whisky, keeping her gaze trained on the mug between her hands.

'God, I'm sorry. You must think I'm insane. I don't know what happened, I just –' she waved a hand towards the window to exonerate herself – 'it was such a beautiful day. There was no one around, I dove in. I guess the tide took me further out than I realised. I'm usually a pretty good swimmer,' she added, in case she had made herself sound like the kind of ditsy hippy-chick who rips her clothes off to get back to nature at any opportunity. 'My leg got caught in some weed or something.'

Or something. The memory of that cold grip rushed at her; she flinched visibly. Reason told her it must have been a tangle of seaweed, but to all her senses it had felt like a hand that had reached for her underwater, trying to pull her down. She thought of the woman in the song, yearning to join her drowned lover; a sudden image of Ailsa McBride flashed before her, washed up along the coast, skin white as china, black skirts waterlogged and swirling around her like an oil slick. 'I owe you,' she added, glancing up to meet his eye. The sentiment seemed inadequate.

'Oh – well,' he blushed and his gaze skittered away. 'It can be dangerous to swim in the bay here, even on a calm day. It's like that all over the island, with the currents. Mick should have told you really.'

'I guess he didn't expect anyone to be so stupid as to try skinny-dipping in October.'

The kettle shrilled and she sprang across to the range, grateful for the distraction.

'Listen, I'm sorry about yesterday too,' she said, trying to throw the words away casually with her back turned as she filled the cafetière. 'It wasn't the stories. I didn't feel too good, I had to get some air. I shouldn't have raced off like that though.'

'It's OK,' he said, with surprising gentleness. 'You don't have to talk about it if you don't want to.'

She turned to look at him. 'There's nothing to talk about.' It came out sharper than she had intended.

'I only meant – I understand.' When she didn't reply, he ploughed on: 'I think Charles was right, the other night, at the pub. When he said everyone who comes here is running away. Or at least, leaving something behind. After Lucy –

129

my fiancée – after she broke it off, I couldn't speak to anyone about it for weeks. I was a mess. I couldn't even be in company. I'd walk out in the middle of meals, I had to get away. Sometimes I'd think I couldn't breathe properly, for the pain. Once I actually thought I was having a heart attack.' He lowered his eyes with an embarrassed half-laugh. 'I'm not suggesting that's what you're— I thought perhaps you'd come to make a new start too.' He left a brief pause and tried again. 'I'm not going to pry. But if there's anything—'

'Do you want milk?' Zoe said, reaching out brusquely for his cup. She twisted away to pour his coffee and felt obscurely guilty. The way he had self-consciously mentioned his ex-girlfriend by name, as an overture of intimacy; he wanted to share his heartbreak and offer her the chance to do the same. She fought a condescending, quasi-maternal urge to pat him on the head and tell him that in a few short years he would look back and hardly remember this Lucy; that life had pain in store for him he could not yet even imagine.

'Please,' he said, chastened.

Zoe hid herself briefly behind the door of the enormous refrigerator, the cool air a relief on her face. She should ask him to leave. This was too fraught, all of it; his attempts to draw her out, to force confidences between them where none should exist, given the difference in their ages and experience. It was only the island that had thrown them into one another's company, and their shared status as outsiders. She could not believe that he would ever have looked twice at her if they had met somewhere they both belonged, at home among their peers. She allowed herself to wonder if he was hoping to sleep with her. Nothing in his old-fashioned courtesy had said as much overtly, but this was the second time he had sought her out; unlikely as it seemed, she found it hard to believe his attentive manner came without ulterior motive. She ought to send him home now before it grew any more

130

awkward, before she had to reject him outright. She took a deep breath and reached in for the milk carton.

'Is this your sketchbook?' he asked, behind her.

Zoe whipped around; the milk slipped from her hand and she swore as it hit the floor. She hesitated, unsure which intervention was the more urgent; eventually she crouched to snatch up the carton before its contents pooled too far over the tiles, and grabbed a dishcloth with the other hand to wipe up the spillage, one frantic eye on Edward. She had left the pad on the kitchen table in the early hours of the morning, after she finished writing, her eyes barely open but her mind and pen racing; he had picked it up and begun flicking through at random.

'Could you—' she reached out a hand for it.

'This one's creepy – who is it?' He stopped at a pen-and-ink portrait of a man standing beside tall arched windows, his face obscured by shadow, a thin birch cane in his hand.

'No one. It's abstract.' She threw the cloth into the sink and snatched the book away from him, closing it before he could turn the page to find her fevered scribbles from the previous night. 'Sorry. I prefer to keep it private.'

'No, I'm sorry. Me being an oaf again. I wanted to see some of your paintings of the island.'

'I haven't done any yet.' Then, realising how harsh she sounded: 'There's this, I guess.' She flipped the pages until she came to the watercolour of the bay she had painted on her first morning, after the first of the dreams. She held the book out towards him, keeping a tight hold of it. Edward whistled.

'That's beautiful. Really stunning. Who's the person on the beach?'

Zoe frowned, turning the page around to face her. She recalled her decision to paint in the figure standing on the beach, at the furthest edge of the cove where the strand curved around towards the cliffs and the sand gave way to a staggered series of sharp-toothed rocks at their foot, but she had no recollection of why she had done so. She rarely put people into her landscapes; the natural world spoke to her more clearly when it was uninhabited. But she had placed this figure – a vague outline of inky-violet – in the exact spot where she thought she had seen someone from the gallery windows after she woke from her sleepwalking that first night. You could not tell, in the painting, whether the person was looking up at the house or out to sea.

'I don't know yet,' she said, closing the book.

Beyond the kitchen window, the sunlight was once more muted by clouds scudding in from the horizon, the sea turned matt and dull as the day faded. Zoe stood at the sink and watched the waves cresting further out as the tide encroached slowly up the shoreline; she was beginning to learn its rhythms now. Behind her, the only sounds were the crackling of wood in the stove and Edward pouring himself another coffee. She half-wished he would leave without a prompt, but at the thought of being left in the house as daylight ebbed, a queasy dread stole up her throat – not so much a fear of the silence as of what might fill it. Why was it so hard to be alone with her thoughts, when that was what she had wanted?

She glanced behind her and noticed the plastic bags from the supermarket lolling against the table leg where she had dropped them earlier in her wild dash to the sea. As she bent to pick one up, she saw a tray of chicken fillets inside. She had planned to make a casserole and keep what was left to eat cold, but there was easily enough food here for two people. In another bag there was a bottle of half-decent red wine.

'Should I go?'

Zoe turned and met his frank gaze through the steam rising from his mug. The question was unnervingly direct, slicing through the veil of his usual diffidence and cautious manners. She sensed a choice laid before her; he was offering her a chance to nip this in the bud before it had even begun, what-ever *this* was. He was handing the decision to her, and all the sense that pertained to her years told her what she ought to say. She leaned down, grasped the bottle of wine by the neck and raised it aloft.

'Unless you want to stay for dinner?'

He held her look, a tentative smile softening his face. It was the response he had been hoping for, she could tell; perhaps it was what he had anticipated all along, as he drove across the moor with her scarf, never imagining that he would have to snatch her naked from the waves. She felt a sudden rush of culpability, so intense she might almost have called it a premonition, if she had believed in such things. She hesitated briefly, and set the bottle down on the table.

'There's a corkscrew in that drawer under the toaster. I'm going to take a shower.' She tucked her sketchbook under her arm on the way out.

'Great. I can chop some vegetables if you like?' Edward said, puppyishly eager. Zoe looked at him. Did he assume dinner included sex, or was it really the prospect of her company making him glow with pleasure? She had no idea what assumptions boys of his generation made any more, though Edward did not strike her as brimming with sexual swagger. Perhaps he was genuinely excited by the thought of an evening away from that spinstery little cottage. She glanced around the kitchen; with the lights on and food bubbling on the stove it would be quite cheerful in here once dusk fell. As long as they kept the conversation safely away from personal confessions, it might be fun to have a guest. And she would send him home right after dinner, she told herself, so there could be no misunderstanding.

Upstairs, a door slammed, though there was no wind.

She was applying a quick dash of make-up in her bathroom mirror – half-amused, half-embarrassed by this capitulation to vanity – when she heard an almighty crash from downstairs, as if something had fallen from a height. Pulling on a hoodie

133

over her bra and jeans, her feet bare and her hair wrapped in a towel, she raced down to collide with Edward rushing out of the kitchen, a potato peeler in his hand, his eyes also wide with alarm.

'Was that you?' she whispered. He shook his head as his eyes flicked towards the corridor that led off the entrance hall. Together they waited, breath held, until it came a second time: a sudden thump and scuffle, the unmistakable sound of a foreign presence. Zoe felt the damp hairs at her nape grow cold. Edward gestured towards a door that led to the drawing room at the north end of the house, a room she had hardly set foot in; on the far side large French windows faced the sea and opened on to the veranda, but it was a cold room, where grey light marbled the walls in wavering reflections. The sound echoed again behind the closed door and she clutched at Edward's arm. Someone was in there; of that there could be no doubt. He took a step closer; she wanted to call him back, to wait at least until he had a proper knife from the kitchen, or a poker from the range, but his hand was already on the handle. She tensed as he pushed open the door, one arm stretched out behind him to keep her back, a protective gesture, though she stuck close, peering over his shoulder, terrified of finding an intruder while half-hoping for it, feeling that she would be vindicated then for the night noises and that recurring sense of a presence in the house.

The room stood empty, its walls washed with slanting amber light as the late afternoon sun dropped towards the sea. The only sign of commotion was a scattering of soot and two fallen bricks around the hearth. Edward motioned to her to stay put as he picked his way to the fireplace; there came another flurry of movement, a frantic scrabbling followed by a cascade of dust and more soot; they both jumped back, startled, and watched as a blackened bird tumbled shrieking out of the chimney and flapped around on the rug.

Zoe laughed aloud with relief, her heart thudding. 'Jesus. He was lucky I hadn't lit a fire.'

'Not so lucky.' Edward crouched closer to the creature as it lurched unevenly in circles. It sounded as if it were screaming. 'I think it's broken its wing. It's only a juvenile, look.' He reached out a hand towards the gull; its hooked beak snapped at the air and he withdrew it in haste.

'Is there an animal rescue place we could take it to?' Zoe eyed the bird doubtfully; juvenile or not, that beak looked vicious. She hoped he would offer to take it outside for her.

He glanced at his watch. 'There's a bird sanctuary with a volunteer centre on the other side of the island, but they'll have gone home by now.' He looked down at the gull thrashing soot across the rug. 'The kindest thing would be to put it out of its misery.'

Zoe shook her head. 'I wouldn't know how. Do you?'

She saw the muscles in his jaw tense. 'Not really. I mean, in theory. But I've never done it.'

'We can't leave it there.'

He looked at her from under his lashes, seeming to weigh up the possibilities. The reflections on his glasses hid his eyes.

'OK. Do you have an old cloth or something like that?'

'Use this.' She pulled the towel from her hair and handed it to him. Reluctantly, he threw it over the protesting bird and tried to bundle it up, swearing as its beak scythed from side to side, catching his forearm. Even his cursing sounded polite, Zoe thought. She hovered, wanting to look useful without having to touch the gull, whose movements were beginning to flag as its cries grew wilder.

'Open the door.' Edward nodded towards the French windows as he scooped up the towel into his arms in one swift movement, scattering feathers over the floor.

Zoe sprang ahead of him, fumbling with the lock, flinging the door wide and jumping back as he ducked past, hunched over his bundle, struggling to contain it. The bird's noises

135

became pitiful. Hurry and make it stop, she thought, with a stab of guilt. She watched as he carried it down the steps and out of sight around the side of the house, then turned back into the room, pulling the door to behind her in the hope of shutting out the sound. What would he do, she wondered – break its neck? Smash its head with a stone? She flinched at the image. He didn't look like the kind of boy who'd ever had blood on his hands; unlike Dan, with his family's near-religious devotion to the great outdoors, at least as imagined by middle-class city dwellers with a fetish for playing at woodsmen a few weeks of the year.

She glanced towards the window. Dan would have had no trouble seeing to the injured gull. He'd have been back in two minutes, wiping his hands on his jeans and grinning. He'd probably have turned it into burgers and have them on the grill by now, she thought, with a twist of her mouth.

She knelt by the hearth and began picking up the feathers, one by one, collecting them in the palm of her hand. Her eyes strayed to the fallen bricks in the fireplace. Curious, she pushed herself to her feet and crouched to look up the chimney. She ought to warn Mick; if one bird's panicked struggle could dislodge loose masonry, maybe the entire stack was unstable and the first winter storm would bring the whole lot crashing down. Holding this thought at bay, she stooped in the wide fireplace and reached up into the dark, trying to judge whether the rest of the fabric seemed liable to crumble. The inside of the chimney felt solid enough. As she patted along the wall, as high as she could stretch, she reached a gap where the bricks must have come out; inside it, her fingers met something that felt like skin. She yelped and jumped back, loosing another shower of soot. With a deep breath, she told herself not to be stupid and reached in again. This time her hand closed over an object, soft and grainy to the touch. She withdrew it into the light and exhaled slowly through pursed lips as she turned it over between her hands in a puff of dust and grit.

A rectangular package, wrapped in treated leather. There was no doubt that it had been there for decades; a century or more, perhaps. Her throat clenched; with clumsy fingers she scrabbled at the knots in the leather thongs binding it, and opened the wrapping to reveal an old book, mottled with damp, its corners foxed and pages crinkled at the edges. She was shaking so hard she could barely open it, her fingers made clumsy by cold and haste. As she moved to turn the first page, she felt a breath on her neck, her skin softly prickling at the presence of someone close behind her, looking over her shoulder at the book.

'Edward?' She half-turned, but there was only a sudden draught from the hallway that sounded like laughter, and the room was empty, as she had known it would be. She looked up to see Edward enter from the other end, closing the French doors behind him. His face was bone-pale; the back of his left hand was speckled with blood, though he seemed not to have noticed.

'I think that might be one of the most horrible things I've ever done,' he said, not looking at her. He frowned and his eyes widened, as if only now realising the significance of it. 'I know it was only a gull, but . . . ' He lifted his head and caught her eye with a quick, guilty smile, trying to affect nonchalance. 'Well, I suppose I saved a life and took a life today. There's probably karma in that somewhere.'

'And you only came to bring my scarf.'

'I know. And I left it in the car. Here, you've got soot . . .' He took a step closer and reached out towards her face as if to brush a smudge away, but stopped abruptly before he touched her. 'I should probably wash my hands. Just there.' A shy dip of his head, indicating her cheek with his finger. Zoe lifted a hand automatically, her eyes fixed on his; the back of her knuckles brushed the spot and he laughed.

'You've made it worse now.'

'You've got blood on you.' She pointed.

137

He looked down at his hand. 'Poor bastard nipped me. I think he could tell I didn't know what I was doing.' He fell silent, then his gaze alighted on the book she was holding. 'What's that?'

A fierce thrill of possession rushed through her; she clutched the book to her chest, unwilling to share it.

'I don't know. It was hidden inside the chimney, where the bricks fell out. I haven't looked at it yet. It's old, though.'

He moved towards her, his face rapt, his attention all on the book. 'My God. That could be valuable – we should show it to Charles. Don't open it till you've washed your hands.'

'I wasn't going to.' Don't talk to me as if I'm one of your kids, she almost added, irritation stabbing at her. She gripped the book tighter. It was hers; she had found it, and she wanted to examine it in private, at leisure, not hand it over to him or Charles or any other man. Because – with a quickening of the blood – she had guessed what it might be, and hardly dared hope she was right. She had been meant to find it, she knew that with a tug of certainty. It had waited all this time for her. She folded the protective wrapper around it again and placed it on a chair by the door. 'Let's eat first.'

He followed her meekly to the kitchen, where she saw that he had peeled all the potatoes and carrots and set the chopping boards out neatly on the table.

'I didn't know what you wanted to do with the chicken,' he said as she soaped the soot from her hands, his tone eager to please once more. She reached for the bottle of wine.

'First things first.'

They had started on the second bottle by the time they finished dinner and moved outside to smoke companionably on the veranda with the dark beach stretching out before them, white frills of waves visible at its furthest edge.

'So you've really not heard a thing?' Edward said. Violet plumes drifted upwards from his lips as he leaned over the wooden rail, his back to her, eyes on the sea. He wore the blanket from her bed wrapped around his shoulders.

On her bench in the shelter of the wall, Zoe huddled into the sheepskin collar of her jacket. 'Someone else asked me the same question today. That boy you mentioned – Robbie. He was in the bookshop. He knew I was living here, he started to ask me if I'd heard anything, but we were interrupted. I don't know if he meant in the sense of noises or rumours.'

'Robbie Logan. Yes, he's got reason to be interested in this place. But then all the kids were obsessed with it, even before Iain disappeared. Nothing more exciting than a ruined haunted house. There's a knowing nod too, the way the older folk tell it. The young men used to try and coax their girlfriends out here for trysts, back in the day when people had to be coy about all that – rumour had it that the McBride house would always get reluctant girls in the mood.' He glanced up and caught her eye before darting his gaze away. 'So for a couple of young boys, the temptation must have been . . . ' He let the thought hang between them, unfinished.

'And then one of them vanishes out here. There's no way that Robbie kid doesn't know what happened.'

Edward shrugged. 'He's kept it to himself for a year, if he does. That's remarkable self-control for an eleven-year-old.'

'Charles thinks he's scared.'

'That goes without saying. I see Robbie every day in the classroom and it's clear he's shutting everyone out. But scared of what?' He held his hands up, empty.

'Being found out?'

'Maybe.' Edward bent to stub his cigarette against the boards and pocketed the butt. His silence seemed to imply a contradiction.

'Well, what else? You don't actually believe this place is cursed, surely?' She was proud of the bravado she put into her voice, though she half-glanced over her shoulder at the kitchen window as she said it.

139

He turned to look at her. 'Of course not. But one thing was odd. Iain – the boy who disappeared – his phone was never found. For a long time the police tried to trace it and there was nothing.'

'That would make sense if he went over the cliff with it.'

'But he didn't, apparently. Over the past year the police have turned up at intervals from the mainland, searching for it. A signal appears intermittently and then vanishes for weeks on end, coming from the island, but always in a slightly different place.'

'Whoa. So they think someone here has it?'

'It's the only explanation. And whoever it is switches it on sometimes. But why?'

'Maybe there's something on it they need to save. Messages, photos – some kind of evidence.'

'That's what the police are hoping for, I gather. It's weird though, isn't it? If Robbie found it, and there was anything on the phone that compromised him, you'd think he'd have destroyed it right away. Besides, he's been questioned repeatedly and his house searched, and they've found nothing.'

'He might be smarter than they give him credit for.' She pictured the flat-faced boy with his shifty gaze.

'Hm.' Edward looked unconvinced. 'He's always stuck to this story that he stayed behind on the beach, and he thought whatever Iain saw in the house made him scream and run away up to the cliff path. He maintains he didn't see what happened after that. But if Robbie was telling the truth, maybe that's why he kept the phone. Iain could have taken a picture of whatever it was before he dropped it.'

'Then surely Robbie would have given it to the police, to prove his innocence?'

Edward shrugged. 'Depends what it was that Iain saw. Ten-year-old children don't always think that logically.'

His assumed tone of expertise needled her; she would have liked to assert her superior knowledge of the ways of ten-year-old boys, but that would have meant revealing too much.

'For God's sake don't say anything to Mick about all this, though.' He leaned back against the rail of the veranda and craned his neck to look up at the house. 'The old stories about his family are one thing – he'll try and laugh those off as superstition. But the business with Iain was different – they knew the family, Iain was at school with their daughters. I get the sense from Kaye that he feels somehow guilty, because it happened at this house.'

'That's crazy. He couldn't be held responsible for a couple kids out here in the middle of the night.'

'I know, but apparently people in the village started muttering about how it would never have happened if Mick hadn't decided to renovate and stirred up the old curse. Some of them were pretty unhappy that he didn't abandon the project after Iain disappeared. There've been mixed feelings about the McBride house being inhabited after all this time.' He gave her a long look, until she understood.

'You mean, I'm not welcome here, by association?'

He shrugged again. She studied his face in the spill of light from the kitchen windows.

'You think they might try to frighten me out? Play tricks on me?' Another possibility she had not considered.

'I don't know. I wouldn't put it past some of them – it's a weird place. People here don't welcome change. But I can't imagine they'd want to upset Mick by driving you away altogether. I think it might make them happy if you were to imply that you'd seen or heard strange goings-on. Act scared, go along with the stories – it might mean they're on your side a bit more.' He picked up his glass and tilted it as if trying to comprehend how it could be empty again.

'Who says I want them on my side? I came here to get away from people questioning me all the time, pretending to be concerned.' *Careful*, said a sober voice from some deep

141

recess in her brain. She had not drunk as much as Edward, though she had drunk enough to be incautious. But she was having fun, damn it; drinking wine and talking inconsequentially with a good-looking man (*boy*, said the uptight voice) whose earnest attention was flattering to her bruised ego. And he was funny, too, more than she'd expected from his serious demeanour; he had made her laugh over dinner with stories about the island parents, the women in the shops, the pub band and their delusions of local celebrity. There had been a sense of collusion in their laughter, the relief of a shared snobbery that she was aware she should not be proud of, but for which she felt no need to apologise. Someone else to whom she could finally say, what *about* these people? She felt lighter than she had in months, and whose business was it to tell her she wasn't allowed that? Only the prissy monologue in her head, it seemed.

'Anyway, I haven't,' she added firmly. 'Heard any strange goings-on. So there's nothing to tell.' She was nowhere near drunk enough to admit to that, not after the neurotic way he had seen her behave two days straight. He seemed friendly enough now – *on her side*, as he put it – but he was the one who had called Mick to tell him about her haring off into the rain yesterday; there was no guarantee he wasn't going to discuss her with Mick in future, or with Charles, or anyone else who seemed interested. Information on other people's business was a kind of currency here, she could see that, and she did not know Edward well enough to trust him on that score.

'You know what we should do now?' Edward said, his voice jolting her back. She raised her head to see him pick up the wine bottle and offer it with a knowing grin. She shook her head, and he upended it over his own glass.

'What?' She watched him with a prickle of apprehension. There was no more wine, dinner was over; they were fast approaching the point of the evening where they would have to decide, tacitly, by inference, how or whether he was going home. He couldn't drive with the amount he'd had, even on a tiny island with no traffic police. She wondered if he had deliberately drunk too much in the hope of being invited to stay.

'We should look at that book.'

It was not the suggestion she had expected. Wrong-footed, she flailed for an answer. That same fierce possessiveness clawed at her; she did not want to share the book, though she knew there was no way she could avoid giving it up. Edward would tell Charles, the first chance he got, and she had no claim on it, besides being the finder.

'Now?'

'Aren't you curious? It's got to be connected with the McBrides. It must have been hidden there since before the house was done up. I remember Mick saying the chimneys and the walls were the only parts that had survived intact, because they were built so solidly.'

Zoe swallowed, her throat scrunched tight. 'Sure, why not.'

Ailsa Mhairi McBride. February 1862.

Inscribed on the flyleaf in a looping Victorian hand, the name and date stood out as a declaration of intent. Zoe concentrated on keeping her hands steady, her eyes on the page, fighting the impulse to slam the book shut, away from Edward's avid attention. He sat next to her on the sofa in the drawing room where they had found the gull and the book, so close that she could feel the heat of his breath on her neck as he leaned in for a closer look, his arm and thigh pressed warm and solid against hers. Without the book, she might have welcomed such proximity; in its presence, she felt a distinct unease, as if she were about to commit a betrayal. Ailsa had purposely hidden her journal away from prying eyes, more than a century ago; if it were to be read at all, it should be by another woman, who would understand and

143

respect the privacy of her most intimate thoughts. Zoe could not shake the sense that she had become the guardian of the book's contents, and that it was her responsibility to protect Ailsa from further slander or misunderstanding.

'Go on.' He nudged her gently, reaching across to turn the page for her.

She put out a hand to stop him. 'Maybe we shouldn't.'

He pulled back and stared at her. 'Are you kidding? It's Ailsa McBride's diary – it might have the answer to the island's greatest unsolved mystery. Charles is going to go *insane* when he sees it.'

As if it were all settled and there could be no dispute about handing it over to Charles; as if he had an automatic right to it.

'He'll know better than anyone what should be done with it,' Edward said, sensing her reluctance. 'This is a piece of history – it ought to be studied properly. I know by rights we should tell Mick, but you know how touchy he can be about the McBride story – I wouldn't put it past him to destroy it, if he thought it might embarrass his family.'

He was canny, Zoe thought; he guessed she wouldn't want to put the book at risk. She wished she had been alone when she found it.

'But it feels intrusive,' she said, stalling. 'Someone's private journal.'

Edward looked at her, frowning, trying to work out if she was joking. 'She's *dead*,' he said, in the voice she supposed he used to his fourth-graders.

Zoe breathed in and turned the first page.

He came to me again tonight, it began.

9

19th February 1862

HE came to me again tonight. Tamhas instructs me to make a note of every such Visitation while he is away, so that he may copy it into his tables and charts, so that every Act may be quantified and measured and the progress of his Success determined. My Husband appears not to entertain the idea that some things might resist his scrutiny. Tamhas cannot comprehend the Passions; his talk is all of obligation and duty, principally mine. But should I condemn him for that, when – until HE appeared – I had no more knowledge of Passion than this table on which I write? I was inanimate, sleep-walking, dead to my own Will and Desire until HE wakened me, and for that I must thank my husband – though he sees only what he wishes to see.

Tamhas intended me to be an instrument, to which I acquiesced, for what else should an obedient Wife do? but my Husband can have no notion of what he has unleashed in our lives. Into our cold marriage bed – shall I say less welcoming to me than a mortuary slab? – has erupted a molten fount of pure animal greed, so fiery I have no doubt it will consume me at the last. Already I

feel myself changed utterly by it – all senses raw, uncov-
ered, alive to the salt air and the rhythms of the tide,
my body opened and laid bare like the most brazen
Jezebel – I, who until the age of four-and-thirty had
barely known the touch of my own hand, still less
another's! And while I do not doubt that HE is pure, I
am certain HE is here not for our benefit but for purposes
of HIS own, which cannot be good. My Husband believes
himself to be Master here, but that was ever his error.
He meddles too deeply with what he only partially under-
stands. Some harm will come of all this, I know it in my
marrow – whether greater or lesser only Time will show
– but I would not go back now – I could not – no, not
for a nursery full of babes and the safety of my cold
sheets.

For my Husband, I will note merely the date, time
and place, so that he may complete his charts for
Monsieur Lévi, and therein my duty is fulfilled. Here I
will set down the particulars, for my own record: how
HE came to me, how HE touched me, what new heights
HE urges me to. If there be harm to come, let it come.

'This is incredible.' Edward half-turned to her, his eyes shining.
'She's written the story of her affair. She might even identify
her child's father in this, if we read on, this mysterious *he*.
God, Charles will be beside himself.' He shook his head in
disbelief. 'It sounds as if it was with her husband's consent,
that's the most extraordinary thing. Suppose all our assumptions about Victorian morals are completely wrong? Why
would he pimp his wife out, though? Maybe he wanted her
to get pregnant, and he wasn't up to it. "An instrument" –
that makes sense, don't you think? Or maybe that was his
kink – asking her to write down all the times she had sex
with her lover while he was away.' He paused for breath and
noticed Zoe's expression. 'Are you OK?'

She had laid her hand flat over the first page to stop him reading any further.

'Fine,' she managed. Again that strange tightness constricted her throat; again she sensed someone looking over her shoulder.

'Suppose the lover killed her and the child, like you suggested?' Edward continued, sitting forward, animated by his own theories. 'She clearly has misgivings about him. It's like she knows it's going to end badly, and this is seven years before she dies, look at the date. If she names him, that could be the key to the whole mystery.'

'Why would he have waited seven years to kill her?' Her voice sounded distant in her own ears.

'She might tell us if we read on,' he said, looking to her for permission. 'Perhaps she started making demands on him as her son grew older. If the lover never intended to acknowledge the child, and it was supposed to be passed off as her husband's, he might have been afraid it would all come out and decided to silence her. Maybe he had a family of his own already.'

'So you believe they were both murdered now?'

'I'm only thinking aloud. I bet it's all in here.' He brushed his fingers lightly across the back of her hand on the book. 'Let's go on.'

Zoe allowed herself to be led. She turned the page and they read on together, flicking through the diary entries: Ailsa's breathless, self-conscious descriptions of her lover's visits, her amazement at her own awakened sensuality. The house fell dark around them as they read, heads bent close over the cramped pages until they were marooned in the pool of lamplight while shadows gathered in corners. A charged silence filled the room, disturbed only by the rustle of paper and the rise and fall of their breath.

In the stillness, Zoe found herself painfully aware of Edward's body, the pressure and solidity of him at her side, the nearness of his slender fingers on the paper, the faint crust of salt on his brow, together with the thudding of blood at her temples, the pounding pulse between her legs as Ailsa's words stirred up memories, though she could no longer say for certain if the images she saw were her own or Ailsa's. But it was the pictures that frightened her. Ailsa had been a talented artist, it seemed; almost every other page held a careful pen-and-ink sketch. Zoe recognised them as the cove outside the house, or the view from the turret. But then Edward turned a page and she saw a drawing of the beach seen from the gallery, through the high windows; there, at the western edge of the sand, Ailsa had sketched in a shadowy figure, looking up at the house. Zoe felt a cold finger trace a line up the back of her neck. She flicked quickly to the next page and heard Edward's sharp intake of breath: half the page was taken up with a drawing of a naked woman draped over a chaise longue, arms raised above her head and crossed at the wrists, her face angled away so that it could not be seen. One leg was crooked up on the chaise, the other placed on the floor, and a man knelt between her thighs, his head buried in her pubic mound. Though it seemed a rough, hasty sketch, the picture had a compellingly lifelike quality; you could almost see the woman's flesh quivering, her muscles braced as she arched her back.

'Looks like Ailsa was definitely getting hers,' Zoe said, to break the tension. 'Good girl.'

It sounded childish; the words echoed around the room. Her face burned and she felt Edward tense beside her as he shifted his weight back, surreptitiously trying to adjust his erection. They had to stop now, she had to send him home, before Ailsa led them into trouble. There was too much awareness between them, too great a charge in the air; it was as if Ailsa's unfettered desires had infected the house with the promise of sex. Zoe tried to move, but a glance at the door and the darkness beyond made her shrink back into the cushions. Edward turned the next page and she saw a picture that made her cry out. A young woman stood, naked, her hands fastened above her head to a hook in the ceiling, her hair hanging down in loose strands that obscured her face. The windows of the gallery were outlined behind her and to her right, the figure of a man holding a thin cane, his features in shadow. It was the image from her sleep-walking dream of the night before – not a vague approximation, but the identical image. But how could it be? Ailsa McBride had sketched this over a hundred and fifty years ago and she, Zoe, had not seen it until this moment. There was no explanation – at least, not one that Zoe was prepared to countenance. Worse still, she feared that if the woman in the picture were to lift her head, the gaunt face beneath the straggling hair would be her own; she could not let him turn the page to find out.

'That looks like the man in your sketch,' Edward remarked.

'Stop.' Her voice rang shrill in the silence. She grabbed the book from him and stood, holding it to her chest. 'We have to stop, now.'

'What's wrong?' He came to stand directly in front of her, a fraction too close, speaking softly. 'Is it because of what happened to her?' When Zoe didn't reply, he nodded, as if answering himself. He reached up to take off his glasses and she noticed his hands were shaking. 'You're right – it feels wrong, reading this, knowing she was so obsessed with the guy that likely killed her. Especially when it's so . . . ' His voice had grown hoarse; he broke off, lowering his head, his hair falling in his eyes. When he lifted his head again she caught the look in his eye: a glazed hunger, barely held in check. For a heartbeat she felt afraid. *Unleashed*, was the word that zipped through her mind: Ailsa's word, and she could not help noting its aptness. A force had been unleashed in this house in Ailsa's time; it had consumed her, as she had

149

predicted, and it was still here. No wonder such stories had grown up around the place.

She opened her mouth to speak, but found no words. Her eyes remained locked on Edward's as their breathing synchronised, quick and shallow. All she could hear was the ticking of the clock in the hall and the drumming of her own heartbeat; she could not take her eyes off his, even when he stepped towards her without seeming to move, and bent his head slowly until his lips brushed hers and she could taste the sea-salt. He placed his hands on her shoulders and drew her in as her mouth moulded to his, hot and open and searching, while disjointed thoughts scudded through her brain: I am twenty years older than you; I have a husband and child; go home, you pristine boy, before I taint you with my mistakes. But she gripped his narrow hips by the belt loop of his jeans and pulled him against her with one hand, still clasping Ailsa's book in the other.

When she felt she might faint with the rush of it, she pulled away to stare at him, snatching gulps of air. He looked back at her with the same frank amazement, as if he could not believe his own boldness. Zoe felt herself shaken, off-balance with desire, all her senses wound tight to a trembling point. She could not articulate to him what she wanted; hardly daring to look at her, he slid down the zip of her hoodie and bent his mouth to the hard tip of her breast. She flexed like a cat, wrapped her fingers in his hair, tipped her head back and opened her eyes to gaze, unfocused, over his shoulder – and let out a scream.

'What?' Edward jumped back as if he had been slapped.

'There.' She pointed at the black window behind him, scrabbling with her zip as the journal fell to the floor. 'I saw a face. Outside.'

She did not miss the flicker of doubt that clouded his expression as he turned to the French windows. The only faces staring back from the glass were their own; pale, wavering discs against the night sky. 'Are you sure it wasn't just the reflection?'

'Someone's out there. I saw them, looking in. Quick, go see. I'll check the front.'

Trying to hide his reluctance, Edward adjusted himself, opened the glass doors at the end of the room and stepped out on to the veranda. Zoe took a deep breath and slipped into the dark hallway, feeling for the light switch, snatching up a pair of boots by the front door on her way out. Triggered by her movement, the security lights blanched the drive with their sudden white glare, but she could see no sign of scuttling in the shadows. She made her way carefully around to the north side of the house where the marram grass sloped down towards the beach. Here, where the path ended and the cone of light did not reach, she found herself swallowed into darkness once more, obliged to guess her way over the coarse tufts, past the steps that led up to the veranda and on until she felt the shift of sand beneath her feet. Scraps of cloud dragged across a faint moon. She stood motionless, arms wrapped around herself, night air chilling her skin. In the distance, waves broke in white frills and the expanse of water beyond was pure, empty black. She might have been sunk in its cold depths now if not for Edward, she thought. The memory of that hand closing around her ankle caught at her and shuddered through her whole body. If she had drowned, how long would it have taken for Dan to find out, she wondered? She had not given Mick and Kaye his number; they didn't even know he existed. How long before someone called him? If Edward hadn't come, they would have found only her clothes strewn across the beach. They might have supposed she had made a deliberate choice. Dan would have been left wondering if that had been her whole purpose all along in coming here.

After a few more cautious, blind paces, the toe of her boot struck a soft lump; she bent to examine a pale shape among

151

the dunes and stifled a cry when she realised it was the dead gull, the wind gently ruffling its feathers, its head bent at an unnatural angle. Beyond her field of vision she sensed a shadow stir; she jumped to her feet, casting wildly around, but could see nothing except the bulk of the cliffs on either side and a thin line of lighter sky at the horizon. Quick footsteps crunched across the gravel behind her; she whipped around, clutching at her sleeves, but it was only Edward, holding out his phone as a flashlight.

'Are you OK? Did you see someone?'

She shook her head. 'I almost stood on the dead bird. Sorry.'

'I honestly don't think there's anyone here,' he said, sounding apologetic. 'I've been all the way round the house. You probably saw a reflection, or a ripple in the glass. The light can do strange things up here.'

Zoe bit her lip; he meant to be reassuring, but that overly patient tone, with its implication that her judgement was unreliable, sounded all too familiar to her. She resented the suggestion that she was imagining things, especially from someone who was far from sober himself. The cold air had drained the wine's glow from her; now she only felt tired and embarrassed by her own dizzy lust.

'We should go in,' Edward said, after a pause.

She nodded and set off towards the front door without looking at him. He trotted close beside her, sweeping his phone light along the façade of the house ahead of them, making a show of being her protector to ward off the awkward silence.

'You've got a message,' he remarked, as they passed the phone on the hall table with its blinking red light. Zoe glanced at it but could not muster the energy to listen, not with him standing there.

'Look, Edward—' she began, as he hovered in front of her in the entrance hall. She sensed he was waiting for permission to continue where they had left off, and was briefly touched by his deferral to her decision. 'I'm really tired. I'm sorry if

– back there, I didn't mean for that to happen. It was all – I don't know – the wine, the book. This afternoon, in the sea. Everything got a little crazy.'

'You could have drowned.' He said it simply, not as a reprimand; even so, Zoe heard the faintest hint of an obligation.

'I know. I'm very grateful. I just think we should . . . ' She rubbed her hands over her face, searching for words that would do the least harm. She could not bring herself to meet his eye; that vulnerable, open look that suggested he would bruise easily. There was such a seriousness about him; he did not seem the kind of boy who was looking for an uncomplicated fling, and what good could it do him to become attached to her while she was here? He would think she had led him on, and perhaps he would be right, but she must be the adult now, before any real damage was done. He had come here to nurse his rejection by a woman; she did not want to add to it. 'Be sensible. You know. There's the age difference,' she finished lamely.

'That doesn't matter to me,' he said. 'I think you're beautiful.'

Zoe laughed, then quickly checked herself. Did he really think that was the source of her anxiety – that she might be self-conscious about her looks? 'Thank you. Look – it's not you. I really like your company. But you're right that we both came here to get away from complications. Maybe best not to add to them, eh?'

He looked down at his hands for a long time and nodded unhappily. 'I should go, then.'

'Should I call a cab for you?'

He gave a brief laugh. 'You haven't really got the hang of living here yet, have you? I'll be fine, it's not far.'

'You're not serious?' She stared at him until he was forced to look up and meet her eye. 'You can't drive home – are you insane?'

He raised his hands in protest and let them fall limply to his side. 'OK, I'm sorry, you're right. If you make some more coffee I'll be all right in an hour or so.'

'There's no way you should drive in an hour, even if you drink a gallon of coffee.' She sighed, pushed a hand through her hair. 'Look, you'd better stay till the morning, sleep it off. There's loads of spare rooms.' As soon as she had spoken, she wanted to bite the words back; there was no guarantee she wouldn't have another of her unpredictable nocturnal adventures. She could not risk sleepwalking naked around the house while he was there – even if he had seen it all already.

'I'll be fine down here on the sofa, honestly,' he said, embarrassed. 'In that room where we found the gull – then I can stay out of your way and leave first thing. You won't have to offer breakfast.' He attempted a smile. 'Sorry I've been such an arse. I like your company too. I'm not usually this forward – it's, I don't know . . . ' He glanced around the entrance hall, as if its carved wooden ceiling might offer an explanation. 'It's been such a strange evening. You nearly drowning, and then the gull, and the book. Those drawings. It's as if this place has had a weird effect on me. Maybe there is something in those old rumours. I feel I'm not acting like myself, but I know that sounds like a terrible excuse.'

'I'd say it's the Malbec that's had an effect on you.' Zoe allowed him a half-smile, but his words stirred an uneasy recognition in her. She thought of Charles and his theory of time overlapping. Could it be true that the house itself might be responsible for her disrupted nights, her out-of-character moods? She dismissed the thought as soon as it took shape; that was as good as saying the place really was haunted, and she would not give in to that when more common sense explanations lay all around her. 'I'll get you some blankets,' she offered, glad of a reason to break away. 'And listen –' she hesitated at the foot of the stairs – 'probably best not to mention this to anyone. That you've stayed here, I mean. It's a small place and I can live without being the centre of village gossip. It wouldn't do you any good either, I guess – to have people speculating about your business.'

'Oh Christ, no, of course not,' he said, stumbling over his words in his haste to reassure her. 'I wouldn't say a thing. I've always tried to keep my private life private here. Not that there's been anything to tell before . . . '

'There's nothing to tell now, either,' Zoe said, and felt a twinge of conscience at the way he hung his head. 'I'll get a pillow too,' she added, in a softer tone.

She stopped to use the bathroom while she was upstairs, noticing as she washed her hands how much soot she had streaked across her face. Had she sat there all through dinner like that and he hadn't said a thing? She smiled to herself; another gallantry that touched her. By the time she had cleaned herself up and fetched a blanket and pillow from one of the unused bedrooms, she found him stretched out on the sofa in the downstairs drawing room, his head tipped back and his eyes closed, breathing in a quiet, steady rhythm through parted lips, one hand loosely holding Ailsa's journal to his chest. She hesitated, watching him for a few moments, feeling more indulgent now that he was asleep. He looked so young, his dark lashes curled on his cheeks. What had she been thinking? Gently she removed the book from his grasp and laid the blanket over him, then crossed to the windows to draw the heavy curtains, taking care not to look at her own reflection: part of her was afraid she would see the face of Ailsa McBride, staring back with those hard, black eyes. Before switching off the lamp she returned to Edward, taking in the smoothness of his unguarded face with an odd sense of loss. He would leave in the morning without saying goodbye, he had said as much, and he should not come back here, she thought. It was for the best. However much she had enjoyed the evening, however much she felt warmed by the idea of his company, they ought not to do this again; he must not

155

feel that she had encouraged him. She leaned across and lifted his glasses off his nose, as delicately as she could, folded them carefully and laid them on the table by his head. She thought briefly of kissing his forehead, the way she always did with Caleb when she checked on him before she went to sleep, but decided that was too weird.

With Ailsa's book under her arm, feeling oddly vulnerable now that she was the only one awake, she made the tour of all the downstairs doors and windows, checking the locks, trying to avoid glimpses of herself in the black glass as she pulled all the curtains against the possibility of faces at the windows. If this were a horror movie, she thought, trying to cheer herself with flippancy, the twist would be that Edward was a serial killer and now she had locked herself into the house with him. She heard herself laugh, too loudly, in the silence, and wished she had not allowed herself to think it. On balance, she didn't think he was a danger – hadn't he saved her life earlier? – but it was true that she hardly knew him, yet she had invited him to spend the night with her alone in a house miles from anywhere. She could picture all too well what Dan would say if he found out – another good reason to keep it quiet. Even if he were to believe that nothing had happened – unlikely – he would not forgive her for being so careless of her own safety, and she had to concede he would have a point.

At the thought of Dan, she remembered the flashing red light on the answering machine by the front door. But when she played the message, it was only Charles Joseph giving her directions to his house for supper the following night. Zoe found she was both relieved and disappointed. She picked up the receiver almost automatically to dial home; an obscure sense of guilt over what she had allowed to happen with Edward, combined with that earlier image of tucking Caleb in as he slept, had triggered an ache that would only be soothed if she could hear her son's voice and reassure him

156

that all was well. It would be early evening at home; perfect timing, if she could steel herself for the inevitable chilly exchange with Dan first. But as her fingers moved to the buttons she remembered that it was Saturday; he would have taken Caleb to his sister's for the weekend. It was what he always did on the rare occasions Zoe had gone away over-night; a way of handing Caleb immediately into the care of another woman, because Dan was unsure of himself, afraid of being left with full responsibility, in case he messed up somehow. Caleb never minded; he was happy enough to be thrown into the general melee with his cousins. There was no way she was calling them at Leah's; she knew what Dan's sister would have to say about her trip, and that was a confrontation she didn't need right now. It would be clear to Leah that she'd been drinking, and on top of that, she couldn't risk Edward waking up and overhearing the conversation. The less he knew of her life, the better. Tomorrow night, then. She would call home tomorrow, after she'd had a chance to sleep.

She barely surfaced from tumbled dreams when she felt the dip in the mattress beside her, the sure touch of a hand on her shoulder. The hand moved softly down the length of her back to the S-bend of her waist and hip and across the curve of her buttock; she stirred, awareness struggling to the surface as if through green water towards the light. In the blur of half-sleep she knew if she fought her way to waking she must push him away, but there was the comfort of another body moulding itself to hers, the particular chime and thrill of it. Perhaps, on some unacknowledged level, this was what she had hoped for when she asked him to stay. To be held, for a while; if that was all that happened, she could pretend she was still dreaming, abdicate responsibility. She wriggled back against him, inviting the pressure of his body. The hand slid a path upwards, across her stomach, under her T-shirt to

157

grasp her breast, pinching her nipple until it stood hard. She murmured a half-hearted protest and his hand moved away, over the sweep of her hip again to ease between her legs, inside her underwear. Drowsy, she felt the familiar swell and opening; she rocked against the pressure as her body responded, even as her thoughts began to crystallise. She wanted this; she must stop this. In a moment it would be too late to stop.

'Oh God, Edward, no,' she murmured, trying to muster the strength to push him away, as his hand moved harder and she became aware, belatedly, that her skin was freezing; the room, too, had acquired a hollow chill. Even under the duvet, where there should have been shared warmth, she could feel only bone-deep cold. Abruptly, his hand stopped moving; she felt the mattress shift. Zoe flung out an arm into that icy air and fumbled for the switch on the bedside lamp. Flinching against its light, she saw that the bed was empty.

She was still screaming when she heard the drumming of footsteps on the boards of the landing, the knock at the door – first tentative, then anxious.

'Zoe? Are you all right?'

She broke off with a hiccupping gasp, as if she were surprised to discover she had been the source of the noise. The handle turned; the door opened a crack. She pulled the duvet up to her throat, fixing her eyes on the darkness revealed in the gap. Edward's pale face appeared, bleary with sleep, a faint pattern cross-hatched on his left cheek where the weave of the sofa had imprinted it. She stared at him and felt the slow turning of fear to anger.

'The hell do you think you're doing?'

'What?' Confusion creased his expression; he rubbed his eyes. 'I woke and heard you screaming. I thought . . . ' He let the sentence hang, as if it was better not to voice what he had thought.

'What kind of fucking horrible trick was that?' She breathed out, hard, trying to master herself. 'How dare you? It's called assault, by the way. And then you run off – did you think that was funny?'

Edward continued to look at her, his perplexity shading into alarm. 'I don't know what you mean. It was only a kiss – I thought you – I didn't mean any—'

'Not then. Now. Getting into my bed and disappearing again. Touching me. You can't just do that, while I was sleeping.'

'What? I didn't.' He pushed both hands through his hair, blinking to focus without his glasses, his face contorted with distress. 'I wouldn't. I was asleep downstairs, I swear. Your screaming woke me.'

Zoe found herself struggling for breath. She wanted to argue, but she knew he was telling the truth.

'Someone was in the room,' she whispered. He left a pause, watching her with an expression of concern, one hand tangled in his hair.

'Do you think you might have been dreaming?'

She pinched the bridge of her nose and allowed her breath to escape. 'I must have been. Jesus. Sorry.'

'It's this house, I swear,' he said, with an air of authority that irritated her. 'Were you reading Ailsa's journal?' He pointed to the pillow beside her where the book lay. 'There's plenty in there to give anyone freaky dreams.'

Zoe glanced at the book and pulled the duvet closer around her. She thought about protesting further but it seemed redundant. After the strangeness of the previous nights, she could no longer say for certain what was a dream and what was really in the house. She wondered if it was the wine; she feared she was losing her grip. She only knew, at this point, that she did not want to lie down in that bed again with the light off.

Edward hovered in the doorway. 'Do you want me to make you a cup of tea?' he offered.

She shook her head. The open door was troubling her;

every time she looked at him, her eye was drawn to the yawning darkness behind him.

'Do you want me to go?'

'No.' She didn't know how to articulate what she wanted. He hesitated, then closed the door behind him and perched tentatively on the end of the bed, as if he expected to be ejected any minute. Zoe watched him, mired in her own confusion. She needed him to stay – like a talisman, she thought; it would not come back unless she was alone – but she was troubled by an uneasy sense that she would be putting him in harm's way if she kept him with her.

'Should I stay, then?'

She saw that he was shivering.

'You're cold. You'd better get under here.' She lifted a corner of the duvet. 'To sleep, I mean. You understand?'

'Completely.' He nodded and slid himself under the cover, seeming grateful for the concession. Zoe turned away, embarrassed, though she was grateful too: for his solidity, his very real human warmth. And why had she thought that, she wondered, as she reached across to turn out the light: *human*. Perhaps because of the lingering sense that whatever had entered her bed earlier had been something else, something less than – or worse than – human.

He reached across and rested a hand gently on her shoulder, and the gesture was so reassuring after her earlier terror that she felt tears prickle in her throat. She laid her hand over his and closed her eyes. A cold draught blew along the landing and under the door, but the house remained silent.

10

'I don't expect anything of you,' Edward said the next morning as they walked along the cliff path, in that frank way of his, keeping his eyes fixed on the line of light where water blurred into sky. Zoe turned to look at him. A salt wind lifted his hair; he squinted into the sun, crinkling the line of freckles over his narrow nose.

'I don't have anything to offer,' she said simply.

The sky arched above them, a high canvas of blue flecked with cloud. Another unseasonably beautiful day, sunlight falling clear as water; up on the cliffs a sharp wind chivvied at their clothes and hair, and the gulls slid along the currents like paper aeroplanes, their wings held still.

'I know you're only passing through,' he continued, kicking at tufts of grass. 'I suppose I am, too. But while we're here . . . ' He pulled his collar up against the wind. 'I like talking to you, that's all,' he said, as if beginning a new train of thought. 'I know the age thing bothers you, but I don't think about it when we talk. I've spent a lot of time on my own since I've been here. Too much, I think. It was useful for a while, to get my head together, but I'm tired of it. I know you've only just arrived, though. You haven't had the chance to get sick of it yet. Stop me if I'm talking too much.'

'I left my marriage,' Zoe said suddenly. It took her by surprise; she hadn't quite meant to say that aloud. It was only as she spoke the words that she realised the truth of it; in coming here, that was precisely what she had done. All her talk of decisions, of needing space, of taking time to think, was rendered meaningless by the simple act of leaving, she could see that now. You could not put a life on hold like that; you could not ask someone who loves you to wait quietly while you decided whether or not you wanted them. Though she was no longer convinced that Dan still loved her in the way that he used to; even so, he had stayed. She could grant him that: he hadn't walked away, when he could have done. She was the one who had shut him out. But in demanding time out to consider the future, she had, in effect, already left – and what did that mean for them all now, that she had chosen to walk away? The shock of comprehension was so great that she stopped in the middle of the cliff path and doubled over to catch her breath, clutching her stomach.

'I thought it might be something like that,' Edward was saying as he walked, before he realised she was no longer beside him and turned to see her folded, a hand over her mouth. 'Are you OK?'

She straightened and nodded. 'Just felt a bit weird. I'm a little hungover, I guess.'

'Me too,' he said, with a self-conscious laugh, though to Zoe he looked as fresh-faced and bright-eyed as if he'd never touched a drop the night before. You can get away with it when you're twenty-three, she thought, with a twist of bitterness.

She was glad now that he had not left first thing as he'd promised. She had woken a second time to the shock of an empty bed, the chill as she remembered her dream of the night before, though the light edging the curtains had given her a shot of courage; she had pulled on clothes and fumbled her way downstairs to find Edward seated at the kitchen table

162

and the air warm with the smell of fresh coffee. He had lain so chastely and quietly beside her during the night, and his presence had reassured her enough to keep the wild dreams at bay; she had slept soundly after her nightmare. At the sight of him sitting there – his narrow shoulders in Dan's cashmere sweater, the tufted hair at the back of his head – she had flushed with pleasure, until she had come closer and realised that he was reading Ailsa's book. That same hot current of anger and jealousy had pulsed through her; she had had to grip the back of a chair to stop herself tearing it from his hands. He must have woken early and taken it from her bedside table to read here, in private, as if he were entitled to it: *her* book! She had breathed hard, biting down her reproaches as she reached for the coffee pot; he had barely glanced up.

'This is extraordinary,' he had said, oblivious. 'She goes for months without writing anything, then there are these long explicit accounts of her nocturnal encounters with the lover. But it's so strange – a lot of the time she makes it sound as if it's all happening inside her head.'

Zoe had felt a shiver run through her. 'You mean – she was imagining this guy?'

'Well, she can't have been, can she? I mean, we have to assume he was a real person, because of the child. But the way she writes, sometimes it's hard to work out whether she's describing fantasies or reality. I'm not sure she knows herself. It's only here –' he had tapped the page – 'towards the end, that you start to get a sense of threat, like she's actually afraid of him. And worried about the child. She says – this is only a couple of months before they died – that she makes the boy wear her silver cross around his neck all day and night so that God will protect him.'

'Jeez, you've nearly finished it. You must have been up for hours reading,' she had said, unable to keep the sharpness of accusation from her voice.

163

'A couple, maybe. I couldn't sleep. I've been skimming lots of it. Her handwriting is so small and cramped, it's taking me forever to decipher it.'

'Protect the boy from what?' Zoe had asked.

'She says HE wants the child.'

'Wants him, how? To take him away?'

'I suppose. She writes that she has made HIM angry, that HE says the child belongs to HIM at seven years, and she knew this all along. And she talks about needing to keep the boy safe from HIM. These are some of the last entries in 1869, written shortly before the murders. She's obviously terrified – she sounds almost deranged with it, poor woman.'

'Maybe that explains it,' Zoe had said, her anger at him momentarily displaced by curiosity. 'The father was threatening to take the child away, she thought he was dangerous and refused. Maybe the father got angry and killed them both to punish her.'

'Or maybe she killed the boy and herself rather than hand him over,' Edward had said. 'She might have believed that was her way of protecting him.'

Charles Joseph had said almost the same thing the day before. The idea horrified her; she could not help but recoil at the idea that any mother would willingly choose the death of her child over any other option, however deluded her intentions. It was then that she had suggested a walk on the cliffs – largely prompted by a desire to get him away from the book.

Now she watched Edward as he turned to gaze out over the silvered stretch of water, the light catching golden flecks in his eyes. There was a tension in his face that had been there since she first saw him that morning; an unspoken anxiety. He was not at ease, and she feared it was her fault. It was easier to remind herself, in the uncompromising sunlight, that he was nearer Caleb's age than her own.

'Is this your husband's jumper I'm wearing, then?' he asked, trying to sound casual, keeping his eyes on the distant head-land behind them.

'Not any more.'

He gave an uncertain laugh, as if he was not sure whether she had made a joke. They continued a while longer in silence. The path was so narrow here that they could not walk side by side, so they were spared the awkwardness of looking at one another. Zoe kept towards the bank of coarse grass on her left; only a few feet to her right, the cliff edge sheered away in a sixty-foot drop to black rocks and thrashing water. There was no safety fence, no warning sign; this was an untamed landscape, and you were clearly expected to look out for yourself if you chose to brave it. She understood now, glancing down, how easily you could lose your footing in an instant, even in daylight, and find the ground gone from under you. She thought with a sick lurch of Iain, the child who had supposedly fallen from the cliffs in the dark the year before. Robbie's friend. Right along this path, it must have happened.

The track dipped and broadened into a natural culvert; Edward turned and reached out his hand to help her down the descent.

'Last night,' he began, as they negotiated the loose scree and mud down to the narrow, fast-flowing burn that had cut the gulley into the cliff face.

'I'm sorry,' she said quickly, grasping at his wrist as her foot turned on a scatter of stones, wishing she had worn proper hiking boots, 'I didn't mean to lead you on. It was an emotional day.'

'No, I meant – when you woke in the night and you dreamed that someone was in the room.'

'Oh, *that*.' She forced a laugh at her own folly. 'Put that down to wine and stress. Jet lag, maybe. I think I can use that excuse for a couple more days.'

He frowned. 'Except that I dreamed the same thing.'

She turned to look at him, questioning; he nodded.

'Though I wasn't even sure it *was* a dream at the time. When I was in your room – I have no idea what time it was, but I woke up. Or at least, I dreamed that I did.' He laughed again, to acknowledge that such a statement made no sense. 'And there was someone standing by the bed, looking down at me.'

Zoe stopped. 'Did they touch you?'

'No.' Edward hopped across the stream and held his hand out to help her. 'They were just standing there, staring at me. I wasn't even sure if it was a man or a woman. But they hated me, I knew that. I felt it.' He struck his chest with his balled fist. 'Like a burning rage at my presence. As if I had no right to be there. It was the most horrible dream. But it was so vivid at the time – I could have sworn I was awake. I wanted to get up and leave, I thought that might make it stop, but they were between me and the door.' He shook his head, rubbed his brow with the heel of his hand.

'Dreams can be unsettling.' She recalled the dip in the mattress behind her, the hand between her legs. It felt like the most grotesque understatement.

'You don't suppose . . . ?' It was the opening of a question; he turned away to begin the ascent up the other side of the culvert, so that he didn't have to meet her eye. She hurried after him, her running shoes slipping on the wet earth.

'We drank a lot last night,' Zoe said, as they reached the top. 'The memory gets scrambled. And we've been primed to think there's something about the house too, haven't we? All those stories they beef up for the incomers. However rational you think you are, they go in on some level. It's not surprising if we start imagining what we've been told to expect.'

'But both of us, in the same night?' he persisted. She looked away.

The path widened and they fell into step, their hands not quite touching. To their left, purple swathes of heather stretched out towards the blue haze of mountains in the distance; to their right, a sheen of mercury slid over the wide sea all the way to the sky. Seabirds chided overhead; the wind stung her eyes and sharpened her senses. The way it swept through the heather gave the impression of movement alongside her, at the edge of her vision, gone if you turned your head and tried to look at it directly. Zoe pulled up her collar and kept her eyes on the path at her feet.

'I could take that book to Charles tonight if you like,' Edward said, after a while. 'I'm having dinner with him.'

'Really? Me too.'

He looked at her, and a bright laugh burst out of him.

'He's a sly old dog. He must think we should get to know each other.' He shot her a quick, shy grin, implying complicity.

'That doesn't seem like his style. I get the sense he respects people's privacy.'

'I didn't mean setting us up,' he said quickly. 'But he likes bringing people together. He understands how cut off you can feel in a place like this, even if you've come here to get away. There aren't many people in the village whose interests go beyond local concerns.' He paused and turned back to the sea, a faint worry line appearing between his brows. 'I go over to his most Sundays for supper. We talk, listen to music. Sometimes we read poetry.'

'Jesus. Am I going to have to recite poems?'

He smiled. 'Not if you don't want to. Charles is the only person on the island I could call a friend, really. I don't think I'd have lasted this long if he hadn't been here. And he does a mean roast.'

'What, better than mine?' She flicked him playfully on the arm. He looked at her solemnly, laid a hand flat over his heart.

'I cannot tell a lie. And it's less trouble – he doesn't make me fish him naked out of the sea first.' That same sidelong glance from under his lashes, as if seeking permission to tease

167

her, confirmation that they were on those terms. She laughed, hearing the ease in it. The terrors of the night seemed to have burned away in the sun, like mist. It might be good to have a friend here, she thought.

'You won't tell Charles, will you? That you stayed over last night.'

'No, of course not, if you'd rather I didn't. Don't you want to ask him about the dreams, though?'

'Absolutely not. He already thinks the place is haunted, like the rest of them – only he dresses it up in bigger words.'

She thought she caught a flicker of disappointment, but he nodded.

'Hey, you can talk about me all you like once I've gone,' she added. She had meant it to sound like a joke, but he looked melancholy. She almost reached for his hand then, but restrained herself.

The sun vanished with sullen finality as the cloud cover reached the coast and dragged above them like an awning. They turned and began to make their way back towards the house, with a tacit understanding that the mood had shifted between them; part of that persistent awkwardness, the fear of misinterpretation, had been left behind. Something – though Zoe could not quite name it – had been implicitly offered and accepted.

Edward held out his hand to help her up the culvert, more out of gallantry than necessity, and as she emerged over the bank she felt him tense, his fingers resting on her arm like a warning. On the path ahead a figure was moving at an unhurried pace towards them. Edward muttered a short curse under his breath and slowed his steps; she turned to him with a questioning glance, but he kept his eyes lowered, his mouth set in a grim line. Evidently he had recognised the newcomer. It took her a few moments longer to understand his reluctance: Dougie Reid, approaching them with his peculiar off-kilter stride, a rangy dog that looked part-whippet trotting at his side, the bitter smoke of his tobacco trailing after him. He acknowledged them with an amiable dip of his head, touching a one-fingered salute to his temple, but there was no mistaking the knowing smirk that twitched at the corner of his mouth as he took them in, the sly tilt of his eyebrow.

'Morning, folks. Lovely day for a stroll.' Everything insinuated but unsaid.

'You're a long way from home, Dougie,' Edward said, too-brightly.

'Might say the same about you, young fella. Thought I recognised your car down there.'

Zoe felt a jolt of unease; he must have called at the house. The idea that he felt entitled to turn up and knock on the door troubled her; supposing she had been there alone? Would he have expected to be invited in? She remembered the way he had looked her up and down; how he had brushed her breast in the car. He might, conceivably, have been the one to find her swimming naked yesterday. The thought made her shudder. There would definitely be no more skinny-dipping.

'Came to see how the young lady was getting on with the car,' he offered, jerking his head back in the direction of the house. 'Everything OK? Oil levels all right?'

'Since yesterday? It's been absolutely fine,' she said pointedly, but the hint of sarcasm appeared to be lost on Dougie.

'That's grand, then. Best keep an eye on the oil with that one. Got to keep her well lubricated.' An unmistakable leer as he caught her eye. She returned his look with a level gaze, unsmiling. 'You often come walking up here, then?' he continued undeterred.

Zoe shrugged, unwilling to share anything about her habits. She did not want him to think this was the place to find her. She was glad of Edward's presence at her side.

'It's a nice wee bit of the coast,' he said, regardless. 'I like the views. Dangerous, though.' He shoved his hands into the pockets of his dirty jeans and gave the sea a cursory nod. 'You a regular visitor round these parts, young Ed?' Again, the insinuating tone.

'There are some good walks, it's true,' Edward said, trying to keep his voice even, but the colour burned in his cheeks and he looked needled. Dougie grinned, as if that were all the confirmation he needed.

'I should be getting back,' Zoe said, wanting to extricate herself from the situation.

'Want me to come and take a look at that oil for you?' Dougie shifted his gaze lazily to her. 'It's nae bother.'

'No – thank you. I'm sure it's fine. I can get in touch if I have any problem with it. There's no need to check up.' She sounder sharper than she had meant; he held up his hands as if warding off an attack.

'All right, hen – only trying to help. All part of the service. Well, I'll leave you kids to it then.' Without displacing the roll-up, he put two fingers between his lips and produced a piercing whistle; the dog jerked its narrow head up and bounded to his side as he gave them another mock-salute and ambled off, still smirking, along the cliff path away from them.

Even when he was eventually out of sight, the discomfort of his presence seemed to hang between them.

'Well, that will be all round the village by tonight,' Edward said, his eyes dark. He seemed angry, as if he should have foreseen Dougie's intrusion or guarded them against it somehow.

'I don't like that guy.' Zoe glanced back along the track. 'He gives me the creeps.'

'You're not the first woman to say that. I've seen him in the pub some nights. When he drinks, he can be properly offensive.'

'What, like harassing women?'

'Mostly comments, that I know of. Things you wouldn't

170

get away with anywhere else, but people here seem to think, oh that's just Dougie, pay him no mind, he doesnae mean anything by it.' He mimicked the local accent, badly. 'I try to avoid him. There's an aggression there under the surface, you know what I mean? One of those guys that's always trying to push you into a reaction. I reckon it wouldn't take much to tip him. Kaye can't stand him – she'd bar him from the Stag if she could, but Mick has some peculiar attachment to him, apparently. They grew up together. He helped Mick fix up the house. Mick feels sorry for him, so Kaye says.'

'I hope he's not planning to check on that fucking car every day,' she said, casting an eye behind her as if Dougie might materialise at any moment.

'Perhaps he won't if he thinks I'm a regular visitor.' Edward glanced at her with a quick, hopeful smile. She avoided his gaze, looking out instead to the darkening sea.

'I should get back.' The thought of Ailsa's book lying on the kitchen table quickened her step. She found herself craving solitude; she wanted to surrender to the particular silence of the house, to immerse herself in Ailsa's story. The pull of it was stronger than any desire for company. If Edward wanted a companionship of sorts while she was here, he would have to learn to share her with the house.

11

What have I become?

I was a respectable woman before HE came. Respectable – ha! What does such a word mean? It means only that a Man would vouch for me and confirm my place in the World. For a woman it means the denial of appetite, curiosity, desire, the body. It means learning how to be less than you are, than you would wish to be, so as not to shame your Father, your Husband, your Brothers, those Men whose reputations are so delicate they may be sullied by an incautious word or glance of yours. How often was I exhorted to make myself less visible, from earliest childhood? "Do not bolt your food, Ailsa. Do not open your father's books, Ailsa. Do not ask so many questions. Speak English, girl, not Gaelic, unless you want to marry a fisherman. Do not run about on the shore, Ailsa, look at your petticoats! Do you forget you are a daughter of the Kirk?"

I never was allowed to forget. It was my duty to be respectable, first because I was the daughter of a Churchman, and later because I was the wife of a rich man. And now I am neither; both are dead, the brittle *Veneer* of respectability is shattered and I am unmoored from *Society*, made an example, cast out, all because HE woke me from my Slumber. And who is to blame for that but my most respected Husband? Who considered me no more than a meek Vessel to indulge his curiosity and designs, with neither Will nor Hunger of my own?

But there is a price to pay for Knowledge; this too was drummed into us as children from the story of Eve, who was seduced by the Devil into disobedience. I always pitied her weakness; now I understand it. I made a Pact, and it will be my undoing.

HE brought me to life, and HE will consume me. It has already begun; I feel myself corroding from the inside. And when my strength fades, what remains for a Child like mine, in a World that has judged and rejected him on account of his birth? How can I abandon my dearest boy, my heart's blood, flesh of my flesh, to the cruelty and censure of Men, or – infinitely more dreadful Prospect – to HIM? For HE will not be denied, at the last. HE will take what HE desires: I have learned this to my cost, and what he wants now is my Son. It will be brought to an end, one way or another.

                                             20th October 1869

Bonar came this morning to discuss my Will. He is canny; he enjoins his Wife to accompany him on these visits so there can be no Odour of impropriety hanging over him in village talk. She brings her sewing and sits meekly in a corner with her lip curled and her eyes averted as if trying to ignore a foul stench. It amuses me to tease her by seeking her opinion on each point of Law her husband elucidates. "Oh, but what do you think, Mrs Bonar?" I say, turning in her direction, all

173

smiles. "I'm sure I have no opinion, Mrs McBride," she demurs. "The Law is my Husband's business. I confine myself to my own Sphere." She knows I am mocking her but must defer to me politely, for I am rich, and her Husband's best client. Mad, wanton, Witch, Harlot: they may call me all these things and I am sure she does, with relish, but I am the one who owns the ground beneath their feet, and that counts for something in this World.

Bonar tried once more to persuade me to sell and move to gentler climes, for the sake of my Health. He observed that I do not look well, more markedly so since he last saw me. "I do not sleep, Mr Bonar," I replied, and he could find no answer to that. He urged me then to think of my Son, and to consider who would care for him if any harm should befall me, God forbid. Those were his words – God forbid. Again I refused. We cannot leave this place; there can be no running from HIM. My brother William is named the child's Guardian, for appearances' sake, but it will not come to that. All material goods my Husband left to me I bequeath to William and his heirs. Perhaps that will make amends. T hid in the Turret during their Visit. Mrs Bonar asked after him, and was itching to see him, I could tell; I explained that he is not like other Children, and will tolerate no Company but mine. Let her make of that what she will.

30th October 1869

I am so afraid. The storms have returned and we have no peace, day or night. All Hallows approaches and it is as if I await my own Execution, listening to the ticking of the clock. I cannot pray – I try, but the words are stopped in my throat. Foolish thought! – I forfeited that solace when I first gave myself so *willingly to HIS embrace. I have hung my silver Cross around the boy's neck, though he pulls at it and I fear takes it off when he is out of my sight, though I try not to let that happen any longer. He has no under-standing of the Danger; he is a mere child, not yet Seven years. And what use am I, if I cannot protect my Son? I would gladly cut my own throat to save him, though I fear that would not be sufficient. But I will not let him be taken from me, I will not! He is all I have, and I am his whole World; we cannot and will not endure separation. I will hold him closer than any lover, for he is the great Passion of my Life; my great enduring Love, and I will keep him from all Harm, now and for eternity, whatever the Sacrifice. This and this alone is my Duty.*

The Day approaches, and I find myself thinking often of my own Father, and the Scriptures he made me learn by rote.

"Ye are of your Father the Devil, and the lusts of your Father ye will do. He was a murderer from the beginning, and abode not in the Truth, because there is no truth in him."

And his favourite, which my Mother embroidered on a Sampler that hung always above our hearth: "For the wages of Sin is Death."

Amen. It is time to go. Let Thy Mercy, O Lord, be upon us.

Zoe closed the book, startled by a sound from below. She had been so involved in Ailsa's words that she had lost all sense of time; now she glanced around the gallery to see that the light outside was fading, twilight glittering over the sea. She stood and stretched; it would soon be time to get ready for dinner at Charles's. Again, she thought she caught a faint noise downstairs, like the creak of a tread. She froze; the sound of footsteps persisted, quite clearly, as if someone were pacing the corridor.

Telling herself not to be absurd, she crept along the landing and peered over the banister at the entrance hall below. The footsteps stopped. She switched on the light and descended slowly, stopping at each step, straining to listen. The pipes made curious noises in this house, she reminded herself, but her heart was jammed in her throat as she tiptoed along the passage and pushed open the kitchen door. The relief at finding it empty washed through her like cold water; she could feel her hands trembling as she clasped the journal to her chest. She let her gaze travel around the room. Nothing appeared to be out of place; there were no footprints on the floor tiles, or none that were obviously not her own. And yet she couldn't shake the sense that someone had been in the room an instant before, and she had just missed them; she almost believed she could feel the air stirring in their wake.

It was those last journal entries, she thought, placing the book on a clean dishcloth on the table. Perhaps Ailsa's fear was infecting her; any mother would be affected by the intimate confessions of a woman in such obvious distress. Zoe leaned on the back of a chair and let out a long, shaky breath. She knew why Ailsa's words had upset her so much: they had pierced her carefully constructed armour to skewer her undefended heart with the guilt she had been trying to avoid. Ailsa was right: what use was a mother who could not protect her child? And what did that make *her*, a mother who had left her child behind because she could no longer hold her marriage together? She should be there to protect Caleb. Perhaps that was what Ailsa's journal had been meant to show her: the way home.

She wrapped the book in the cloth to take to Charles, unable to shake the sense of distress. What had Ailsa done on All Hallows after she had closed her journal for the last time? Perhaps no one would ever know the truth. A sudden noise jolted Zoe from her reverie, like a door slamming in the wind, but distant, as if outside. It's nothing, she told herself, glancing at the clock.

12

Charles opened the door to her in a striped apron, his sleeves rolled up and flour on his hands. A rich smell of meat trailed after him. Horace loped at his heel, took her in with mild curiosity, let out a single desultory bark as if giving her clearance, and padded away in the direction of the cooking.

'You found us! Come on in.' Charles twinkled, nodding her through to a small hallway paved with uneven stone flags. 'Edward says you have a surprise for me?'

Zoe felt caught off guard. Edward had pre-empted her; there was no prospect of keeping the book to herself now, even if she had decided to try.

'He told you, then?'

'Only that you'd be bringing something I'd be extremely excited to see. He's been very cryptic about it, I was about to move to advanced interrogation techniques. Could he have meant that bottle of wine, I wonder?'

Zoe smiled, handing her gift over as he led her into a well-proportioned kitchen where a vast casserole dish simmered on an Aga and Edward leaned against a counter, a glass of red in his hand. He flashed her a secretive smile as she entered and she felt obscurely pleased to see him, despite the book.

'You stole my thunder,' she said, mock-reproachful. He held up his hands in self-defence.

'I haven't told him a thing about it – I left that for you.'

'Is one of you going to put me out of my misery? Red or white?' Charles turned to Zoe with a bottle in each hand.

'Water for me, thanks. I drove,' she added, by way of apology.

Charles gave her a long look, his head on one side. Again she was struck by the extraordinary clarity of those blue eyes in his weathered face, bright as a husky's. 'Very sensible,' he said, setting the bottles on the table. 'Best to be safe.'

'Are you going to show him?' Edward asked, impatient.

She hesitated, turning to Charles. 'You'll need to wash your hands first.'

He complied while she fished the package from her bag, a cloth wrapped around its leather binding. Though she had spent the afternoon immersed in Ailsa's journal, it was not enough; she wanted more time to re-read every entry and scrutinise the disturbing, familiar sketches, until she could understand what had happened to Ailsa and her son in that house. The answer was somewhere in the writing, she felt certain.

She placed the package into his open hands and watched his eyes widen, exchanging a glance with Edward. Whatever the old bookseller had been expecting, it was not this. He half turned away, hunched over it as if protecting a newborn, and peeled back the wrapping quarter by quarter, between finger and thumb. In the silence that fell as he opened the first page she could hear only the bubbling of the casserole and the slow rhythmic thud of Horace's tail on the tiles. Charles's knees seemed to buckle; she and Edward stepped forward, ready to catch him, but he righted himself, looking back to her with an expression of wonder and disbelief and she saw, to her surprise, that his eyes were filled with tears.

179

'I can't believe – so many years I've looked for this. I thought it must have been destroyed. How did it come to you?' he asked, his voice shaky.

It struck her then, how odd the phrasing was; as if he knew without being told that the book had found its way to her by its own volition.

'It was hidden in the chimney,' Edward chipped in, eager to claim his part in the discovery. 'We found it last night.'

Zoe shot him a pointed look. Charles raised his eyes to her; she did not miss the mild quirk of his eyebrow that told her he could make an educated guess about their having spent the evening together but would not dream of asking.

'A gull fell down the chimney,' she said, to clarify. 'It dislodged some bricks while it was struggling. There was a cavity behind them with the book inside.'

'Extraordinary.' Charles smoothed a hand over the cover, shaking his head fondly and gazing down at it with paternal tenderness. 'I asked Mick to check every possible structural hiding place when he was rebuilding. I thought she might have found somewhere, you see, but Mick didn't want me poking around. I think he'd lost patience with my quest by then. You haven't told him about this, have you?' He glanced up, anxious.

'I told Zoe you should see it first.' Edward moved across the kitchen to join them, his face open and beaming. He wants to please Charles, Zoe thought, the way you want to impress a favourite teacher; but it was she that Charles fixed with his grave expression.

'Thank you,' he said, inclining his head in deference. 'You can't imagine how much this means to me. And now, let's eat.'

He handed Zoe the book while he picked up the casserole and led them through to a dining room where a heavy oak table had been laid for three with silver cutlery and candlesticks, pleasingly old-fashioned. Charles's house was large, rectangular, built from the local brown stone; its frontage appeared symmetrical from the outside, though inside all the rooms, while well-proportioned, felt slightly crooked, off-kilter, the timber beams warped from centuries of standing sentinel at the edge of the village. It was the former manse, he explained, setting the pot down on a trivet and lighting two fat beeswax candles; sold off twenty years earlier when the kirk needed to save money by putting the minister in a small, modern terrace on the new estate.

'So this would have been Ailsa's father's house?' Zoe asked, her gaze roaming over the bulging plaster, the pocked stone lintel over the fireplace, the window embrasures which showed the thickness of the walls. 'When he was the reverend here?' She wandered past the table to a mahogany dresser at the far end of the room, beside the window, where shelves of curios glinted behind warped glass.

'That's right. A pleasing synchronicity. I find it remarkable to think of her growing up in these rooms.'

Zoe's eyes swerved to the doorway, as if she might catch the child Ailsa standing there. It was difficult to picture that severe woman with her tightly pulled bun and obsidian eyes as a little girl.

'Did she have a happy childhood?' She was not quite sure what had prompted her to ask that.

Charles grimaced. 'I fear not. She was ten when her mother died giving birth to William and her father was a severe disciplinarian, as befits a Victorian minister. From what survives of his writings, I suspect the concept of sin, and a woman's particular susceptibility to it, loomed large in her upbringing.'

'Poor kid,' Zoe murmured, as she laid the book on the dresser and her eye was caught by a silver object in a velvet-lined box on one of the shelves.

'I always wondered,' Edward asked, 'did you buy this house

because of Ailsa, or did you become interested in her because of the house?'

Charles smiled. 'You can't live on this island and not be interested in Ailsa, however hard the Drummonds have tried to erase her. I've been involved with her story for a long time.'

'This is Ailsa's cross.' Zoe tapped the window of the cabinet with a fingernail. 'The one she's wearing in the photograph.'

Charles looked surprised. 'That? No, that one belonged to my grandmother. It's a traditional design made by a local silversmith – they were very popular with the Victorians. You can buy cheap replicas now in the gift shop at the ferry terminal. You're not vegetarian, are you? I ought to have checked.' He lifted the lid of the casserole and stirred the gloopy brown liquid inside.

Zoe bent to peer in through the bubbled glass. She had only seen the photograph once, but she was convinced that it was Ailsa's pendant, not merely a similar design. She remembered it vividly from the night she had seen Ailsa's face in the window: every tiny engraved scroll, every patch of tarnish. But that had been a dream, she reminded herself, a memory of the photograph. Still, she was certain that she was not mistaken. She thought of Ailsa in her final terror, hanging it around her son's neck.

'Even if I were, I'd turn for that,' she said, taking her seat at the table. 'It smells amazing.'

'Venison,' Charles said, ladling a large helping on to her plate. 'I have an old friend with an estate in Ayrshire. He sends me a very generous gift at the beginning of the season when it's freshly butchered and it usually lasts me through the winter. This is a traditional local recipe, with my own secret ingredient.'

'Magic mushrooms,' Edward hissed, behind his hand, in a stage whisper.

'Oh great – now I'm going to start hallucinating?' She laughed, playing along.

'You'd hardly know the difference, in the McBride house,' Edward said. 'Like poor old Ailsa. Maybe that's what she was on.'

Zoe stopped laughing abruptly; she noted how Charles froze for an instant and his eyes flicked sharply to Edward, though he covered it with a smile.

'I'm afraid you two have the advantage over me, as I haven't read any of the journal yet. You think Ailsa suffered hallucinations?'

'It's hard to say, there are parts where . . . ' Edward hesitated, the colour rising in his face. He glanced at Zoe for confirmation. 'Well – it's very explicit. But when she describes her encounters with her lover, it's not clear whether it's real or all in her head. It often reads as if she doesn't know herself.'

'Interesting.' Charles finished serving and replaced the lid of the casserole. 'Extreme isolation can have profound effects on the psyche, you know. It's well documented. If you look at accounts by lone yachtsmen, mountaineers, prisoners in solitary confinement, medieval hermits – they all testify to the same phenomena. Auditory and visual hallucinations, and a pervasive sense of unreality – a sort of disappearing, where the boundaries between the self and the material world begin to blur. I've experienced it myself. Help yourselves to vegetables.'

'You have? Where?' Zoe leaned in, her fork poised halfway to her mouth.

'Many years ago I walked a pilgrim trail through Bhutan,' he said, waving a hand as if it were too far back to consider. 'I was alone for three months, and even in the monasteries it was almost wholly silent. The mind performs extraordinary somersaults in those circumstances. I walked for a whole day in deep and fascinating conversation with a man who I later came to realise, by all objective measurements, was not there.'

'And you didn't think you were going crazy?'

'Naturally, one wonders.' He smiled. 'But as I mentioned

183

to you before, our culture has decided upon a very reductive definition of reality, and therefore of dreams and madness. I've always been interested in experiences that challenged those boundaries. Have you ever taken ayahuasca?'

Zoe shook her head; she could not work out whether Charles was a delusional old hippy or a sage. But she liked the way he wrong-footed her expectations, though she felt her own life appear small and narrow in the light of his stories.

'Well, it's not for everyone,' he continued cheerfully. 'Anyhow – I wrote a detailed journal entry recounting everything I talked about with my walking companion that day. We discussed the soul, it was all entirely lucid, and when I told the monks at my next monastery stop, they simply nodded, didn't bat an eyelid. Different understanding of reality, you see. So I have no need for stimulants, I assure you. Beyond this, in moderation.' He lifted the bottle, winked at Edward and poured him a large glass.

'Auditory hallucinations,' Zoe repeated, wondering. 'Hearing voices, you mean?'

'Exactly. There's sound scientific basis for it too. The human brain is hard-wired to convert sound into language. If there's an absence of actual language for a period of time, it starts interpreting other available sounds as speech. So you find frequent accounts of polar explorers or sailors hearing singing or cries in the wind. Hence the legends of mermaids and sirens, perhaps. Charles Lindbergh, the aviator, described hearing a voice speaking clearly to him during his flight, though he knew it was only the noise of the engine.'

'They heard singing, but it was the wind?' Zoe took a sip of water; for the first time in days, she was beginning to feel reassured.

'Do you think that's what happened to Ailsa?' Edward asked. 'The isolation drove her to madness?'

'But it's not madness, Edward, that's the point.' Charles set his glass down and turned to him, his face solemn. 'There are numerous psychiatric studies of prisoners who have been kept in isolation and the symptoms they present are not typical of mental illness, as we would usually define it. Silence and solitude have very particular effects on the brain. It's more akin to the experience of religious mysticism. Or, conversely, what we might call being haunted.'

Zoe stared at him. 'You're saying – people might have thought Ailsa was crazy, and she maybe even believed she was being haunted, but really she was just suffering scientifically proven effects of isolation?'

'I'm offering up one explanation,' Charles said evenly. They ate in silence for a few moments while they contemplated what the alternatives might be. Zoe had the unsettling sense of movement from the corner of her eye, at the edge of her vision. A moment later she felt something warm and heavy against her leg; she started and looked down to see Horace's muzzle resting against her thigh, his mournful chocolate eyes pleading with her.

'Ignore him, he's a terrible drama queen. Anyone would think he's never fed.' Charles clicked his tongue and the dog lay down under the table, his gaze fixed reproachfully on Zoe.

'She didn't imagine the child though, did she?' Edward put down his fork and looked around the table as if addressing a debating panel. 'So there must have been a real lover at some point too. Maybe he left her and she was so grief-stricken that she started hallucinating sex with him.'

Charles made a non-committal noise. 'It's very explicit, you say? Unusual for a woman who would have been raised with such a strict sense of sin and shame. I wonder.'

The wages of Sin is Death, Zoe thought. 'Perhaps all that repression only made her fantasy life more dramatic,' she suggested. 'Forbidden fruit, and all that.'

Edward turned to Charles.

'What about this reputation that the house is somehow associated with sexual disinhibition?' he asked, avoiding Zoe's eye. 'Did that come before or after the McBride story? I mean – could Ailsa have been responding to the atmosphere of the place, or at least influenced by its reputation?'

Charles took another mouthful and chewed for a while, considering. 'In its present form, I believe that aspect is a later embellishment. But that piece of land has always had curious associations. It was certainly a pre-Roman sacred site, with all the inevitable associations.'

Zoe leaned forward. 'Like what?'

'Human sacrifice,' Edward said, his eyes glittering with delight like a schoolboy's.

Charles pointed his fork at him. 'You're an educated man, Edward. You should know very well that there's no conclusive proof to suggest that the Celts practised human sacrifice.'

'But you said there were bones found there in the nineteenth century, when McBride pulled the old chapel down to lay the foundations,' Edward protested. 'They're in the museum on the mainland.'

'I also said there's no reason to believe that they were the result of ritual murder.' Charles glanced at Zoe. 'Of course, the legends have more traction than historical evidence. Then there was a hermit living in the chapel in the twelfth century, a mystic, who supposedly resisted daily torments by demons in the form of beautiful maidens and wrote rather spicy poems about it. But I think it's far more likely that if Ailsa found herself awakened in that respect, it was the influence of her husband's pursuits. He could have conditioned her to expect certain results.'

'His *experiments*,' Zoe said darkly.

'You haven't told me about this.' Edward sat up, alert. 'I mean, I knew about the séances, but why would they have – *that* kind of effect on Ailsa? What was he doing – hypnotising her?'

Charles took a long draught of wine. He appeared to be weighing his words. 'I wouldn't want to speculate further

186

until I've had a chance to study the journal. By rights, I should send you both home this minute with a doggy bag so I can get to work.' He smiled, but Zoe saw the hunger in his eyes, and recognised it; if he possibly could, he would have shut the door on them then and there. Ailsa's book exerted a powerful pull on all those who came within reach of it.

'I think Charles knows more than he's telling us,' she said.

Charles turned to her, his eyes unreadable. '*I* think we should finish this up and have some apple crumble,' he said, in a tone that gently but firmly closed the subject of Ailsa McBride for the present.

It was almost ten thirty when Edward stretched and shifted in his place by the fire and murmured that he ought to think about getting back to look at his lesson plans for the following day. The crumble had been followed by coffee and a game of Scrabble in the living room, which Zoe had been persuaded to join despite her protestations; she had acquitted herself better than she had expected, though it became clear that the game was only the latest skirmish in an ongoing and fiercely competitive war between the two men, which Charles won comfortably – as, she gathered, was usual. She had enjoyed the good humour, the companionable sparring between them, but felt only half-present, watching the flames leap in the hearth as the wind rose outside, her mind tangled in thoughts of Ailsa and her book, and the nature of Tamhas McBride's experiments, which Charles seemed so unwilling to discuss. Though she could hardly blame him for withholding, she thought, as she toyed with an unpromising row of letter tiles, since she was doing the same. He had subtly asked her more than once if she had experienced anything unusual at the house, and pride had made her lie to him. She decided to offer him a trade-off: her information for his. But this was not a conversation she wanted to share with anyone else.

Edward hesitated, shrugging on his jacket.

187

'I can walk you to your car if you like?' It touched her, the studied casual politeness of his tone, that failed to disguise his eagerness. At the same time she felt a needling of anxiety; she hoped he would not expect to be spending the night with her as a matter of course.

'I'll stay and help with the dishes,' she said. Charles caught her eye.

'Well, that would be most kind.'

Edward's narrowed gaze flitted from one to the other. 'Do you need me to . . . ?'

Charles held up a hand. 'You have more important demands on your time, my friend. Young minds to be shaped. You are excused such mundane chores.'

'Well, they're only colouring in maps tomorrow, to be honest,' Edward said, evidently fearful of being left out. But Charles insisted, ushering him out to the hall with a momentum that left Edward throwing her urgent glances over the old man's shoulder, making a phone shape with his hand as the front door closed behind him.

'Now then.' Charles ran hot water into the deep porcelain sink and rolled up his shirtsleeves. 'I'll wash, you dry. There's a clean dishcloth in the second drawer behind you. And then you can ask me about whatever's on your mind,' he added.

'OK.' Zoe found the cloth and took up her position by the draining board, determined to keep her voice steady. 'I don't believe in ghosts, right?'

'Of course not.'

'Or magic.'

'Very sensible.'

'*But*. The house. There are things I can't explain.'

'Ah.' He passed her a soapy dinner plate and nodded.

'What you said earlier – about people hearing voices in the wind because they've been alone for too long. That made sense to me. It's a rational explanation, right?'

188

'Quite rational.'

'But I've only been there three nights. And last night I wasn't even alone, and it still happened.'

'I didn't like to pry,' he said, handing her a wine glass. 'Careful with those, they're very old.'

'I mean, Edward came over for dinner.'

Charles said nothing, though she caught the hint of an indulgent smile.

'And then I wondered if these things are happening – the dreams, I mean, and hearing voices – because I've been told these stories about the house, so my brain's conjuring them up out of nothing because I've been primed to expect them.'

'Well, the human mind can play extraordinary tricks with perception,' he said evenly.

'But then, when I looked at Ailsa's diary . . . ' She laid the dishcloth down and turned to face him. 'I've been having these dreams, since I got here. Unlike anything I've had before. And they're exactly like the dreams she records. But they started before I found the journal, so there's no way I could have been influenced by it. So – how do you explain that? Since you know about this stuff.' She heard her voice rise as she spoke, until she sounded almost accusing.

Charles considered her calmly. 'It may be that you are unusually sensitive to – *atmosphere*,' he said, though the word seemed deliberately ambivalent. 'That can happen if one is in an especially vulnerable emotional state.'

She stared at him. 'I'm not in a state. There's nothing wrong with me.'

He held up his hands in defence, his forearms sleeved in suds. 'I meant only, being a long way from home. Away from your family.'

'You don't know anything about my family.'

'Forgive me. I meant no offence. It's the bad habit of those who live in a small community to speculate about what might lead a stranger here. We lack incident, you see.'

189

She nodded, wary, and picked up another plate to dry.

'That first night I arrived – you said everyone who comes here is running away from something,' she said. Charles acknowledged the truth of this with a tilt of his head.

'Well – wanting space is not the same as running away,' she continued. 'You make it sound like cowardice, when sometimes it's the opposite. People have their own reasons. It's not for you to judge.'

'Of course not. Again, I ask your pardon. I expressed myself clumsily. It's true that distance sometimes brings clarity.' After a pause, he added: 'Though it's also true that the things we try to distance ourselves from end up following us. It's not always simple to escape.'

Zoe did not reply. She felt that same unsettling sense that Charles knew more about her than she would have liked anyone here to know, impossible as that seemed. They worked in silence for a few minutes, broken only by the soft slosh of water and the chink of crockery.

'But the house,' Zoe began, after a while. 'It feels like there's . . .' She broke off, unsure how to articulate it. 'You don't really think it's possible for a place to hold on to – I don't know what you would call it. Bad vibes doesn't quite cover it, but you know what I mean?'

'Are you asking if I believe a place can retain memories of events?'

'I guess.'

'Absolutely.' Charles put his cloth down and leaned against the sink. 'You've heard of the *genius loci*, of course – the Roman belief in the particular spirit of a given place. The fact that it's become a metaphor now doesn't make it any less true.'

'But there's a difference, isn't there? Between a bad atmosphere and *actual* spirits, the kind Tamhas McBride was trying to summon. You can't really believe in that?'

He sighed. 'Zoe – when you've been around as long as I

190

have and travelled as widely, you realise that most of what we importantly believe to be self-evident is built on sand.'

'So what *was* Tamhas looking for?'

Charles paused, peering ahead at the dark window as if the answer might be found in its depths.

'This is conjecture, based on my own reading of certain references in the letters. I have no corroboration, though naturally I'm eager to see if Ailsa's journal bears out my theory in any way.' He glanced over his shoulder to the doorway, as if someone might be lurking there to snatch the book away.

Zoe nodded, impatient.

'Do you know what I mean by an incubus?'

'Isn't that a rock band?'

'I wouldn't be surprised.' He smiled. 'The incubus is supposedly a night-demon who seduces women in their sleep and can impregnate them. The figure recurs through a number of mythological traditions – the earliest mention comes from Mesopotamia, but Saint Augustine and the medieval demonologists discuss them at length. Even King James, in his *Daemonologie*. They crop up in a lot of witchcraft trials, as late as the seventeenth century.'

Zoe sucked in her cheeks. 'Sounds to me like the Mesopotamians came up with a smart excuse for raping sleeping women.'

'You may not be far wrong. One theory is that the myth evolved in societies where families would have slept in the same room, as a means of explaining away unwanted pregnancies. And later, in the Christian tradition, sexual desire, especially in women, was so bound up with the notion of sin that it often went hand in hand with accusations of heresy and congress with the Devil.'

'But this is pure medieval misogyny,' Zoe said, indignant. 'I thought Tamhas was supposed to be an educated man – surely he didn't believe this bullshit?'

'Many of the leading Spiritualists were highly educated men

191

– yes, and women,' he added, seeing her expression. 'Tamhas regarded himself and his fellow practitioners as pioneers. He was interested in testing the limits of human knowledge, like any scientist. And we mustn't forget he had more personal reasons. He wanted an heir. He complains repeatedly to Lévi in his letters that his wife had not conceived after almost a year of marriage.'

'You mean he was trying to summon one of these demons to get his wife *pregnant*?' She stared at him.

'I am merely saying I believe that could have been Tamhas's intention, based on my reading of his letters. His writing is so carefully ambiguous it's all open to interpretation.'

She shook her head. 'That's the most insane thing I ever heard. Poor Ailsa – no wonder people talked about her having the Devil's child. The servants must have figured out something weird was going on.' She picked up the dishcloth, considering. 'It's strange, though – for such an intimate journal, it's oddly cautious too. She never mentions her son or her lover by name, that I could see. There's only one place where she refers to the boy as *T*.'

'There was no name registered for the child in the parish records,' Charles said.

'So, it must have meant a lot to her to protect the boy's father, if she was prepared to endure all these witchcraft rumours rather than identify him. He must have been someone important. What about the solicitor, Bonar? He had regular meetings with her, it seems?'

'It's a thought,' Charles said mildly, though his tone suggested it was one he had dismissed.

'How has no one considered this? It was probably him putting all the rumours about in the first place to discredit her, so he could save his reputation. Yes – it makes perfect sense.' She stabbed the air with a dried fork, triumphant. 'He was married. And he'd have known all the legal rights – towards the end, Ailsa says she's afraid the child's father wants to take him away. Maybe he was spreading the story that she was losing her mind so he could paint her as an unfit mother and get custody of the boy—' She stopped, breathless. 'What? What's so funny?'

Charles was smiling. 'Nothing – I'm sorry. It's only that you stayed behind because you wanted to ask me about things you couldn't explain away. Now you've talked yourself back to an entirely rational explanation.'

Zoe studied him. His expression was indulgent; he did not appear to be mocking her, though she could not help hearing a slight condescension. Eventually she laughed and shook her head.

'Well, that's your fault. I was almost ready to go along with the house having a memory, but the demon that impregnates you while you sleep was a step too far.'

'I suppose that's fair enough.' He took the fork from her hand. 'And now, you've been very kind, but I can manage the rest. I don't like to think of you driving back too late.'

'You mean, you want to get back to the book,' she said, smiling. 'Thanks for dinner. My turn next time.'

An odd shadow passed across his face. 'Oh, there's no need for you to go to any trouble. It's my pleasure to have guests. You're welcome here anytime, you know. I do mean that.' He flipped the dishtowel over one shoulder and walked with her to the front door. 'I hope you'll come back once I've had a chance to study Ailsa's book, and we can talk more about it.'

'What will you do with it? Will you give it to Mick?'

'I must, in the end – it belongs to his family.' He hesitated. 'But perhaps you'd be discreet and not mention it to him just yet? It's an important find – one that needs careful study. You understand that, I know. I'm sure you'd like the chance to look at it again.' He raised an eyebrow, inviting complicity.

'I'd love to. But really, I'd be happy to cook for you some-time too. Come and visit the house. You must want to see it, if you're writing about all this.'

'Oh, I've spent enough time at the McBride house over the years,' he said. His gaze drifted as if to distant memories, before snapping back to her. 'But it's kind of you to offer. I wouldn't like to put you to any trouble.' He held out her jacket and helped her into it. Horace snuffled around her feet as she stepped out into a surprisingly cold wind, pulling her collar tight around her face.

'Take care of yourself, Zoe.' He laid a hand briefly on her arm; she thought she detected a note of urgency in his voice. 'And Edward,' he added, as she turned to go. 'He's more fragile than he appears, as lonely people often are. Take care of him too.'

She offered a curt nod in farewell, needled by the implicit reproach. But as she reached the end of the path she thought perhaps she had been mistaken, and what she had taken for disapproval was in fact concern, or a veiled warning.

She glanced back at the gate to see Charles silhouetted against the warm light of the doorway, one hand raised in farewell, the dog wagging its tail slowly at his side, and felt the insistent prodding of unanswered questions about her host. She had found herself wondering about Charles all evening: his solitary, self-contained life, and the way he managed to appear so open and congenial while giving away so little of himself. There had been no evidence of children or grandchildren, past spouses, family or friends, neither in the form of photographs nor anecdotes. She had thought more than once that he might be gay, though he had said nothing to confirm that either; rather, he gave the impression of keeping himself separate from everyone, male or female, of holding back. She could not quite analyse why she had trusted him so implicitly, even from the beginning, and yet she had. It was not his obvious learning but the way he seemed to offer that far rarer quality, wisdom. Now she wondered if she should be more cautious. She questioned again what could have brought him here, this man of such broad horizons and experience, who could have chosen to make his home anywhere in the world. What was *he* running away from? She lifted her hand to mirror his gesture and watched as he closed the door to shut out the last of the light.

The road out of the village took her along the green and past the School House. Its curtains were drawn and edged with lamplight; she slowed the car and considered pulling up outside, knocking on the door. Edward would not hide his pleasure in seeing her; she could tell him of Charles's lunatic theories, they could laugh about them together, and she could offer her new conviction that Ailsa's mystery lover was the lawyer, Richard Bonar. Edward would have Wi-Fi; she could search to see if there was any more to be discovered about Bonar, and even Google 'incubus', since she could not deny that she was curious to know more about Tamhas and his experiments. Edward would attempt to kiss her again, and part of her would welcome it. But as she drew level with the gate she looked away, set her gaze ahead and pressed the accelerator until the lights of the village faded in the mirror. What had passed between her and Edward last night, in the isolation of the McBride house, had seemed entirely inevitable, wildly romantic even, sparked into life by Ailsa and the erotic force of her forgotten writings. Zoe found she did not relish the thought of trying to repeat it in that dingy little cottage, with her car parked outside for all to see; having to sneak out in the same clothes the next morning, sheepishly, before the children arrived for school. It would seem squalid and desperate. Charles's parting words had lodged a splinter of guilt in her mind too; though she had been tempted to tell him it was none of his business, he had only voiced what she was already uncomfortably aware of: that she must be careful with Edward. She must not use him as a distraction. Driving on past his house struck her as the responsible decision, and she was pleased with herself for resisting. Besides, Dan and

Caleb would almost certainly be home from their weekend away by now; she could call, and the prospect of hearing her son's voice spurred her to put her foot down.

A strong wind had risen during the evening; it buffeted the car as she followed the road out on to the open moor, towards the line of hills against the inky sky. Shreds of cloud breezed across a fat gibbous moon, haloed with a ring of haze against the dark. Though she felt confident of her way this time, she could not help but be conscious of the vast emptiness of the landscape all around her and the night pressing in. The car gave her cause for concern, too: one of the headlamps appeared permanently dimmed and turned inward, even on full beam, and the heater produced nothing but a smell of burnt dust, while a curious knocking occurred intermittently from somewhere under the chassis. Even so, it was better than being out here on the bike, in the rain. She set her jaw and concentrated hard on the road ahead, alert to movements in the corner of her vision. Something streaked out of the heather into her path, pausing for the space of a heartbeat, its bright eyes two hard gems in the reflected light. Zoe stamped on the brake but it had melted away into shadow on the other side of the road. She breathed hard, cursing aloud, waiting for the pounding under her ribs to settle; a fox, probably, she told herself, stupid to be so jittery. But she cut her speed, leaning forward over the wheel to peer into the thick darkness. It would be easy to go off the track here, if you allowed your attention to wander even briefly.

She almost missed the fork in the road; it appeared sooner than she expected. Zoe glanced in the mirror and signalled, though there were no other cars, and in that instant she saw, unmistakably, a figure blocking the view through the rear window, the silhouette of a person in the back seat. She stifled a cry, tried to look over her shoulder but turned instinctively the wrong way; wildly she wrenched her head back to the left, certain that someone was there, motionless, in the corner of her eye. But in trying to steer into the turning and see behind her at the same time she took her eyes off the road, swerving enough that the nearside wheels missed the tarmac and the car pitched slightly into a shallow ditch that ran along the verge. She braked hard, heart hammering, as she turned fully to look at the back seat. It was empty; of course it was.

She swore loudly, slamming the heel of her hand against the wheel, as she tried to bring her breathing under control. The Golf was half on the road, one of its back wheels in the ditch, but listing only a little. She put it in first and tried to accelerate away, but heard the frantic spinning of the tyres on mud, unable to find purchase. Sweat prickled on her palms; she wiped them on her jeans and breathed deeply, in for two and out for four, the way Dr Schlesinger had shown her. It's fine, she told herself; everything is going to be fine. Again, she was distracted by that sensation of movement at the edge of her line of sight. She snapped around and saw through the rear window, some way back along the road, the figure in the long coat she had seen two nights earlier, when she had been stranded on the bike. Most likely a shepherd, Mick had said. The person was walking unhurriedly towards the car, the skirts of his or her coat whipped by the wind, whose gusts seemed even louder out here. Zoe unfastened her seatbelt and reached for the door, thinking she would ask the stranger to help her push the car back on to the road, but even as her fingers closed on the handle she was gripped by an over-whelming sense of dread.

The figure continued to approach at a curiously slow pace, but in the mirror Zoe could see that what she had taken for a long waterproof riding coat was more like an old-fashioned cloak, with a hood that obscured the person's face; they also held their hands wrapped inside the flapping material, so that no part of them could be seen. She knew, inexplicably but with no trace of doubt, that she must not address the figure, above all not allow it to lift up its hood. She put the car in

197

gear and stamped on the pedal, but was met only with the futile spinning of wheels until the engine cut out. She glanced behind; the person in the cloak was about twenty yards away and narrowing the distance with their steady, lurching gait. She wrenched the key again in the ignition; the starter strained and strained before hiccupping into silence. *You're flooding the engine*, said Dan's voice in her head, in a familiar, weary tone. She tried once more, with greater desperation and the same result. In the rear-view mirror, the person had almost reached the car; as the wind snagged at their cloak, Zoe had the impression of long skirts billowing beneath it, caught around bone-thin legs. Fear spread coldly along her limbs until her hands and feet prickled with loss of feeling; it's a shepherd, she told herself, just a shepherd, though she had the presence of mind to jam her elbow down on the button beside her to lock her door. The car was so old it didn't have central locking; she lunged across to hit the lock on the passenger door as a shadow fell across the rear window. She tried to swallow but her throat had clenched shut; she bowed her head in a gesture of submission and waited for the rap on the window, the rattle of the handle.

Instead, the car was flooded with sudden light. Zoe looked up, surprised, to see a pair of headlights approaching at speed from the opposite direction. A dark-blue pickup truck slammed to a halt alongside; her initial relief ebbed away when she saw that Dougie Reid was driving it. Beside him, in the passenger seat, sat Annag, the barmaid from the Stag, who shot Zoe a brief look of sullen contempt before turning away.

Dougie jumped down, grinning. He lifted the cigarette stub from his lip and shouted through her window.

'Got yourself in a wee mess then, eh?' He was delighted to find her in need of rescue, she could tell. He tugged at the handle of the driver's door; reluctantly, Zoe lifted the lock. Then, remembering, whipped her head around to look behind, to left and right. There was no sign of the figure in the cloak.

That was absurd. But she had no time to ponder an explanation before Dougie opened the door.

'I think I took the turning too fast,' she said. 'The back wheel's stuck.'

'Aye, that's a nasty bend if you're no used to it.' He sounded unexpectedly placatory. 'You'll need a wee push. Start her up for me.'

'I can't get it to start.' She had slipped into her default apologetic tone, the one she had so often found herself using to Dan, and was angry at her own weakness. It was Dougie who had sold her a car that wouldn't start; he should be apologising to her. Dan would make her feel it was her fault. The car was fine before, he would say. She twitched her head, as if the voice could be shaken off like a fly.

Dougie sized her up. 'Aye, there's a knack. Hop out.'

She climbed out of the car and exchanged places with him. The wind snapped her hair into her eyes; she pushed it away and turned slowly, searching the dark expanse of the moors and the hills beyond. There was no sign of anyone out walking. She wondered if she could have imagined it – but twice, the same figure? She glanced at the truck. Annag had pulled down the sun visor and was stretching up to apply lipstick in its mirror. Shadow obscured half her face; Zoe could not see, but suspected it was her own Chanel lipstick and that the girl was deliberately trying to provoke her. She looked away.

The car made a throaty sound and coughed into life. Dougie jumped out and gestured for her to take his place.

'I'll give you a good hard shove from behind, eh?' He winked. Zoe responded with a feeble smile. She would have liked to tell him to fuck off, but was aware that she was at present in his debt. He tapped his knuckles on the window of the truck as he passed. 'Oi, you! Make yourself useful and help me push.'

Annag looked at them through the smeared glass with a hauteur that suggested she could not believe this was being asked of her. Eventually she climbed down with an exaggerated show of resistance, tugging down her very short tube skirt.

'I'm no getting shite all over maself because she cannae drive properly,' she said, aggressively champing gum. Zoe noticed a long run in the girl's tights and dirt crusted over her studded ankle boots.

'Chrissakes.' Dougie rolled his eyes. 'All right – you get in there and steer and Mrs Adams can help me push. That OK with your ladyship?'

Annag darted him a sour look and wedged herself primly into the driver's seat.

'You OK?' Dougie asked, through his roll-up, as Zoe braced herself against the rear bumper beside him. It seemed a perfunctory enquiry; she nodded. 'No going to do your back or anything?'

'I'm fine.'

He banged on the rear window with a fist. In response, Annag revved the engine; Dougie nodded to Zoe and she shouldered the whole of her bodyweight against the car, willing it to move. Mud sprayed up from the trapped wheel, spattering their faces; Dougie heaved until veins stood out at his temples, and as the whine of the engine reached an unbearable pitch, the car jerked forward on to the road, flinging Zoe and Dougie into the rut it left behind.

'Thanks.' She picked herself up, rubbing at the mud on her jeans. 'Sorry to put you to all this trouble.'

'No trouble at all, hen.' Dougie patted her on the shoulder, as the car door opened and Annag's thick legs swung out. 'Lucky for you we were passing by.'

Zoe made a non-committal noise. That Dougie, who must be in his mid-forties at least, should be out so late with a sixteen-year-old girl in the middle of nowhere, made her uncomfortable if she paused to think about the implications, but she told herself it was not her problem. The girl didn't seem at all troubled; if anything, she carried herself with a kind of insouciance, bothered only by Zoe's imposition on her time. They might be related, Zoe thought, for all she knew; half the islanders seemed to be. She must not become like the village gossips, permanently alert to scandal. He was probably giving her a lift, that's all. Though she could not help wondering where they could have been coming from when they found her; as far as she knew, there was nothing along that stretch of road until you came to the McBride house. The thought unnerved her; she hoped Dougie had not taken it upon himself to drop by and check on the car again. But if he had sought to find her there alone, he would not have brought the girl, surely? She decided to ask Mick to have a quiet word with him about turning up unannounced. Now was not the time to risk giving offence.

'Did you see someone walking along the road just now?' she asked, effortfully casual, as Dougie brushed his jacket down. He looked up, interested.

'Out here? No. Why, did you?'

'I thought I might have. A shepherd, maybe.' She watched as Annag climbed back into the cab of the truck and ostentatiously lit a cigarette from a pack on the dashboard.

'I doubt that, hen,' Dougie said. His usual mocking expression had turned serious. 'No shepherds on the moor, this time of night. They don't use the bothies up here any more.'

'I guess I was mistaken.' She smiled politely and moved towards the car.

'Maybe you've started seeing things.' He was watching her with a sly grin. 'They say the McBride house'll do that to some folk.'

'It was probably a fox. I don't have my glasses on. Thanks for your help. I should get going.' She eased herself back into the driver's seat. A ghost of cheap perfume and minty gum hung in the air. Dougie interposed himself before she could close the door and leaned in, one arm resting on the roof.

'Aye – fox, shepherd, easy mistake.' His tone was half-amused, half-mocking. 'I'd best come out and take a look at that ignition sometime, though. Don't want you to have any trouble getting her going.'

'Oh – I'm sure it'll be fine.'

'Like I said, no bother at all. I'll be seeing you, then.' He bent his head down to give her a parting smile that looked like a leer in the half-light; she caught a whiff of tobacco and something sharper, more animal. Before she could protest further, he slapped the roof twice, as if giving her a signal to depart, and walked away to his truck. Zoe slammed the driver's door, her hands shaking, and pulled away so quickly that the tyres squealed on the road.

13

She rounded the final bend in the drive, expecting the white shock of the security light as the car approached, but the house remained stubbornly dark even as she pulled up outside. At once she felt a torsion in her gut, a knife-twist of apprehension. Before she set out for Charles's that evening she had remembered to leave the light on in the entrance hall, so that she wouldn't have to enter a dark house when she returned, but now she could see no welcoming glow through the windows either side of the front door. Perhaps she had only thought about leaving on the light, but not actually done so; she rummaged in her memory but found nothing certain. The disrupted nights were fraying her concentration; more than once in the past day or two she had let the kettle boil dry or left the bath to overflow, with no recollection of having put either on. She was not unduly worried; she had been through this before, and besides, she was probably still a little jet-lagged. Nothing a good night's sleep wouldn't solve.

She sat with the engine running, not wanting to switch off the headlamps which were currently her only source of light. Wind shook the little car vigorously, like a dog with a rabbit between its teeth.

The wind must have caused a power failure, she reasoned.

That would make sense. She spread her hands on her thighs and looked at them, weighing up what to do. If she hadn't been so jittery from the events of her journey across the moor, she might have felt better able to think clearly. She should call Mick, ask him to come out and take a look, see if he could fix the problem; if not, he could at least start the generator for her. Although he would not be pleased; he had already given up a morning to show her how to work the generator herself, precisely so that she would be able to manage if bad weather affected the power. She recalled, with a flush of shame, how she had been so distracted by the dream of her first night in the house that she had barely paid attention to his careful instructions. Even if she had been able to remember, she felt an instinctive reluctance to venture down into that cellar on her own, in the dark. She glanced at her watch; it was ten to midnight on a Sunday. Mick and Kaye would no doubt be in bed; they had children who needed to be up for school in the morning. It was hardly fair to disturb them now, when she should be able to do this for herself. She would not have them thinking she was so helpless. In any case, she had intended to go straight to bed. She could do that well enough by the light of the storm lantern; if the power was still down in the morning she could call Mick then, when the gale had blown over.

She looked out at the house. As always, night lent its eccentric aspect an air of menace, the sense that it was somehow off-kilter. The blank windows betrayed nothing. A lone gull stood sentinel on the gable above the front porch, keening like a widow in mourning. The thought of spending a night alone there without light sent a thick chill rippling up to her nape and that same tingling numbness through her limbs. A brief image of the figure on the moor, the particular flapping of its cloak, flashed behind her eyes and she realised her hands were shaking. This was ridiculous. She needed to get inside, light the lantern, make herself a hot drink. The wood burner would not be affected by the power cut; at least there would be warmth and hot water. She could make it cosy. She toyed with the idea of calling Edward; she was sure he would jump straight in his car and come out to spend the night if she asked him. Almost as quickly, she decided against it. If she must be careful not to use Edward as a distraction while she was here, she must guard equally against using him as a crutch, to take the edge off the hardship of being alone. She took a deep breath, rummaged in her bag for the keys, and stepped out to unlock the front door, leaving the headlights on while she did so.

She pushed the heavy door open into an expectant hush that made her think of churches, an effect heightened by the thick scent of lilies, now past their bloom. A red dot flashed on the telephone table. She flicked the light switch a few times; nothing happened. Fumbling for her cell phone, she held out its small blue glare while she crunched back over gravel to turn off the headlamps. The darkness pressed in closer, though she was surprised to see, after a few moments' adjustment, how much the moon illuminated when there was no artificial light to compete. She locked the front door behind her and shot the iron bolts, pushing from her mind the foolish notion that there might be someone in the house. Now that she was inside, she became aware of another smell, stronger than the lilies; a smell of decay, of something dead and rotting. Must be a problem with the drains, she told herself; another thing for Mick to fix in the morning.

To delay the inevitable progress through the dark corridor beyond to the kitchen in search of the storm lantern and matches, she pressed a button on the answerphone and Dan's voice filled the hallway, echoing strangely.

Hey, Zo, it's me. So – I just picked up your message, I was at Leah's for the weekend. You could have tried my cell. A pause, a rustling while he shifted the receiver, a faint sigh, as if he were considering how to proceed. *I hope you're doing*

OK. I've been worried about you, obviously. Another pause; then, more decisive, as if he had prepared a speech: *Look, I found your pills. And I know you didn't leave them behind by mistake, because they were stuffed down the side of the mattress on your bed. The bed in the spare room, I mean. So – I called Dr Schlesinger.* Zoe felt her scalp constrict. *And – of course, you know this – she said she hasn't seen you for a couple months. She was surprised because she was under the impression that I knew.* He left a pause, to allow for impact. *So you can see why I'm worried. You're not supposed to stop taking them like that – she said the side effects can be pretty bad. I didn't know what to do so – I know you'll be mad about this, but I called your mom. She's upset because she's been emailing and you haven't replied and she doesn't know how to get a hold of you. So – I thought maybe I could give her this number and if you won't talk to me, maybe she—*

Zoe jammed her finger on the button, cutting him off. *Fuck him.* Not a word about Caleb; only that imperious, school-teacher tone he had taken to using with her lately, that implied he knew best in all things, and it was all for her own good. He had no idea – how could he, when he wouldn't listen – what that medication had been doing to her head, how muddled and disturbing it had made her thoughts, how it had affected her sleep. He could not know how liberating it had felt to leave the pills behind, and with them the blunt-edged, stifled person she had become. Here, on the other side of the ocean, she had determined that she would be free of them, she would face the world without that layer of cladding, like sodden wool, that muffled all her feelings, so that she no longer trusted her own responses. She had known she would likely feel a little strange for the first few days; that was to be expected, but it was a small price to pay, and she was coping, wasn't she? She was coping fine. It was only the broken nights affecting her. And to give her mother the number here, to give *her* an entry to her sanctum – that was an unforgivable betrayal. He must have known how she would feel about that; but as always it was couched in the language of concern. She pressed her fists to her temples. Why was it so hard to make them all understand that she wanted time away, on her own, without their needs and their fussing? Why was her desire for solitude such a threat to them? She could understand how Ailsa must have felt out here, a century and a half earlier, fending off interference from her brother, the minister, the solicitor, the villagers, all the men telling her to doubt her own sanity, wanting to bring her autonomy under their control.

Anger had displaced Zoe's earlier fear; she turned away from the answerphone on its polished table and strode out towards the kitchen, holding her phone up so that its wavering beam could illuminate the end of the corridor. She could not call and speak to Caleb now without first confronting Dan, and she couldn't face that yet, but there was always the capricious McBride network; if it appeared again, she could try Skyping Caleb. He might be able to talk to her without Dan's knowledge.

A message flashed up on her phone screen to indicate low battery. Her pulse kicked, but she was sure she had enough left to keep the flashlight app working while she found the storm lantern. Directing the light straight ahead meant leaving the floor immediately before her in darkness; she had not taken more than two steps when her boot struck a soft, fleshy object underfoot. She felt it give with an unpleasant crunch and jerked the beam down; at the sight, she let out a yelp and stumbled back in horror. It was the body of the juvenile seagull Edward had killed – at least, she assumed it was the same one, its wings spread out in a stiff parody of flight. Its head was missing. The flesh around the neck had turned stringy and blackened where it had been severed.

Zoe froze, staring, a pulse thudding in her throat. She put a hand out to the wall, fearing that her legs might not hold.

After the initial revulsion, a colder, infinitely more frightening realisation dawned: someone had placed the bird there deliberately. Meaning someone had been inside the house while she was out. Meaning, perhaps, they could still be here. She held her breath, straining for a sound, but there was only the fierce gusting of the wind and the incessant cries of the gull outside. She stood for what felt like minutes, unable to move in any direction, rigid with fear, and perhaps would have remained there if her phone had not smoothly shut itself down, plunging the house into complete darkness. The shift brought her back to herself. She could make a dash for the front door, jump in the car, drive back to the village, wake Mick or Charles or Edward, let them know there had been a break-in, ask one of them to return with her or notify the police. She glanced back at the entrance hall, now coldly lit by the moon through the narrow windows either side of the front door. But that would involve a drive back across the moor, and she could not shake the image of that figure in its cloak wandering out there. Suppose she stalled the car again in her panic, and couldn't restart it, out there, with no phone? No: better to call Mick from here; she could reasonably justify it now, with the gull. But Mick and Kaye's number was in the folder with all the information about the house, and she had left that in the kitchen. She had no note of Edward's number except in the memory of her phone, which she could not now charge with the power down. Even if she managed to call Mick, it would take him at least twenty minutes to reach her, and before she could do anything, she was going to have to venture through the house in search of a light – and some kind of makeshift weapon.

Skirting the bedraggled corpse, she began to feel her way with tentative steps along the passage that led to the kitchen, half-fearing the further discovery of the bird's head, pausing at every step to listen for sounds of movement elsewhere. There was no sound but the wind and the now-familiar creak and shift of old timbers. Her eyes began to grow accustomed to the dark; as she progressed, she tried to muster her thoughts into a logical sequence, only to find the voice of her fear countering every rational argument. It could have been a cat, she told herself. But where would a cat have come from, out here? And how could it have got inside? She tried to recall whether she could have left the back door unlocked, or the French doors in the drawing room, but she was so tired, it was growing harder to pinpoint memories with any clarity; she dredged up an image of turning the key in the lock, but could not be sure it belonged to that day. Every attempt to calm her own fears led back to the same, dreadful probability: that someone had been in the house, that they wanted to frighten her, that they quite possibly wished her harm. It struck her that there might not be a power cut at all, that whoever had been in the house – might *still* be in the house – had cut the electricity deliberately. At this thought her strength failed and she fell against the wall, snatching for breath that would not come, her legs turned to dough beneath her, telling herself over and over that she had watched too many movies. Everything else that had happened in the house since she had arrived could be explained away as tricks of a fraught mind: sleeplessness, stress, her period, even – though she hated to admit it – withdrawal from the meds she had recklessly abandoned. But the beheaded gull in the hall was indisputably real, and the concrete threat it implied pushed all stories of ghosts and night-demons from her mind.

She edged open the kitchen door; it let out a long, ratcheting creak. Breathing hard, she faltered in the doorway, unwilling to take a step inside in case someone was waiting there to ambush her. When nothing happened, she shook herself briskly and threw the door back so that it banged against the wall and revealed the room empty, patterned with milky light through the diamond-paned windows at either end. She found, to her great relief, a small but powerful flashlight in the dresser

drawer, which she propped up while she busied herself lighting
the hurricane lamp, her hands trembling so badly that she
spilled paraffin over the work top. The homely glow of the
lantern, when the flame took, restored a calm of sorts, though
even in here she could discern that faint smell of decay. She
checked the back door to the veranda and confirmed that it
was still firmly locked, the key secure on its hook. Then she
took down the folder from the dresser and turned its laminated
sheets, with all Kaye's carefully printed local maps, marked
with walks and sites of interest, until she found the page with
their emergency numbers. It was only as she picked up the
storm lantern to make her way back to the telephone that
she noticed her sketchbook open on the table. She was sure
she had put it away safely after Edward had picked it up the
other night, to stop him leafing through it. But the picture on
the open page looked unfamiliar; she reached across and pulled
the book into the light.

The drawing facing her was not one of her own. It was a
crude pencil sketch, the figures no more than stick-people,
such as a child might draw, but what it showed was unmistakable. At the top of the page, wavy horizontal lines suggested
the sea. Below them, the figure of a woman, naked, her breasts
and pubic hair crudely outlined, her arms reaching toward
the surface with vertical lines rising upward from her head
to show her hair rippling above her like weed under the water.
Her eyes were round circles, her mouth stretched wide in a
dark scream. Below her, at the bottom right-hand corner of
the page, another figure, its hand reaching up from the depths
and grasping her ankle. The face was barely visible, but
suggested a death's head grimace with a malicious smile.

Zoe pushed the book away, almost dropping the lantern,
the same cold cramps wringing her gut. This was meant to
be her, there could be no doubt about it. Whoever drew this
had seen what happened on the beach, with Edward; her
foolish swim, her near-drowning. Someone had been watching

her that day. It was an attempt to frighten her, as Edward had said; they had broken into the house and left the drawing and the dead gull to scare her off. She thought again about Dougie and Annag driving back across the moors, away from the coast – what else was there along this road except the house? Could they have been here? The naked spite on the girl's face whenever she saw Zoe suggested she would be entirely capable of such tricks, but Dougie's motive was harder to imagine; perhaps a wish to make her feel vulnerable, so that she would be more receptive to his attentions, grateful for his presence? Even so – *even so*, she thought, her mind racing – how could they have known about the hand? How could anyone have *seen* what she had felt, underwater?

She grabbed up the lantern and the folder and dashed back along the passage to the entrance hall, where she dialled Mick and Kaye's number with shaking fingers. It rang for a long time before she heard Kaye's sleepy voice murmur, 'Stag, hello?' in her ear. She was about to speak when a sound interrupted her from the kitchen; she froze to listen and recognised the familiar space-age bing-bong of an incoming Skype call. Dropping the receiver in its cradle, she ran back to the kitchen, all fear driven from her mind by the thought of Caleb.

Her laptop stood open on the table, though she was sure she had closed it before she left; she rushed to accept the call and in an instant the sight of her boy's dear face eclipsed everything. He looked pale and anxious; her heart swelled to see him.

'Mommy?' His voice sounded distant, muffled. 'When are you coming?'

'Soon, sweetie. I'll be back before you know it.' Then, because she felt she owed him more than that: 'You know Mommy's just having a little vacation. To help me get better. Because I was sick, you remember?' He did not reply; only continued to blink at her with his serious dark eyes. She willed the connection not to fail now. 'Mommy and Daddy have to think about a few things, honey, and sometimes it's easier to do that if one of you goes to a different place, so you don't end up fighting.' No, that was too much. She forced a smile. 'But everything's going to be OK, I promise. Where are you? Are you hiding under the covers?' She could not identify the background; it was dark, the white of his skin stark against it. His eyes seemed to have moved away from her face, though it was hard to tell with the delay on the picture. 'Don't let Daddy catch you, he'll be mad,' she whispered, trying for a conspiratorial tone, wanting to make him laugh, but Caleb was looking past her. His eyes had grown wider, his face rigid, jaw clenched. 'What's wrong, honey?' she asked gently. 'Caleb?'

'Mommy?' His voice emerged from the speaker, small and fearful.

'What is it, baby?' She leaned closer to the screen.

He paused, as if unwilling to speak.

'I don't like that person behind you.'

She whipped around to find the kitchen empty, sunk in flickering shadows cast by the flame of the hurricane lamp. 'Caleb? Who did you see?' She heard the rising panic in her own voice. 'There's no one here.' But the screen froze; his face fractured and vanished and only her own hollow-eyed reflection stared back at her. She clicked frantically on the Wi-Fi icon but it showed no available networks; she snapped the cover shut and laid her hands flat on it, as if to keep his last words trapped inside.

She lost track of how long she sat at the table in a state of paralysis, rocking slightly and staring at her hands, unable to raise her head for fear of what she might see in the room or reflected in the dark windows. Fear had rendered her mute, incapable of movement; all her whirling thoughts reduced to one: who – or *what* – had Caleb glimpsed in the room with

212

her? The stirring of a shadow cast by the wavering lamplight, or a real figure? All around her the house guarded its silence, while outside the wind chased around the eaves with increasing menace. She wanted Edward there, or even Dan, but most of all she wanted Caleb: his lithe, warm body in her lap, anchoring her; his head tucked under her chin, the familiar smell of his hair. She ached for him so urgently that she felt her face contort from the sheer pain of it, though the tears would not fall.

She should never have come here. The brief contact with her son had unmoored her, tugged memories loose; the whole purpose of her flight to the island now appeared foolish, self-indulgent. Charles was right: there were things you could not outrun. She should go back. Tomorrow, she would call Dan, admit she was wrong, change her flight.

A sound from the hallway roused her; in her stupefied state, it took her a moment to realise that the phone was ringing. She hesitated briefly before grabbing up the poker from the kitchen range in one hand and the lantern in the other. There was no sign of anyone in the corridor; she averted her eyes from the dead gull and reached for the phone, hoping it might be Kaye returning her earlier, aborted call, understanding that something was wrong. There was always a chance, she thought, as she set down the lantern and picked up the receiver, that it could be her mother, but even *her* voice might seem oddly comforting right now.

'Hello?'

She thought she heard a woman greet her by name, but the words were buried under a rush of interference on the line, as if the person on the other end were speaking on a cell phone outside in the gale. This segued into a slow, rhythmic static, like the turning of an old gramophone record after the music has ended.

'Hello?' Zoe repeated. She was about to hang up when the singing began.

It was the same voice as the first night: thin and sick with sorrow and longing, cracking on the high notes, almost whispering on the low, the ancient guttural language hissing in her ear. She listened in disbelief, half-wondering if it could be a crossed line, until the song grew fainter and, as it faded, a woman said, low and clear:

You won't take what's mine.

In the instant before she dropped the receiver, Zoe registered, with a detached curiosity, that the voice had spoken in the local language, but that she had understood the words perfectly.

'Leave me alone!' She snatched the lantern and ran up the stairs, holding the poker out in front, her only thought to lock herself into her bedroom and hide there. From what, she could hardly articulate; she no longer knew if the blind fear that constricted her throat and hammered in her chest was of a real intruder or the voices in the house, in her head. *It's not real*, she told herself, followed by another thought, almost calm: *I'm going crazy*. She was about to open the door to her room when another sound cut through the wind's roar.

It began as a woman's scream: sudden and sharp, followed by another. As Zoe listened, pinned to the spot, she realised, with a flush of blood to her face, what she was hearing. These were unmistakably the abandoned cries of a woman in the throes of her climax, the noises of extreme pleasure at the very edge of pain tearing from her throat, the very sounds Zoe had made during those wild dreams when she had sleep-walked to the gallery. The screaming came from beyond the upper landing, from the direction of the turret room; she craned her neck up but could see nothing in the blackness. The hairs prickled along her arms; she found herself unwillingly mesmerised by the sounds, caught in an uneasy mixture of guilt and arousal. As the woman appeared to approach her fever pitch, a subtle change in the tone of her cries caused Zoe to realise, with dawning horror, that she was no longer

214

moaning in pleasure but in real pain, or terror. It was not her imagination this time; a woman was up there, and she was being hurt. Zoe took the next set of stairs two at a time, poker in hand, and rattled the handle of the turret room. It appeared locked, as it had on the night when she first heard the song, and she might have given up then if she had not heard, beneath the woman's wild screaming, another sound, the desperate voice of a child:

Mother! Mother, stop!

Zoe rammed her shoulder against the door, wrenching at the handle until it gave suddenly, flinging her forward into the dark of the spiral staircase. She hesitated, one foot on the bottom step, her nerve failing; the cries continued, though strangely they seemed quieter and further away now that the door was open. Moonlight filtered down from the windows above. She climbed the stairs, shaking with adrenaline, to find the room empty. Turning slowly full circle, she peered with the lantern held out to see under the wooden shelf that ran around the observatory, but she knew there was nowhere for anyone to hide here. Wind shook the glass in its frames; she crossed to the window and looked out across the beach to see the marram grass pinned flat to the sand like a crouching animal, while towering waves smashed in plumes of white spray against the rocks at the foot of the cliff. On a pinnacle of roof immediately below her stood a black-backed gull uttering relentless, urgent screams.

Zoe set the lamp down and rubbed her knuckles into her eyes, leaning against the ledge. The gull's cries were eerie; at times they sounded like a human scream, almost orgasmic. Was that what she had heard? Had her mind done the very thing Charles had spoken of earlier – interpreted the sounds around her to fit a narrative? But then what about the child's voice? That at least could not have been a gull. The bird opened its hooked yellow beak and screeched to the empty air. She wondered if it was the mother of the dead juvenile

215

downstairs, mourning her baby. The thought of that feathered corpse with its mangled neck set her skin crawling. She pulled out a stool from under the shelf and settled herself directly opposite the staircase, so that she could see out over the water and at the same time catch the first glimpse of anyone attempting to breach the tower room. Like a princess in her fortress, she thought, wrapping her fingers around the poker. A fitful silence seemed to settle over the house. Even the gull gave up its vigil and flew away, its breast flashing pale in the moonlight.

She began to feel safer after a while, in her tower. She could not have said how long she sat, watching the sea, one eye on the dark hole where the stairs descended. Clouds chased across the face of the moon as if speeded up; the turret shook under the wind's onslaught but stood firm. Each time her eyes grew heavy and her head slumped to her chest she jerked herself upright; she needed to stay awake, in case whoever was in the house tried to come up here, into her sanctum. She must have dozed a little, though, because on one of these occasions when she snapped her eyes open, the lantern had burned lower and she could hear the unmistakable tread of footsteps on the stairs below. She had grown so numbed with fear now that she realised she had been expecting it; half in a daze, she slid from the stool and crouched, gripping her improvised weapon with both hands, her arms trembling with tension. The shadow of a human figure crept up the wall as the footsteps progressed, grotesquely elongated by a shaky light.

'I'll kill you if you come any further,' she managed to shout, from a cracked throat, as a man emerged from the darkness of the stairwell.

'Zoe? Jesus Christ!' Mick Drummond shone his flashlight in her face; she put up an arm to hide her eyes from the glare but held the poker out level, its point towards him. 'Are you OK? I didn't mean to frighten you – I was ringing the doorbell

216

for ages down there and when there was no answer I thought I'd best let myself in and see that nothing's happened. Kaye said you rang and hung up on her, and when she tried to call you back she thought you might be – having some difficulties. She told me to get myself over here and check you were all right.'

'Someone was in the house.' The poker shook in her hands; she could imagine how she must look to him, wild-eyed and insane, hiding up here from shadows. 'They cut the electricity.'

Mick rubbed a hand over his mouth and gave her a long look, assessing her. 'Nah, your fuse box has tripped, that's all. A bulb must have gone somewhere. It's easily fixed – did I no show you before?' There was a faint hint of reproach in his tone. 'In the cupboard under the stairs.'

'They left a dead gull on the floor,' she said. Her voice sounded hoarse and wired. 'They cut its head off.'

'*What?* Who did?'

'Downstairs. I'll show you.'

'Come on, then. You're all right to put that down now, eh.' He spoke gently, as if to a spooked animal, nodding to the poker. She looked down, briefly confused as to why she was holding it, and lowered it slowly, gesturing for him to lead the way.

At the foot of the stairs on the ground floor he disappeared into a cupboard with his flashlight.

'Here's your fuse box, see? Yeah, there we are – the bath-room's tripped on the first floor. They don't last five minutes, those bulbs. You need to push this wee switch up, OK?'

Zoe couldn't see what he was doing – she had pressed herself flat against the wall, away from the dead bird – but she murmured assent and the hallway was flooded with sudden brightness.

'There.' She pointed. The speckled corpse looked merely pathetic now, under the electric light, with someone else in the house.

217

'Bloody hell. That would explain the smell, anyway.' Mick poked it with his boot and crouched to look closer. 'I'd say a cat did that,' he said carefully. 'Horrible thing to find, though. No wonder you're upset.'

'Where would a cat come from, out here? How would it get in?' She disliked the condescension in his tone; besides, he was not a good liar.

He straightened up, lifted a shoulder in a half-shrug. 'Wildcat, maybe. Did you leave any doors open?'

She stared at him. 'You're telling me a fucking *wildcat* got in the house?'

He looked panicked. 'Well, no a real wildcat, as such. You don't get them on the islands. I meant more like a housecat that's run off and gone feral. You'd be amazed the gaps those buggers can squeeze through. Even a window open a crack—'

She shook her head. 'There was someone in the house. My son saw them,' she added, catching his sceptical frown, and regretted the words before they were out.

'Your *son*?'

'On Skype. He saw someone in the kitchen.'

'But . . . ' the crease in his brow deepened and he rubbed at it with the knuckle of his thumb; he seemed troubled now, as if he felt unequal to this female non-logic. 'How could you get Skype? There's no connection here, I told you. You can't have—'

'There's a network that comes and goes. I've found it a couple times. It's called McBride.' It was the wrong thing to say, she saw that immediately. *He thinks I'm crazy*, she thought.

'It wouldn't—' he began, but stopped himself. When he spoke again his voice was gentler. 'Look, you've had a nasty shock. You could do with a cup of tea and a wee dram. It's no surprising, with this mad weather and the lights going off and all *this* business.' His foot nudged the bird. 'Kaye said if you were upset, I was to bring you back with me right away and you can stay at the pub tonight. We've a couple of the guest rooms empty. I'm under strict instructions,' he added, seeing her demur.

Zoe sensed that he did not want to extend this invitation any more than she wanted to accept it; neither of them wished to acknowledge that there might be a problem with the house. But she lacked the energy to argue. When she responded with a limp nod, he seemed relieved.

'Right. Good. Let's find a bin bag and get this poor old fella out of here,' he said, with a brisk artificial smile.

Before they left the house, Mick checked all the downstairs doors and windows while she trailed through the rooms behind him like an anxious child.

'No, everything's locked up tight as far as I can see,' he said eventually, shaking his head with the same furrowed expression. 'I can't understand how a cat could have got in anywhere.'

'Someone drew a picture in my sketchbook,' Zoe said, remembering. 'I left it on the kitchen table. I'm pretty sure that wasn't a cat.'

'Seriously?' For the first time since he arrived, Mick appeared unnerved. He ran a hand through his sparse hair until it stood up in tufts. 'A picture of what?'

'I think it was supposed to be me drowning.'

'Christ. Are you *sure*, Zoe? There's no sign of anyone forcing the doors or windows, I promise.'

She wondered if he knew very well that there were some among his neighbours who would like to punish him for resurrecting the house by frightening his tenant away, as Edward had told her. Perhaps he could even guess who was responsible. Was it in his interest to persuade her that she was imagining things?

'Am I sure there's a picture in my sketchbook that I didn't draw?' She stared him down until he dropped his gaze to the floor. 'Is there any other way into the house?'

219

He scratched a thumbnail over the stubble on his chin. 'No. Unless—'

'What?' A chill prickled her neck.

'There's a coal hatch outside that opens into the cellar. But I padlocked it when we finished all the work. Better give it a wee look, I suppose.'

Outside, the wind was so fierce she could almost believe it would hold her weight if she leaned into it. She pulled her hair from her face and followed Mick around the south side of the house, guided by the light of his powerful flashlight. He stopped at a wooden hatch with double doors set into a raised box on the ground among the rough seagrass, large enough for a man to fit through with a sack of coal. Its central metal clasp was held together by a shiny steel padlock, so new it had not yet been tarnished by weather or salt. Mick knelt to examine it in the flashlight beam.

'Looks pretty solid,' Zoe offered, peering over his shoulder.

'Yep.' He raised his head to look at her and she thought she caught a flicker of anxiety in his eyes. 'No cats have chewed through that, anyway.'

'So how did the gull get in the hall then?' She folded her arms.

Mick stood and brushed sand from his trousers. 'I can't explain it, Zoe.' He looked profoundly uncomfortable. 'I just don't know. I can only think there must have been a window open somewhere earlier.'

'But we checked.'

'Aye, but maybe . . . ' He shifted his weight from one foot to the other and glanced out towards the beach, avoiding her eye. 'Maybe you don't remember closing it when you came home. If you were a bit – you know. Preoccupied, or something.'

He means drunk, she thought. *Or crazy.* She wanted to assure him that she would have remembered closing an open window, but realised she could not make this assertion with any conviction. She had thought an angry gull was a screaming woman. She had mistaken a crossed line on the phone for a voice threatening her in Gaelic. She had heard a child speaking in the tower room. But the dead bird and the drawing were solid, tangible; those she had not imagined.

'Someone broke in somehow,' she said stubbornly. 'There's evidence.'

Mick sighed. 'OK. I'll come and have a proper look at all the locks tomorrow, in daylight. But I honestly couldn't see—'

'Does anyone else have a key?' she asked, struck by a sudden thought. 'Any of your friends, maybe?'

'Course not. We've got the only spares, in case of emergencies.' He patted his pocket. 'Come on, let's get you back for that cup of tea. Some of us have got to work tomorrow.' He made a show of looking at his watch. 'Or today, I should say.'

'How old's your son, then?' Mick asked, eyeing her sideways as they drove the narrow road back across the moors. The dashboard clock showed a quarter to two. There was a sly note to his voice that suggested he was pleased to have winkled out some personal history at last.

Zoe leaned her forehead against the window, furious with herself for her carelessness.

'He's ten.'

'Och, that's a nice age, same as our Megan, though she can be stroppy as a teenager when she wants. Then we've got wee Josie, she's seven. Where have you left him, then?'

'He's at home.'

'Oh, aye? With his daddy, is he?'

'Yes.'

'And your other half doesn't mind you going off like this?'

'Nn-hnn.'

She could feel Mick looking at her. Eventually he sniffed and turned his eyes back to the road.

'Bugger me. Well, don't you go giving Kaye ideas, eh. I bet she'd only love to get away from the girls for a wee holiday. I don't think I'd cope, if I'm honest. Your fella must be a better man than me, all credit to him.'

Zoe gave a weak laugh, to reassure him that she understood it was a joke. Let him think she was a selfish mother. Everyone else thought so.

'I saw your friend Dougie driving his pickup along here earlier when I was on my way home,' she said, to change the subject.

'Dougie? Coming this way, was he?' He didn't appear unduly surprised.

'Into town, same as we are now. He had your young barmaid with him.' She shifted in her seat to watch his reaction.

He kept his eyes on the road ahead, but she could see he was frowning, as if engaged in difficult calculations in his head.

'Annag does a bit of waitressing up at the golf hotel on her nights off. There's no many jobs here for the young folk, you can imagine. She'd like to leave the island really, poor lass, but she's stuck looking after her wee brother. Dougie'd be giving her a lift home, I expect.'

'I thought the golf course was out the other side of the village?'

Mick hesitated.

'Aye, but this wind's probably brought some trees down. Sometimes it can be easier to take the coast road.'

Zoe's grasp of the island's geography was not firm enough to argue with this, though it seemed unconvincing. She felt Mick was resisting the obvious explanation.

'I didn't think there was anything on this road apart from the Mc— your house?'

He half-turned to her, his expression grown wary. 'What's your point?'

She looked at her hands in her lap. It had occurred to her

that Edward had said Dougie helped Mick work on the house; she wondered if he could have held on to a key, but she didn't feel she could say this to Mick without more evidence.

'I just thought it was unusual to see anyone coming from this direction. From the house.'

'Wait – you're no suggesting it was *Dougie* breaking and entering?'

'No, of course not. I only—'

'There's no way it could have been Dougie. He can't draw to save his life.' He let out a barking laugh; she glanced at him and joined in, to smooth over the tricky moment, but the laughter died away quickly, to be replaced by an awkward silence. They drove on without speaking, each looking ahead, listening to the wind punching at the windows.

'Did you really find a Wi-Fi network?' he asked, as they approached the sleeping town. 'You're no making that up?'

Zoe was too tired to be offended by the implication. 'Honest to God. Only a couple of times. It doesn't seem to last long.'

'I can't understand how that could happen.' He shook his head.

'I'm pretty dumb about tech, but isn't it to do with satellites moving overhead?'

'But how could it be called McBride? I'd never set that up. That's like a sick joke. You swear you're no winding me up?'

'Why would I?'

'No reason. Except—' He shot her a sideways look, heavy with reproach. 'You've been spending a lot of time with Charles Joseph, haven't you? Listening to his tall tales. I thought maybe the two of you had decided to pretend there was funny business going on up at the house so you could have a bit of a laugh at my expense. He knows I don't like people going on about those old stories.'

'I wouldn't do that, Mick.' She laid a hand on his arm. 'Seriously. I can't imagine Charles would, either.'

'Oh, you don't know Charles. Don't be fooled by all that

223

twinkly-eyed professor act. He's wily as a fox. He wants to write a book about my family, I'm sure he's told you. He thinks it would make money.'

'But you don't want him to?'

He made a dismissive noise. 'Well, they didn't exactly cover themselves in glory back then. Would you want someone writing that you had a child-murdering witch for a great-great-aunt? It's bad enough the islanders repeating it, but Charles's books sell all over the world. I'm no having a load of numpties from America or whatever coming to take photos of the house. There's my girls to think of. No offence,' he added, as an afterthought.

'I don't think that's the kind of book Charles would write, though,' she ventured. 'It might clear her name, if it was investigated properly.'

He snorted. 'You think that would make a blind bit of difference to anyone round here? People like the legend. No one's interested in the *truth*, whatever that may be.'

'Charles would be the person to find out.'

'Oh, aye?' Mick glanced at her as he turned into the Stag's car park. 'I see he's got to you already.' He turned off the engine but made no move to open the door. 'See, that's why I was worried about you talking to him. I was afraid he might put ideas in your head. Make you start imagining things. We didn't want you to feel anxious about the house when there was no need.'

'The stories don't bother me.'

'Really?' He looked at her, one eyebrow briefly raised. She could see he was thinking of the way he had found her in the turret.

'Look – I know I probably seemed a little hysterical back there.' She was surprised by how calm she sounded. 'But I know someone broke into the house. *That* bothers me. Old ghosts, no.'

'*Ghosts*.' Mick gave a thin smile. 'No, you seem too smart

224

to believe in all that. I'll get the locks checked over tomorrow, like I said. I might see about getting an alarm too. We didn't bother because it's always so safe out here.' He broke off and glanced up at the pub, where a light shone in one of the upper windows. 'Come on, Kaye's waiting up for us. You'll have to keep your voice down, the girls will be fast asleep.'

'Do you want me to do you a sage smudging before you sleep?'

'Sorry – what?' Zoe wrapped her hands around her steaming mug and looked at Kaye, whose face appeared oddly young and naked without the heavy eye make-up, her pink hair scrunched into a ponytail.

'It's a cleansing ritual. You burn white sage and it absorbs darkness and helps to cleanse your aura if you've had a traumatic experience.' She appeared to be entirely serious.

'Oh – no, I'm fine, honestly. It wasn't really traumatic, I just . . . ' Zoe smiled, wanting to find the words to make Kaye go away as quickly as possible without offending her. 'I probably overreacted. I'm so sorry to have woken you – I feel like an idiot. I'm a little hormonal,' she added, confidentially, thinking Kaye was the sort of woman who would appreciate this.

Kaye inched closer to her on the single bed and pulled her pink fluffy dressing gown closer over her chest. She fixed Zoe with an earnest gaze. 'Did you actually see someone, or was it more of a *presence*?'

Zoe leaned her head back against the wall and took in the furnishings: the cheap pine wardrobe, the floral curtains, the white flat-pack bedside table between the twin beds with its old-fashioned clock radio. She vaguely remembered an old horror movie about a guy who had stayed in a hotel room with twin beds and woken in the night to find the other bed had been slept in. She closed her eyes and tried to look fine; there was a very real risk that Kaye might offer to stay in the

225

room with her if she diagnosed a troubled aura. The stuff in her mug smelled revolting – bits of unidentified leaf floated on the surface – but the hefty measure of whisky Mick had poured her when they arrived had been welcome; now all she wanted was to lie down.

'See, I heard you on the phone.' Kaye lowered her voice. 'Before you hung up, you shouted, "Leave me alone." I knew you weren't talking to me. I said to Mick, it's started. I knew you were in trouble.'

'Actually, I thought you were my mother,' Zoe said, trying to raise a laugh, but it sounded hollow. She opened her eyes; Kaye wasn't smiling. She laid a hand on Zoe's arm.

'Don't take this the wrong way, but I told Mick you weren't the right person for the house when you first emailed. I said to him – a woman on her own, she shouldn't be there. Wait and see is there someone more suited to a place like that. But you were the first one and he so wanted to get a tenant in, he was fretting about the money. He wouldn't listen to me.' She pursed her lips and shook her head.

'Why didn't you want to live there, Kaye? That beautiful big house Mick's so proud of.'

Kaye hesitated, clearly torn between loyalties. 'It's not—' She stopped and began on a different tack. 'See, the thing you have to know about me, Zoe – I'm very *sensitive* in that regard. My grandmother had the gift, and it's passed down.' She leaned closer, her eyes searching Zoe's for a sign of recognition. 'Course, Mick doesn't believe in any of that. Or he doesn't want to. But for someone like me, it would be a torment, to live in a place that had psychic disturbances. And I have to think of my girls too – I don't know if either of them have the gift yet, but I wouldn't be surprised, and children are highly attuned to energy fields.'

Zoe blinked. Part of her wanted to laugh. 'So, you think the house really is haunted?'

Kaye tilted her head from one side to the other as if to

avoid outright confirmation. 'Look, Zoe. You've heard the old story by now. You can't tell me a place with that kind of history isn't going to hold it in its psychic memory. Now, some folk – that sort of thing won't affect them at all, they could live there and not even notice. Others . . . well.' She held out her hands, palms up, as if the conclusion was self-evident. 'And I think you're the second type, Zoe. You can sense things. Like me.'

'Like Charles,' Zoe murmured, without quite meaning to speak aloud. Before she came to the island, she would have regarded a woman like Kaye as a dippy crank, as unlike her as it was possible to be, with her crystal amulets and her auras and her gross herbal tea. Now, she was not so sure. Perhaps Kaye was right; she certainly seemed to have developed the ability to sense things she could not explain since she had moved into the house. Charles had suggested it was because she was vulnerable; even now, his presumption caused her to prickle with anger, largely because it was accurate.

'Aye, Charles is a very dark horse,' Kaye whispered, with a smile that betrayed reluctant affection. 'He dresses it up in all his intellectual language, but he's got the gift and then some. I can always spot people who have. That's why I knew about you.'

'You mean, he's psychic?' She pictured Charles's precise professorial manner and almost laughed, until she also remembered his knowing eyes, and the unnerving way his offhand references seemed designed to suggest he knew more about her than she had been willing to share. No – it was impossible.

'Psychic? He's a fucking *wizard*, if you ask me. Don't tell him I said that.' Kaye grinned. 'Listen to me – it's two in the morning. You'll be wanting to sleep.' She pushed herself to her feet and yanked the belt of her robe tighter. 'I'll fetch you a clean towel. Do you want me to stay in here with you tonight, if you're worried? It's no trouble.' She indicated the spare bed.

227

'I wouldn't dream of it,' Zoe said, smiling reassuringly until her jaw hurt. 'I'll be out like a light. I'm so sorry again for disturbing your night.'

'Don't be daft. Like Mick said – you can call us anytime. I totally understand,' she added, in a confiding whisper.

Zoe waited until the door had closed and reached for the small bag she had brought with her. Though all her muscles felt drained and her eyes gritty with exhaustion, her racing thoughts refused to slow and she knew sleep would elude her here. She tried to curl up under the floral duvet but a peculiar dull ache persisted in the pit of her stomach and she recognised it as homesickness. To distract herself, she took out the few items she had grabbed before leaving: a toothbrush, a clean T-shirt, her cell phone and charger and the copy of Charles's book on world myths. She opened it at the end and flicked through the index until she found what she was looking for, then turned back and began to read the chapter headed *Incubus*.

14

'I saw that shepherd again last night,' she told Mick as he drove her back through the village the next morning. The wind had dropped and high, white clouds drifted across a pale sky; the small town with its pastel-washed cottages looked benign against the distant hills. In daylight, the events of the night before appeared painfully foolish to Zoe. She had slept until eleven thirty, when Kaye had woken her with a cup of tea, pressing her to stay longer. She would have liked to ask for their Wi-Fi password so that she could pre-empt Dan's next intrusion with a blandly reassuring email, but it had been clear that Mick was impatient to give her a lift back and deal with the locks, as he'd promised, so that he could return to work. She would call home later, she told herself, once she'd figured out what she wanted to say.

'What shepherd?' he said.

'Out on the moors. The one I saw the night you rescued me on the bike. But he vanished.'

Mick looked blank.

'I don't know who that would have been. There's no sheep on that side of the hills.'

'You were the one who told me it was a shepherd. Someone must live out there, right? He seems to walk off the road into nowhere. Or she,' she added, recalling with a flicker of unease the impression of long skirts.

Mick gave her a sidelong glance. 'Aye. Well. The old crofters know the paths across the moor better than anyone. There's no many of them left now. Look, Zoe –' he turned to her, his face anxious – 'we were talking, me and Kaye. You don't have to go back to the house if you're no comfortable. I'm going to call a guy I know on the mainland and see about getting an alarm put in, but it might take him a week or so. I never thought about it before – like I say, this is the kind of place people really do leave their doors unlocked. But if it would make you feel safer . . . And you're welcome to stay with us at the pub till it's done. Or –' he shifted his gaze back to the road, his mouth set in resignation – 'if you've changed your mind altogether, we can refund the rest of the month. I'd understand.'

'I'm not going anywhere,' she began, before her attention was caught by the row of shops on the village's main street. 'The bookshop's closed,' she remarked, as they passed. 'Is that normal, on a Monday?'

'Don't ask me what's normal when it comes to that man,' Mick said. 'So, you're saying you're happy to stay?' His surprise was evident in his tone.

'I hope he's OK.' Zoe craned her neck back to watch the shuttered windows of the bookshop disappearing in the rear window. A twinge of alarm caught her; she thought about asking Mick to let her out so that she could go back and check, but feared she had tested his patience far enough.

'Why wouldn't he be?' Mick put his foot down as the road left the village and straightened to rise across the broad expanse of moorland ahead. 'You saw him last night, didn't you? You and young Ed Sinclair.'

There was an undercurrent of reproach in his voice, and Zoe could not discern whether his disapproval was directed at her for accepting invitations from Charles, or because there was already talk in the village about her and Edward.

'He invited us for dinner,' she said mildly. She could hardly tell Mick that the cause of her anxiety was having left Charles alone with Ailsa McBride's journal.

'Aye. Poking over the old story, no doubt.' His jaw flexed. 'See, I know I can't stop you taking an interest, it's only natural. But for Charles to be indulging his obsession at your expense – that's no fair on you or me.' He shook his head. 'And then it's no surprising if you get back there in the dark and start imagining things, and we all have to—' He broke off, pressing his lips together.

'Run around after me.'

'That's no what I meant. It's no problem for you to call us anytime if you're bothered about something, I've told you that. I'm only saying maybe spending all that time listening to Charles is no exactly helping you feel at home in the house.'

Though Zoe had spent the night trying to find rational explanations, frequently doubting the evidence of her senses, she found Mick's insinuations insulting. He would not have said the same thing to a man, she thought, anger knitting tight in her chest. If a man had said he suspected a break-in, Mick would have taken him seriously, whereas she could be dismissed as a credulous hysterical woman.

'You really don't believe there's anything in those old stories about the house?' she asked, turning to him. 'In all the time you were growing up here, and then working on it, you never encountered anything unusual?'

'Course not.' He answered so quickly and decisively that Zoe knew he was lying.

'Kaye believes it,' she persisted. 'She gave me a whole bunch of white sage to ward off evil.'

'Aye, well.' His mouth tightened. 'That's an ongoing bone of contention, believe me.'

'I heard about the kid who disappeared up there last summer. That must have been terrible.'

231

She watched Mick closely, noting how his knuckles whitened as he gripped the wheel, and the way the colour ebbed from his face. It took a while before he seemed composed enough to reply.

'Aye. It was a dreadful accident. That's what it was. Couple of boys messing around at night, trying to spook each other. And they wouldn't have been up there in the first place if people here weren't obsessed with the past. So you can see why I get pissed off with all this haunted house shite.' He was struggling to keep his voice under control. 'But I blame myself too, how could I not?'

'Why?'

'Should have paid a night watchman to keep an eye on the place. It seemed like a waste of money at the time – I didn't think anyone would bother going out there to rob the building supplies and I had men on site all day. I never thought about kids playing games. There's no a day goes by I don't think about that wee boy.' His voice closed up and Zoe saw that he was fighting to contain his emotion.

'It's not your fault,' she said gently. 'No one could think that. They shouldn't have been there.'

'Course they fucking shouldn't. But they were ten years old.' His shoulders slumped, the defensive posture leached out of him. 'I used to ride my bike out there with my mates when I was that age, same as them, daring each other to call up the witch's ghost. It was a ruin back then. I should've remembered the attraction.'

Zoe wanted to ask him about the boy's phone, and what he thought about the theory that Robbie Logan had killed his friend, but she could see how distressed the subject made him and decided to leave it.

'The boy was never found?' she ventured, after a while.

'No. They think he must have gone off the cliff. Nothing supernatural about it at all.' Mick swallowed hard. 'It was a terrible thing for the whole community, you can imagine. The family left the island in the end, they couldn't stand to be here. There was no way I was ever getting Kaye to move out to the house afterwards, so there was the end of that plan. All that money.' He flinched, as if the memory caused him physical pain. 'And there were plenty of folk who did think it was my fault, you know? Said I'd stirred up trouble by not leaving the old things buried. As if they hadn't all been out there in their day, hunting for ghosts or trying to get laid, one time or another. Folk said no one would last long out here, and I suppose they'll be proved right.'

Zoe heard the bitterness in his voice. 'Not by me,' she said firmly. 'Why trying to get laid?'

The colour rose in his face. 'Oh, nothing. One of the old wives' tales, when I was young. The lads used to say that if you could get a girl out to the McBride house, she'd go wild for it and you'd get your way. Something to do with the spirit of Ailsa McBride. Her being a wanton one, I suppose. The village lads were forever trying to convince girls to go there with them at night.' He gave a self-conscious half-laugh.

'You and Dougie?'

His expression changed. 'Ah, we never had much success in that department. The girls were too smart.'

As they descended the cliff road and rounded the final bend into the driveway of the house, the sight of a dark-blue pickup parked outside sent her heart plummeting to her stomach. Mick pulled the Land Rover up beside it; she saw the Golf's hood propped open and Dougie Reid bending over it, poking about inside. He straightened up at the sound of the engine and grinned, showing his tobacco-stained teeth.

'Morning, Michael.' He wiped his hands on his carpenter trousers. 'Should you no be at work instead of driving around with beautiful women? Does your wife know?'

Mick did not return the smile. 'What are you doing here?'

'Mrs Adams was having a bit of trouble with her starter motor yesterday, did she no tell you? So I brought my big

233

tool round to see if I could sort her out. I'm a Good Samaritan like that.' He waved a spanner with a wink at Zoe; she gave him a fleeting, sarcastic smile. 'Were you hoping to do the same, Michael?' he asked, raising an eyebrow as Mick lifted a toolbox from the back of the car.

'I'm checking on the locks,' he said, giving Dougie a look that seemed loaded with warning.

'Dearie me – I hope you've no been getting peeping Toms or any of that?' Dougie eyed her as he took a pouch of tobacco from his back pocket and rolled a cigarette dexterously between two fingers. He sounded as if the suggestion amused him. 'You're a long way from civilisation out here, mind. I can see why you'd be nervous.'

'Fuck's sake, Dougie. Get on and mend the car. Don't you have a job to go to as well?' Mick pushed past him to the front door with a noise of exasperation. Zoe felt a stab of pity for her landlord, combined with guilt; the lack of sleep and the anxiety about the house, her, the money, were all written plainly on his face. He looked frayed, his eyes pouchy.

'Can't leave a lady out here all on her own with a temperamental motor.' Dougie removed the cigarette and spat a gob of brown phlegm on to the gravel. 'Milk and two sugars if you're putting the kettle on, hen.'

Zoe glanced at Mick as she unlocked the front door; she found his surreptitious eye-roll reassuring.

'I'll start with all the windows and doors at the back,' he said, wiping his boots on the mat. Then he stopped, nosing the air like a dog. 'Christ, that smell seems to have got worse overnight. Don't you think? Not sure how that could be, when I got rid of the gull.'

'Maybe there's another one I haven't found yet,' she said drily. 'Do you want coffee?'

'Only if you're making some.'

'Sure. It's not like I have anything else to do.' She picked up the vase of browning lilies from the hall table and set off

234

towards the kitchen, shedding petals as she went. At this hour, washed with bright coastal light, the room appeared homely and welcoming, despite that persistent smell of decay. She moved her laptop and sketchbook off the table and wondered if she should try to show Mick the McBride Wi-Fi network, but knew instinctively that it wouldn't appear while he was there, and would only make her look doubly foolish. She filled the kettle and set it on the range, emptied the dead flowers into the bin and the brown water down the sink. As she glanced out of the window down the beach, she saw a seal basking on a rock and the sight lifted her spirits briefly. She measured out spoonfuls of coffee into the large cafetière, and when the kettle started up its whistle, she opened the fridge to look for milk, and let out a scream.

Mick and Dougie hurtled down the corridor within minutes to find her standing in the light of the open door, trying to catch her breath. Staring out at them from its one frosted eye was the severed head of the gull.

'Is that your signature dish?' Dougie said, peering over her shoulder.

'Jesus Christ.' Mick reached in and picked it up. 'Was this here last night?'

She shook her head. 'I don't know. I didn't look in the refrigerator after I found the body.'

'It's been in there a while.' He weighed the frozen lump in his hand.

'The Gullfather,' Dougie said, in a bad Brando accent.

'Will you fuck off away outside, Dougie? Seriously. You're no helping.'

'Sorry, pal. Here, let me.' Dougie took an empty carrier bag from the back of the door and bundled the offending item inside. 'My dog'll think it's Christmas,' he said cheerfully, before heading back down the passageway to the front door.

Zoe sat heavily at the table. The kettle shrieked unattended until Mick moved it off the heat.

235

'You're going to tell me your feral cats have learned to open refrigerators,' she said, not looking at him.

Mick pulled out a chair and slumped into it, pressing his fingers into his eyelids. 'I don't know what to say, Zoe. I can't see that any of the locks have been tampered with, not the windows or the doors. I can't explain it.'

'Well, then it seems pretty obvious to me. It was someone with a key. Or someone who knows how to pick a lock, or remove one. Some kind of handyman, maybe? Someone who seems to think it's all a big fucking *joke*?'

Mick followed her furious gaze to the door. 'No. No, you're wrong. I know Dougie. He wouldn't do anything like this.'

'He keeps turning up here uninvited,' she said, lowering her voice to a hiss. 'This is the second time, and then I saw him driving back from here last night. Always this excuse about the car – I wish I'd never rented it.'

'That's just how folks are round here, Zoe.' He dropped to a whisper too, mollifying. 'We keep an eye on each other. He's trying to help, in his clumsy way. Make sure you're OK.'

'It's intrusive. I'm on my own out here, I don't want some creepy guy I don't even know showing up all the time. I didn't ask anyone to keep an eye on me.' She considered telling Mick of her conviction that someone was watching her, that the crude drawing in her sketchbook bore that out, but suspected he would find that too easy to blame on her paranoia and hysteria.

'I know Dougie can be a bit . . . ' he searched for the right word ' . . . *crass*. But he's harmless.'

That was not Edward's view, she recalled – nor Kaye's, according to him. She wondered if Mick was blinded by a long unquestioning loyalty.

'Look – I don't want to offend anyone, but you need to tell him. He can't keep coming here.' She glared at Mick until he gave a defeated nod. 'Are you going to report this break-in to the police, then?' She gestured to the fridge. After the initial

236

shock, the discovery of the gull had lent her a brief sense of triumph; Mick was more deferential now that he could no longer accuse her of imagining it all, and she felt herself on surer ground.

He pushed his hands through his hair and sighed. 'They'd have to come across from the mainland. It's an awful bother to call them out for this, when there's no real harm done. I mean, you've no had any of your things taken, right?'

She thought of her laptop left open on the table, untouched, and reluctantly shook her head. 'Wait – there's no police at all on the island?' She stared at him, hearing the note of fear in her voice.

'Well, there's Bill. He's a Special Constable. But he's getting on for sixty now.' He caught her look and held out his hands as if in apology. 'We've only got a hundred and thirty residents. And everyone knows everyone. That's why looking out for each other has always worked – the crime rate's almost zero.'

'Except that someone broke in here and put a dead bird's head in my fucking fridge,' she said stubbornly. 'Or does that not count as a crime? Is that considered a fun prank around here?'

'What you have to understand,' Mick said wearily, 'is that it's not directed at you. Maybe that's no much comfort, but there's nobody here would actually *hurt* you, I guarantee it. This is about some folk punishing me for going against their wishes.'

'But I'm the one who's going to get terrorised until I give in and leave, so they can score their point against you.'

'*Terrorised* is a bit strong,' he began, but she cut across him.

'How would you feel if someone had put that thing in your kids' bedroom? Well, then.'

'OK.' He pushed his chair back. 'You're right. I'll see about getting that alarm fixed up. I'm going to take a look at that

237

padlock on the coal hatch too, maybe you could do with a stronger one. And I'll have a word with Dougie.'

'Oh, aye, will you now?' Dougie breezed into the kitchen and rinsed his hands in the sink. 'Am I going to have to make this coffee myself while you two sit there gossiping like old wives?' In answer to his own question, he picked up the kettle and poured water into the cafetière, then sat himself down next to Zoe. 'That starter motor's running fine now, hen. Just treat her gently.' He turned to Mick and grinned. 'This is like old times, eh, pal – the two of us out here? Though we're no used to having such a good-looking lassie for company.'

Zoe caught the look that passed between them; she recognised Mick's evident unease – she might even have said *fear* – and the cockiness on Dougie's face, and though she didn't understand the coded reference, she read the balance of power between the two men. Dougie had some kind of hold over Mick, and she guessed it had been that way since their youth. The thought caused a cold knot to tighten in her gut; if Dougie was the one creeping around trying to scare her, as she suspected, Mick was less likely to confront him. He was right to think she had not been persuaded by his reassurances that no one would actually harm her. She saw all too clearly the lascivious glint in Dougie's eye, the greedy way he allowed his gaze to rove over her body; she was certain that he was also aware of the house's reputation for heightened sexual atmosphere, and that he would be entirely capable of exploiting it.

'Course, I fear we're a wee bit *mature* to interest Mrs Adams,' Dougie continued, slurping at his coffee. 'Her tastes run to the younger gentleman, I hear.'

'Right, come on then.' Mick ignored him and stood, his drink barely touched. 'We should be getting back. I'm sure Zoe would be glad of some peace.'

'Peace. Aye, I'm sure she would.' Dougie knocked back the last of his coffee and fixed her with a pointed smile. 'I hope you don't get any more nasty surprises.'

238

Mick's eyes flicked to Zoe, his face tight with anxiety. 'I'll let you know about the alarm. And I'll sort out the other business too,' he added, giving her a meaningful nod behind Dougie's back as he ushered his friend out. She heard the front door slam and from outside the sound of raised voices carried, though she could not make out the words. After a few minutes the engines growled into life, followed by the skidding of tyres on gravel.

After they had left, the house felt oddly blank and empty. She let herself out of the kitchen door on to the veranda to escape the smell and pulled off her boots to walk barefoot down the sand to the water's edge. The tide was out and the beach strewn with driftwood and ribbons of seaweed where the wind and wild water of the night before had cast them up. She picked up a pleasingly smooth, twisting piece of wood about eighteen inches long and ran her fingers over the grain, enjoying its heft and texture. It was a while since she had submitted to the discipline of a still life; she decided to take it back to the house to sketch. Wet sand squeezed between her toes, shockingly cold; she stepped deliberately into the lacy edges of the waves and reminded herself that she was connected to the earth, the sea, the elements, all tangible and real and present. She allowed herself to breathe out and push the thoughts of her unquiet night to the corners of her mind. Above her, from a ledge on the cliff, a gull let out a cry so bleak and human, so like a woman in pain, that it set her heart racing again; she turned, suddenly afraid, her gaze skittering from one side of the cove to the other, unable to shake that sensation of being watched. She looked back at the house and thought she caught a shifting of the shadows by the veranda, a flicker of movement, there and gone; she remembered that she had not locked the kitchen door behind her. If someone had been hidden there, watching her, they might have let themselves in while her back was turned; even now, they might be *inside the house*, waiting for her.

239

She ran back up the sand, clutching her piece of driftwood like a cosh, her pulse pounding. There was no sign of anyone where she had imagined she saw movement. Slowing her pace, she lowered the wood and crept around the north side of the house, where Mick had shown her the outside hatch for the cellar. The sand was soft and dry here, amid the tufts of grass, and constantly shifting; she thought she saw the blurred outline of footprints, but there was no way of knowing if they were recent. As she proceeded, her bare foot struck something cold half-buried in the sand. She knelt to examine it, and brought out a steel padlock, its surface patched with rust. The shackle had been neatly snapped in two, evidently with a pair of bolt-cutters.

Zoe raised her head, alert for a tell-tale sign of anyone's presence, but only the wind and the seabirds offered any sound. She stood, brushing the sand from her jeans, and stamped up the slight incline to the cellar hatch. The wooden doors remained closed, firmly fastened by their gleaming silver padlock. She looked down at the one in her hand as understanding slowly registered. Someone must have cut the original lock and replaced it with one of their own – to which, presumably, they had the key, giving them access to the cellar, and through it, the house, at any time they chose. And Mick had realised this yesterday, she thought, as cold anger displaced her fear. He had known when they checked that the lock on the hatch was not the original; he had guessed at what had happened, which must be why he had offered to fit a new one, though he had not acknowledged it to her. It was not hard to imagine who might have a set of bolt-cutters among his tools, and who Mick might be protecting. She shuddered, her thoughts racing through all the possible implications. She had no doubt now that it was Dougie who had left the dead gull and drawn the picture. A wave of nausea gripped her at the idea of him looking through her sketchbook, reading her tumbled, breathless account of her erotic dreams. Another thought occurred: had he hidden himself inside the house while she was *there*? The unexplained noises, the lights going. That fleeting impression she had had of a figure by the bed, watching her while she slept – could that have been *real*? Was he trying to fuck with her and frighten her away, or might he be more dangerous than that? She had seen the look in his eyes when he told her he hoped there were no more nasty surprises.

She had to confront Mick with it. Dougie ought to be arrested, though she did not suppose Mick would take it that far. She closed her fist over the broken padlock, wishing she had had the sense to wrap it in a cloth before picking it up; she had seen enough cop shows to know that, if there was evidence that Dougie had cut it, her own fingerprints would be all over it by now, perhaps obscuring his. Even so, she would insist that Mick call the police this time and show them, whatever his protestations.

15

An hour later, showered and dressed in fresh clothes, she drove back across the moorland to the village with the padlock wrapped in a handkerchief in her pocket. The darkening sky threatened rain by the time she reached the main street. She had intended to drive straight back to the pub and present Mick with her evidence, but as she passed the bookshop, the sight of the shuttered windows sparked a flare of anxiety in her chest. It seemed unlike Charles to take a day off, and it troubled her that his absence coincided with his possession of Ailsa's journal. Instead of continuing to the Stag, she pulled in alongside the green, feeling that she ought at least to check if he was all right. First, she walked up to the bakery and bought two chocolate croissants; that way, she would not look too foolish if he was fine, and she could pretend she had simply come to hear his verdict on Ailsa's account.

The path through the churchyard offered a shortcut from the green to the lane leading up to the old manse. Zoe pushed open the rusted gate and stepped through on to an uneven path cobbled with clumps of moss. There were few trees here, only two boxy yews flanking the gate and a line of four tall pines at the periphery. A cold wind sliced unchecked across the rows of crumbling headstones and leaning Celtic crosses.

242

The boundary wall was veiled in tangled ivy, obscuring plaques whose inscriptions had long been smudged by age and weather. The kirk itself, an unprepossessing building of dark stone with a steep gabled roof, huddled in a far corner with the hills at its back. All was green and grey: hills, grass, graves, trees, sky. She struck out towards the far wall, pleased at her own boldness – no one seeing her crossing a graveyard so purpose-fully could suppose her a woman afraid of ghosts – when a flash of red caught her eye and she turned. A figure sat cross-legged on one of the stone tombs in the lee of the wall, hunched over a phone, the hood of his red sweat-top drawn down around his face. Zoe quickened her pace, but the boy looked up and their eyes met; she saw that it was young Robbie Logan. Without quite knowing why, she left the path and picked her way through the wiry grass between the graves towards him. She saw him glance to left and right, assessing his chances of escape. As she approached, he flinched into himself, pulling his hood closer, and she saw that he had a welt on his cheek where the skin had split over a fresh bruise.

'Hey,' she said, stopping a few feet away.

'A'right.' He would not raise his face to look at her.

'What are you doing out here?' As she said it, she glanced down and saw the inscription on the headstone next to the tomb he was sitting on. It read 'Brigid Logan, Much Loved Wife and Mother'; the date of death was three years earlier. An empty jam jar had been placed at an angle on the grave, containing a few inches of scummy water and a straggling bunch of wild flowers. 'Sorry, dumb question. Is that your mom?'

The boy nodded, shrouded inside his hood. His breath made small puffs in the damp air.

'Jeez, she was young. Only thirty-six. Was she sick?'

'Cancer. She didnae go to the doctor in time.' His voice was flat.

'I'm so sorry. Do you come out here to talk to her?'

243

Robbie glanced up at her from the tail of his eye, visibly surprised. 'What if I do?'

'Nothing wrong with that.'

He looked down. 'Ma sister says it's mental.'

'Talking to someone you love and miss? I'd say that's the most normal thing in the world. It'd be mental if you didn't.'

He bit his lip, considering this. 'Do you think they can hear us? The dead?'

Zoe allowed her gaze to sweep quickly over the rows of graves. She couldn't tell from his tone whether he was goading her, or making some dig about the house, or if the question was genuine. 'I don't know,' she said, opening her hands in apology. 'What happened to your cheek?'

He reached up and touched the bruise gingerly with a fingertip, but his face closed up. 'Banged maself on the climbing frame.'

'You should get some ice on that, it looks painful.'

He shrugged, as if to say it was no big deal. It was the shifting of his body language, the way he avoided her eye, that told her he was lying. She realised, with a sudden cold plummet, that he must have been hit, and had learned not to speak of it. She wondered if Edward knew; surely he would have some responsibility for the boy's safety. Robbie may be an unappealing child, but he was only eleven, and it sounded as if life had dealt roughly with him so far. She held out the paper bag from the bakery.

'Want one of these?'

He eyed the offering with suspicion, until desire overcame his wariness and he reached in for a pastry.

'You were going to ask me a question the other day, before we were interrupted,' Zoe said, perching beside him on the edge of the tomb and taking out the other croissant. 'About the house.'

Robbie's gaze dropped to his lap, instantly guilty. 'Only if you'd heard anything weird out there.'

'What, like ghosts? It's famous for them, right?' She laughed, but he didn't join in, only shrugged. She glanced around again. The kirkyard was empty. A lone raven watched them from the wall. 'I don't believe in ghosts,' she stated, picking off a chunk of pastry.

'You just said it's normal to talk to the dead,' he shot back, as if he'd caught her out in a lie. 'So you must believe they're still around us. What's that if it's no a ghost?'

Zoe looked at him. She did not want to rip away the meagre comfort of confiding in his dead mother. 'I don't know. I guess I meant we try to keep people's memory alive by talking to them.' She paused; he went on glaring at her accusingly. 'I didn't think I believed in ghosts before I came here. But it seems like everyone's determined to convince me I should be scared of the McBride house.'

'It's a bad place,' he said, spraying croissant crumbs, his small eyes suddenly fierce. 'It's cursed. You shouldnae have come.'

'Are you saying that because of your friend?'

He shunted himself down from the tomb, wiped his mouth on the back of his hand and brushed the flakes of pastry from his top. 'I haftae go.'

'Wait – Robbie.' She grabbed at his sleeve; caught off balance, he swung around to face her, alarm in his eyes. 'If you know about the house, don't you think you should tell me? I mean, it sounds like you know more than Mick does, right?'

A spasm of fear flashed across his face before he yanked his arm away. 'I told you. Bad things happen there. You should go home while you still can.'

'What do you mean by that? What bad things? Am I in danger?'

He had already begun to walk away. She hurried after him, catching him easily with her long stride, and blocked the path so he was forced to face her.

'What happened to Iain? Was it something he saw? I *know* you know.' She heard the aggression in her voice, saw his lip tremble.

'Let me go. I haftae get home.'

Zoe stepped back. 'Shouldn't you be in school right now, anyway?'

It was the wrong thing to say; his face curled into a scowl.

'What are you gonnae do – tell your boyfriend?' He ducked past her, eyes lit up with the knowledge that he had scored a direct hit. 'He won't do shite – he's scared of ma dad.'

'You mean – Mr Sinclair isn't – he's not my boyfriend.' She faltered, caught out, wondering at the same time if it was the dad who had taken a swing at Robbie's face.

'That's no what everyone's saying. Ma sister said he stays out at yours.'

'That isn't true.' She pressed a hand to her cheek, powerless to stop the colour rising to her face.

'She says you don't waste any time. You've no even been here a week. You must be a desperate old slag, she said.'

In his gleeful contempt, his features had grown uncannily reminiscent of Annag's. Zoe retreated another pace, shocked to hear such malice from a child.

'That's a horrible thing to say, Robbie,' she managed, but the boy had turned on his heel and started up a lumbering run towards the gate. She was tempted to hurl herself after him, demand to know what else had been said about her, what else he knew about the house, but it was clear that he would give nothing up voluntarily and it would hardly help her reputation to be seen harassing a child. She now wished, as she quickened her pace towards the far gate with one last glance over her shoulder, that she had not given him the pastry meant for Charles.

There was no response to her repeated knocking at the old manse. After a few minutes she shaded her face with her hands and peered in the dining-room window, but could see no sign of life. She knocked again, and tried the brass knob of the front door; it swung open as if by invitation, and she remembered Mick's words about people leaving their houses unlocked here. Pulling it shut behind her, she called Charles's name tentatively from the hallway. The only reply was a mournful whine from overhead. Slowly, she climbed the uneven stairs to see Horace lying on the landing, grey muzzle resting on his paws, his eyes fixed on a closed door directly ahead. He raised his head a fraction at her approach, thumped his tail once on the carpet and let out the same plaintive moan, his gaze returning to the door as if to direct her attention. She bent and ruffled the dog's fur.

'Good boy. Is he in there?' She forced a cheerfulness into her voice to push away the fear that had stolen up on her as she took in the dog's resigned vigil and the forbidding barrier of the door. Charles must be inside; but if he were, why was he not responding? In the pit of her stomach, she knew her instinct had been right; something had happened, and it was connected to Ailsa's book. Dreading what she might find, she knocked, at first gently and then with increasing urgency, calling Charles's name. When this yielded nothing, she turned the handle and stepped inside.

He was slumped over an antique desk, his white head resting on his arm as if he had fallen asleep, except that he seemed unnaturally still. Horace followed her into the room but hung back, keeping his distance, only emitting now and then another melancholy whimper. The room was long and narrow, stretching the width of the house at the front, and crammed floor-to-ceiling with bookshelves. A threadbare Persian carpet was the only covering over uneven boards which creaked under Zoe's boots as she crossed to the desk and laid a tentative hand on Charles's shoulder, her throat closed tight, praying that she would find him sleeping. His skin was icy, even through his shirt.

247

She looked around, unsure of what to do next. He did not seem to be breathing, but she could not be certain. She ought to go for help, she supposed, or call a doctor, if they even had one on the island; anything to shift the responsibility of being the one who found him, but she felt frozen to the spot, horribly aware once more of that sense of being watched – and not only by the dog, who was cowering by the door and seemed unwilling to approach his master.

Zoe cast her eyes over the material on the desk, as if seeking an explanation. There, under Charles's left hand, was Ailsa's journal. Under his right, he had pinned down a sepia photograph. She slid it out and recoiled. It was a portrait of Ailsa, but one she had not seen before, taken – she guessed – some years after the last. In this, Ailsa was pictured reclining on a sofa, her hands clasped over the bodice of her black dress, the silver Celtic cross pendant arranged above them. A curious sharpness defined the lines of her face against the backdrop; her hair was pulled back and her eyes stared straight ahead, as they had in the earlier picture Charles had shown her, but in this one the direction of her gaze appeared indefinably wrong. They were, somehow, not Ailsa's eyes, and they altered her face in a disturbing way Zoe could not quite pinpoint.

She was scrutinising the photograph, trying to determine why she found it so unsettling, when Charles snapped his head up so suddenly that she let out a small scream.

'Is she still here?' He cast around wildly, as if struggling to focus.

'Jesus! Are you OK?' Recovering herself, Zoe laid a hand on his arm until his eyes came to rest on her, confused and fearful. He looked, in that instant, older and more frail than she had seen him, and she wondered if she might have vastly underestimated his age.

'Zoe?' He squinted, reaching for her hand and covering it with his. His grasp was freezing and papery. 'What time is it?'

She glanced at her watch. 'Just gone two thirty.'

'In the afternoon?'

She nodded, watching him carefully as he let out a trembling breath, smoothed his hair and replaced his glasses, his face furrowed with incomprehension.

'You gave me a hell of a scare there. I thought—' She decided to leave it unsaid. 'Who did you think I was? Who did you mean by "she"?'

'Oh.' He waved a hand and looked around the room with apparent relief. He had begun to seem himself again. 'The woman who cleans for me. She always comes on a Tuesday. I thought you were her.'

'It's Monday.' It was clear to Zoe that he was not telling the truth, but she did not press him. 'I saw the shop was closed this morning. I was going to drop by and see how you got on with the journal.' She gestured toward the desk. 'I didn't mean to barge in – I got worried when there was no reply. And the door wasn't locked.'

'It never is. People don't, here.'

'So I understand. Anyone could have walked in, though.' She gave him a look of reproach.

He laughed. 'Locked doors are not necessarily proof against unwelcome guests, as you well know.' Before she could ask what he meant by that, he levered himself up from the chair, rolling the stiffness from his shoulders with a grimace, one hand cradling the small of his back. He was wearing the same tweed jacket, corduroy trousers and sweater he had had on the evening before. 'Long past time to put the kettle on. I seem to have missed breakfast *and* lunch. Shall we have some toast to make up for it? And the poor dog must be starving. He'll punish me for it, you watch.'

Zoe followed Charles downstairs, though she noticed Horace still hanging back, as if uncertain of his master.

'I thought you were dead up there.' The words burst out of her in a rush.

'Oh dear.' He offered an apologetic smile and busied himself with filling the dog's bowl and putting the kettle on. 'No, you don't need to worry about that. I had a bad night, I'm afraid.'

'With the diary?'

'It's a disturbing read. I don't need to tell you that. But there are things—' he stopped and turned to face her. 'I'm glad you're here. I must ask you. You say you experienced identical visions to Ailsa's, even before you read her descriptions?'

She felt herself blush. 'I'd call them dreams, but yes, essentially.'

'And are there physical manifestations?'

'I've been sleepwalking. I wake and find myself in a different room. And there are other . . . ' she hesitated, dropping her gaze to the floor. 'The first night, I thought I found bruises on myself. But they were probably just from travelling.'

Charles was looking at her with his head on one side. There was no trace of any salacious curiosity in his expression, rather a reluctant concern. 'Do you hear voices in these dreams?'

'Sometimes I hear a man talking to me. But it's as if he's speaking directly in my thoughts. I know that doesn't really make sense.' Her voice had grown quieter.

'What does he say?'

'The same things Ailsa records.' Her face was burning.

He only nodded, as if this was what he had expected to hear, and turned his attention to measuring out tea leaves into an enormous blue-glazed pot.

'Those drawings in her book,' she continued, when the silence became uncomfortable. 'I've seen the same images, in the dreams. I drew them in my sketchbook too, before I saw the journal. It's like some weird déjà vu. I don't even want to believe it myself, but it's there. I can't explain it.'

He gestured for her to take a seat at the kitchen table. 'And you've experienced other phenomena in the house too, you said?'

250

'A woman's voice, singing that song about the drowned fiancé. I keep imagining it coming from different rooms. Once from the telephone. And a woman's voice speaking to me in Gaelic.' She shook her head. 'I sound insane even saying it aloud. And someone's broken into the house, trying to scare me – I know that for a fact, so I don't know how much I'm imagining, or—' She broke off and clasped her hands to her temples. 'I'm very tired, you see. I haven't slept well in a long time. And I was on these pills that made me – but I'm getting better now. I feel like my head's clearer. That's why I can't understand why, now—'

'Have you experienced anything like this before?'

'No.' She raised her eyes to meet his steady gaze. 'Except – years ago, after . . . ' She paused; what was the point of concealing it now that Mick and Kaye knew about Caleb? 'I had postnatal depression very badly when my son was born. Well – postpartum psychosis, they called it. I heard voices, saying terrible things. I imagined all kinds of stuff . . . I was in the hospital for a while. But it passed. I thought I was doing OK.'

The kettle shrieked; Charles lifted it from the hob and poured water into the teapot.

'I had wondered, reading the diary, whether Ailsa experienced something similar at the beginning,' he said softly. 'It wouldn't have been recognised in those days, of course. She might have thought she was going mad, or believed it was the effect of her husband's séances.'

'But her son was seven by the end of the journal, and her husband was long gone.' Zoe pulled at the ends of her hair. 'She couldn't have had postnatal psychosis for that long, surely? And that doesn't explain how we had the same dreams.'

'Then we must consider the other possible explanation,' Charles said carefully, setting a mug of tea in front of her.

'You mean, that the house is actually haunted.' She wrapped her hands around the mug and fixed her eyes on the table. It was not framed as a question.

'I mean that Tamhas McBride, knowingly or unknowingly, unleashed a force there whose psychic influence has persisted.'

'That's an academic way of saying he did summon a demon.'

Charles merely tilted his head.

'You really believe that?' She wanted to sound sceptical, but could not muster the necessary energy. There was too much that remained unexplained, and she was left with only two possibilities: either she was losing her mind, or what she had seen and heard in the house was real, and Ailsa had seen it too.

'I've made a life's work out of studying the history of occult and esoteric beliefs, and I've concluded that certain experiences can make us more receptive to what might be deemed supernatural influences. Trauma, loss, despair. Consider it – Ailsa had been suddenly widowed, she was left alone, then an unexpected pregnancy and the resulting social isolation. All that would have left her extremely psychologically vulnerable.'

Zoe considered this. 'But you said that, according to Tamhas's letters, she'd already been affected by his experiments even before she was widowed.'

'True. Perhaps she was always susceptible.'

'You mean unstable.' She found she did not want to acknowledge this possibility. She had seized on the idea of Ailsa's independence and her ferocity to bolster the idea that the dead woman had been maligned by history; she had liked the theory that Ailsa had become a victim precisely because of that independent spirit, because she had lived in a society that needed to punish a woman for wanting to determine her own fate. But what if hearsay had been right all along, and Ailsa really was an unbalanced woman who had lost her mind and killed her child? Zoe had to concede that the journal, particularly towards the end, read like the outpourings of a mind that had been thrown off-kilter. And if Ailsa was crazy, and she was suffering the same delusions as Ailsa, that would

252

mean she was also crazy. Dan had tried to tell her she was unstable. Dr Schlesinger never used such loaded words; she talked of 'mood shifts' and 'unhelpful cognitive patterns'. But it amounted to the same thing: attempts to make Zoe believe her mind was not securely anchored, that her judgement could not be trusted. Charles was too tactful to say it openly, but he was inevitably drawing an implicit parallel between her experience and Ailsa's.

'I see you found the photograph,' he said, nodding at the portrait of Ailsa that lay beside her on the table where she had set it down. 'Have you worked out what's strange about it?'

'Her eyes.' Zoe picked it up, grateful for the swerve of subject.

'Well spotted. They've been painted on afterwards – do you see? It was often done with Victorian death portraits.'

'Wait – she's dead in this?' She recoiled, holding the picture at arm's length. 'That's so creepy. Why would they do that?'

'It was a common custom. Macabre to us, but the Victorians saw it as a way of honouring the loved one. Usually commissioned by the family, but in this case, the portrait was taken by Bonar, the solicitor, who was a keen amateur photographer.'

'Bonar again, huh.'

'He sent a copy to William, but it seems he rather sneakily also gave it to a doctor friend of his who came over from the mainland to look at the body. It later became quite celebrated in scientific journals of the time.'

'Why?'

'Well – look at her. What do you notice?'

Zoe held the picture up to the light. 'Apart from the eyes, nothing special. It's very sharp.'

'That's due to the long exposure. Most portraits from that time are slightly blurry, because living subjects can't help moving even minutely while the picture is being taken. The dead, on the other hand, are obligingly still. Where you have living relatives posing with a corpse, the dead person appears much more clearly in the photograph than those around them – it's an uncanny effect. But that's not what's curious here.'

'She looks like she's resting.'

'*Exactly*. Remember, she'd been missing for three days before her body washed up on the shore. Have you ever seen a drowned corpse?'

'God, no.'

'Well, I promise you they don't look as serene as this. And everyone in that community would have been familiar with the state of a body that had been in the sea for three days. You can imagine – this extraordinary state of preservation only fuelled the idea of supernatural intervention.'

'But . . . ' Zoe stared at the picture, frowning. 'Surely this strengthens the argument that she was murdered? Obviously she didn't drown at all – someone must have hidden her body and dumped her on the beach to be found as if she'd washed up. And the forensics weren't good enough back then to prove otherwise.'

'It won't surprise you to learn that that line of enquiry was not pursued,' Charles said. He unwrapped a loaf from the larder and cut two thick slices, which he trapped between the two halves of a mesh disc and imprisoned under one of the steel lids on the range. 'Though much energy was devoted by Bonar's doctor friend to investigating how a body might feasibly be preserved in salt water. The same doctor, incidentally, who ruled death by drowning – the local physician was indisposed at the time.'

'Convenient. See – everything points to Bonar.' She slammed the photo on the table as if to close the case. 'He even gets his buddy to say she drowned when it must have been clear to everyone that she couldn't have. How come no one challenged that, if they all knew what drowning looked like?'

'This is a small island community,' Charles said patiently. 'Few people were educated beyond childhood back then.

Fishermen and crofters didn't question the authority of doctors and lawyers – at least, not aloud. People were inclined to believe the explanation that suited them, anyway.'

'You mean, they'd rather accept that her body was in perfect condition because she was a witch than because she didn't really throw herself in the sea.' She bit her lip, angry on Ailsa's behalf. 'You must have looked into Bonar.'

'Of course.' The smell of toast had begun to warm the air. 'There's not much to discover. He left the island with his wife and four children shortly after Ailsa's death, even before her estate was settled. He wrote to William Drummond saying he had taken up a position in Canada and could no longer represent the family.'

'That's a long way to run. As good as a confession.'

'It would be a neat solution, wouldn't it?' Charles slid the wire disc from the hotplate, flipped the toast on to a plate and inserted another two slices. 'Of course, an alternative view might be that he was so distressed by the deaths of Ailsa and her son that he felt unable to stay here.'

'I don't buy that.'

'It's merely conjecture. As is your theory. I'm simply saying there is no shred of evidence to prove that Richard Bonar was the father of Ailsa's child. By all accounts, he was an entirely upright man, a pillar of the community, and a devoted husband and father.'

'Exactly – someone like that would have the most to lose, and the most need to hide the truth.'

Charles gave her a tired smile. 'You've got it in for Bonar, haven't you? You can make his very probity argue against him. He never made it to Canada, incidentally. Died of pneumonia on the journey, less than a year after Ailsa's death. She left him a small bequest in her will, which passed to his widow.'

'So,' she counted the charges off on her fingers, 'he's the only man that ever sees her, he knows she's leaving him money,

255

he vamooses the minute she dies, he gets his friend to say she drowned in spite of all the evidence – but you still think he's innocent.' She twisted her mouth. 'OK – say he is. You must have some other idea of who the lover was? Did you get anything from the book?'

'Ah.' He slapped a chunk of yellow butter on to the toast and pushed the plate across the table to her. 'When you have eliminated the impossible, whatever is left, *however improbable*, must be the truth. Sherlock Holmes,' he added, catching her expression.

'Oh, OK. We're back to the incubus, are we? I'd say that falls squarely in the realm of the impossible.'

'Would you?' He crooked an eyebrow. 'In spite of everything you've told me?'

A chill stole over her skin. 'Yes. I mean, there's the child. Who must have had a human father, whatever the legend says. I was reading your book about it last night.'

'Oh? At Mick and Kaye's?' He had turned his back to refill the kettle.

She frowned. An odd sensation spread under her ribs. 'How did you know I was at theirs?'

'You told me.'

'I don't think I did.' Tired as she was, she felt certain she hadn't said anything about where she had spent the previous night. Charles appeared not to have moved from his desk until she found him – he could not have spoken to anyone that morning.

'Or else – I was at my desk most of the night. Perhaps I saw the Land Rover coming down the lane and returning late. That must have been it.'

Zoe gave him a long look. An uncomfortable tension had entered the room, affecting their earlier ease. She pushed the plate of toast away. 'You know Kaye says you're psychic, right?'

He laughed. 'Dear Kaye. I'm afraid like many city folk she

rather romanticises the history of the islands. She thinks anyone who was born here must be part Druid.'

Zoe tilted her head. 'You can't blame her – it's not like the islands don't invite it. All those legends . . . I always thought, you know, when I was a kid and my grandmother told her stories, that there must be a kind of magic here. I guess that's why I wanted . . . ' She dipped her head, left the thought unfinished.

Charles gave her a searching look before returning his attention to the range.

'True. Though Kaye would have us all cavorting around standing stones at the solstice if she could.' With a deft movement he whipped out the next round of toast. 'I'm flattered you read my book. Dare I hope it was in some way informative?'

'I can see where the rumours around Ailsa's son might have come from. The coincidences, I mean. The way the incubus is supposed to impregnate women with the – whatever the child is called.'

'You mean the cambion.' He nodded, reaching for a jar of dark home-made marmalade. 'A child fathered by an incubus on a mortal woman is called a cambion. Always a male child, said to have certain distinctive traits. Merlin in the Arthurian legends was supposedly a cambion, hence his magical powers.'

'But the legend says the baby appears stillborn. Then it's mute as a child. Like Ailsa's son.'

'Until the age of seven years, yes. At which time he fully assumes his true nature and comes into his powers.'

'Ailsa wrote in the journal that at seven years he becomes his father's son. Towards the end she believes the boy is in danger, she says his father wants him, she makes him wear her cross for protection. Do you think . . . ' she hesitated, the hairs prickling on her arms ' . . . she convinced herself that it was true? If she was losing her mind, maybe she really started to believe that her son was evil in some way.'

257

'I think there is no doubt from the diary account that Ailsa loved her son fiercely and would have made any sacrifice for him. It also sounds as if she was suffering from some illness towards the end, and was terrified of what might happen to the boy when she was gone.' Charles took a bite of toast, his eyes fixed distantly on the window. 'As I said before, she wouldn't be the first mother to kill a child considered abnormal, under the illusion that she was sparing him a lifetime of suffering. More than a lifetime, in this case.' He turned back to her, his face grave. 'The cambion is supposedly immortal. He ages, but cannot die or father children. She would have known the legend from Tamhas, I'm sure of it. Still, there's one thing we *have* learned from the journal.' He paused to pour another mug of tea.

'What's that?'

'The boy's exact birth date. All Hallows, 1862 – a good six days before the date officially registered by Bonar. Which means the final entry with those ominous verses of Scripture was written two days before the boy's seventh birthday.'

'You think that's evidence that she killed him? To save him?'

Charles held out his hands, empty. 'I think it's significant. Not conclusive either way. But I feel the journal is an extraordinary testament to a mind at its limits. It's deeply disturbing to read. You must have found the same.'

She nodded, hearing an echo of profound sorrow in his voice, and thought again how he seemed so much more invested in the story of Ailsa and her son than Mick, her direct descendant, who wanted only to disown her.

'Will you tell Mick?'

'In time, of course. I would like the opportunity to study it in more detail. Perhaps you would be kind enough not to mention it to him for a while longer?' He lifted an eyebrow, looking for complicity.

'Of course not.'

'Not that I suppose he'd have a great deal of interest, but he'll worry about the content being made public.'

'Would you do that?'

'I couldn't, without his permission. The book rightly belongs to him. That's why I'd like time to read it thoroughly before he makes any decisions. I'm sure you understand.'

She nodded, scraping her chair back. 'I should get going. Thanks for the tea.'

'Zoe – there is one more thing.' He stepped forward, as if to intercept her. 'Humour an old man, will you?' He fixed her with his serious blue gaze; she felt a flicker of alarm. 'There is an influence in that house that I believe is dangerous. It drove Ailsa McBride to her death. Perhaps you might reconsider whether it's wise for you to stay on there. A woman in your position—'

The muscles tightened in her jaw. 'What position is that, then?'

He sighed. 'Alone. A long way from those you love. You may be susceptible.'

'*Susceptible*. You mean you think I'm crazy like she was.' She stared him down.

'I meant only, in your circumstances, there would be no shame in choosing—'

'You know nothing about my circumstances. Unless – have you been spying on me? Googling me?' She exhaled hard through her nose, trying to keep her composure. 'Jesus, what is wrong with this place – don't you understand privacy? Can't any of you leave other people the fuck alone? What's funny?'

'I'm sorry.' Charles suppressed a smile. 'Says the lady who walked into my house while I slept.'

'You left your door unlocked! Anyway, I was worried about you.'

'And I'm also concerned about you. I'm not interfering for my own amusement, I promise you.'

'You think I'm nuts.'

'Far from it.' His face grew serious. 'I think you could be in danger.'

'You're not the first person to tell me that. Mick warned me there are people in the village who want to scare me off.'

'I'm not one of them. But you were right to say earlier that I know more about the story than Mick. On the strength of that knowledge, and the evidence of the journal, I'm asking you to trust me when I suggest you think carefully about staying there alone.'

'Come back with me and have dinner tonight, then,' she said, folding her arms. She thought she saw him flinch, so quickly she could not be sure.

'I don't think we ought to give the gossips any more ammunition, do you?' He gave her a paternal look, gently chiding. 'Besides, I have a lot of work to catch up on. Thank you for the offer, though.'

'You won't, will you?' she said, a knowing smile stealing over her face. 'You won't set foot in that house. You're scared.'

He lowered his eyes. 'Let us say that I also regard myself as susceptible in some ways.'

'So you *are* psychic.'

'You see, I knew you were going to say that.'

They looked at one another; Zoe caught the twitch at the corner of his mouth and burst out laughing. She put her hand in her pocket and closed her fingers around the cold metal of the broken padlock.

'I know exactly what I have to be afraid of in that house, and I'm going to deal with it,' she said, determined.

'Very well. But since I can't accept your kind invitation tonight, let me send Horace in my stead. He'll even bring his own food.'

'Seriously?' Zoe glanced down. The dog was lying on the floor under the table. At the mention of his name, he raised his head and thumped his tail on the floor. 'I'd love to have him, but – he won't like to be away from you, will he? He'll be miserable – I couldn't do that.'

'He's a trouper. He'll do what's asked of him. Won't you, old chap?' He reached down and scratched the dog between the ears. Zoe privately doubted whether ponderous, faithful Horace would prove much of a deterrent to someone like Dougie Reid – she could not imagine him leaping for an intruder's throat under any circumstances – but the dog's presence might at least lend her a shot of courage, and she was grateful for the offer.

On the doorstep, Charles handed her a bag containing dog food and Horace's favourite blanket. Horace himself seemed quietly accepting of his secondment; he stood beside her, gazing wistfully at his home.

'You can always call me, you know,' Charles said, his face earnest. 'If anything disturbs you. Anything at all.'

'I'll keep that in mind. So you don't think I'm crazy, then?'

'Not in the slightest. I think you're as sane as I am.' His blue eyes glinted in the low light. Zoe smiled.

'I don't know if that's reassuring.'

At the gate she turned to look up at the house. The long window on the first floor at the front must be Charles's study, where she had found him. A thick screen of pine trees inside the garden wall shielded the house from the lane. He could not possibly have seen Mick drive past last night, much less have identified who was in the car. That same unease tightened in her sternum; not for the first time, she found herself questioning her instinctive trust of the old bookseller. Horace nudged her leg with his nose, as if to reprimand her for such disloyal thoughts.

16

In the last light of the afternoon, the saloon bar of the Stag appeared stale and shabby. The tarnished horse brasses arrayed above the bar; the worn carpet patterned to disguise decades of stains; the sepia prints with their faded mounts, depicting the fishing industry of yesteryear: all wore a self-pitying air of neglect by day that she had not noticed in the hot crowds of her previous visit. Two elderly men slumped in a window seat, clutching full pints on a table slick with spilled beer, rheumy eyes glued to a soundless shopping channel with subtitles on the wall-mounted television. The ghosts of woodsmoke and old cigarettes lingered in the air. Behind the bar, Annag Logan clicked her thumbs furiously on her phone, barely raising her eyes to register Zoe's entrance.

Horace trotted ahead to the back door and turned to look questioningly at Zoe, evidently on his way to Charles's bench in the garden.

'Hi,' she said brightly, though the girl had clearly decided to ignore her. 'Is Mick around?'

'Nope.' More clicking. Zoe leaned forward and saw coloured shapes zipping across the screen.

'Well, do you know where he is?' She was determined to keep her temper despite the girl's manner, though Annag's words, as reported by Robbie, ran through her mind like a news ticker.

'He's away to the mainland.' Annag bothered to look up for this; she clearly wanted to see how it landed.

Zoe felt a flicker of fear. She folded her fingers around the broken padlock in her pocket. 'I didn't know. When's he back?'

Annag shrugged. 'Tomorrow, maybe. Or Wednesday. Can't remember. He's gone to see the brewery. He usually stays over a bit, goes to the cash and carry and that.'

'OK. Thanks. Is Kaye here, then?'

This time there was a distinct hesitation. 'She's at a rehearsal. With the band.'

'Where?'

She could see Annag wrestling with herself, could tell how much the girl wanted to tell her to mind her own business. Zoe laid her hands flat on the bar and leaned closer. 'It's important,' she said pleasantly, locking eyes until Annag flicked her gaze back to her game.

'At the school hall. You'll know where *that* is.' There was no missing the malice in the last words. Don't rise to it, Zoe told herself.

'Thanks. Come on, Horace.' She clicked her fingers. Horace lumbered to his feet and padded over to her. She had not thought it possible for a dog to roll its eyes, but Horace seemed to favour her with a particular expression of weary tolerance that was as near as dammit.

'Must get spooky out there all on your own,' Annag remarked, as Zoe reached the door.

She turned. 'Not really.'

'Why've you got Horace, then?'

Zoe forced a smile. 'Company, I guess.'

'You're no short of that, from what I hear.' The girl's attention was deliberately fixed on her screen.

'Do you know the house well, Annag?'

263

'What?' Her head jerked up; she stared at Zoe.

'Are you familiar with the McBride house? Have you spent much time there?'

'No.' The girl's small eyes shrunk further; her face had grown wily and guarded. She even put the phone down. 'Why would I want to go there?'

'It's very beautiful. A lot of bird life.'

She saw no spark of recognition; Annag only returned her stare with the same careful blankness.

'So?'

'I thought maybe you liked seabirds?'

'Do *you* like them?'

'I've kind of gone off them.'

'Well, you've come to the wrong place, then.' She resumed her game, to demonstrate her lack of interest in the conversation. She was good, Zoe thought; if Dougie had roped Annag into helping him, she was not going to give it up that easily.

'You should probably take your little brother to the doctor, by the way,' Zoe remarked, as she was leaving. 'That cut on his face looks nasty.'

At this, Annag raised her head. 'He's a clumsy wee bastard. He's always falling off things. You should probably mind your own business.'

'OK. Here's an idea. Why don't we all try doing just that?'

She pulled the pub door closed behind her, but the victory of the last word felt hollow; a pulse of anxiety started up at her temples. If she had achieved anything, it was only to set Annag more determinedly against her by suggesting she knew who was behind the gull incident. She regretted mentioning Robbie's bruise, too. Families were tight-knit here; she should have realised that any attempt at interference from an outsider would only meet with a closing of ranks. But the real unease, she realised, as she opened the passenger door for Horace like his personal chauffeur, came from the knowledge that Mick

264

was away from the island. If anything happened in the house that night, no one was coming for her.

On her way to the school she stopped and swore loudly, causing Horace to prick up his ears like a maiden aunt; in the heat of her exchange with Annag she had forgotten her intention to ask for the Wi-Fi at the pub. She could hardly go back in now and ask a favour; it would have to wait until she had spoken to Kaye.

It was almost four when she reached the school hall; the children had long gone and she could hear Kaye's laughter as she pushed the door open into that familiar smell of floor polish and gym shoes. Edward stood under the semicircular window at the end tuning his violin, his eyes closed, the last light of the afternoon gilding his hair. She allowed herself to watch him for a moment, conscious of the whispers and glances of the other men as they unpacked their instruments. Belatedly, she wished she had thought to put on make-up, and found herself ridiculous for thinking it.

'Kaye! Annag said I'd find you here.' She made her voice brisk and cheerful, to quell any doubts about her reason for showing up. But she could not suppress the small charge of excitement when Edward snapped his eyes open and turned to her with a smile disarming in its frank pleasure at seeing her. She acknowledged him with a brief nod. 'Can I have a quick word?' She lowered her voice and gestured Kaye to the door.

'Course. Back in a jiff, fellas.' Kaye took her by the elbow and led her into a corridor lined with children's paintings carefully mounted on coloured sugar paper. Zoe tried not to look at them. The stick figures surrounded by spiky trees and wobbly seas made her think of Caleb, with a predictable pull in her chest, but they also reminded her of the sinister drawing left in her sketchbook.

'I'm glad you've come – I was going to ring you after this,' Kaye said, squeezing Zoe's arm, her fingers now plated with

265

long silver rings. In her bold eye make-up and fuchsia lipstick she appeared entirely alien from the soft creature of the night before in the fluffy robe, a Valkyrie armoured in Celtic jewellery. When she next spoke, she lowered her gaze; the purple glittering lids and thick lashes a shield against evident embarrassment. 'Do you want to stay at the pub tonight? You can come for dinner. I think it's best.'

'Uh – well . . . ' She was going to explain about Horace, but Kaye cut in.

'It's only – this is a bit awkward, I wasn't sure if I should tell you, but – I had a phone call. From your husband.'

'*What?*' Zoe stared at her.

Kaye glanced up in discomfort. 'He was a wee bit worried about you. He said he hasn't been able to get through on the number for the house and he's left messages but hasn't heard back.'

'But – how did he get your number?' Anger spread coldly through her limbs; she felt her fists curl. Dan must have found a way to look through her computer again before she left, though she had changed her password after the last time.

'I thought you must have given it to him, for an emergency contact.' Confusion clouded Kaye's face. 'Maybe he got it from the website, then. Anyway, he only wanted to check you were OK – he said you hadn't been well lately, so he asked if . . . ' She tailed off, seeing Zoe's expression. 'I know – they're babies, aren't they? I take the girls to my folks' for a couple of weeks in the summer and, honest, Mick's on the phone every five minutes – he cannae work the drier, where are the spare towels, all that. I'm like, you're forty-six, man, did you no manage to wash your clothes before I came along? Actually, I'm no sure he did.' She laughed, trying to lighten the mood. 'It's like having an extra child, I'm no kidding. Sounds like yours is the same, eh?'

'He's not – he wants . . . What did he ask you?' A thought

266

occurred. 'You didn't tell him about last night? That I stayed with you?'

Kaye was not quick enough to hide the flash of guilt. 'I might have mentioned that you were a wee bit upset. Only because he was worried,' she added, defensive.

'Did he say anything else? Did he mention Caleb?'

'Easy there.' Kaye pulled her arm away; Zoe realised belatedly that she had grabbed the other woman's sleeve with more force than she had intended. 'Is that your wee boy? No, I don't think so. He only said you weren't quite yourself, on account of being ill, so he wasn't sure how you'd be coping on your own . . . '

'And you had to tell him what happened last night. Fuck's sake!' Zoe wheeled around, her hands in her hair, and found herself face to face with a child's painting of a ruined house, outlined in black, a white stick figure with wild hair depicted in one of the windows. It was captioned, in clear, round, teacher's writing: 'The Haunted House, by Iain Finlay, age 10'. The green background was faded and curling at the edges. She started; how had Edward allowed this to stay on the wall, a year after the boy's disappearance?

'Look, Zoe – I'm really sorry.' Kaye was trying to sound placatory. 'I wasn't to know what I should or shouldn't say, to be fair. You've no told us anything about your life back home. And fair enough, you've come here for a bit of peace.' She held up a hand as if to fend off protest. 'Your marriage –' she lowered her voice, with a quick glance back to the hall, and Edward – 'and whatever you get up to here, that's your business. I'm no like these old village wives that have nothing better to do than gossip. I felt sorry for him, that's all. Your husband. He sounded really upset that he couldn't reach you, like he'd been imagining the worst. I know Mick would fret like mad if I went off to America on my own, he'd do the same.' She paused, grinning. 'Chance'd be a fine thing, eh.'

'Don't feel sorry for him.' The words came out curt and

clipped. 'He's manipulating you. We're separating, if you want to know. He doesn't like me being here, obviously. This is his way of trying to control me from three thousand miles away. If he does it again you can tell him you're not my babysitter. And I'm not *getting up to* anything.'

Kaye clapped a metalled hand to her mouth. 'Oh my God. I had no idea.' Zoe could tell she was pleased with the added layer of drama.

'You didn't tell him any of that stuff about the house being cursed or me being *sensitive*?'

'Course not.' Kaye pulled herself up, affronted.

'Did Mick tell him anything about last night?'

'Mick was away to the mainland by the time he called.'

She felt a wash of relief. 'When's he back?'

'Tomorrow. That's why I wondered if you wanted to stay in the guest room for tonight. It's only that . . . ' Kaye hesitated, 'if you have another bad night, I wouldnae be able to leave the kids and come out to you. It might be best, just in case.'

Something in Kaye's expression troubled her, the way her gaze swerved away. She was not good at hiding. There had been more to her conversation with Dan than she was admitting, Zoe was certain.

'Did he ask you to keep an eye on me?'

'No! It's not that. I'd feel better if you were at the Stag tonight, that's all.'

Zoe looked at her. If she hadn't learned about the phone call she would have taken Kaye up on her offer, especially in Mick's absence. But this changed everything. She had not imagined Dan would stoop so low – intruding directly into her attempt to find some space for herself, asking her landlords to monitor her behaviour. If she gave into it now, she would never make the break. He would know that, however far she travelled, he could look over her shoulder as if he were in the same room.

'Thanks for the offer, but I'll be fine at the house. There's really no need to worry.' She hated to sound like a bitch when

268

Kaye had been so generous the night before, but she guessed from the other woman's face that she had made some kind of promise to Dan to take charge of her welfare and report back. No doubt Kaye meant well, but Zoe could not bear the idea of them conferring over her as if she were a wayward adolescent going to her first high school party. Dan had been the same after the postnatal depression when she came out of hospital, except then it had been her mother he had corralled into acting as his informer. Whatever it cost her, this time she would not accept his supposedly concerned surveillance. Her freedom was at stake.

Kaye looked alarmed. 'I really think Mick would be happier too,' she began.

'Well, as much as I hate to make either of you feel bad, you didn't sign up for babysitting duties and neither did I. I'm your tenant, and that's the deal. And my paranoid husband has no right to call you and misrepresent me and make you feel you're responsible for me – and by the way, I'm the one paying for the house, not him. So I'd appreciate it if you treated me like an adult.'

'That's not what—'

'I don't care what he told you. I can guess. He's a control freak. And he's really good at it, so I don't blame you if you were convinced.'

'I'm sorry, Zoe.' Kaye twisted her rings, keeping her eyes fixed on her hands. 'Like I say, I didn't know any of this. I don't want to get involved in your business—'

'You're not. I'm fine.' There was a long pause. Zoe knew they were both thinking of the state Mick had found her in the previous night. She was glad Dan had not managed to speak to him, or he would no doubt be on a plane right now.

'What did you want to ask me about, anyway?' Kaye said, flicking a quick glance to her watch.

'Oh – it was nothing, really.' She could not mention the padlock now; that would have to wait for Mick's return. She stuck her hand into the pocket of her jacket and felt for it, but found nothing. Panic flared briefly in her chest; it must have fallen out in the car, or maybe at the Stag, or in the car park . . . She would have to find it before Mick returned; without evidence, he would never admit that Dougie had tampered with the cellar hatch. She realised, with a twinge of fear, that Dougie must know Mick was away overnight, and might well decide to use the opportunity to his advantage; the thought was almost enough to make her back down and ask for a room at the Stag after all. If not for Dan, she would have done, but she could no longer be sure whose side Kaye was on. 'Have you spoken to Charles today?'

'Charles? No – why?'

'No reason.' She did not want another knowing talk from Kaye on the subject of Charles's psychic powers, about which she had her own suspicions.

'Are you sure you're OK?' Kaye laid a hand on her arm. Zoe thought again how pretty she was, under the defiant make-up.

'I'm fine. Honestly. Last night was – out of character. I'm sorry you got dragged into this business with my husband, too – that was unfair of him.'

'No, I'm the one who should be sorry. I'll know next time.' But there was a wariness in her tone that told Zoe she was not sure who to believe.

'Kaye?' A bearded man with a grey ponytail stuck his head around the door. 'Hate to interrupt, but if you're no joining us Bernie'll have to start singing for you in a minute, and naebody deserves that.'

'Away to fuck with you,' called a good-natured voice from the hall, presumably Bernie.

'Whisht, I'm coming. Here.' She looked at Zoe and, in one swift movement, lifted one of her silver chains over her head. A jagged black stone like a lump of shiny coal hung from it. 'Take this. It's black tourmaline. Very powerful protection against evil spirits and negative energies. Go on, do this for me at least, I'll feel better. And you've got the sage, haven't you? Don't forget to burn that.'

'OK. Thanks.' Zoe dipped her head like an Olympic medallist to receive the pendant. 'Don't suppose you have anything that keeps ex-husbands away?'

'I think those are called lawyers,' offered the ponytailed man, who was leaning in the doorway. She laughed, and raised a hand in farewell, but Kaye did not smile, only continued to watch her with that same intent frown. Zoe thought she saw Kaye's lips moving silently as she turned to go and wondered if she were saying some kind of prayer or incantation for her safety, and whether it would work.

'Zoe!'

She snapped around as she unhooked Horace's lead from the gate, still braced with anger, to see Edward jogging across the playground towards her.

'Oh – hey.'

He stopped a few feet away. They looked at one another, unsure how to proceed.

'They're going to hate me,' she said, gesturing to the hall. 'I've already kept Kaye out for ages. You should get back.'

'They can manage without me for a minute.' He pushed his hair out of his eyes and she thought, with a pang of conscience, how young he looked. 'I see you've got Horace. Is Charles OK?'

She was touched by the concern in his face. 'He's fine. Horace is staying the night with me, for company.'

Edward reached out a hand to the dog, who licked it once, as if for the sake of etiquette. 'I can't see him being much of a guard dog.'

'That's what he wants you to think. Underneath he's a ruthless killer.'

He smiled. 'I wondered if you might care for any other company tonight?'

271

'Well, it's . . . ' she hesitated, taking in his earnest brown eyes, his smooth skin. Then she thought, fuck it. Why not? Dan thought he could watch her, even here; she would make it clear that her choices were her own now, and beyond his reach. 'Sure. Don't expect anything fancy. It'll only be pasta.'

'That sounds good. I'll be a couple of hours at most. I'll bring some wine.'

'If you want.'

'OK, great.' He hovered a moment longer, bouncing on the balls of his feet, his eager smile betraying his pleasure.

'You should get back to your friends.'

He nodded, tousled Horace behind the ears, and ran across the playground, waving.

Zoe watched him disappear into the school and glanced along the green to the row of shops. She ought to pick up some fresh salad, at least. Next to the bakery there was a small drug store, its windows crammed with support stockings and cures for indigestion, where she had bought her tampons; she toyed briefly with the idea of stopping for a packet of condoms. But that would be tantamount to deciding in advance that she meant to have sex with Edward, and part of the charm of their interaction was the not-knowing, the gentle acknowledgement that it was a possible, but not inevitable, conclusion. Part of her felt she would rather indulge the fantasy than ruin it with the disappointment and self-consciousness of experience; even so, she could not help feeling a rush of relief that her bleeding appeared to have stopped. Perhaps her body was so out of practice that she could not manage a period of more than a couple of days; still, it meant she could be open to the possibility of sex. *Real* sex, she thought, wryly.

But even as she considered it, she understood fully what it meant to live in a community like this; if she bought condoms, or if Edward did, the entire village would know. They might as well sky-write it over the island. She wondered if Kaye had

272

told Dan anything about Edward, about the rumours circulating. There was no way of knowing, now, how far Kaye could be trusted. Zoe had not dared ask her how Dan had introduced himself on the phone. Had he said, 'Hi, I'm Daniel Bergman', thereby giving Kaye her married name, and the means to Google her? She had not dared look herself up online lately, but she was sure there must be stuff out there; about the accident, if nothing else. She walked past the drug store; it was closed, in any case. Fate, Zoe thought, and laughed.

17

The light was fading as she drove back across the hills to the house, but the earlier cloud cover had broken to reveal an unexpectedly vivid sunset. By the time she turned the corner of the drive, the sky was banded in fiery reds and golds and edged with smudges of charcoal cloud, the water lit like burnished metal, and her first thought was to capture it on film so that she could later transfer the colours to a larger canvas.

She raced up to the first-floor gallery where she had moved all her painting things and dug out her camera. The battery was low, but ought to be enough to catch the sun before it slipped away below the horizon. She had intended to take her pictures from the beach, but now she looked towards the sea and saw that the neon colours framed through the dark outlines of the gallery's tall Gothic windows made a more dramatic photograph. She fired off a few frames, squinting back at the tiny screen to assess the results – and stopped. It was dark enough outside for the windows to capture her reflection; she could make out her own silhouette holding the camera. But that was not what made her scalp tighten. In the image on the screen, the reflection in the window clearly showed a figure standing in the doorway to the gallery, behind her. She turned, slowly, knowing full well there would be no one there. The door was empty. She zoomed in on the camera's screen and saw that it appeared to be a figure in a cloak, like the shepherd she had seen on the moor. But the image blurred the more she zoomed; it was impossible to see any detail of a face.

She was surprised by how calm she felt as she walked back downstairs, switching on all the lights as she went. She could attempt to rationalise it away – some double exposure of her own silhouette – or she could simply accept that this house played tricks on the eyes and the mind, why not on the lens too? Horace sat patiently at the foot of the stairs, sniffing; she guessed he could also smell that strange odour. His presence steadied her and she ruffled his ears as she passed. In movies, she thought, animals are always sensitive to the paranormal; if there was anything in the house, Horace would be whining and barking inexplicably, his fur standing on end. But perhaps Horace had not seen those movies and didn't know his role. He padded after her to the kitchen, where she opened one of the bottles of wine she had brought back and took a large glass out to the veranda. The sun had dropped with remarkable haste; a few last streaks of orange hung above the horizon.

The wind was sharp and fresh, out here; it whipped her hair and stung her eyes, clearing her head. Gulls circled above the cliffs, barely moving their wings on the shifting currents. The water had turned to hammered steel in the last light of the day. She had walked out of her life to be alone here, with the salt wind and the sky and no certainty of what awaited her; there would be consequences, but not yet. She felt suspended, almost peaceful. Edward would be here soon; the prospect caused a small stab of heat in her groin.

When she grew too cold to stay outside she locked the kitchen door carefully behind her and poured another glass before wandering back to the entrance hall. She ought to call

Dan and make clear how she felt about him speaking to Kaye behind her back, but she felt unprepared for a confrontation. The message light on the answerphone flashed accusingly; after a few moments' indecision, she pressed the button and her mother's breathless voice echoed around the hallway, as if she had begun midway through a public address:

'. . . *so completely selfish . . . not how marriage works . . . don't you think Daniel's had enough to deal with . . .* '

Zoe dived for the machine and hit 'delete' before she could take in any more. She fully expected the second message to be a continuation – the brief recording window would hardly have been sufficient for her mother's charge sheet – but instead she heard only that strange crackle of static, like the turning of an old record, that she had heard the previous night. It seemed to go on for minutes; she was about to erase it, thinking someone had dialled the number by accident, when she heard a woman's voice, soft and indistinct, repeating the same phrase in Gaelic. At first all she could make out was the strange cadence of the words, which seemed menacing and soothing at once, but as she listened she found that she understood the meaning, though she could not have explained how. *Time to go*, the woman was saying, over and over. *Time to go.*

Her skin grew cold. She reached out for the delete button but thought better of it; if someone was making prank calls to frighten her, she would need this recording as evidence for the police, along with the padlock – she would search for that in daylight. A sound in the kitchen startled her, so that she cried out, but it was only Horace, knocking a chair as he came in search of her. She knelt beside him and buried her face in his wiry fur, which he bore as patiently as he had endured all the changes in his routine so far. She fetched the rest of the bottle and took it up to the gallery, where she made sure to shut the door behind her. Edward would be here soon. There was nothing to be afraid of.

*   *   *

276

She must have drifted off, because when she opened her eyes the room appeared strangely lit, and it took her a few seconds to realise that night had fallen outside. Struggling to sit up, she found herself on a day-bed at the side of the gallery, but the rest of the room was unrecognisable. Yellow light fell unevenly from oil lamps placed on tables and benches around the walls; an odd smoky taint hung in the air, mixed with a bitter, vegetable smell, and she could hear a man's voice murmuring as if to himself, low and preoccupied. She rubbed her eyes and made out a tall figure with his back to her, his shirtsleeves rolled above the elbow, bent over a workbench ranged with glass beakers and a pestle and mortar. As a reflex, she reached up to clutch the pendant Kaye had given her and found, as she touched it, that she was not wearing a lump of black tourmaline but a silver Celtic cross. The discovery alarmed her; she looked down and saw that she was barefoot and dressed in a floor-length cotton shift tied with ribbons across her chest. A woollen shawl was wrapped around her shoulders, her hair hung loose. She shook her head, as if this might clear her vision; she was dreaming, this much she realised, even within the dream, but she felt so unusually aware that she could not see how to wake herself from it. The man at the table turned to her, holding out a glass. His face was not quite in focus, as if she were seeing him through a smeared lens, though she had an overwhelming impression of hair: bristling eyebrows, dark sideburns and a full moustache. When he spoke, his voice came to her distantly, as if underwater. He was urging her to drink; she surprised herself by obeying. The solution tasted brackish, slightly fermented, of vegetable matter and stagnant water; she retched more than once as she swallowed it, and wondered, in some detached part of her mind, how it was that she could taste so vividly in her dream. He led her gently to the day-bed and laid her on it; her vision was beginning to blur, dizziness unbalanced her, and she was grateful for the solidity of the bed beneath her head. *Don't*

277

fight it, the man said, not unkindly, in a broad Scots accent, and he undid the ties of her shift at the neck, though she made a feeble scrabbling attempt to bat his hand away. *Good girl, Ailsa*, he whispered, as he stepped away to extinguish the lamps. She tried to raise her head, which now felt alarmingly heavy on the frail stalk of her neck, and saw that the only remaining light came from a branched candelabra behind him. He stood over her and struck up a low incantation in a language she could not understand but from which she instinctively recoiled, moving his hands peculiarly across the candle flames, the strange cadences building momentum until the words reached a crescendo of invitation. The candles blew out all at once and she felt her body – which was both hers and not hers; her breasts were heavier, the springy hair between her legs unfamiliar – turn suddenly cold, as if a window had been opened to let in an icy blast.

An age seemed to pass before she heard a gathering sound, soft at first, a rush of air like the onset of a gale or the retreat of the sea before a vast wave crashes. She opened her eyes (or had they been open all along?) to see another figure taking shape out of the shadows. He knelt beside her and though she could not see him clearly, she knew that he was the one she had been waiting for, and that she must not look directly at his face, because he was so terribly beautiful. He parted the fabric of her shift and she felt his breath raise goosebumps on her skin. His fingers circled her breasts as he moved his mouth to each in turn, tugging lightly and then harder with sharp teeth. She was pinned under him, arching her body to him, unable to move, feeling her own arousal growing and with it an indefinable dread and excitement, the knowledge that she was about to cross a threshold and that afterwards it would be impossible to return. It was a transgression that promised enlightenment, a new understanding of herself, but she was not sure who had made her that promise, or if it could be trusted. She knew, too, in some dim recess of her

278

mind, that these were not her thoughts, or not hers alone; they had been Ailsa's first.

He moved his mouth down her body and pulled the shift up to her waist. She closed her eyes and clasped her hands around his head as he worked his tongue into her, drawing back, circling, expertly edging her closer; she became conscious that she was on some level holding her breath, resisting him, refusing to let herself go, for fear of what would follow. *That's it; give in*, she heard a voice say, and she realised that the man in the shirtsleeves had been standing in the shadows all along, clinically observing. The understanding did not dampen her desire; instead the sense of performance emboldened her and she did as she was told, and let go.

Rising to her climax, she opened her eyes as he entered her and looked into his face, for the space of a heartbeat. Her fingers scrabbled for the cross around her throat; the cry she uttered was one of exquisite pleasure and horror in the same instant.

When she woke – for she supposed she must have been asleep – she realised first that she was freezing. She was lying on the couch in the gallery, with the electric lamps casting shadows up the wall. She looked down at herself; she was wearing her own clothes, though her jeans were unzipped and her T-shirt pulled up over her breasts. Her head felt foggy, her mouth dry and sticky; when she tried to sit up, her foot knocked an empty bottle and sent it clattering across the bare boards. She pulled her hair back and twisted it into a ponytail, troubled by an obscure sense that something terrible had happened, something she would have cause to regret, the memory of it hanging just beyond her grasp. Did she finish the bottle of wine? She had no recollection of drinking it, but it was empty, and her clothes were in disarray. She slid a finger inside her underwear, experimentally; her pubis felt tender, her skin chilled.

It was exactly the kind of situation – that nagging, cold

unease – that, had she been on a date, would lead her to fear she'd been slipped a roofie. But she had been alone – hadn't she? No one could have drugged her. She had dreamed – though the details of the dream were hazy now – of Tamhas and Ailsa; she had seen Tamhas's experiments through Ailsa's eyes: the concoction, the summoning, the visitation. Except that, of course, no one knew the nature of Tamhas's experiments, not even Charles. She had witnessed nothing; her fevered imagination had conjured images out of her own preoccupations and Charles's mythical theories. As she tried to gather her thoughts, she became aware of a noise from beyond the door; a rhythmic scratching of nails against the wood. She pressed her thumbs into her eyes, forcing herself to focus, but the sound continued, soft and insistent, until she could not stand another second –

'Go away.' She tried to shout, but her voice came out cracked; she was answered by a low whine, and relief sluiced through her, weakening her limbs so that she slumped back against the couch. After a deep breath, she pushed herself to her feet, righted her clothes, and opened the door to see the dog looking expectantly up at her. He made a reproachful noise.

'God, sorry, Horace – you must be starving.' She had no idea what time it was, nor how long he might have been sitting outside. At that thought, her sluggish brain caught up and she remembered Edward. He too might have been outside knocking while she was asleep in the gallery. She stumbled downstairs, steadying herself against the smooth wood of the banister, disorientated by drink and sleep, trying to blink away the gritty sensation under her eyelids. The grandfather clock in the entrance hall told her it was ten to eleven. She paused to listen; the house seemed caught in an uneasy silence, the ticking of the clock unnaturally loud. Outside the wind had risen again; she felt it buffeting the old walls as if seeking entry.

280

She paused by the telephone. Perhaps Edward had given up and left; she would not have heard a car from the gallery on the beach side of the house. She ought to call him and explain, apologise. She pressed her fingers to her temples. The dream had left her shaky, disorientated; she felt post-orgasmic, but depleted by it, rather than elated or satisfied. She could not shake the conviction that she had not been alone in the room, despite any evidence to support the idea. This uneasy mix of paranoia and guilt, the gaps in memory and the desire to convince yourself that you are being absurd; this must be what the fear of date rape feels like, she thought. The horror of being violated while unaware of it, that was it; she could not rid herself of the sensation that something had been done to her while she slept, without her knowledge, and that its effects would prove irrevocable.

Her stomach cramped with hunger and she realised she had barely eaten since the morning. She put a hand out to the wall, to feel the cold, smooth plaster solid beneath her palm. A new message light flashed on the answerphone; Edward must have called to apologise or explain. She hesitated briefly before pressing 'Play'. The recording began with that same drawn-out silence and hiss of static; immediately she switched it off, in terror of hearing that distant, guttural voice intoning *Time to go*. Instead she picked up the receiver, but there was no dial tone. She clicked the button repeatedly, with increasing frenzy, but the line remained dead. Maybe the wind had brought the lines down, she thought, listening to it gusting round the corners of the house, worrying at the window frames. She would have to walk up on to the cliffs with her cell phone, see if she could get a signal. But first she and Horace needed food. One foot in front of the other; these were the practical steps she could focus on.

In the kitchen, the smell of decay had grown stronger; a sharp, cloying taint to the air that made her think of dead things. The dog seemed aware of it too; he began nosing

281

around the skirting boards and radiators with a throaty whine as if following a scent; she found it reassuring, if only for the confirmation that the odour was not merely in her mind. She made a peanut butter sandwich and was taking the first bite when she was startled by a sound. Muffled at first, but close by, like a heavy object falling to the floor. She froze, her eyes drawn to the low door at the back of the room that led to the cellar. Someone was down there. Her bowels turned to water; her throat closed tight. She had guessed right, then; Dougie had waited for Mick's absence to come for her – and he had cut the phone line to make sure. Her gaze was fixed on the door handle, expecting any moment to see it turn; she couldn't make herself move. In a second or two he would be in here with her. As she thought this, an almighty crash sounded from below the house, the grating of metal hitting metal. The noise snapped her out of her trance; she saw that the cellar door had a keyhole, and an iron key hanging next to it on a hook at head height. In two strides, she had crossed the room and turned the key in the lock. Quickly she let herself out of the kitchen door on to the veranda and down the steps. She had not stopped to put on shoes and the sand was cold and damp through her socks; she scurried around the south side of the house to the cellar hatch, which she found closed but unlocked, as she had guessed. He would be on his guard now, she thought; he would know that what-ever had fallen might have alerted her to his presence. But when he found he could not get into the kitchen from the cellar, he would have no other way out but through the hatch. She cast around on the ground to see if he had left the padlock lying around; her idea had been to lock him in and fetch help from the town, but her resolve was faltering. There was no light out here except the moon through rips in the cloud, and she could see no sign of the lock; she realised he would likely have put it in his pocket. She might have panicked then, but as she turned to hurry back inside her foot struck a solid object and she bent to find the driftwood she had carried from the shore earlier. It felt weighty and reassuring in her hands; she lifted it and practised a swing through the air. It would do, she thought. It was all she had.

So she waited in the shadows, balancing the piece of wood, testing its heft like a batter waiting at the plate, until she saw the hatch lift. She raised her weapon and steeled herself; a hooded figure climbed out in the wavering beam of a flashlight and before he could turn she brought the wood crashing down with all the force she could muster. Nerves skewed her aim, or perhaps he sensed a movement, because he twisted away as the blow fell and she caught him across the back of the head. He crumpled to the ground with a shrill cry. Zoe dropped the wood and fell to her knees in the cold sand beside the prone body; the pitch of his scream had filled her with a different kind of dread. She pulled the hood back roughly and stared into the white face beneath it.

'Jesus Christ, Robbie. What the fuck?'

The boy didn't answer, only kept up an insistent crying, the hiccupping sobs of a child in pain. There was blood on the back of his head. He was wearing one woollen glove, his fist balled against his mouth; the other hand was bare.

'*Shit*.' She sat back on her heels, pushed her hair out of her face and looked around, as if someone might have been watching. 'Let's get you inside.'

18

'How are you feeling now?'

She had emptied the ice cube tray into a dishcloth and knotted the corners for a makeshift ice-pack, which Robbie held pressed to his head at the kitchen table, his other hand absently scratching at Horace. The dog sat between the boy's knees, as if understanding that his warm presence was a useful consolation. She had made Robbie some hot milk with honey and crumbled a couple of painkillers in it, while she was on her second strong coffee. Now she leaned back against the sink, watching him. Her earlier wooziness had passed, to be replaced by a pounding ache in her temples.

'It hurts behind my eyes.'

'Is your vision blurry?'

'Sort of. Cannae tell really.'

'You might have a bit of concussion. I didn't hit you that hard.' He shot her a barbed look. 'OK, I guess that's not for me to say. Look, I'm sorry – I thought you were an intruder. I mean, technically you *were* an intruder. What were you *thinking*?' When he didn't reply, she shook her head. 'You were lucky. Where I live, people would shoot you for breaking into their house, ask questions later.'

His face registered a flicker of alarm before he returned his attention to his mug.

'Don't your—' She stopped herself in time, before she said *parents*. 'Your dad – does he know you're out?'

'He's in Belgium.'

'Belgium?'

'Or one of those. France, maybe.'

'Since when?'

He shrugged. 'Last week.'

'So who looks after you when he's away?'

'Ma sister.'

She noted the curl of disgust as he said the word; the undisguised resentment in his voice. No love lost there. Her eyes wandered to the bruise on his face as an idea formed.

'Does she know you sneak out at night?'

'She wouldnae care. She's too stoned to notice anything when she gets home.' He picked at a splinter in the table, not meeting her eye.

'Really? Where's your sister getting pot, out here?' She hoped she sounded suitably disapproving, rather than interested.

'Off Dougie.' He snapped his head up, stricken. 'Dinnae tell him I said that.'

'I wouldn't dream of it.' So Dougie was dealing drugs to a sixteen-year-old; another charming attribute to add to his list. 'Does your dad know?'

He snorted. 'Course not. He wouldnae believe it, anyway. Dougie's his pal.'

She nodded. They looked at one another in silence for a few moments.

'How do you even get out here?' she asked eventually. 'It's five miles from the village.'

'I've got a quad bike.'

She frowned. 'But – don't your neighbours hear you driving it off? I've never heard it either.'

285

'It's ma da's. He keeps it in a lock-up behind the boat yard. There's nae houses out there. Then I cut off across the moors before your turning and leave it up on the cliffs.' He pointed in the general direction. 'You wouldnae hear it. I'm careful.'

'So you've been out here a lot?' When he didn't reply, she pulled up a chair to the corner of the table and sat across from him. 'Robbie – was it you all the time? Did you cut the padlock and put a new one on?'

He nodded miserably, staring into his mug.

'And the dead gull – was that you too?'

A pause, then another nod. 'And the mice.'

'*Mice?*'

'And the burgers.'

'What are you talking about?'

'I caught a couple of mice in ma trap. And I took some burgers out the freezer. I stuffed them behind the radiators the other night, when I did the gull.'

She stared at him, trying to comprehend. '*Why*, Robbie?'

'I thought they'd rot and smell like dead meat but you wouldnae know where it was coming from so you might think there was a dead body under the floor and you wouldnae want to stay here.' The words tumbled out in a rush; he wouldn't look at her.

'No, I mean – *why*? Why do you hate me so much, to play those tricks? What have I done to you?'

He lifted his head then and she saw that his eyes were filled with tears, his lip trembling.

'I wouldnae have hurt you, honest. I was trying to save you.'

She stayed very still. 'From what?'

'I told you – bad stuff happens here.' He dragged the back of his hand across his nose. 'I thought if I could scare you enough you'd leave before they could do something really bad.'

'Who?' A chill crept over her skin. 'Who do you think was going to do something to me?'

His gaze slid away; he pressed his lips together until they turned white and began scratching at the tabletop. She tried another tack.

'Did you draw the picture in my book too?' He nodded again. 'So you were spying on me that day?'

'I wasnae *spying*,' he said, indignant. 'I was on the cliff. You don't *own* the cliff. I used to come out here all the time, before you ever came. To talk to Iain.'

'Like you talk to your mom?'

He made a non-committal movement with his shoulders. Zoe watched him, unsure how to proceed. She recalled reading somewhere that murderers often returned to the scene of their crime, through fixation or guilt. This child was the only one who knew the truth about what happened to his friend in this house, last summer; in this unexpectedly intimate setting, he seemed on the point of letting it spill out. She was conscious that a clumsy or ill-judged question from her would make him clam up for good; she felt an unwelcome responsibility not to screw this up. She wished her head were clearer.

'Did you think . . . ' she hesitated, weighing her words carefully, 'that if you could stop something bad happening to me, it might make up for what happened to Iain that night?'

He was silent for a long time, picking at the wood. 'There was nothing I could have done,' he said in a small voice. 'If I'd have gone after him, it would have been me as well. I wouldnae be here.'

'But you feel guilty, because you didn't try to save him?'

'It should've been me,' he said fiercely, after a further pause. 'It was my idea to come out here at night and film in the house, see if we could prove it was haunted. Then I was the one who was too scared to go in. But it was only because—'

287

'Because what?' she prompted gently, when he fell silent.

'You'll take the piss.'

'I promise I won't.'

His eyes flickered up to meet hers briefly. 'I heard Mam,' he whispered. 'I never told Iain, he'd've said I was mental, but we were down there on the beach and I heard her voice like she was standing right beside me. She said, *Don't you go in there, Robert Logan*, like when she was really cross and she wasnae messing about. And it freaked me out so much I couldnae move, so Iain went on his own, and that was when—' he broke off, his face white.

She knew better than to press him on the details; what Iain did next was the part he had successfully kept to himself for over a year.

'Was Iain filming when he went in, like you planned? Do you think he caught what he saw on his phone?'

A mute shrug, his gaze fixed on the table.

'I wonder what happened to his phone,' she said idly.

'They never found it. He must have had it with him,' Robbie said. But in the split-second before he spoke, she saw it: the way his eyes flicked in the direction of the cellar door. She felt a tingle of excitement.

'Well, I guess we'll never know,' she said. He rubbed a knuckle into the corner of his eye.

'It should've been me,' he repeated quietly. 'And then naebody would've cared.'

'Oh, Robbie, that's not true. What about your dad and your sister, for a start?'

He huffed out a small, bitter laugh. 'Ma sister would be glad if I was dead. She could leave the island then.' He reached up, absently touching a finger to the mark on his cheek.

'Did Annag do that to your face?' Zoe asked.

'Fell off ma bike.' He spoke in a tone so expressionless, it seemed to acknowledge the evident untruth of the statement. He had not even bothered to keep his lies consistent.

'This afternoon you said it was the climbing frame.'

'I cannae remember. I'm always banging maself. I'm clumsy like that.'

Annag had told her the same thing, she recalled. Her dislike for the girl hardened further. Surely Edward must have observed the child's injuries; she made a mental note to speak to him about it. 'Doesn't your dad notice all these bruises when he comes home?'

'He sleeps most of the time when he's home, or goes to the pub. He hates being there without Mam.'

She saw then how much effort it was costing him not to cry. Instinctively, she shunted her chair closer and put an arm around his shoulders. She felt him tense, before his muscles slackened and he leaned his head against her. His clothes smelled of stale cigarettes; she was shocked by the sudden pang of tenderness she felt for this unhappy child, who she guessed had not been cuddled by anyone since his mother died. The soft, snuffling sounds he was making into her sweater told her he was crying. They remained there in silence for a while, the house unusually quiet and motionless around them. Zoe found herself almost laughing at the irony; she had half-imagined she would spend the night with a younger lover, and instead had ended up mothering an unhappy boy. On reflection, she did not regret the turn the evening had taken, though the thought of Edward brought her back to the gravity of her present predicament. She had assaulted and injured a child she barely knew and had no means of getting him back to his family or letting anyone know where he was.

'Listen, Robbie. We've got ourselves a situation here. Your sister might not notice you sneak out at night but she's sure as shit going to notice if you're not there in the morning, right?' She drew back to look at him; when he raised his head from her shoulder she saw that he had been drifting off to sleep and her heart clenched again. 'You can't possibly ride home on that thing after a whack on the head, and I'd drive you –' she saw the flash of fear across his face – 'but I can't right now because I've had too much to drink. And I can't even make a call because the phone's not working.'

At that he shot her a guilty look from under his lashes. 'I know. That was me.'

'You cut the phone?'

'Aye. With ma da's bolt-cutters. I thought you'd be scared if you couldnae call anyone so you'd have to drive into town.'

She sighed. 'Well, nice job, Robbie, because we're screwed now. Unless you have a phone with a signal?'

He shook his head. 'There's no signal anywhere along this part of the coast.'

'Great. Well, all we can do is sit tight for now.' She hesitated. 'Mr Sinclair might be on his way out – he was going to come for dinner. He could take you home. Although it's getting pretty late.'

'He won't come.' He sounded certain.

'How do you know?' She let her arm slip from around his shoulders and looked at him with growing suspicion; he hunched into himself and winced as he shifted in his chair. The moment of intimacy was broken.

'I knifed his tyre.'

'Jesus.' She passed a hand across her forehead. 'Any particular reason?'

'I heard the two of you talking in the playground. When you invited him for dinner. I thought, if he couldnae come out, it would be easier to scare you alone. I'm sorry,' he added, into the neck of his hoodie. 'Can't I stay here with you for tonight?' When he looked up, his eyes were pleading.

Zoe sighed. 'Doesn't look like we have a choice. As long as you don't put any dead animals around the place.' She pointed a stern finger in his face, but he spotted the twinkle in her voice and responded with a tentative smile. 'And no more of that singing either.'

290

The boy's smile faltered. 'What?'

'All the music and the singing, and the prank phone calls. That's got to stop too.' But she saw the seriousness of his expression and her chest tightened.

'I never did any singing,' he said, shaking his head. 'Or the phone. That wasnae me, I swear it. I don't know what you're talking about.'

She watched him; the fear in his eyes appeared genuine, though it might have been no more than a fear of being caught out.

'Never mind. I'll take you into town first thing in the morning – we should get a doctor to look at you. But you'd better back me up, dude. You tell them everything you've been doing out here, all the pranks, and why I acted in self-defence, OK? Now – you want some toast?'

Robbie nodded, wincing as he adjusted his ice-pack. Horace let out a reproachful noise as she stood and crossed to the fridge.

'One other thing,' she said, turning to Robbie as she crouched to empty a pack of the dog's food into a bowl on the floor. 'How did you know about the hand?'

The boy frowned, his eyelids drooping with fatigue. 'What hand?'

'In that picture of yours. You drew me in the water and a hand pulling my ankle. How could you have seen that, from up on the cliff?'

He only looked further confused. 'I didnae see anything. It's just part of the story.'

'What – the McBride story?'

'Aye. Her son. The wee boy. Because they never found him, folk say he's under the water waiting to pull you down to live with him. It's what they tell kids to stop them swimming there. People at school said it was him that got Iain. I drew him getting you as well.' His face closed up briefly, before he looked back at her, curious. '*Was* there a hand, then?'

291

'No, of course not, don't be silly. Strong currents, that's all.' She heard herself give a high, false laugh. 'I wondered where you'd got the idea, that's all.' She turned her back while she cut a few slices of bread, but she could feel his eyes on her, sceptical, and knew that he could tell she was lying, the same way she was certain he had not told her the whole truth.

'It'll happen to me in the end, I know it will,' he said, suddenly, as if to himself, while she slipped the bread into the toaster. She turned slowly to face him.

'What will?'

'Same as happened to Iain. They'll get me too. One day I'll disappear, and naebody will know why.' He did not sound especially fearful, only resigned. Zoe felt a cold tremor along her arms.

'Who, Robbie? Does someone want to hurt you? Is it the same people you think will do something bad to me?' She shook him by the shoulder and felt him flinch away from her. He folded his arms on the table and hid his face; she couldn't tell if he was crying this time or falling asleep. With a deep breath, she smoothed a hand over his velvety close-cropped hair, relieved to see that the wound was only superficial once she had cleaned it up. But she was worried that the blow might have given him a mild concussion, though he seemed lucid enough; she could not really remember how hard she had swung the piece of wood.

There was nothing to be achieved by pushing him further now. It was nearly midnight. Instead she led him upstairs, helped him off with his damp sweatshirt and tucked him into a bed in one of the spare rooms on the second-floor landing. His eyes closed almost as soon as he lay down, and his pinched, wary face softened in sleep; watching him, she felt another stab of maternal pity and guilt. It was heartbreaking to think that a child should have so little kindness in his life. She bent and planted the ghost of a kiss on his forehead before she left the room, the way she always did with Caleb when he was sleeping, but even as she straightened, she was conscious of the wrongness of it, in every sense. What was she doing here, so far from home, kissing this unknown child goodnight, when she should be with Caleb? Her mother was right; she had been selfish. She switched off the light and left the bedroom door ajar. When Mick returned, she would tell him of her decision: she needed to go home.

The kitchen was still warm from the range; she found Horace curled in front of it on his blanket, dozing gently with his muzzle on his paws, twitching occasionally in his dreams. She plucked a cold slice of toast from the toaster and bit off a corner, chewing it dutifully, though it had turned rubbery and she no longer felt hungry; the wine and coffee churned in her stomach. She was too wired now, too uneasy for sleep; the loss of the phone line troubled her more than she wanted to admit, though she could not deny the relief she had felt on learning that Robbie had been behind the snapped padlock and the dead gull, rather than Dougie Reid. At the thought of the lock, her eyes strayed to the cellar door, and she recalled the way Robbie had glanced towards it when she had asked him about Iain's phone. Was it possible, she wondered?

The key turned easily and the door opened on to a flight of steps descending into musty darkness. She reached inside to flick the light switch, but nothing happened. She almost lost her nerve at that and considered retreating, but her curiosity over what Robbie had been doing down there overcame her fear and she returned with the storm lantern, holding it carefully ahead of her to illuminate the rough stone steps as she moved down, one hand on the wall to steady herself.

She had not taken in the cellar properly on her previous

visit with Mick to look at the generator; she had registered only that it gave her an unpleasant feeling. Now, as she shone the lamp around the walls, she realised that this dank room must be the oldest part of the house; much older than the structure that had been built over it. Two of the walls appeared to have been hewn directly out of the rock of the cliffs, and shored up with worn and ancient-looking stone pillars. As the wavering light slid over the walls, she noticed unusual marks carved into the stone, and recalled Charles's story about Tamhas McBride building on the foundations of an old chapel, itself erected to sanctify a pagan site. She shivered, largely because the cellar was so cold; the air held a chill, mineral taint that seemed to seep into her skin, and a faint smell of decay. Probably more of Robbie's rotting burgers, she thought, almost smiling at his childish attempts to frighten her. She would have to clean all that out in the morning.

Because the house was so newly rebuilt, the space was relatively empty; there was only the detritus of building work, stacked in corners. She saw immediately what had caused the crash that had alerted her to Robbie's presence; he had knocked over a tall metal shelf unit that had held half-empty paint pots, a tray of tools and off-cuts of electrical cables. The paint did not appear to have spilled; most likely it was all dried out. She stepped over the fallen shelves, deciding she would not attempt to right it until the morning. There was the silent generator in the centre of the floor, cans of fuel ranged along the wall on the other side. The only other item of interest was a large Victorian dresser with a mirror on top, pushed into the corner opposite the set of steps that led up to the coal hatch. Zoe wondered why it had been left here; perhaps it had miraculously survived the decades of neglect in the house and Mick intended to sell it, but had not yet had the chance to transport it. But the many drawers were all pulled out haphazardly, and the body of the dresser had been inched away from the

294

wall – recently, to judge by the scrape marks in the dust. A frisson of fear and excitement sparked through her, as it had when she discovered Ailsa's book. Robbie had clearly been searching for something down here, before he had given himself away.

She brought the lamp closer and looked into all the drawers, to see nothing but a couple of old screws and a dead spider. Next, she set the light down beside her and proceeded to take out all the drawers, one by one, to check if anything could have fallen down the back. When she was satisfied that the dresser was completely empty, she sat back on her heels and saw how it had been worked away from the wall; she crouched and dragged it – even empty it was a considerable weight – far enough that she could squeeze into the corner. It took her a moment to realise that the flagstones beneath her feet bore blurred inscriptions in curling, archaic letters, too badly worn to read now, but clear enough to see the shapes of Celtic crosses and dates. She recoiled, realising that these were tombstones, meaning that the cellar must have been built over the crypt of the old chapel. Perhaps that would account for the smell that seemed to be growing stronger. She took a deep breath and reprimanded herself; if there were bodies here, they were centuries old and long since crumbled to dust. The thought was not altogether reassuring. She peered in with the light but could see nothing on the floor behind or under the dresser, and was brushing off her jeans when, looking closer, she noticed that the stone flag in the corner was uneven. She crouched to press it and found that it rocked easily under her hand, though it was fitted too tightly for her to prise up with her fingers. Among the fallen tools she found a thin scraper, the kind used to remove old paint and wallpaper; its blade fitted neatly into the crack between the stones, and though it bent alarmingly, she managed to lift the loose flag. Beneath it, she could see a cavity, and inside this was a

295

child's woollen glove. She lifted it out, unsurprised to find a hard, oblong object inside; she shook the glove and a scratched mobile phone in an orange plastic case covered in Star Wars stickers fell into her hand.

She remained crouching, motionless, for what felt like several minutes, while her hands shook uncontrollably. There was no doubt in her mind that this was Iain Finlay's phone, the one the police had tried unsuccessfully to find, and that Robbie had hidden it down here, perhaps thinking this was the last place anyone would look once the initial search was over. There were even grains of sand stuck inside the edge of the casing. He must have found a number of hiding places for it over the past year; Edward said the police had traced the signal to different locations each time it was switched on. But why had Robbie kept it? She could only think that it must contain evidence of some kind; she would confront him when he woke. No; at once she realised what a mistake it would be to let him know she had found it. He plainly did not want any adults to see what was saved there, or he would have handed it in long before.

At this thought her gut twisted, remembering what he had said about the mysterious 'they' he feared would do something bad to her, and make him disappear. Whoever 'they' were, the answer was on this phone, she was certain. She heard her blood thudding in her ears as she pressed the power button, but the screen remained dark; the battery was long dead. She turned the phone over in her hands. It was an old model and her own charger would not fit; she would need to buy or borrow one without arousing suspicion. She knew that she ought to hand it over to the police as soon as possible, and she fully intended to do so, once she had seen for herself what the boy was so afraid of. She would show Edward, too; she needed to talk to him about Robbie and the mark on his face. She slipped the phone into the pocket of her cardigan and picked up the lamp.

The cellar had grown unbearably cold, or perhaps it was simply that she had not moved for a while, and the smell was worse; there must be a problem with the drains, or else mice had got in here and died, if they hadn't been planted by Robbie. She stood, hearing her knees crack, and was distracted by a slight movement in the glass of the dresser. Glancing up, she froze as she looked in the mirror to see a figure in a hood standing at the foot of the stairs that led back to the kitchen.

She surprised herself by not crying out; her voice had stopped in her throat. Her heart skittered, a bitter cold enfolded her whole body and her limbs stiffened, but she could not tear her eyes from it. With shaking fingers she scrabbled at the neck of her shirt for Kaye's pendant; as she drew it out, she thought she heard the figure laugh softly. She could see them clearly in the mirror; what she had taken for a shepherd's waterproofed cloak looked more like an old-fashioned lady's hooded cape. The figure's hands were folded inside its sleeves and its face could not be seen in the shadows. *Don't turn around*, she told herself, in her head, but she knew without seeing. Once more, she sensed that the figure had heard her, and was laughing at her naiveté.

I was on your side, Zoe thought, her eyes fixed on the mirror. She did not think she said the words aloud. *You loved your son; I understand that. I only wanted to defend you.*

She thought then that the figure smiled under its hood, but it was not a reassuring smile. *Time to go*, it said, softly, in Gaelic, the words echoing through her mind; *time to go*. It seemed to take a step towards her, one hand outstretched; panic rushed up through her chest to her throat, she backed away towards the coal hatch steps, thinking she might still outrun it if it moved towards her, but she had forgotten the fallen shelf unit; her foot caught it behind her and she could not stop herself falling. She put a hand out; as she looked up,

297

she glimpsed a gleam of pale skin and hard, dark eyes that fixed on her, unmoving, as if they had been painted. In the next instant, the lamp crashed to the floor and she heard the sound of breaking glass as everything turned to black.

19

It was still dark when she woke to feel hot breath on her face, in her ear a heavy, panting sound. Something cold and damp touched her chin; she yelped and brushed it away, but it was followed by a wet, rasping touch along her cheek and a soft moan. She blinked her eyes open to see two bright pinpricks staring back at her from the gloom, and a black snout quivering an inch from her nose.

'Jesus, Horace.' She laughed shakily, her limbs slack with relief. 'You scared the shit out of me.'

A blade of light pierced the gap between the doors of the coal hatch above; gradually her sight adjusted to the shadows. Raising her head painfully, she put out a hand to lever herself up and drew it back instantly with a cry; she had leaned on a shard of glass from the broken lantern. The memory brought a rush of panic; she peered around the cellar, but could see no sign of anyone except Horace. She hauled herself carefully to her feet and kicked the splinters of glass aside, hoping he had not cut his paws in the dark, before pausing to inspect herself for injuries; besides this new shallow cut to the base of her thumb, there seemed to be nothing worse than minor bruises, though she noticed that she felt unusually tender between her legs, as if she had been penetrated. She could not find an explanation for this, except to think it must be connected with the end of her period. But none of these bruises could compete with the thudding in her head from the wine she had drunk the night before; white-hot bolts of pain shot behind her eyes as she moved. Fragments of memory rushed at her; her hand flew to her pocket to find the outline of the phone. A quick check reassured her that it had not been damaged by her fall. Today she would drive into town and buy a charger for it, and at least one of the island's mysteries might be solved. Then she remembered: *Robbie.*

Cursing, she picked her way across to the steps that led up to the kitchen, where the door at the top stood open. Horace trotted gamely after her. She had no idea what time it might be; she had to get the child back to town, take him to a doctor, explain as best she could what had happened. A sickly light fell through the kitchen windows; the sky outside was heavy and overcast, with bloated clouds pushed across the bay by a gusting wind grown fiercer overnight. Drizzle spattered the panes. The clock above the range showed twenty after nine.

Shit, she said, aloud. The poor kid must still be sleeping, but he should have been at school by now; Edward would have noticed his absence, even if Robbie's negligent sister hadn't. Panicking, she raced up the two flights of stairs to the second floor, calling his name gently, so as not to wake him with too much of a fright, but when she opened the door of his room it was empty, the bed neatly made.

'Robbie?' Her first thought was that he might have gone to the bathroom. She hurried from room to room, calling him, checking all the toilets and washrooms, once catching a glimpse of herself in the mirror and starting at the wild-eyed woman who stared back, her hair tangled and unkempt, a smudge of blood on her face from a cut above her eyebrow where she must have struck her head on the cellar floor when she fell. She called more frantically, telling him the joke was over, there was breakfast waiting, but the house remained silent. She tried the tower, but found no sign of him there either. She revisited the first floor, and the ground, until she had searched every room and even the larger cupboards twice and was forced to concede that Robbie had gone. Perhaps he had woken early and not wanted to face her, she told herself, in an effort at reassurance, or else he wanted to avoid a confrontation with his sister. He was probably even now warm and dry in Edward's classroom, with no one any the wiser about his nocturnal adventures. But the front door remained bolted on the inside, the back door of the kitchen that led out to the veranda was also locked, with the key hanging on its hook. His single woollen glove still sat on the table; Zoe's eyes travelled uneasily to the cellar door. Had he let himself out that way? She could think of no other explanation, but that meant that he must have crept past her unconscious form. The thought troubled her, as did the one that followed on its heels: if he had come through the cellar, he must have seen that she had discovered his hiding place for Iain's phone, though he had evidently not attempted to search her for it. Perhaps it was the knowledge of that discovery, and the fear it bred, that had caused him to flee.

'Come on, Horace,' she said, unlocking the back door and grabbing up her boots and jacket, pausing to stow the phone safely in an inside zipped pocket. The dog looked at her with that same expression of resigned exasperation, but loyally followed her down to the beach.

The wind was stronger out here than it had appeared from the shelter of the house. Towering grey waves gathered pace and smashed against the foot of the cliffs; the gulls appeared tossed like confetti on the high currents that whipped her hair across her face and into her mouth. She yanked it back and twisted it inside her collar as she set off up the cliff path, battling into a gale that grew stronger the higher she climbed, flattening the heather and hurling rain into her eyes,

301

until she feared it might pluck her off the face of the rock and fling her out into the whirling air. As she crested the final rise of the path where it levelled out at the top, she looked to her left and there, on a patch of clear ground, she saw a muddy quad bike. Her stomach plummeted; she ran over, to find a helmet secured to the seat. If Robbie had not taken the bike – she tried to untangle her thoughts in the bellowing wind – then how had he returned home? Or had he not gone home at all?

She hurried back towards the cliff edge, remembering the boy's ominous words the night before, his gloomy certainty that 'they' would make him disappear like Iain. What had he been trying to tell her? Tufts of bleached grass and uneven erosion conspired to play tricks on the eye; it was hard to tell, right there at the edge, where solid ground ended and the drop began. Panic gripped her. Suppose she had hit Robbie harder than she realised? If he had been concussed by the blow after all – worse, if she had caused some internal head trauma – and he had come up here in search of his bike but he'd been dazed, or his vision had been affected, up here, in this weather – if he'd strayed too close to the cliff, there was every chance he might have—

She stopped, steadying herself, and hooked a finger inside Horace's collar to pull him back; when she was sure he was sitting obediently, she shuffled close enough to the overhang that she could peer over to the boiling white mass at its foot, where the sea smashed over black teeth of rock. The wind gusted dangerously and, looking down, she experienced a moment of vertigo; the sensation of a hand in her back, between the shoulder blades, pushing her forward. She stumbled, caught off balance; dizziness clouded her vision and briefly, as she pitched forward, she thought she glimpsed a shape below, under the waves. But she righted herself and dropped to her knees, clutching at clumps of grass, until the giddiness passed and she felt stable enough to edge herself backwards on to the

302

path. Her pulse beat wildly in her throat; the storm wind, rather than blowing away the fog of her hangover, seemed only to have intensified the pain. She was starving too, almost faint with hunger; that would explain how she had almost lost her balance. She needed to eat before she could think clearly. Horace stood beside her, his tail thumping against her side; she slung an arm gratefully around his neck.

'Come on,' she muttered, hauling herself to her feet. 'Breakfast. And then we have to find Robbie. Otherwise . . . ' She left the thought unfinished.

She drove first to the Stag, snatching bites from a piece of toast in her lap on the way; guilt had stopped her lingering over food in the kitchen. In the car park she sat for a few minutes in the car, watching the rain lash at the windscreen.

'You'd better stay here in the dry,' she told Horace, switching off the engine. 'I'll get you home in a minute, I promise.'

The public entrances were locked, though she could hear a vacuum cleaner dimly droning from the unlit interior. It was unlikely that Annag would be here at this time, but Zoe could think of no other way to find her. Making her way around the back of the pub to the beer garden, her jacket pulled up over her head against the squall, she found the Drummonds' private entrance and rang the bell. As she pressed it for a second time, Kaye opened the door, breathless in loose-fitting workout clothes, her pink hair tied up in a scarf.

'Caught me doing my Pilates— Oh my *God*,' she said, as she looked Zoe up and down. 'Come inside. What happened – have you had an accident?'

Zoe stepped into a narrow hallway at the foot of a flight of stairs, touching a hand to her face; she had forgotten that she had not stopped to clean herself up before jumping in the car, and that her appearance might be liable to cause alarm. The cut on her thumb had bled down her wrist and on to

303

her sleeve; the wound on her brow was also sticky with congealed blood, and her jeans were muddy at the knee where she had collapsed on the cliff path.

'It's worse than it looks,' she said. 'Is Annag here?'

'Annag?' Kaye blinked. 'She doesn't come on till eleven.' She grinned, as if to make light of the situation. 'I know we've a reputation here in the isles, but even we don't open the pubs at breakfast time.'

'Where can I find her?'

Kaye's face grew serious. 'She'll be having a lie-in, if I know her. What do you want Annag for?'

'I need to ask her something. Where does she live?'

Kaye rattled off the address, but bit her lip, clearly anxious at Zoe's manner. 'Do you want me to call her for you? It's no bother.'

'No, it's fine. I'd better go.' She didn't want to upset Kaye with thoughts of Robbie's disappearance if he was safely at home or school. 'Is it far?'

'Stonecutters' Row? Not at all – it's the wee lane of cottages behind the green. Not the pretty coloured ones facing the kirk, but the road behind that, where the tourists don't go. Zoe,' she called, as Zoe turned to leave, 'are you sure you won't come in and have a cup of tea while I call Annag for you? You look . . . ' she hesitated ' . . . like you might need one.'

Zoe rubbed at the blood on her sleeve. 'No – really. But there is one thing – there's a problem with the phone up at the house. I think the line's broken.'

Kaye frowned. 'Broken? What, come down in the wind, you mean?'

'I guess. Anyway, it's not working. Can we get someone out to fix it?'

'In this?' Kaye gestured to the door and shook her head, with a hint of indulgence, as if humouring a tourist. 'These storms are set in for the next couple of days, they say, and

304

it's going to get worse tonight. They've cancelled all the ferries – the last one left at eight this morning. Mick rang to say he's stuck there till they're back up and running. We'll no get anyone out from the mainland now, I'm sorry. If I were you, I'd stock up on fresh milk and bread while you're in town – there might not be any deliveries for a wee while.'

Zoe nodded, pressing the knuckle of her thumb to her teeth as she processed the implications. Catching her expression, Kaye laid a hand on Zoe's arm.

'The invitation still stands, you know – if you want to come up to the pub tonight, that room's waiting for you. I know I'd be happier if you were here than worrying about you out there in the storm, with no phone working.'

'Thanks, that's kind.' She left Kaye with a wave and a forced smile, but all she could think of was that roiling water at the foot of the cliff, and the shape she thought she had seen.

As she turned into Stonecutters' Row, she saw what Kaye meant about it not being a street for tourists. Unlike the carefully preserved holiday rental cottages facing the green, done up in their pastel colours with neatly tended gardens, the houses here sagged under a weight of neglect, and looked more melancholic in the rain. Roof tiles were missing; old bicycles rusted in the front yards, and in one an unwanted fridge slumped against the wall with its door hanging open. Zoe pushed open the gate of number two, neither the worst nor the best of the row, and pressed the buzzer. Rain poured in a cataract from a blocked gutter at the side of the front door. She could not hear whether the bell had sounded, so to be sure she jammed her finger on it while hammering on the glass with her other hand. After a disproportionately long time, she heard shuffling steps from inside, accompanied by creative swearing.

Annag opened the door and stared at her with undisguised

resentment. She was wrapped in a dirty towelling dressing gown, her hair hanging in dank strands around her face, which bore smudges of make-up she had not bothered to remove before bed. A smell of stale cigarettes gusted out from the house behind her.

'Is Robbie here?' Zoe asked, trying to keep the panic tamped down.

'What the fuck?' Annag folded her arms. 'He's at school, isn't he? Why would he be here?'

'But – you *have* seen him this morning?'

'No.' The girl regarded her with scorn. 'I was literally asleep until you woke me up. I was working till gone midnight last night,' she added, defensive. 'Robbie gets himself to school. What's it to do with you?'

Zoe realised her mistake; she should have checked the school first. If Annag had been asleep, Robbie could have come home, changed and got himself there without her knowing any different. There was the matter of the bike, but she pushed that to the back of her mind; maybe he had run out of gas.

'Nothing – I'm sorry. I'm sure he is.' She began to back down the path. Water ran in rivulets down the inside of her collar; her jeans were soaked through. Annag let out a theatrical sigh.

'He's no in fucking school again, is he? Did they send you to find him? Running errands for your boyfriend now, are you?' Without waiting for an answer, she held the door wider and made an extravagant, sweeping gesture with her hand. 'Well, he's no here. You can check if you want. Try the kirkyard, or the bookshop. Or down at your place –' she raised a knowing eyebrow – 'he sometimes bunks off out there. He's obsessed with it.'

'He's run off before, then?' Zoe tried not to sound too hopeful.

'All the time. Wee fucker wants attention.' Annag fixed her

with a defiant stare while she rummaged in the pocket of her dressing gown and brought out a packet of cigarettes.

I'd run away too if I had to live with you, Zoe almost said, but reined herself in. She was too sharply aware that she could be held responsible for losing Robbie, and if he didn't return soon, she would need the family's understanding; it would not be smart to make a further enemy of his sister.

'He'll turn up,' Annag said airily, propping the unlit cigarette in her mouth as she closed the door. 'He always does.' Adding, under her breath but loud enough for Zoe to catch, 'No that it's any of your fucking business.'

Zoe half-ran the short distance across the green to the school, hampered by the various aches in her knees, groin and head from the night before. The rain was so dense now she could barely see across the playground; whipped by the wind into billowing curtains of water that hit the ground so hard it rebounded up to waist height. She was surprised to find the playground gate and the front door unlocked, so that she walked in unhindered, her clothes dripping over the colourful welcome mat. She hesitated in front of a glass-fronted office with one small desk and chair and a sign that read 'Mrs L. McCrae, School Secretary'. Of Mrs McCrae herself, there was no sign. Zoe continued along the corridor with the children's paintings where she had spoken to Kaye the previous afternoon until she caught sight of Edward through the window of a yellow door at the end; he was making animated gestures, apparently doing an impression of a lunatic gorilla. From behind the door she heard peals of childish laughter and found herself smiling; she watched him with a sudden surge of affection and thought again how much Caleb would be delighted with him, so that she almost forgot the gravity of her purpose there.

She knocked on the classroom door and walked in; Edward started, clearly caught off guard. He moved towards her, but her gaze raked the room, scanning for Robbie. She could not see him, though she noticed a sturdy girl with purple-ribboned braids lean across to her companion and whisper ostentatiously in her ear behind a cupped hand; both girls burst into loud giggles, staring at her with knowing expressions in identical wide blue eyes that marked them as Kaye's daughters.

'That's enough, Megan,' Edward said, over his shoulder. He pushed his hair out of his eyes and lowered his voice. 'What's happened? You look—' he stopped, taking in her cuts and bruises.

'Like shit. I know,' she whispered back. 'Where's Robbie?'

'He's not in yet. Why?' His eyes registered her urgency. 'Let's talk out here.' He took her by the elbow and guided her towards the door. 'Mrs McCrae, would you keep an eye on them while I deal with something?' This last was directed to a stern-faced woman in a Fair Isle sweater who sat in one corner, helping a curly-haired boy with his reading. She responded with a curt nod, but her eyes on Zoe were narrowed and disapproving.

He led Zoe to the end of the corridor, but kept his voice to a whisper. 'Robbie truants all the time. There's not much I can do without involving Social Services, and I'm reluctant to do that at this stage – it's hard to get his dad to acknowledge there's a problem. Why are you so worried about him?'

'He came to the house last night. He's the one who's been prowling around, playing tricks. He hurt himself and I put him to bed, but this morning he was gone and his quad bike's still there.' The words tumbled out; she paused to draw breath. 'He seemed really unhappy – I was afraid he might have taken off and . . . ' She let her hands fall empty to her sides.

Edward nodded, processing this.

'He's probably afraid he's in trouble, that's all. Let's give him till the end of the day – if he's not home by four, we'll have another think. Looks like you hurt yourself too.' He raised a hand as if to touch her face; she flinched away.

'How can you be so calm? This is an eleven-year-old kid, out there somewhere in *this*.' She gestured to the window, opaque with running water. The sky outside had grown so dark it appeared to be almost dusk.

'Because it's not the first time,' Edward said wearily. 'He'll have found somewhere warm and dry to hide away. You should try the bookshop – Charles has been known to harbour him, though I've asked him not to encourage it.' He shook his head, as if there was nothing to be done about Charles. 'Look, I'm sorry about last night. Some bastard slashed my tyre. I tried calling you but the line was completely dead. I didn't want you to think I'd stood you up.' He offered her a nervous smile.

'I know. Robbie did it. He wanted to stop you coming out to the house.'

'Little shit.' Edward balled his hand into a fist. 'I won't get that money back then. Did he try to attack you?'

'No, he was—' She broke off, her attention distracted. The semicircular window that overlooked the playground offered a view right across the green to the kirkyard beyond. Though the window was blurry with rain, she was certain she could make out a figure in a hooded cloak standing motionless between the gravestones. Her throat tightened; she put a hand out to the wall to steady herself.

'Are you sure you're all right?' Edward touched her arm gently. 'That cut on your head looks pretty nasty.'

'You can see that, right?' She clutched at his sleeve, her voice hoarse. 'That – *person*, in the graveyard?'

He squinted and peered through the glass, then gave her an odd, sideways look. 'Of course.'

'Really?' She could hear her voice shaking. 'Do you know who it is?'

He rubbed the pane with his sleeve and looked again.

309

'Unless I'm mistaken, that's Charles. It looks like his big coat. Although I can't see any sign of Horace . . . '

'Damn.' She let go of his arm. 'Horace is in my car. I left him there out of the rain.'

'Hold on, then – I'll come with you. We can ask Charles if he's seen anything of Robbie.' He darted a glance over his shoulder at the classroom. 'She'll be all right with them for a few minutes. They're more scared of her than they are of me. Wait there.' He dashed back down the corridor and returned a couple of minutes later with a waterproof jacket.

They ran across the playground through the downpour together, setting their shoulders against the wind. The figure in the kirkyard had not moved, as far as Zoe could see; it stood there, gaze fixed on the ground. Her gut tightened; she tried to swallow against the familiar sensation of nausea rising in her throat as last night's memories of the reflection in the mirror jagged across her mind. In the road alongside the green, the drains had started to overflow; brown water gushed in torrents through the gutters. She stopped by her car and let Horace out of the back seat, keeping one eye on the hooded figure; the dog flew out like a greyhound from a trap and sped across the road with an energy she had never guessed him to possess. She tried to call him back, but her voice was lost in the wind; he was lucky that there was no traffic. At his frantic barks, the figure in the kirkyard turned; she felt a momentary twist of horror until she saw, as they approached, that it was indeed Charles, in exactly the kind of long waxed coat she had supposed the person out on the moors to be wearing, the first time she saw them. The old bookseller drew back his hood and crouched, smiling, to meet his berserk dog, who hurled himself at his master as if they had been separated for years. Her heart thudded at her ribs with relief, and once more she sensed Edward looking at her oddly.

310

'What are you doing out here, Professor?' he asked Charles, when they reached him, standing by a tall Celtic cross.

'On my way to open up the shop.' Charles eyed him carefully. 'What's brought you away from the children in this? And Zoe – my goodness! You look a little the worse for wear, if you don't mind my saying so. Has Horace not been looking after you?' He tousled the dog's ears; Horace was leaping around him like a puppy.

She glanced away, embarrassed. 'He's happy to get away. It's been a bit of a morning.'

'Robbie Logan's run off again,' Edward shouted, over the gale. 'He was out at the McBride house last night, and this morning he'd vanished. You haven't seen him, I suppose?'

'Ah.' Charles wiped the rain from his face. 'I'm afraid not. I'm a little late opening today, as you see. I didn't sleep too well.' He glanced at Zoe, almost apologetically. 'I suggest you and I get warm and dry inside, Zoe, and you can tell me what's happened. Robbie might decide to turn up once I'm open. I'll let you know, Edward, if he does.'

Edward turned to Zoe. 'I'll see if I can get my tyre fixed at lunchtime. If not, I'm sure Charles will lend me his old jalopy – one way or another, I'll come out and see you once school has finished, let you know what's going on. Don't worry – I'm sure we'll have heard from Robbie by then.'

He smiled, and laid a hand on her arm; she knew that Charles had noticed it. She thanked him, and turned to follow Charles towards the gate. As she did so, she glanced down at the granite plinth of the cross where he had stood and saw, with a quick shiver, that it was a memorial to Tamhas McBride. A thought struck her.

'Where's Ailsa?' she called after him. He stopped abruptly, turning to look at her through the squalls of rain, and cupped his hand to his ear, though she was sure he had heard.

'Pardon?'

'Ailsa – where's her grave? Is she here?'

He smiled as he waited for her to catch him up, and swept an arm around the kirkyard. 'A suspected murderess, suicide and witch, in consecrated ground? What do you think?'

She swiped water from her brows. 'So where was she buried, then?'

He hesitated – a beat too long, Zoe thought.

'No one knows. Come on into the shop and dry off, and I'll tell you the story.'

'The villagers didn't even want her buried on the island,' Charles said, setting a steaming mug of coffee before her. She sat at the broad table in the bookshop's back room with a selection of pastries from the bakery, a blanket tucked around her shoulders and her jacket on the back of a chair in front of the radiator, while he pottered about in the kitchen, feeding Horace. 'Bonar wrote to William to say that the reverend had understandably refused burial in the kirk and it was thought best that unconsecrated ground be found somewhere on the mainland. Even then, you see, they worried about her grave becoming a focus of unhealthy fascination. Bonar offered to take responsibility for the discreet interment of the corpse, if William would meet the bill. He had to pay labourers from the mainland to carry the coffin, as none of the islanders would touch it.'

He pulled up the chair opposite and helped himself to a croissant. Horace flung himself across Charles's boots as if to prevent him leaving.

'But there's no record of where she was taken?'

'We know the coffin was taken off the island by boat, accompanied by Bonar. After that, nothing official.' Charles rubbed crumbs from his moustache with his thumbnail. 'There was a paupers' graveyard in the grounds of the lunatic asylum in Inverness. That's the most likely, from hints Bonar gave William afterwards. It would have been fairly easy to have her buried there anonymously, if sufficient money changed

312

hands, and William seems to have been glad to pay to make the business disappear.'

'That's so sad. An unmarked grave.' She looked up at him. 'And yet you don't sound convinced.'

'There's one curious thing. A story grew up, recorded by a local magistrate in his diary, that the two men who were hired to bring her coffin over on the boat went around afterwards saying they thought it was too light to contain a body. Of course, they may have just enjoyed spinning a good yarn in the pub, but the rumour certainly took hold at the time.'

'What do you think Bonar did with her, then?'

He hesitated. 'It's always possible that he donated her corpse to his doctor friend, either for payment or as a quid pro quo for signing the death certificate. A medical man at the time would have given a great deal for the opportunity to study a healthy corpse in such an unusual state of preservation after death, you can imagine. All completely illegal, of course, which is why Bonar would have had to concoct a story for William. But there's no way of knowing for certain.'

'Or maybe she never left the island.'

Charles gave her an odd look. 'Where would you get that idea?'

'I've seen her.' She glanced up to meet his eye, but met only with a quizzically raised brow. 'Out on the moors, walking, in a kind of hooded cloak. And last night. I saw her in the cellar, before I fell.' When he said nothing, she set her jaw and fixed him with an accusing stare. 'So have you – I know you have. That's why you won't come to the house, isn't it – because you see her too?'

'You're very tired, Zoe, and you're understandably worried about Robbie—'

'Don't give me that! You're the one who's so sure about ghosts, or whatever you want to call them. Yesterday, when you first woke up, you said, "Is she still here?" You didn't mean your cleaner, you meant Ailsa. Well, didn't you?' She

313

heard her voice growing high and strained. Charles merely regarded her for a long time.

'Did you see her face?' he asked eventually.

'Not really.' She lowered her eyes. 'It was more a *sense*.'

'But you're sure it was Ailsa?' He spoke very gently, as if to a distraught child.

'Yes! I just *knew*.'

'Had you – forgive me for asking – but had you had a drink?'

She flushed. 'Yesterday – a little. But the first two times, not a drop. I was cycling or driving across the moors.'

'Could it not have been someone in a long hooded coat, like mine?' He gestured to the kitchen, where his coat was hanging on the back of the door, rainwater puddling on the floor beneath it.

'I thought of that, but they seemed to vanish into thin air.' She had begun to feel foolish, like a patient who comes to the doctor convinced they have a life-threatening condition, only to be diagnosed with a common cold.

'Hm. Any more of those unusual visions you mentioned?' he asked, taking a gulp of his coffee. 'The ones that match Ailsa's?'

This time she felt the colour suffuse her entire face and neck. 'Last night, I dreamed—' She broke off, covering her eyes with her hands, as if to hide herself from his searching gaze. 'I dreamed I *was* her. And I saw the whole thing – the séance, or whatever it's called, through her eyes.'

'Well – she describes it in some detail in the journal. It's not surprising if that's lodged in your imagination—'

'Tamhas was there, and then someone else appeared. Or some*thing*. And he—' She shuddered and lowered her hands to the table.

He leaned forward, intrigued. 'You saw Tamhas in this dream?' When she nodded, he frowned. 'Wait there.' He crossed the room to the glass-fronted cabinet where he kept the box with the photograph of Ailsa he had shown her the first time he told her the story. When he returned, he laid a sepia portrait on the table in front of her, and watched with a shrewd expression as she gasped.

'That's him!' She stared up at Charles, her mouth hanging open, and tapped her finger on the heavy, bristled face that glared imperiously into the lens. 'That was the man I saw. He was wearing that same patterned waistcoat, though not the jacket. He was in shirtsleeves.'

'Interesting. I haven't shown you this photograph before, have I?'

'I don't think so. No, I'm sure you haven't.'

'And you couldn't have seen him in a book, perhaps?'

'I haven't read any books about him.'

Charles nodded, and this time his manner reminded her of a doctor reluctantly making a diagnosis about which he had hoped to be proved wrong. She pressed her hands to her face again, steepling her fingers over her nose and mouth.

'In these dreams – visions, whatever – I feel like I'm *becoming* her. Like she's taking me over.' She felt tears rising; all the exhaustion of the previous night rushed in on her as she fought them back. 'Charles – why is this happening to me?'

He gave her a long look, stern but compassionate. 'I think you could answer that yourself, Zoe, if you put your mind to it.'

She picked up her coffee and avoided his eye. Horace padded over amiably and laid his muzzle on her thigh, apparently having forgiven her for the night's disruptions.

'Hey, boy,' she said weakly, fussing with his ears. 'I bet you're glad to be home, eh. Sorry I was such a lousy mom.' As she said it, the words struck her with unexpected force; she found herself blinded by sudden tears and a choking sob that jammed in her throat as she tried to swallow it down.

315

'You're not a lousy mother, Zoe,' Charles said, his expression deadly serious. 'Far from it.'

'Don't say that. You don't know anything about me.' The sob fought its way to the surface; she made a hiccupping sound as it burst out. 'Look at me. A little boy was in my care and I couldn't keep him safe. I failed him. Don't you understand that?'

She glanced up at him through her tears and almost recoiled; his ice-blue eyes seemed to pierce her and lay her open, and in that instant she had the sense that he understood everything, and always had, from the beginning. He reached across the table and laid a cool, dry hand over hers.

'It wasn't your fault,' he said quietly.

'It was completely my fault,' she whispered.

A long silence unfolded; they sat like that for a few minutes, listening to the slash of the rain against the windows and the roaring and sucking of the gale. Eventually, Zoe withdrew her hand and rummaged in her pocket for a tissue.

'Robbie will be all right,' Charles said firmly, gathering up the coffee mugs as he pushed his chair back.

She frowned at him briefly, as if she had forgotten what they were talking about.

'You said before that he was scared,' she murmured. 'You were right. He thinks he's in danger. He told me last night *they*'ll get him sooner or later.'

Charles turned at the kitchen door. 'Did he really? That's more than he's ever said to me. He didn't say who, I suppose?'

'Whoever got Iain. Or *what*ever.' A shiver ran through her. 'He knows what Iain saw in the house that night, that's for sure.' She felt conscious then of the phone in her jacket. She ought to turn it over to Charles, she knew, but a stubbornness in her needed to see what had terrified Iain so badly that he had run up on to the cliff edge in the dark, before she showed it to anyone else. If whatever was in the house could be captured on film, it would be confirmation that she was not losing her mind.

'He'll confide in us eventually,' Charles said, from the kitchen. She heard him pouring more coffee.

'If he comes back.'

'Oh, he will.'

She stood, shrugging on her sodden jacket, suddenly irritated by his blithe optimism. 'You say that like you know where he is.'

'What I know is that Robbie Logan has a strong survival instinct,' he said calmly. 'He's needed it, in that family. You mustn't blame yourself – he obviously trusted you.'

'Not enough to stop him running away,' she said, grimly. The photograph of Tamhas stared at her from the table; she turned it face down before she left. She had seen enough of those eyes the previous night.

On her way back to the car she called in at the hardware store and scoured the rack of phone chargers, but the model she wanted was not on display. When she asked the stout, grey-haired man behind the counter for the one she needed, he narrowed his eyes and she feared he could read her thoughts, or see the outline of Iain's phone in her pocket.

'Hold on – I'll see if we've any left out the back,' he said, tucking a pencil behind his ear. 'Not much call for them these days, see – naebody's got those phones now.'

But he shuffled back a few minutes later with a packet in his hand.

'You're in luck,' he said, sliding it across the counter as she scrabbled in her purse for the right money. 'I thought you Americans were all up to date with the latest technology,' he added, with a grin.

'Not me, I'm afraid.' She forced a smile. 'I'm old-school. I'm not even properly American,' she added, growing flustered as she riffled through the unfamiliar notes, 'so maybe that

317

explains it. My grandmother was Scottish. From round here. Not this island, I mean, but this area.' She was talking too much, she knew, because she could feel him watching her closely and it was making her nervous.

'You're practically a local, then. Here—' He leaned over and pointed out the correct bill. She couldn't tell if he was being sarcastic.

'That storm's getting worse,' he remarked, nodding to the door, as she tucked her change away. 'Must be bleak out there at the McBride house, with this wind.'

'Oh, it's quite cosy once you're inside,' she said brightly, keen to get away as fast as possible and avoid any questions about the house. It was only as she zipped up her purse that she realised there was money missing. She paused in the doorway to recount. She could not be entirely sure how much had gone – not a huge sum, but enough to make a difference; thirty or forty pounds, perhaps. Her stomach somersaulted; Robbie must have taken it from her bag before he slipped out that morning. But whether the theft suggested anything about his intentions, she had no idea.

20

It was nearly midday by the time she returned to the house and shut herself in against the weather. The rooms looked flat and ordinary in the overcast daylight, all the skewed, dancing shadows of the previous night vanished. She went straight to the kitchen and tore the plastic cover off the new charger, cutting her finger on the jagged edges in her haste, and plugged the phone into a socket above one of the counters so that she could keep an eye on its progress. For a while she stood over it, impatiently expecting to see the battery light appear, but the phone must have been so damp, or else had not been charged for so long, that there was no immediate sign of life. Eventually she forced herself to give it time, and made her reluctant way upstairs to strip off her soaking clothes in the bathroom.

Under the stinging needles of a hot shower, she became aware of how many places she hurt from the fall the night before. Looking down at her naked body through the streaming water, she noticed dark, painful bruises blossoming on her knees and elbows, as well as the cuts to her hands and arms where the glass of the hurricane lamp had caught her. But she could not explain the marks across her breasts and thighs. Peering closer through the steam, she saw that they looked

319

exactly like the bruise she had found on her hip that morning after the first of her dreams; like nothing so much as small bite marks, livid crimson welts where the skin had been sucked hard or tugged by teeth. She must have fallen harder than she thought, she told herself, and caught her chest on the sharp edge of the metal shelves on the way down. Afterwards, with a towel wrapped around her hair, she examined her face in the misted mirror. How haggard she looked, with that great bruise swelling to purple on her eyebrow, and shadows under her eyes as if she hadn't slept in a year. She ought to rest now; there was nothing more she could do as far as Robbie was concerned until Edward came over at the end of the school day.

But she could not stay idle for long; she put on clean clothes and wandered the house, returning to the kitchen every few minutes to check the progress of the phone, missing Horace and the reassuring padding of his paws on the wooden floor. She could not settle to reading, and the thought of taking out her sketchbook, with its pictures that seemed to have come straight from Ailsa's journal, sickened her. She heated a carton of soup on the stove, more for something to do than from any real appetite, and left it to go cold after a few spoonfuls. Outside, the wind slammed against the window panes and chased around the gables and the turret like a woman crying.

On one of her tours, as she passed the telephone table in the entrance hall and saw that the message light was still flashing, she remembered that she had not listened to the new message from the night before; she had switched it off in a panic, fearing the recurrence of that sickly voice intoning *Time to go*. Now, in this muted daylight, she felt braver, and hesitated only briefly before pressing the button.

It began with that same strange, rhythmic static, like the turning of an old record; her skin prickled coldly, but the words, when they came, flooded her with relief: Caleb, his

320

voice high and peevish, the way it sounded when he was overtired and not getting his own way.

'Mom-*my*! When are you coming? You said it was soon!'

She smiled at the familiar whiny tone; Caleb could be exhaustingly stubborn when he wanted his own way. But she was knifed with guilt too; she had had barely any contact with him for days. She had thought it might be easier to talk freely to him while she was here, with the advantage of distance; now it only felt that her journey had put another obstacle between them. Of course he couldn't understand her absence. It was selfish and deluded to have imagined he would. She should call right away; he would wind himself up if she didn't. Nearly six in the morning there, she thought, checking her watch; Dan would be getting him up for school in half an hour anyway. It was only when she picked up the receiver that she remembered the severed phone line. She couldn't call them, and if Dan tried to ring again and found the line dead, he would assume she had cut herself off deliberately; he would start harassing Kaye, or quite possibly jump on a plane and come out to check on her in person. She must stall that at all costs. Maybe it would be best, she thought, replacing the receiver, if she took Kaye up on her offer to stay at the pub that night. She could use their phone; that might at least appease Dan for now, and she couldn't deny that after the previous night the prospect of an ordinary room, surrounded by other people, offered a certain comfort. She decided to drive into town in the afternoon, to save Edward the journey, and take an overnight bag with her.

She supposed she must have slept, because she became aware of the doorbell echoing through the house, followed by a furious hammering; she opened her eyes, momentarily disconcerted, to find herself lying on the sofa in the downstairs drawing room, where they had discovered Ailsa's book. Rain lashed steadily against the French doors, with greater ferocity than before; the gale had worked itself up to a vicious temper and the room was almost dark. Shivering, she pushed herself to her feet as the bell rang again; her watch told her it was quarter to four. She raked her hands quickly through her hair as she hurried along the corridor, wishing she had woken in time to tidy her appearance before Edward arrived, conscious of how washed-out and downright old she must look to him. But when she opened the front door, she was surprised to see Dougie Reid standing in the porch in full waterproofs, his pointed features scrunched against the rain streaming from his hood. Instinctively she stepped back. He dangled a car key between his thumb and forefinger.

'A'right, hen. Christ, what happened to your face?' He pointed at her eye.

'I hit my head.' She waited.

'Looks nasty. You want to be more careful. Listen – I need a favour.' He grinned at her wary expression. 'No that kind of favour, don't look so worried. I've been sent to get wee Robbie's quad bike back.'

'Have they found him?' She almost stumbled forward in her eagerness for good news. His face turned serious.

'No. And that's no like him at all – folk are starting to get worried. Bill McCrae's called a meeting in the pub in half an hour, everyone's to go along. He wants to organise search parties. He wants you there and all, since you were the last to see him.'

She didn't like the way he looked at her as he said this, the weight of implication in his tone. 'OK, I can be there. So what's the favour?'

'I need you to drive my truck to town while I take the bike.' He jangled the keys at her.

She backed away, shaking her head. 'I can't drive your truck. Besides, how would I get home?'

'I can give you a ride after.'

She did not miss the lascivious glint in his eye. 'I wouldn't want to put you to the trouble.'

'Nae bother. It's either that or you bring me out here later to collect it.' He waggled the key more insistently.

'I – I'm not good with big vehicles. I had a car accident earlier this year,' she added quietly. 'I'm still a little shaken by it, I get nervous. And with this weather—'

'Ach, you'll no meet anything on the roads tonight. It's dead easy, you know the way.'

'I was kind of – expecting someone.' She glanced at her watch.

'Edward, you mean?' His mouth twitched in a smile. 'He's gone on up to the pub for the meeting. Lucky coincidence – he came round to see Annag after school, I was there and we decided it was time to talk to Bill. He mentioned he'd promised to come out and tell you what was happening. I was coming for the bike so I said I could kill two birds with one stone.'

She didn't like the way he said this, nor the way he rested his gaze on her; there was an impertinence to it, a knowingness. When she hesitated, his eyes narrowed. 'A wee boy's gone missing, Zoe. Folk muck in when something like this happens. That's what we do round here.'

There was a long silence, full of unspoken implication.

'OK. I'll get my bag.' If she grabbed a toothbrush and change of underwear now, she thought, there would be no need for him to drive her home later; she could stay at Kaye's and avoid that situation at least. She hovered on the mat, watching the wind blow gusts of water on to the tiles inside the front door, aware that she could not very well leave him standing outside. 'Wait in here, then, I won't be a minute.'

'Nae rush.' He stepped inside and drew his hood back, pulling the door shut behind him. 'If you've got the kettle on I'll have a brew while I'm waiting.'

'I'll only be a second,' she said, anxious, but he had already begun strolling towards the kitchen. She hurried to get ahead of him.

'I wouldnae mind a cup anyway,' he said pleasantly, but with an edge that suggested he expected to get his way. 'There's nae hurry. It's going to be a bitch of a ride across the moor on that bike – I'd like to get some hot liquid inside me first.' She saw the grin and waited for the inevitable. 'Bet you wouldnae mind that either, eh?'

And there it was. She turned on him. 'What are you, fifteen?'

'All right, hen, only having a laugh. No need to be so uptight.'

'Did Annag ask you to collect the bike?' she asked, to change the subject, setting the kettle on the range and rinsing a mug, hoping to get this delay over as quickly as possible. Being alone in the house with Dougie and no working phone was inducing a kind of muted panic which she felt she must disguise, in case he should sense her fear and toy with it.

'Aye. Poor kid's going out of her head with worry.'

Zoe recalled Annag's attitude that morning when she had learned that her brother was missing. 'Give her a joint, then,' she said crisply. 'That'll calm her down.'

Anger flashed across his small, colourless eyes for an instant, but he produced a thin smile. 'Sounds like someone else round here could do with one and all.' The smile vanished. 'Seriously, I don't like what you're implying there. I wouldnae like to think you're repeating that to anyone.' He pointed an oil-stained finger at her. 'Big Jim Logan's one of my oldest pals. I keep an eye on those kids for him when he's working.'

'Well, you didn't do a very good job last night, did you?'

His mouth curved back to a grin, and this time there was malice in it. 'Wasnae my roof he was under when he disappeared. It's no me the police want to talk to.'

They stared at each other, until the silence was broken by a liquid electronic bleep. Zoe jumped, and turned; it had come from the phone on the counter, and suggested it had finished charging. She yanked the lead out and tucked it hastily into the back pocket of her jeans, but she knew that Dougie had spotted it.

'How do you take your tea?' she asked, to distract him.

'So strong you could trot a mouse on it,' he replied automatically, but his eyes had narrowed again. 'That your phone there?'

'Yep.'

'Looks like a kid's one. I'd have thought a lady like you'd have something a bit more sophisticated.' He kept up the easy smile, but she didn't like the way he was looking at her.

'Just a big kid at heart,' she said, with a shrug. 'The teabags are in that jar. I'll go get my stuff so I don't keep you waiting.'

'Take your time. Like I said, there's nae rush.' His gaze had started searching the room now; she disliked leaving him alone there, but could think of no other way to hasten him out of the house.

When she returned a few minutes later with her overnight bag, he was leaning against the range sipping a mug of tea. Her eyes flashed around the kitchen to see if anything looked disturbed or out of place, but all was apparently as she had left it. The phone weighed down the inside pocket of her jacket; she had not yet dared to try switching it on, for fear the sound would attract his attention.

'Do you think Robbie's OK?' she asked, to steer the conversation back to safer ground. 'I heard it's not the first time he's run away.'

'Trying to make yourself feel better?' Dougie rubbed a hand over his mouth and unshaved chin, and an expression she could not read passed across his face. 'Aye, he's a wee truant. Doesnae have much time for school, since his pal vanished. But it's no like him – staying out for hours in weather like this. He likes his home comforts, our Robbie. So, aye, folk are worrying this time.' He took a sip of tea, his eyes fixed on her over the top of the mug. 'What was he doing out here last night, anyway?'

'Playing pranks on me. Pretending to be a ghost.' She sighed.

Dougie nodded, as if that made sense. 'Odd that he'd leave the bike behind, though. I cannae understand that. Makes me think you know more than you're telling us.'

A sick chill spread through her gut; was he going to accuse her of doing something to the boy?

'That's all I know,' she said, trying to keep her voice steady. 'I said he shouldn't ride back in the dark. I was going to take him home this morning, but when I went to wake him, he was gone. I thought maybe the bike was out of gas.'

Dougie drained the last of his tea and ran the mug under the tap. 'Well, I'll soon find out. You can tell all that to the police, eh. And open a window, hen. Smells like you're hiding a corpse in here.'

Outside, he handed her the key to the truck as the rain battered their faces. 'Try not to run her off the road,' he said, with a knowing grin. She waited until he had switched on his flashlight and set off along the cliff path towards the place where Robbie had left the bike, before scurrying around the side of the house to the cellar hatch with her collar pulled up around her ears. Her thoughts chased one another so fast they tripped themselves up; Dougie's insinuation that she was hiding the truth about Robbie's disappearance had frightened her, and she was aware that any blurring of the facts now could compromise her later. Should she tell the police that she had hit Robbie with the driftwood, believing him to be an intruder? But then they might suspect that she had accidentally hurt him badly – killed him, even – and hidden the body, or pushed him off the cliff to hide the evidence. She rubbed the rain from her eyes and felt the weight of her tiredness. She was being ridiculous, melodramatic; no one would think that. Even so – better to say he had hurt himself in the cellar, and that

326

was why she had asked him to stay; better not to admit responsibility. She suspected the islanders would rally together against a stranger, if she gave them grounds for suspicion. She scrabbled around in the wet grass and sand until she found the wood, where she had dropped it in shock the night before. She turned it in her hands, but it was too dark to see clearly; it was sodden from the rain, but if it still held traces of Robbie's blood the police would surely find them, and that would look damning for her. The best solution would be to burn it in the range before anyone came out to search the house. There was no time to do that now; instead, she lifted one side of the coal hatch shutters and dropped the piece of wood through the hole, hearing it thud wetly on the stone floor below.

The saloon bar of the Stag was as full as she had seen it the week before, on the night she arrived, but without the easy ambience of good cheer that had accompanied the band. Instead, a close, febrile air hung over the small huddles of people clutching pints or hot drinks and murmuring to one another in low, urgent voices. The atmosphere shifted palpably as she entered; there was no mistaking the way the conversations petered out as heads turned to register her arrival. Again, she felt those stirrings of fear, an awareness of the pack closing against her. They think I'm responsible, she thought, as her gaze skimmed the room, snagging on eyes eloquent with mistrust. If Robbie had come to any harm, she realised, they would blame her squarely for it; her and the house.

She saw Annag sitting on a stool by the bar, her face pink and puffy from crying, a tissue pressed to her nose. Oh, *now* you can put on a show of being upset, Zoe thought; now there's an audience. The look that passed across the girl's face when their eyes met told Zoe she could hope for no sympathy from that quarter; it would suit Annag in various ways to

327

shift the responsibility for her brother's welfare on to someone else, especially her. Kaye stood beside Annag with her arm around the girl's shoulder; when she glanced up, Zoe saw in her face a mixture of confusion and suspicion, and realised in that instant how serious her situation had become. To her great relief, she turned to see Edward pushing his way across the bar towards her. He reached out and squeezed her elbow surreptitiously; she felt the pointed stares of the islanders and was grateful for his solidarity.

Before they could speak, the whispering and nudging was interrupted by a tall man in police uniform, who clapped his hands and took up a position in front of the bar. This, she supposed, must be Bill McCrae, the Special Constable. He wore his grey hair close-cropped above a high forehead, and took in the assembled crowd with an air of suppressed relish that he was attempting to hide behind a stern professionalism. An expectant hush fell over the room.

'Friends,' he began portentously, clasping his hands together. 'Today our community must brave another difficult situation involving one of our children. Wee Robbie Logan has gone missing overnight from the McBride house.' He paused to allow the flurry of gasps and appalled murmurs, punctuated by Annag's gulping sobs, to subside. 'I know we're all familiar with Robbie's mischief –' another pause for indulgent smiles and nods – 'but I fear we must take it seriously this time. He took his father's quad bike out there last night, but left it up on the cliff. So wherever he is, he went on foot. I'm going to suggest those of us who are fit and able divide up into search parties. Some can check his usual haunts around the town, but I want the strongest men out on the moor and along the cliffs – I've taken the liberty of dividing you up into groups. We can't get reinforcements from the mainland at the present time, with the weather, and it's too bad for the coastguard to search along the foot of the cliffs . . . ' here he paused and bowed his head, to acknowledge what had been implied; there was an audible intake of breath, ' . . . but if we pull together, I have every faith that we'll bring him home safe.'

'That's what you said about Iain Finlay.' All heads swivelled to look; the defiant speaker was the old lady with tea-cosy hair Zoe had once seen in the bookshop; her expression was ominous. Annag produced an obliging wail.

Bill's air of authority faltered.

'Now, Mrs McDaid, let's not be hasty—'

An old man with white brows and weathered skin the colour of walnut pushed himself to his feet and glared straight at Zoe before turning to point an accusing finger at Kaye.

'This is your Michael's doing,' he said, and a chorus of murmurs backed him up. 'He was told he should leave that place to rot. He cannae say he wasnae given warning. Greed – that's what it was.' More murmurs, heartier this time. The speaker raised his voice. 'His father wasnae cold in his grave before Michael started talking about incomers.' He paused to look back at Zoe, as if she were also implicated. 'And now two wee boys gone. How many more, before he'll see what he's done?'

Kaye let go of Annag and drew herself up, her face flushed with indignation and distress.

'How dare you say that, Malcolm McEwan – when Mick's no even here to speak for himself! And you're happy enough to take one on the house from him when he is.' The white-haired man looked down at the glass in his hand, somewhat sheepish. Kaye planted her hands on her hips, her breath coming in shallow gasps, making her bosom tremble. 'How can he be responsible for Robbie? You tell me that, eh?'

'He stirred up the old curses,' the man said, to a ripple of mumbled affirmations, but Bill cut in with his serious policeman voice.

'Now then, Malcolm, let's have no more talk of curses, that's no going to help anybody. Nor is pointing the finger.' As he said this, he glanced across and his gaze rested on her; she felt

329

the islanders' eyes follow and forced herself to look down, lest her face convince them of her guilt. 'What's past is past. We've to think about Robbie now, not Iain. And we're practical folk here, aren't we? We know how to get things done.' Another smattering of agreement, though with less conviction. 'Right. Well, we're going to get our torches and waterproofs and bring wee Robbie safely home. Who's with me?'

He was answered by a scrape of chairs and a reluctant nodding of heads, but clearly not the enthusiasm he had hoped for. Undaunted, he took his list of search parties and set about the room, organising groups, quashing protests, dispersing instructions with an air of thwarted military ambition. Zoe couldn't help noticing that, excepting the one sent to look around the village, Bill's search parties consisted exclusively of men, while the women volunteered to stay by the phones and make tea for the searchers. She also realised, belatedly, that there was no sign of Charles.

Edward was attached to a group dispatched to search the cliffs near the house.

'I'll come and see you afterwards,' he whispered as he zipped his jacket.

'I have something to show you,' she hissed back, shaking her head quickly when he raised a questioning eyebrow. 'I can't tell you here.'

She hovered uncertainly by the bar as one by one the groups of men left, armoured in squeaking oilskins against the weather. Dougie had not yet returned; she left his keys with Kaye, who smiled kindly and offered her a cup of tea, but with a wariness in her eyes that Zoe had not seen before. Or perhaps she was imagining it. She had just accepted the tea, with thanks, when Bill McCrae approached, his face solemn in the yellow light.

'Ms Adams? I'd like your assistance, if you don't mind.'

'I was going to offer – I could go out with the guys on the cliffs, if you want help—'

He gave her a brief, patient smile. 'Oh dear me, no. You need a local knowledge of those cliffs to be up there in this weather. It's much too dangerous – we don't want you going missing as well.' The smile faded, to be replaced by the expression he used to show he was taking his responsibilities extremely seriously. 'But there is one thing you can do for me. I'd like to take you back to the house now and have a look around, if you don't mind. And you can talk me through exactly what happened with Robbie last night, see if we can piece it all together.'

'Sure.' She smiled tightly, but all she could think of was the driftwood on the cellar floor, and how, without her car, there would be no time to hide it.

'Good grief, it smells like rotting flesh in here,' Bill said, wiping his feet carefully on the mat before stepping into the entrance hall and raising his head to sniff the air.

'Yeah, that's Robbie.' Zoe, less fastidious, shook off her jacket as rainwater streamed from it over the tiles. She turned to catch the look on his face. 'I mean – that's one of the tricks he played on me. He's put dead mice behind the radiators – I haven't managed to get them out yet.'

'Tell me about these pranks, then,' Bill said, following her along the corridor to the kitchen.

She related the history of her encounters with Robbie: the face at the window, the gull, the padlock, the burgers – here even Bill allowed the briefest twitch of a smile – right up to the noises that had alerted her to the boy's presence in the cellar the night before, though she omitted any mention of the driftwood or the phone. While she spoke, Bill nodded and made affirmative noises, as if her account confirmed a hypothesis, while jotting methodically in his notebook.

'Do you want tea?' she asked, when she had finished, turning away to the sink so that he could not see her face, since she feared he would somehow be able to detect in it the incompleteness of her story.

331

'No, I'm up to here with tea, to be honest. I want to get on and catch up with the searchers. I'd like to take a look in that cellar, though.' He looked at the door in the corner.

'Sure.' She set the kettle down and forced a smile. 'You'll need a flashlight – the bulb's blown, I think.'

'I've a powerful one in the car. You wait here.'

As soon as he had gone, she rushed to the cellar door and peered into the thick shadow. Almost without thinking, she flicked the light switch and, to her surprise, the bulb buzzed briefly and flickered into life. She steadied herself against the door jamb; she was certain it had not worked the night before. With a glance over her shoulder, she took a few hesitant steps down into the gloom; the light was dim, and failed to reach the furthest corners, throwing them into deeper shadow as a result. The wood must be right over the other side, under the coal hatch steps; she would have to pass that dresser, with its mirror. A cold sensation slid between her shoulder blades and she lost her nerve, hesitating long enough that Bill's heavy footsteps could be heard behind her on the kitchen flagstones and it was too late.

'Right we are.' He stopped at the top of the stairs. 'Looks like that light's working fine.'

'I – I guess it must be a loose connection. It's not very bright, though.'

'Aye, well – let's take a look then. You've no touched anything?' He eyed her oddly; she wondered if he thought she had lied about the light to create a diversion. She shook her head, and he edged past her to sweep the beam of his flashlight around the walls.

'Looks like there was a bit of a scuffle down here,' he remarked, taking in the fallen shelves and broken lamp.

'Like I said, the light wasn't working. Robbie knocked the shelves over in the dark.' Her voice sounded high and hectic, even to her.

'It must have been very upsetting, to have all these tricks

played on you,' he said evenly, as if she had not spoken. 'Very frightening. Out here on your own, in a house with this reputation.'

'Well – at first, I guess. Then I was just pissed about it, you know? That anyone would do something so pathetic.'

'Understandably. So you must have been very angry when you discovered it was Robbie. Anyone would be, in your position.'

She saw where he was leading. He crossed the floor carefully, scouring it with the beam of his flashlight, his boots crunching over broken glass.

'Actually, I was more relieved.' She descended another couple of steps, unsure whether or not she should keep out of his way. 'That it was only a kid messing around, I mean. I'd worried it was—' She broke off. Bill turned to look at her.

'What?'

'I don't know. An adult. A man, I mean, who might want to—' She stopped, afraid she was digging a deeper hole. 'Anyway, I wasn't angry with Robbie, once I knew it was him. I felt sorry for him.'

Bill had crouched to examine the flagstones underfoot. He touched a finger to the floor and raised it to his nose. 'These are bloodstains here.' He looked up expectantly.

'That was me.' She indicated the injury on her brow. 'I tripped over the shelves and hit my head – see? And then I cut my hand on the broken glass.'

'While you were chasing Robbie?'

'No – he was in bed by then, upstairs.'

'So what were you doing down here?'

'I – I came down to clean up.' But she knew he had caught the hesitation. 'Clean up' had been the wrong choice, too; he would assume she had been trying to erase the evidence of her crime. He picked his way across to the coal hatch steps and shone the flashlight upwards at the wooden shutters. The wind rattled them in their frame and rainwater was leaking through the gap. He peered up at the hatch for a long time; Zoe could tell that he was doing it for dramatic effect, but she felt rooted to the spot by his stillness, his intent gaze, as if she did not have permission to move until he did. Finally he stepped back, as if satisfied that some question had been answered, and his foot struck the driftwood.

Even in the dim light, she could see the muscles of his face working as he made his calculations while he stooped to pick it up, first taking a handkerchief from his pocket and wrapping it around his hand.

'How did this get here? It's soaking wet.'

She tried to explain, offering him a version of the truth, a version in which she had been scared by sounds in the cellar and ventured down armed with the piece of wood, only to trip up the intruder and discover it was Robbie. Bill dutifully jotted down her answers, but it was clear he didn't believe her; he made a show of taking the piece of wood upstairs, holding it carefully in his handkerchief, and wrapping it in a plastic bag to take to his car. She wouldn't have believed herself either, she thought, listening to her panicked replies. He wanted to see the bed where Robbie had allegedly slept; when she led him up to show him, she was appalled to find bloodstains blooming on the top sheet and pillow.

'But those are mine!' she protested. She was certain Robbie had not been bleeding when she put him to bed, but her memories of the previous night were blurred and confused. 'I cut my hand this morning, like I said – it must have dripped. You can get it tested.'

Bill cocked an eyebrow and gave her a look that suggested she should not attempt to tell him how to do his job. 'Oh, we will, Ms Adams, I'm sure, but you'll appreciate I don't exactly have my own forensics lab out here.'

He took some photos of the bed on his phone, picked up the pillow gingerly by one corner and led her back downstairs, where he wrapped it in a clean garbage bag and tucked it under his arm.

'Now. I need to get out and see how the search parties are doing on the cliffs, and I've no signal here,' he said, as if this were her fault. 'Maybe you should come with me.'

'Why?' She followed him to the entrance hall and leaned against the wall. 'Am I under arrest?'

He looked doubtful. 'No, of course not. But you'll appreciate there are things worrying me here I need to clear up. You won't go anywhere, will you?'

'Where would I go, in this?' She gestured to the rain hammering against the windows. Tiredness squeezed her temples; all she wanted was to be left alone. She had no desire any more to return to the Stag, to the whispers and stares of the islanders, to Kaye's appalling tea and that light of suspicion in her eyes. Besides, Edward had said he would come and see her. She would wait here for him; it was all she could cope with now.

'Fine. Well – perhaps someone will have good news, and there'll be nothing to worry about. I'll drop by later and let you know what's happening.'

'Mr McCrae – I didn't hurt Robbie. But he was frightened. He thought someone wanted to get him.'

Bill's head jerked up. 'Did he say who?'

'He wouldn't tell me.' She thought, with a flash of guilt, about the phone in the pocket of her jacket, hanging on the back of a kitchen chair. There was no doubt in her mind that Robbie had run away because he realised she had found the phone; perhaps he feared she had already seen what was on it. She could hand it over to Bill right now, let him deal with whatever mysteries it held. She had a duty to do so, she knew; there would be consequences for keeping it back, if it offered any clue about Robbie's disappearance. But a perverse instinct stopped her; perhaps it was Bill's manner, the self-importance and the implied accusation, or perhaps it was loyalty to Robbie himself and the secret he had so stubbornly protected from the police all these months. She felt, the way she had with Ailsa's diary, that it had come into her hands for a reason after being hidden so long, and that she should be the one to unlock its contents. Not least because she half-dreaded, half-hoped, that she would find confirmation that Iain Finlay had seen what she had seen; that it would offer proof beyond doubt that the terrors of the house were not all in her mind.

'Whoever it was that got Iain, he said.' She lowered her voice. Bill's face tightened with anxiety and she realised he was afraid; another vanished child, on his watch, the first one still unexplained and the islanders angrily looking to him for answers. It must have shaken his sense of his own position, to think that Robbie had confided more to her than he had told the police in a year.

'Right.' He seemed about to say more, but turned his attention instead to the task of assembling his multiple layers of waterproofs. 'As I say, please don't go anywhere for the time being. I'll come back and let you know when there's news. And I'll have more questions for you, I'm sure.'

'I'm sure you will,' she said, with careful politeness, and closed the door behind him.

When she was certain that the sound of his engine had died away through the wind, she took the orange phone from her jacket with trembling hands and ran upstairs to her bedroom, where she locked the door of the en suite bathroom and sat on the floor by the heated towel rail. To her amazement, the screen crackled into life when she switched it on, the blankness forming into a selfie of a grinning ten-year-old, with gappy teeth and freckles, flipping the bird at the camera. No passcode; she mouthed a silent thank you and clicked through to videos. There was only one saved. With her breath caught in her throat, she clicked play. As the images began to unfold on the screen, poorly lit and wavering with the

336

young cameraman's efforts to hold a steady focus, the sound obscured by his own muted breathing, she clamped a hand over her mouth and watched as her eyes widened; a terrible sickening cold spread through her as she understood exactly what Iain had seen in the house that night, and what Robbie had been afraid of ever since.

21

By the time she became aware of the doorbell echoing through the house, the screen had long faded to black. Around her, the room slowly gathered shape and she realised she was still sitting on the floor, her back against the bath, Iain's phone on the floor beside her. She had no idea how long she had been there. Pushing herself to her feet, she stumbled on to the landing, bleary as if she had woken from a deep sleep, as the bell went on ringing, followed by a furious hammering on the front door. It would be Bill, she supposed, back to ask her more insinuating questions. Well, now she had an answer for him, of sorts.

But when she pulled the door open she saw Edward on the threshold, rain pouring from his clothes, his glasses so spattered she wondered how he could see. At the sight of him, her legs almost buckled with relief; he stepped inside and took off his waterproof coat, slinging it on a peg inside the door. He wiped his glasses on the hem of his shirt and replaced them, frowning at her.

'Are you OK? You look like you've seen a ghost. Sorry – bad choice of words,' he added, catching her expression.

'What's the news?'

He pressed his lips together and shook his head. 'Nothing so far. I suppose that's got to be positive, hasn't it? I mean, they haven't found a—' He stopped, looking down. 'But it's hard to do anything useful in this weather. Can I warm up a bit? I'm frozen to the bone.'

'God, sorry – of course.' She led him to the kitchen and put water on to boil while he settled himself against the range. But as she reached for the mugs the fear took hold of her again and she began to shake uncontrollably, so that the china rattled in her hands and she had to set it down. She turned away, breathing hard, unwilling for him to see her like this, but she heard him move to stand behind her; his arms circled her and she found herself leaning into him, for the relief of having someone to hold her up. She twisted around to face him; her head sought the curve of his neck and she felt his mouth press against her hair as she inhaled his scent of rain and earth and warm skin. They stayed like this for a long while, close together. She felt the pulse in his throat quicken as his lips touched her temple and strayed down to her ear; the heat of his breath tickled her skin and her face tilted to his, unthinking, deliberately avoiding thought, opening herself to blind need. His mouth met hers and he tasted as she'd remembered, clean and boyish, though this time he seemed more confident, more certain of his desire and how to assert it. And so she let him slide his hand under her shirt and pull down her bra, slipping his thumb inside to circle the goosebumped flesh, while she reached for his belt and loosened it. His erection, when she took it in her hand, was silky, hot, pulsing. She moved her hand and his breathing grew hectic against her hair; he unzipped her jeans and she closed her eyes as he eased them down over her hips with her underwear, hardly knowing what she was doing, refusing to let her mind engage or think ahead. He turned her urgently to face the sink; she gripped the edge of it as he nudged her legs apart and pushed his way inside her, reaching around at the same time to touch her, so that they rocked together with the same gathering rhythm.

339

She tried to give herself over entirely to the physical sensation, to detach herself from the thoughts crowding in, full of reproach; instead she concentrated on the mounting pressure, the slick movement of his hand and his hips together, working herself hard against his fingers so that her climax, when it came, was swift and shocking, causing her to clutch at the cold enamel of the sink and cry out as if ambushed. His was not far behind; she heard the discreet gasps of his pleasure gaining in volume and had the presence of mind to arch her neck back and whisper, 'Not inside me,' so that he groaned and withdrew sharply, leaving her with a sudden ache and the inevitable warm wetness against the small of her back, that turned immediately cold and clammy on the hem of her shirt. She leaned against the counter, limbs heavy, senses unravelled. In the dark window above the sink her reflection stared back at her, wild-eyed and flushed. There was a window at the other end of the kitchen too, facing the drive; neither had curtains drawn. Anyone could have seen them. Her blood hummed with the release; her throat was damp with sweat. She could not quite believe how reckless she had been; for an instant the audacity of it almost made her laugh.

But the weight of responsibility returned with the awkward business of tugging up her jeans, turning to face him, remembering the discovery she had to share. He was staring at her from under his fringe, eyes bright with wonder and alarm.

'I'm sorry,' he said in that very English way, his voice almost a whisper. 'I didn't expect—'

'Shh.' She laid a finger on his lips. His earlier confidence seemed to have ebbed away with his erection; he looked now as if he was waiting to be told off. 'We both needed it. It's fine.'

He did not appear reassured; in fact, he seemed barely able to look her in the eye. Self-consciously, they straightened their clothes.

340

'What did you want to show me?' he asked, replacing his glasses.

'Wait there.'

She ran up the stairs to her room, where Iain's phone lay on the bathroom floor. Here she paused to tidy her hair and wipe herself with a tissue. In the mirror she thought she looked more startled than blissfully post-coital.

When she returned to the kitchen, Edward was hunched at the table, staring at his hands.

'Zoe, I – I don't know what happened there, I'm sorry. I don't usually behave like that – I want you to know. It was as if – something took me over.'

She laid a hand on his shoulder. 'There's nothing to apologise for. It was going to happen sooner or later, right?'

He raised his head with a wan smile. 'Well, I hoped, but now – in the middle of all this, with Robbie, it seems . . . '

'Look, don't feel bad. There are other things to think about.' She set the phone down in front of him.

'What's this?'

'It's Iain Finlay's.' He jerked his head round to look at her, eyes wide. She nodded confirmation. 'Robbie tried to hide it in the cellar here. I guess he's been keeping it different places all this time. I need your advice – I don't know what to do about it. Watch the video – then you'll understand.'

He appeared surprised, and somewhat hesitant, but he touched the screen obediently, his brow furrowed in concentration. Zoe moved to the sink and stood with her arms clasped across her chest, watching the rain battering the panes of glass. She couldn't bring herself to see it a second time, though she could tell, from the scratchy soundtrack, exactly what was happening. In the dark window she saw Edward press his hand over his mouth, just as she had.

The shaky video shows three people having sex in the unfinished gallery of the house: two men and a young girl. The girl is bound at the wrists from a hook in one of the

341

roof beams, though she appears to be participating willingly, her skin milk-white in the moonlit room. Empty bottles can be seen on the floor beside them. Though the quality of the film is poor and her hair half-obscures her face, you can easily identify the girl as Annag Logan. One of the men – the one behind her – is Dougie Reid, the other is Mick Drummond. The sex takes its course without much imagination, in the manner of amateur porn; what happens next, it seems, is that Iain inadvertently makes a noise. The actors in the squalid little scene snap to attention, looking around, conscious of an intruder. It's Dougie who first sees and points; what he shouts is lost in the rush of Iain's panicked breathing. At this point the film falters and pitches, to be replaced by fragmented images – of the stairs, upside down and jolting; a quick flash of a child's white trainers as he runs; the ground outside, splintered glimpses of moonlit sand and seagrass; shouts can be heard, distantly, until the phone thuds to the ground and the screen goes dark. But it is enough to guess at how the scene might have ended; enough, certainly, to mean the three participants would have questions to answer about what had happened to Iain after they pursued him.

'Jesus Christ,' Edward said, barely audible, his head propped on his hand. He pushed the phone away as if he could distance himself from the images. 'That was last summer. She would have been fifteen.'

Zoe nodded. 'Robbie told me he was scared. He said *they* would get him, like they got Iain. That poor kid's been living in terror for the past year. They must have threatened him, don't you think?'

'They don't necessarily know he's got the phone.'

'But surely they've guessed he saw something. And he's run away now because he thinks I've found it – he's afraid the secret's out and he's in trouble. What do we do with it?'

He looked at the phone warily, as if it might make a sudden move. 'Give it to Bill. That's all we can do.'

'Can he be trusted?'

He turned to her with a questioning frown; she made an impatient noise. 'I mean, everyone's pretty tight here, right? And they don't like a scandal. Bill's not even the real police – they won't get here until the storm's over. What if he decides it's better for the island if he makes this disappear?'

Edward hesitated. 'You mean we should hold on to it until the mainland police arrive? But that might be a couple of days. And if Dougie or Annag knows anything about what's happened to Robbie, then we'd be withholding evidence.' He paused, his mouth curling in disgust. 'You don't think they could have – not her own brother?'

Zoe shrugged. 'He told me she wished he was dead, so she could leave the island. I'm pretty sure she hits him.'

He dropped his gaze to the table. 'I thought so too. I went to see the father about it – Robbie would turn up with bruises whenever he was away on a job. Not an easy man to reason with – he said he'd send me back to England on a stretcher if I suggested anything like that about his family again. I should have reported it, I know, but it seemed to stop for a while after that. Annag's hated me for it ever since.' He shook his head. 'Maybe you're right. I could take the phone to Charles – see what he thinks is best.'

'Good idea – you and Charles could call the mainland police before you give it to Bill, tell them you have it. He'd think twice about tampering with it then.' She looked at the phone and chewed her lip. 'Poor Kaye. Jesus. How's she going to cope with this? Mick always seemed like a good guy.'

'It's this house,' Edward said, with sudden animosity, lifting his eyes to the ceiling. 'It has an effect on you. It's not just that you forget your inhibitions – it's more like something takes over, some spirit of – I want to say *lust*, but that sounds absurdly Victorian.'

'It's not the fucking *house*,' she said, turning on him. 'That's

343

two middle-aged men exploiting an underage girl – you can't excuse that with folk tales.'

'I wasn't excusing it,' he began, riled, but his defence was interrupted by a loud noise from somewhere beneath their feet. Both froze, looking at one another.

Zoe pointed to the floor, mouthing the word 'cellar'.

'Someone's down there?' he whispered. She shrugged; the sound came again, a hard bang, like a door slamming. She cast around; in a panic she grabbed a carving knife from a block on the counter and handed it to Edward, motioning for him to go ahead. He swallowed, but dutifully pushed the cellar door; it swung open with a slow groan. She hovered at his shoulder as he flicked the light switch; the bulb fizzed into life and he let out a self-conscious laugh as he crouched to look around.

'It's only that hatch on the other side there – it's blown open and the wind's banging it, that's all.'

She heard the tremor of relief in his voice.

'Robbie must have taken the padlock. I'll go out and see if I can wedge the catch closed.'

'A lot of rain's come in,' Edward called up, as he descended further into the shadows. 'Why don't I make a start on cleaning that up while you do the hatch?'

She hesitated at the top of the stairs. 'Maybe we shouldn't. Bill told me not to touch anything.'

'Why not?'

'He thinks—' She stopped; the discovery of the video had temporarily allowed her to forget that she was under suspicion for Robbie's disappearance. 'There was blood on the floor where I cut myself. He thinks it's connected with Robbie.'

'Well, there's water all over the steps now. That's not going to help anything.'

'It will look like we've tried to clean up.'

'Zoe.' Edward sounded faintly impatient. 'You've got nothing to hide, so what are you worried about? At least let's

344

get the hatch closed and the worst of the water up. I can explain to Bill, if I have to.'

Zoe felt that was optimistic, but she lacked the energy to argue. She pulled on her jacket; it was a fight even to open the kitchen door. Outside, the wind and rain showed no sign of abating; a rumble of thunder rolled towards her over the sea. She tried not to think of Robbie as she battled the hatch against the gusts, finally forcing it shut and fitting the clasp over the metal loop that held the two shutters together, hoping it would hold without a padlock. Was he out in this somewhere, hiding on the moor or up on the cliffs? She remembered the dark shape she thought she had seen that morning in the churning water and bile rose in her stomach.

By the time she returned to the cellar, squeezing out her wet hair, Edward had brought down a mop and bucket. But instead of clearing up the water, she found him crouched by one of the walls, stroking his fingers over the stonework.

'Come and look at this,' he called, his voice bright with excitement. 'Bring a torch, if you have one?'

She returned to the kitchen and rummaged in the drawers until she found the one Mick had shown her for emergencies. Edward pointed and she directed the beam to one of the pillars of the old chapel built into the cellar wall.

'See that?' His eyes were lit with childish enthusiasm, as if he had forgotten their present dilemma. The flashlight illuminated a series of overlapping circles carved into the stone, so that they formed a geometric shape like the petals of a flower. It reminded her of patterns she had drawn as a child, she thought, with a plastic gizmo you could spiral around with a pencil.

'What is it?'

'Witch marks,' he whispered with satisfaction. She took a step back. 'People carved them on to doorposts and windows to keep witches and their spells away. These must go back to the sixteenth century or earlier. This place is amazing. I've never seen down here before.' He took the flashlight from her and shone it around the floor of the old chapel, showing up the worn inscriptions. 'And look what else I found.'

He led her to the corner where she had pulled out the old dresser the night before; instinctively she averted her eyes from the mirror. Even now, with Edward beside her, the memory of that reflection unnerved her. He was scuffing a patch of plaster on the floor with the toe of his boot.

'See here? I think this has been covered up,' he said. 'Look at the shape of this plaster – it's a perfect rectangle, like a tombstone.'

'So?' She felt a prickle along her arms.

'There are graves all over this floor – none of the others has been plastered over. Ask yourself – why this one?'

'I don't know. Right now I'm asking myself what we do about that phone. Bill said he's coming back here sometime tonight.'

'Don't you want to find out?' His eyes shone up at her in the flashlight; he looked like a boy planning an adventure, and her heart squeezed again, with a pang of guilt, at his enthusiasm. 'Why would anyone want to hide a grave, down here?' He kicked at the plaster. 'It's old, too, you can see it's cracking. We could chisel it off in no time.'

'You can't start taking the floor up,' she protested weakly, but he had already sprung over to the scattered tools that had fallen from the shelf and pulled out a chisel and hammer.

'Come on – hold the torch steady,' he said, and she found herself crouching beside him while he chipped away at the ancient plaster in a kind of frenzy, sending up clouds of dust that stung her eyes and lodged in her throat.

'Bill's going to go nuts,' she said, watching him, but he swept the fragments aside and continued with increased fervour.

'You could get a brush if you wanted to help,' he remarked, not looking up.

She was grateful to return to the kitchen, though the sight

346

of the orange phone in the middle of the table set her pulse skipping in panic. She drank a glass of water; by the time she returned with a dustpan and brush, Edward was white with dust and wearing a triumphant smile.

'Check this out.' He took the brush from her hand and flicked the piles of chipped plaster aside. She pressed her sleeve over her nose and mouth and peered down as he shone the flashlight on letters carved into the stone beneath.

'I can't read it.'

He cast around with an impatient exhalation, before grabbing the mop and dunking it in a puddle of rainwater from the hatch. He ran it over the uncovered stone and the moisture caused the dust to settle, revealing the words that she had feared they would find:

In Memoriam
Ailsa Mhairi McBride
1831–1869
Teàrlach Seosamh McBride
1862–1869
Let thy mercy, O Lord, be upon us

Zoe stared at the inscription, unable to speak. Had Ailsa been here with her, in the very foundations of the house, all along? She felt her blood had stopped moving.

'Do you think she's really buried there?' she asked eventually, in a whisper. 'Or did someone do that as a memorial? Was it Mick that covered it up?'

'This was done long ago.' Edward traced his finger over the letters. When he raised his head to her, his face was deathly pale with white dust, his eyes dark and solemn. 'Don't you see? The boy's name,' he said, pointing, when she shook her head. The words emerged as a croak.

'Charles said there was no record of his name. Someone evidently knew it. Whoever put this stone here.'

'Charles told you that?' His voice sounded distant. 'But look at the names.'

'I can't even pronounce them.'

'They're Gaelic.' He read the boy's names aloud, faltering on the consonants.

'Yeah, I guessed that. What? What is it?'

'Zoe.' He sucked in his cheeks and looked at her as if she were being deliberately obtuse. 'In English, her son's name was Charles Joseph McBride.'

Above them, the coal hatch gave a sudden rattle, as if someone were shaking it; a chill wind knifed through the gap. They shivered at the same time.

'Could be a coincidence,' she said.

'Hell of a coincidence, though.' Edward pushed himself to his feet and stretched his back. 'Do you suppose he's some kind of descendant? He must be, don't you think? That would explain why he's so obsessed with the story.'

'They never found the boy's body. It's possible that he didn't drown, I guess.' She glanced at him for confirmation. 'He could have been picked up by a boat. Maybe he survived to grow up and have kids of his own.'

'It's pretty far-fetched. And Charles would acknowledge the connection, surely?' He frowned. 'Why would he keep it a secret? Maybe it makes it easier for him to write about it, if he appears to be objective. Perhaps he shares Mick's fear of being tainted by association with her.'

'He's got her necklace,' Zoe said, remembering. 'Ailsa's cross – it was there in his cabinet. He told me it belonged to his grandmother, but I would have sworn it's the one Ailsa's wearing in the photographs.' Another possibility struck her, but it was so outlandish, so clearly crazy, that she shook her head to rid her mind of it before she made a fool of herself by suggesting it aloud.

She held Edward's gaze; they watched one another for a long while, as if trying to read the other. It seemed absurd to think that half an hour earlier they had had frantic, urgent sex against the sink; when she tried to conjure the memory, it felt faded, like an incident that had occurred years ago. 'I've had enough of this place,' she said abruptly, turning for the stairs. 'Let's get back to the light.'

'Come into town with me,' Edward said, gathering up his waterproofs. 'We can ask Charles together.'

She peered out of the window by the front door; the wind continued to pummel the house and she thought she had seen a flash of lightning. 'You and Charles need to talk about what to do with that video. Dougie should be arrested, at the very least – I'd bet he knows where Robbie is. Anyhow, I don't want to go back to the pub. Did you see the way they all looked at me? Even Bill thinks I've got something to do with it.'

'Come back to mine, then,' he said, laying a hand on her arm. 'I don't like to think of you being here alone. I'd like to be with you tonight anyway, after . . . ' He offered a shy smile by way of a reference to their earlier encounter.

'I ought to stay here – Bill said I mustn't go anywhere until he came back. I should probably do as I'm told for now, until he's convinced I'm innocent.'

'OK.' He seemed reluctant to leave. 'Well, why don't you come over later, after Bill's been? At least you'd be in town then, with a working phone, so we can find out any news. Better than being cut off out here.'

'People would talk, wouldn't they? If I stayed at yours?'

He tilted his head. 'Do you really care about that, now? Do you think I do?'

His eagerness was touching, she knew, though at present she only felt wearied by it. But there was nowhere she could go, she realised, that would ease her restlessness or allow her to sleep; she may as well spend the night in Edward's cottage instead of staying here, wandering from room to room like a wraith, worrying about Robbie and conscious of the uncovered gravestone beneath her.

'Sure. I'll drive over as soon as Bill's been. You get that phone safely to Charles, OK?'

He seemed reassured by this. He nodded and kissed her goodbye – tentatively, on the lips, though she pulled away before he was tempted to linger. As he braced himself against the storm, the sky was lit for the space of a heartbeat, by a flash of sickly, greenish light, and the roll of thunder that followed sounded like a threat.

22

Zoe closed and locked the cellar door, shutting out the image of that disturbing tombstone and its implications. She recalled Charles's story of the labourers hired to take Ailsa's coffin to the mainland, and their conviction that the box had been empty. What if she had never left? Suppose she had been buried, in secret; suppose she had remained here, *in the house*, all this time? And what did it mean that the boy's name was engraved there too? *Teàrlach Seosamh McBride*. She tried to whisper the names aloud. Charles Joseph. Ailsa's son.

She made another pot of coffee and a cheese sandwich and sat at the kitchen table with them, her back to the cellar door. The storm raged on outside, but the house itself remained quiet; no strange scratchings or singing, no voices, no ringing phone. It was almost ten when she was disturbed by the doorbell, and she could not say how she had passed the time; it seemed to have washed over her as she sat, like a stone in a slow-flowing river, numb to thought and feeling.

It rang a second time, insistent now, as if someone were holding it down, and she pushed her chair away from the table, dragging herself back to awareness. The front door was snatched by the wind as she pulled it open, braced for another

351

dose of Bill's heavy-handed questions, but the figure in oilskins on the doorstep shouldered roughly past her, slamming the door behind him, and when he lowered his hood she saw with a dropping sensation in her stomach that it was Dougie Reid.

'Anyone else here?' He peered past her into the hallway.

She glanced over her shoulder, anxiety tightening her chest. His manner was brusque, with none of the sly insinuation he usually employed with her. 'Bill's coming any minute.'

She knew he had caught the fear in her voice. A smile curved across his face. 'He'll be a while yet, hen. He's out with the searchers on the moor. You and I need to have a wee chat.'

'It's late, Dougie. I was about to go to bed.'

He raised an eyebrow. 'You're lucky you can think about sleep. There's no one else in the town'll be sleeping tonight, for worrying about that wee boy.'

'I'm worried too. I'd prefer to be on my own, if you don't mind. We can chat tomorrow,' she added as a concession. She heard how polite she sounded, and hated herself for it; why was she tiptoeing around him, as if afraid to give offence?

'Won't take a minute,' he said, his voice light.

She gathered her courage and folded her arms, her heart scudding. 'No. I'm not feeling well. I'd like you to leave, please.' But he pushed past as if she had not spoken and headed down the corridor in his waterproofs, his boots leaving muddy footprints over the tiles. She had no choice but to follow him. 'Did you hear me?'

'They're saying all kinds of things in town,' he remarked over his shoulder as he reached the kitchen. She watched the way his gaze scoured the room, as if searching for something particular.

'About Robbie?'

'About you. People are saying you're no right in the head.'

She rolled her eyes. 'Well, it's good to know this place hasn't

352

changed since the nineteenth century. A woman who chooses to live on her own, you all decide she must be crazy. Nice going.'

'Well, it's your own husband who says so, hen, and he's no from around here.' He shrugged off his coat and threw it over a chair. The run-off pooled on the stone floor. Underneath he was wearing overalls and a leather tool belt around his waist.

'What?' Her pulse quickened; for a sudden, awful moment she thought Dan might have turned up, and even now might be sitting in the bar at the Stag, holding forth about her failings to an eager audience.

'Aye. Kaye's spoken to him. She says he asked her to keep an eye on you. Says you've had some kind of breakdown and you're no taking your pills. You've no got a firm grip on reality, apparently.' His eyes glittered; the smile curved like a blade. He took a step towards her.

'My husband wouldn't say anything like that. You need to leave now.' But she could see he had caught the tremor in her voice.

'It's a worry, though. A wee boy goes missing, last seen in the company of a nutter. Folk are talking, you can imagine. I mean, why would anyone keep a stranger's child at their house overnight? Why would you no take him straight home?'

'Maybe I thought he was safer here than at home.'

'Well, turns out you were wrong about that, eh. Looks like he wasn't safe with you at all. Who knows what a mental woman might do to a child.'

'That's crazy – I would never hurt a child.' She heard her voice rising. 'I'm a mother, for Christ's sake.'

'Aye, we've heard that too. And folk are saying, what kind of mother leaves her child behind in another continent and fucks off to live on her own? Eh? You've got to admit, you're no going to win Maw of the Year for that.'

He moved another step closer; she found she had backed

herself against the sink. She tried to draw herself upright and put her shoulders back; she was at least as tall as him.

'Get out.' She made her voice as hard as she could. 'Get out of my house, or I'll call—' She broke off, seeing his smile widen to a grin.

'Will you? Who will you call?'

He knew about the phone line, she realised; it was that knowledge that lent him his bravado. They were alone here; there was nothing she could do. She saw him register her understanding of her predicament, saw the satisfaction he got from her fear. He stepped forward once more until he was inches away from her. She felt his breath on her face, with its smell of stale cigarettes.

'If you touch me, I will fucking kill you,' she said through her teeth. He gave a sour laugh.

'Don't flatter yourself, hen. That's no what I'm here for. I'm a wee bit old for your taste, anyway, eh?'

'Likewise,' she shot back. She saw the naked flash of anger in his eyes and wished she could spool the word back and swallow it; she had betrayed a knowledge she should not have possessed, and they both understood the implications. He reached out and placed a hand deliberately on her breast, his grip tight, his eyes fixed on hers, challenging her to provoke him.

For a few seconds she stared back at him, unable to move, her breath stopped in her throat. She could see his face as if in high definition: every acne scar, every blackhead on his nose, every bristle on his lip seemed magnified, his ridged teeth and pale eyelashes appeared to her as if she were seeing them on a screen. She tensed her jaw, concentrated hard and, in one swift movement, brought her right knee up to connect sharply with his groin.

He yelped and jumped back, but the cry was more outrage than pain; he had seen an intimation in her face somehow, and angled his body away as she moved, so that her knee had struck the inside of his thigh instead of her true target. Before she could react, he had grabbed her wrist and twisted her arm hard behind her back, so that she heard a click in her shoulder as she screamed.

'You fucking slag. Don't ever try that again. Where's the phone?'

'In the hall.'

'Not that one. You know what I mean. The other phone.'

'What other phone?'

'Fuck's sake. The one I saw in your kitchen today, the orange one. I want to see it.'

'Why? It's just my phone. Why should I show you?'

He wrenched her arm harder and she cried out. 'Because I'm asking you nicely. Do as you're told, eh, and we'll be done without any trouble.'

'OK, OK . . . ' She let out a jagged breath. 'If I give you my phone, you'll leave?'

He hesitated. 'Aye. Where is it?'

'In my bag. On that chair over there.' She nodded, but he did not let go of her arm; instead he dragged her across the room until she could reach into her purse with her free hand. She held out her phone in its black leather flip case, but he only pulled her arm higher. 'Jesus, fuck, let me go. Here's the phone.'

'That's an iPhone.'

'I know. That's the only phone I have.'

'Don't fuck with me, hen. I want the one I saw this afternoon. In the orange case. The Nokia. Where is it?'

'I don't have a Nokia phone,' she said, her voice tight with pain.

He slackened his grip and pulled her chin around with his free hand to face him. 'Then why did you go to Dickey's this morning and buy a Nokia charger? Aye, don't think you can have any secrets here. Now let's try one more time – where is it?'

'I—' She shook her head.

'Did you show it to anyone? Does anyone else know you have it?'

'I don't know what you're talking about, I've told you.' She kept her face turned away.

He paused, leaning back to look at her.

'All right, hen, if you want to make this harder for yourself.' He slapped her across the face, a hard crack with the back of his hand that so astonished her as it rang out that the pain took a moment to register. Tears sprang to her eyes; she blinked them back as he pushed her up against the wall, gripping her other hand and pulling her wrists together behind her, so that she was pinned, unable to move, her back to him and her cheek pressed against the plaster. She heard the sound of a zipper and feared the worst, but it must have been the tool belt opening. A tearing noise followed, and she felt the sticky pressure of duct tape against her skin. She cried out as it was wound around her wrists until she could feel nothing but the burning in her shoulders.

'Now then,' he said, in her ear, when she could no longer move her arms, 'I won't ask nicely next time. Where's the cunting phone?'

'I don't have any other phone,' she repeated, the words coming out staccato with the pain, but she allowed her eyes to travel towards the ceiling. Dougie followed her gaze. She tried to keep her thoughts ordered; if she could lead him to believe the phone was somewhere in the house, he would waste time searching for it, and Edward and Charles would have a chance to call the police before Dougie thought to go after them.

'Right,' he said, appearing to make a decision. He pushed her towards the door of the cellar.

'What are you going to do to me?' she asked, struggling against him. 'Do you really think you can get away with this?'

356

He grinned, but the novelty of taunting her appeared to be wearing thin. 'Reckon I can get away with anything I like,' he said, clamping a hand around her breast again. 'Who would believe what you say now? You're mentally unstable, remember.' He let go and shoved her hard between the shoulder blades. 'You're lucky I think you're an ugly bitch. Although maybe I should give you a seeing to anyway, put you in your place.' He unlocked the cellar door and affected to consider it. 'Nah. I've got better things to do. And I don't want that wee posh boy's sloppy seconds.'

'Bill McCrae will be here any minute,' she said, fighting to keep her voice even. 'What will you tell him?'

'I'll tell him I've no idea where you are.' He smiled, showing his stained teeth. 'I'll say you must have gone out in the storm. That's the sort of thing a mental woman would do.'

'I'll scream the fucking place down.'

'I don't think so. Whisht your noise now.' He shoved her against the wall next to the open door and held her with his forearm across her chest; she tensed, fearing he meant to push her down the steps. But he tore off another strip of duct tape and brought it towards her face, even as she tried flailing her head to avoid it, imploring him to spare her that, promising to keep quiet. With the tape across her mouth, she felt herself crumple, the fight gone out of her.

'That's better. Get yourself down there.' He nudged her forward to the cellar steps, holding her by the shoulders until she had reached the bottom. 'I'm going to find that phone. And if I don't, I'm going to come back and ask you again. So you have a wee think about whether you want to be more helpful when I come back, because I will teach you a lesson if you're not.'

He retreated back up the stairs and slammed the door. Zoe was plunged into darkness as she heard the sound of the key turning in the lock.

*   *   *

She breathed in and out hard through her nose, trying to slow her thoughts while her eyes adjusted. As if for the first time, she began fully to comprehend the danger she was in. Dougie was volatile, but he was also, she now realised, sharper than she had given him credit for. If he suspected her of having Iain's phone – if he thought she had seen what was on it – he would regard her as a threat. There was too much at stake for him. And he was right: she was alone with him in the middle of nowhere, with no means of communication. Was he capable of killing her? She could hardly say what was possible now; if he hadn't killed Iain Finlay with his own hands, she was sure that at the very least he had pursued the boy to his death on the cliffs. And had he killed Robbie too? It was not impossible. She had no doubt that he would be prepared to rape her; hadn't he taken pleasure in explaining that the islanders thought she was unstable, crazy, hysterical, a slut? No one would believe her version, if she ever got to tell it. In the midst of her fear she found a reserve of anger for Dan, for trying to undermine her from three thousand miles away. Would he be pleased with the result, if he could see her now, if he could see the effects of his interfering phone call to Kaye? Her throat pinched tight at the thought, so that she had to remind herself to keep breathing.

Gradually she found she was able to make out shapes among the shadows. There was the dull gleam of the dresser's mirror; there the skeletal outline of the fallen shelves. Ailsa's grave was somewhere in that corner, she thought, noticing how calmly she acknowledged the fact. It was not the person beneath her feet who frightened her now, but the one whose footsteps she listened for overhead. *It's the living you have to be afraid of*; hadn't she said that once to Edward? Thunder kettle-drummed outside and the gale rattled the wooden shutters above her in the far corner.

Of course; the hatch! Dougie could not have known it was not padlocked on the outside; all she had to do was free her hands and force it open. She stepped gingerly across the floor, feeling her way with her feet, listening for the crunch of broken glass, glad that she had taken to wearing sneakers around the house because of the cold floors. She needed to look somewhere on this side of the cellar, near the steps; Edward had had the carving knife in his hand and must have put it down when he'd discovered the water damage. She kicked around, trying to make as little noise as possible; she had no idea how thorough Dougie would be in his search, or how soon he would be back. At last her toe struck an object that gave a metallic scrape against the stone floor. She crouched and eased herself around so that she could grasp the handle of the knife behind her back with her free fingers. She managed to manoeuvre the blade towards the tape binding her wrists, though it was difficult to keep it steady and apply enough pressure to pierce through the tightly wrapped layers. More than once the knife slipped and she felt a burning pain, followed by the warm trickle of blood down her hands, making the task harder as her fingers grew slippery. But she kept sawing away, and eventually she felt the fibres fray and give under the blade, until she could force enough of a gap to wrench her wrists through. Though she could not see properly, there seemed to be a quantity of blood running down her arms, but her heart was pounding so hard now she could hardly register the pain, only the thrill of relief as she ripped the tape off her mouth and sucked in air. She groped her way up the steps to the shutters of the coal hatch, and pushed hard; at first they resisted, and she cursed herself for having secured the catch so effectively earlier. She heaved again, climbing higher so that she could put her shoulder against the wood, and suddenly it gave, flying open so abruptly that she almost lost her footing, but at the same time she felt the rain lash

359

her face and launched herself upwards, into the welcome snarl of the gale.

For a few seconds she stood in the full force of the storm, in the shadow of the house, uncertain as to her next move. She had been so bent on getting out of the cellar that she had not given any thought to what she would do if she succeeded; quickly she realised that she was not much better off outside. She had no car keys – they were in her bag, in the kitchen, beyond her reach; she was still cut off here, alone with Dougie, who might glance out of the window and see her at any moment. And how could she get away? There was only the road across the moors, but he would realise she was missing and come after her long before she could reach the town, and there was nowhere to hide out there, in that exposed landscape. Her other option was to conceal herself here somehow and hope that Bill McCrae kept his word and returned, though it was more likely Dougie would find her before Bill arrived. She must not let Dougie corner her out here, in this weather; there were too many ways to make a plausible accident happen to someone who didn't know how treacherous the coast could be.

While she stood crippled with indecision, another furious jag of lightning tore a trail through the clouds, so that briefly she saw the length of the beach illuminated, the churning waves rising and crashing in pyramids tall as houses, the cliffs towering on either side of the cove. The shock of it galvanised her. She was shivering now, her sweater soaked through, jeans sticking to her legs, hair plastered across her face, but she knew she had to move. She glanced up at the house; it was fortunate there were not many windows on this side. The sky seemed strangely lit from behind the clouds with a greenish, sickly glow; some effect of the moon and the storm, she supposed, which allowed her a little visibility but would also make it harder to hide.

A dull ache throbbed in her right wrist; when she looked down, she could see that blood was pumping from the wound. The knife must have gone deeper than she had realised, in the first flush of adrenaline; now that she stopped to catch her breath, she began to feel dizzy. She crouched and took off one sneaker and sock, then bound the sock around her wrist and knotted it as tight as she could manage with one hand. It occurred to her, as she straightened up and pressed herself against the wall, that Dougie would have parked his truck at the front of the house, and might have left his keys in the ignition. If she could get to it before he caught her, she might at least have a chance of escape, and of getting to town; she might even meet Bill on the way.

As she hunched in the shadows, working up the courage to launch herself around the corner of the house to the truck, she became aware – she could not quite say how – that she was not alone in the darkness. She held herself very still, listening, but could hear no sound of breathing, no shifting of wet sand underfoot or rustling in the marram grass. She was conscious only of a presence, close behind her, silently watching. She tried to swallow, not daring to turn around in case he had come out to find her. But nothing stirred except the rush of the wind and waves and the hard scrabble of rain against the walls and windows. Her body tensed from her scalp to her feet, every nerve ending humming with a dreadful anticipation; she felt a shift in the air around her and braced herself for a blow to fall, but in that instant the screaming began, from somewhere above her.

She had heard it before; that same abandoned cry of a woman's ecstasy that had brought the colour to her face the other night. It was hard to make out where it was coming from. Slowly, she allowed herself to turn. There was no sign of anyone in the darkness, though the cries continued, rising

361

to that feverish pitch where they ought to reach a climax but instead shaded from pleasure into pain, as they had before, the anguish awful to hear. Zoe edged along the south side of the house until she reached the corner facing the beach; by this time the sound seemed to surround her, echoing over the bay, and with each new cry fear gripped her tighter, dark and sinuous, wrapping around her until she could barely draw breath. She pressed her hands against her ears in an effort to shut it out, but it pierced her defences. Was Dougie terrified too, she wondered, inside the house; would the cries bring him running out here in panic? Surely no one could hear that agony of human suffering, and not be plunged into blind terror? And then the monstrous thought struck her that maybe Dougie could not hear them at all. Maybe they only existed for her. The sheer horror of this idea caused her to stumble over the grass, but her attention was distracted by another sound, from further away; a child's voice, shouting. She could not catch the words, but the tone was electric with terror.

Blinking into the rain, she strained to listen; it was almost impossible to hear through the storm, but the shouts seemed to be coming from the shore. All at once another sheet of lightning showed her the beach, unnaturally lit, and the unmistakable outline of a child at the water's edge. Forgetting Dougie, she broke cover and ran down the wet sand. As she drew closer, she thought she heard her name being called.

'Robbie?' Her voice was lost in the gale, but she yelled again. 'Robbie, is that you? Wait there, I'm coming!'

She paused to look back at the house, wondering if Dougie had heard, and thought she glimpsed a figure looking out from the central window of the gallery, lit from behind. The child screamed for help; she spun round and in that eerie green half-light she could make out the shape of the boy against the thrashing white of the breakers, though she was

362

not close enough to see his features. She ran towards him, but as she closed the gap between them, he jerked his head away and began to walk into the water.

'No! Robbie, stop!' She hurled herself towards him; as she reached the frill of foam along the sand he turned, chest-deep, to look her full in the face and she saw, with a jolt that seemed to stop her heart, that it was not Robbie but Caleb, his eyes wide and pleading.

'Mommy! Help me! I don't want to go with her.' He glanced fearfully over his shoulder, to the crashing waves, as if someone were calling to him. Instinct blinded her; she could not stop to ask herself how he came to be there.

'I'm here, baby – it's OK, you're safe. Come to me.' She held out her hands to him, the water snapping at her ankles.

At the same time, another voice cut through the wind, from high above them. Lightning tore through the sky and she craned her neck to see Charles Joseph standing on the cliff above the beach, his white hair blown back so that he looked like an Old Testament prophet.

'Zoe! Stay where you are. Don't move. Do as I say, you'll be all right.' And then, raising a hand, he seemed to address someone else, someone she could not see, and what she thought he shouted into the storm, in a commanding voice, was: 'Leave her! It's not her you want. I'm here.'

'Zoe!' She whipped around at the sound of another urgent cry and saw a man racing down the beach towards her; at first she thought it was Dougie and her stomach turned over, but as he approached she realised the voice was Edward's, and he was sprinting over the sand to her. 'Zoe, come back, what are you doing?'

'*Mommy!*' Caleb screamed again, at her back, and the naked terror in his cry undid her; she turned and flung herself after him. He lunged for her, their fingers almost touched, until a wave broke over his head and pulled him under; she could see only his white hand, like a pale starfish, flailing above the water. With a scream she launched herself into the waves, oblivious to Edward's cries behind her; the cold slammed into her chest, knocking the breath from her as she was wrenched out of the air and into the black depths.

The force of the wave sucked her under; salt scorched her nostrils as they filled with water, but she opened her eyes and saw Caleb, sinking slowly, his hand still stretching for her. She lunged towards him, but as she did so she saw, with horror, another pair of white hands emerge from the darkness below to clutch at his leg, dragging him down. She could not make a sound; nothing but a stream of silver bubbles emerged from her mouth. Caleb's face sank deeper, blurring into the dark, transfixed in a rictus of pure terror; his grasping fingers were the last to fade. Her lungs burned and burned, until the pain grew so great that she thought she would burst with it; but in the instant that it became impossible to bear, so it subsided, to be replaced by a strange calm. She had a glimpse of billowing black material, of long, dark hair swaying like weed in the water; she saw the white hands close around her wrists and this time she submitted to them, allowing herself to be tugged gently downwards. She could go to him now, follow him to the deep. There was no need to fight it any more.

But in that moment of blissful surrender she felt the grip of another pair of hands in her armpits, a sudden rush upwards, a shattering of warmth and calm as she broke the surface to the cruel truth of cold air and water. The rest came to her in splintered images, like the snatched video on Iain's phone: a flash of lightning over the peaks of the waves; the scrape of shingle under her legs; the glimmer of Charles's eyes as he laid her on the sand, shivering so hard she thought her bones would shatter; his voice, as if from a great distance, intoning words she could not understand; the sour taste of vomit in her mouth as she rolled on to her side. An explosion of thunder, and somewhere behind it, as she slipped back into the dark, the pale voice of a woman singing a lament for her lover, lost to the sea.

23

A regular electronic beep intruded through the murk behind her eyes. It came to her as if from a great distance, along with the curiously intimate sound of inhalation and exhalation that made her think someone was breathing steadily in her ear.

Overlaying both these noises was the low rumble of a man's voice. She tried to raise her head, but a bolt of pain shot through like a white-hot needle from temple to temple, so she remained immobile, waiting for the pain to recede. Gradually, the fog in her brain began to clear. She became aware of a pressure around her mouth and nose, an uncomfortably claustrophobic sensation, and realised the breathing noises were her own, oddly amplified inside a plastic mask. The voice she could hear reminded her of Dan's. Her dreams had been such a tangle of familiar faces and voices that it took some moments before she became convinced that it *was* Dan she could hear, she was certain of it, though she could not quite bear to open her eyes and confirm.

'My wife is mentally fragile,' he was saying, in the special over-loud tone he used for explaining things. 'So I think it's best you keep the worst of it from her, when she wakes. You know she had a previous attempt . . . ' He faltered here; she heard him pause to compose himself, before continuing: 'A previous suicide attempt, about six months ago. Last May. She drove her car across a red stop light at an intersection, into the path of a truck. If the driver hadn't . . . ' Another pause to swallow. 'It was a miracle she survived. Broken collarbone, that was all she got. She tried to claim it was an accident, but the guy said she looked right at him and accelerated. I knew what she was trying to do.'

She caught the murmur of another male voice, though she could not make out the words. Dan sounded as if he were right beside her; as she began to feel a tingling in her limbs, she became aware of a weight on her left hand, the pressure of fingers squeezing hers.

'Well, what was I meant to do – have her committed?' Dan sounded defensive now. 'She was on medication and in therapy, I hoped that would be enough. I wasn't happy about it, of course not, but I couldn't exactly stop her. Tell you the truth, I thought maybe a break would do her good. She'd seemed better lately – I thought she was out of danger. As soon as I realised she hadn't taken her meds with her—'

The other voice cut in, rising in a question.

'Depression, mostly. But a kind of mania, too. Persistent delusions. So, in answer to your question, Doctor, I'd say there's no doubt this was another go. The cuts to her wrists, trying to drown herself—'

Drown herself. The words triggered a landslip in her memory; fragments of images surfaced like debris from the mud: the storm, the waves, the pale hands, Caleb. *Caleb.*

Her eyes snapped open to a white glare that bleached her vision; she sat bolt upright, ignoring the tearing sensation in the skin of her hand, and the pain in her chest and head. The sedate beeping that had first woken her speeded up, its rhythm urgent. She tried to speak but her words were stifled inside the mask. From both sides blurring figures rushed forward to take hold of her, easing her back to a supine position. A

367

woman barked a few words, brisk and professional; a man's voice snapped back. She heard the word 'ventilator'.

'Zo, honey, can you hear me? You're going to be OK.'

Slowly, her focus returned; through the blinding light a face loomed into view, inches from hers, and took shape as Dan's: square-jawed, solid, concerned. He had grown a beard since she had last seen him; it softened his features. She could feel him pressing her left hand while someone else was messing with her right.

'She's trying to say something,' Dan said, glancing over his shoulder. 'Can we take this off her for a minute?'

Another white figure appeared; the mask was lifted.

'Where's Caleb? He went under—' Her lungs tightened as if squeezed in a vice; she snatched frantic breaths, panicking as she found herself unable to gulp the oxygen she needed.

'Zoe.' Dan spoke quietly, with a trace of weariness, as if the effort of repetition pained him. 'Caleb's dead, honey.'

The cry that tore from her was primal, inhuman; a long sustained note that only faded when she had no air left and her chest seemed to close in on itself. Quickly the mask was replaced; she took shallow, gulping breaths until the pain eased. Someone leaned over her; she felt the pinch and slide of a needle in her arm, then a familiar sluicing of warmth and heaviness through her veins. For a long time she lay with her eyes closed. She had to force them open. She could barely hear her own voice. Dan bent his head closer.

'Take it off again, will you? I can't hear her.'

The mask was raised.

'She took him,' Zoe whispered. Her tongue felt waterlogged. 'I tried to save him. She dragged him underwater. It was Ailsa. I couldn't reach him in time.'

'Sweetheart.' Dan was looking at her with infinite sadness. 'Caleb wasn't in the water. He died last year, remember? Right before Christmas. He had meningitis. You know this, Zo.' She thought she caught an edge to his tone, a trace of

368

impatience. Did she know this? It sounded like something he had told her before, something he wanted her to believe.

'I spoke to him the other day. He called me.'

'No, he didn't. You've been speaking to him all year, but he's not there. He's gone, Zo. I can't lose you as well.' His voice faltered; she felt him squeeze her hand.

The mask was snapped back over her mouth. She closed her eyes and let her head sink back into the pillow. The warmth pulled her down. The machine was breathing for her now; in, out, steady as a heartbeat.

'This is what I'm talking about, Doctor.' Dan sounded almost plaintive. 'All year, the same thing. She talks about Caleb as if he's still alive. She keeps doing it. She tells me quite calmly about conversations she's had with him and I don't know if it's a wilful self-deception or if she's really losing her mind with grief. I don't know if I'm supposed to encourage it or be firm with her. She can sound so lucid and normal the rest of the time – you wouldn't think she was delusional, if you met her.' He sighed; she heard the rasp of his hand across his stubbled chin. 'She blames herself, that's what it comes down to. She thought it was just a fever – she gave him ibuprofen and put him to bed so she could finish a painting, she said. Four hours later he was in a coma. I'm not a shrink but it seems pretty obvious to me.'

The low murmur of the other man's voice carried across the room.

'No,' Dan said, indignant now. '*I* don't blame her, of course not. I'm not saying I would have recognised those symptoms any better if I'd been there. I mean, I like to think I'd have taken a second look but we'll never know, will we, so it's kind of moot. I was away working, on the other side of the country – first I knew was a phone call. She got him to hospital in the end, but it was too late. She never even sold the fucking painting, either. She put a knife through it.'

The second voice cut in, its tone soothing.

'I already said, I don't blame her,' Dan repeated. 'But she blames herself. I think she always will. Who the fuck's Ailsa, anyway?'

As she slipped back into the dark she could hear the waves crashing: in, out, in, out.

The next time she opened her eyes Dan had gone. In his place there was a man in a white coat looking down at her with dark, shrewd eyes. She lifted a hand limply to pull at the mask. The man held up a palm in warning; he peered at the machine, checked its display, hesitated briefly and nodded, before removing the plastic from her face.

'How are you feeling?' His accent was polite, clipped, Scottish.

'I don't know yet.'

He gave her a brisk, professional smile, but his brow remained creased in a frown.

'I'm Dr Chaudhry. You're making good progress. I'm hoping we'll have you off this in a few days, if you continue.' He indicated the machine beside her.

'Was my husband here? Or did I dream that?'

'No, he was here. I expect Sister's made him go home for some rest. He's been by your bedside for the best part of three weeks, you know.'

'Three *weeks*? But—' She struggled to sit up; immediately the burning started up in her lungs. Dr Chaudhry pressed her shoulder gently until she sank back to the bed.

'You've been very ill, Mrs Bergman. We had you in intensive care for the first ten days.'

'What—'

'Pneumonia resulting from hypothermia, and Acute Respiratory Distress Syndrome. You nearly drowned, you know. A lot of people don't recover from that, but I'm pleased to say you're doing better than I'd hoped. You were lucky they were able to get the air ambulance out to you quickly.'

370

'I don't remember . . . ' She looked at him; images tumbled back out of the darkness. 'Wait – Charles was there. He pulled me out of the water.'

'You were very lucky,' he repeated, more firmly this time, as if that was an end to the discussion.

'What's the worst of it?'

'You're through the worst of it now, Mrs Bergman,' he said, in that same crisp voice. 'The antibiotics have been very effective. I've had to be careful with the dose, because of—' He stopped abruptly and glanced down at her notes. 'As I say, I think we'll have you breathing on your own very soon.'

'No, I mean – I heard my husband tell you to keep the worst of it from me. I don't want anything kept from me. I need to know what happened. Charles and Edward – they were both there, on the beach. Are they OK?'

He took a long time to answer. He perched on the side of the bed before he did so, as if he had been taught that this position conveyed sympathy. She knew what he was going to say before he spoke.

'I'm afraid the two men who went in after you weren't so lucky. The younger one was pulled out of the water, they brought him here too, but – there was nothing we could do for him. The older man – they think he was swept out to sea. They called off the search after two days. They didn't find his body. I'm so sorry, Mrs Bergman.' He stood and rearranged his clipboard.

'What about Robbie?' she managed to say.

He frowned. 'Who's Robbie?'

'Robbie Logan.'

'I'm afraid I don't—'

'Oh, that's the wee boy that went missing from the island,' said a woman's voice, from the other side of the room. Zoe turned her head and saw a round-faced nurse with neat black braids wheeling a trolley piled with towels and plastic bowls.

'Nurse Andreou keeps up with the local news better than I do,' the doctor said, dipping his head in apology.

'They found him that evening over here on the mainland,' the nurse said.

'Oh, God. What happened?' Zoe craned her neck to see her.

'Oh no – he's safe and well.' She dropped a towel on Zoe's bed and smiled. 'He'd managed to stow away on the last ferry out that morning – can you believe it? Hid in the back of a van – the driver didn't find him till he stopped at a petrol station. They were halfway to Glasgow by then. But he took the lad straight to a police station.'

'Is he OK?'

'Last I read, he'd gone to stay with relatives in Inverness. Well, they'd reopened the case about the other wee boy that went missing up there and the family's all caught up in that, so he's in the best place. He's got to testify and all the rest of it, poor mite. Time to give you a wash, if that's all right?'

'I'll leave you to it,' Dr Chaudhry said. 'Try to get some rest, Mrs Bergman. You survived. What you need to do now is get yourself well.'

'Wait, Doctor.' She flapped at his sleeve and he turned back. 'Did you see Edward? Did you treat him?'

'Edward?'

'The guy who drowned.'

'No, I didn't treat him. He died at the scene, I was told. I'm sorry.'

'He was trying to save me. They both were.' Her eyes stung with tears and her chest constricted; she felt her breath grow shallow and fluttering, like a panicked bird caught beneath her ribs.

'So I understand. The police want to talk to you about it. I've told them you're not well enough yet. I shall continue to tell them that for the time being. Meanwhile, try not to upset yourself.' He replaced the mask before she could protest.

'I'll dig out the paper if you like,' the nurse whispered, leaning in with her flannel as the door closed behind him. 'You can read the story for yourself, if it won't upset you too much?'

Zoe nodded. The nurse lifted her right arm and began to sponge her down, but she hardly registered it. She felt numb with misery. Edward *and* Charles. And it was her fault. She had never intended to take anyone with her. Ailsa had only wanted her, she had been sure of that.

24

They kept her sedated for a few days afterwards; it was felt that her distress was impeding her recovery. Then, one evening, she woke to find all the lights dimmed and Charles sitting by her bed, watching her. Violet and gold streaks showed in the sky through the window beyond him. He wore a tweed coat and held an old-fashioned brown trilby hat in his lap.

'Are you real?' she asked, pulling the mask down and easing herself up on one elbow.

'Quite real, I assure you.' He took her hand; his touch was warm and dry, and entirely solid. 'Reports of my death have been greatly exaggerated.' He winked.

'I can't tell any more. They've been giving me these drugs.' She tried to focus on him. 'They said you were lost at sea.'

'No, no. I chose not to be found. Not quite the same thing.'

'But no one could have survived in that water, surely?'

'Mm. That's what they said last time. But they can be mistaken.' He gave her an indulgent smile.

She opened her mouth to ask what he meant by last time, before she remembered her sight of him on the cliff, the words he had shouted into the storm, the grave in the cellar.

'It's you, isn't it?' she whispered, after a while. The hospital had fallen unnervingly silent around them; only a distant set of footsteps could be heard tapping down a far-off corridor. 'You're Ailsa's son. That's why they never found his body. He didn't die.'

Charles gave a soft chuckle. 'Who would believe that, Zoe? A man who can't die, like the Wandering Jew of legend? Besides, that would make me a hundred and fifty years old. Although there are days when I feel like it, I can tell you.'

'It's true, though, isn't it? You're a – a cambion.'

'What do *you* think?'

She gave a dry laugh. 'I think I'm maybe not the most reliable judge of what's real and what's not right now.'

'Oh, I don't know.' The corners of his mouth twitched mischievously. 'A brush with death is thought to convey great insight. In another age, you'd have been hailed as a visionary or a prophet.'

'Or burned as a witch.' She tried to laugh again, but it died on her lips. It seemed to her that Charles's face had aged since she had last seen him, in some indefinable way, but his blue eyes remained as sharp and knowing as ever. 'I think,' she said slowly, watching him, 'it's like you said. There are more things in heaven and earth, *etcetera*.'

'Then perhaps that's all the answer you need.'

The silence deepened.

'You saved my life,' she said after a while.

'I played a part. You have Bill McCrae to thank too.'

'Bill?' She frowned.

'We all came back to the house together. He wanted to talk to you about the phone. We arrived in the nick of time to find you down there on the beach. I thought I understood what was happening. Edward hurled himself after you. I had to follow you both. But there wasn't time – all I could do was leave you on the shore and go back for Edward.' His gaze moved away to the window. 'It was Bill who gave you first aid and called the air ambulance. Without him, you'd likely not have survived.' He passed his hands over his face as if washing it, and a long sigh shook his frame. 'But I was too late for Edward. I can't forgive myself for that. It seemed better to vanish. That's not so hard if you know the coast.' When he lowered his hands she saw the pain in his eyes. The room darkened around them.

'You warned me to stay away from Edward. I should have listened. He'd be alive now if I had.'

'But I was the one who understood the danger. It was my fault – I should have spoken more plainly when I had the chance. I was a coward, and so I failed you both.'

She wanted to ask him what he meant by that, but she realised she was afraid to hear the answer.

'What about Dougie?' she asked, instead.

He shifted in his seat and turned back to her. 'He tried to run, in all the confusion, but he couldn't get off the island with no ferries, and Bill had a few of the village men primed to detain him when he got to town. They've been arrested, for the video. Both of them. Mick confessed everything – he's in a terrible way, by all accounts, though they both maintain that Iain's death was an accident – they say he was frightened at being caught, they chased him up to the cliff and the next they knew, he'd lost his footing in the dark.' He lifted one shoulder in a helpless shrug. 'Even so, that means they've been concealing information, and of course there's the business with Annag. Her father beat Dougie black and blue when he came home. It will come to trial, eventually.'

'Christ. Poor Kaye.' She looked down at her hands.

'Yes. She's taken the girls back to Glasgow, to her parents'.'

'You've been back, then? To the island?' She struggled to sit up, curious.

'Of course not.' He smiled. 'I'm missing, presumed dead. I've picked all this up from the local papers.'

'But – can't you tell them you survived? Let people have some good news, out of all this. They'd be so relieved to see you.'

He shook his head. 'They'd be frightened, Zoe. People there are superstitious, underneath. I'd become an object of curiosity and speculation. No – I'm an old bachelor, with no ties – it's easy for me to slip my moorings. It won't be the first time. They'll remember me fondly for a while, perhaps, and then they'll forget. It was time to move on, anyway.'

'No ties – what about Horace? He won't forget.'

'Dear Horace.' His face creased with sadness. 'My house-keeper will have taken him in. I made her promise she would, if anything ever happened to me. She'll spoil him rotten in his old age. I miss him terribly, of course. But he's not the first companion I've had to leave behind.'

She gestured to the door. 'You can't just disappear. I mean, someone must have seen you come in here, tonight.'

'Oh, I'm quite practised at slipping past unnoticed.'

'Because you're a shape-shifter?'

'If you like.' His blue eyes glittered with a mischievous light, and the lines around them deepened.

'You knew about Caleb all along, didn't you?' she asked quietly.

His expression sobered. 'I could see that you had suffered a great loss. That was all, at first. The kind that opens up a crack that lets the dark in. I feared the house would prey on that.'

'It was my fault. I was working on a painting – I resented losing a day on it because he was sick and off school. I sent him to bed to get him out of the way. I told him, "I'm going to finish my work while you sleep." That was the last thing he ever heard me say.' She gulped back tears. 'Not even "I love you".'

'But he would have known that.'

'Did you see him?' She grasped his hand. 'When you were on the cliff, and you looked down and saw me. Did you see Caleb too, in the water?'

'Caleb wasn't there, Zoe. That was a trick played on your mind. A cruel trick.'

'You saw someone, though.' Her eyes narrowed. 'You spoke to them. You said, *Leave her*. You saw *her*, didn't you?'

When he offered no reply, she nodded, as if in answer to her own question. 'You knew she was buried there. Ailsa, I mean. That's why you wouldn't come to the house.'

He sighed. 'Yes. Poor Bonar. He loved her, you know, in an entirely chaste way. He felt he had failed her, and the boy. That was his way of making it up to her, in death – to defy the minister and bury her secretly in the old crypt, so that she would be in consecrated ground after all. He thought it was what she would have wanted. In fact, it was the worst thing he could possibly have done.'

'Because she could never leave.'

He dipped his head as if in acknowledgement. 'Consecration never meant much in that place anyway. Older, darker forces had claimed that ground long before the Church came.'

'So the house *was* cursed?'

He tilted his head as if weighing the question. 'I wouldn't use that word. Things were done there, over the centuries, that had left their imprint. So when Tamhas began his experiments, the atmosphere was primed to act as a conduit. But he didn't understand the nature of what he had unleashed. Neither did Ailsa.'

She shifted against her pillows and pushed herself upright. The last streaks of twilight through the window had faded, turning the oblong of sky deep indigo. Shadows moved over the hollows of his face. Zoe wondered, briefly, why the nurses had not switched the lights on yet, and hoped they would not, for a while; it was more companionable this way. 'What do you mean?'

'She acted out of love, as I told you before. She believed that at seven years the boy would inherit his father's nature. To her – a minister's daughter, steeped in Victorian Presbyterian

378

theology – that meant only one thing – evil – and she felt she must protect him from it, at any price. She didn't understand, you see, that he would have a choice.'

'I don't understand either.'

He fixed her with a serious look. 'Ailsa believed that her husband had succeeded in calling up a demon. But it's only New Testament Christian theology, which is really a very young religion in the history of human stories, that equates that word with pure evil. Older traditions knew that the *Lilin*, the night-spirits, were ambiguous. In the Old Testament they are called simply *the Watchers*. She forgot, you see, that even in the Bible they are rebel angels, and that rebellion is an act of free will.' He paused and pulled at his beard. 'That was what she failed to understand – that her son would have a choice. There is always a choice to turn to the light. Remember that, when the time comes.'

The tone of his voice made her shiver, and she had to look away.

'Why do you talk about her son in the third person like that, as if he were a stranger?'

Charles bowed his head. 'Because it's a story from long ago, and that boy is a stranger to me. And now I must go. Better not outstay my welcome.'

He pushed his chair back and stood, pressing a hand to his lower back, as if his old joints pained him. Zoe clutched at his other hand.

'*Wait* – I'll see you again, won't I?'

'Never doubt it.' He smiled. 'Not for a while, perhaps. We have our journeys to make, you and I. But we'll meet one day, of course.'

'But – how will we stay in touch? Where are you going?' Panic rose in her voice.

'Don't worry. I'll know how to find you, when the time is right.' He bent and placed a dry kiss on the top of her head. 'Be brave. It's not over yet.'

Despite his words, an unexpected warmth spread through her, tingling along her limbs; she sank back on to the pillow and watched him set his old hat on his head before buttoning his coat.

'I'd like you to have this, until we meet again.' He reached for her hand and dropped a cold object from his bunched fist to her open palm. She looked down to see Ailsa's silver cross pendant and jerked her head up, fear in her eyes.

'Won't this bring bad luck?'

'On the contrary.' He gave her that same earnest look, and she thought how out of time he looked, like a classical actor from an old movie. 'I like to think it will bring you courage.'

'Will I need it?' She heard the waver in her voice.

'One always needs courage.' His eyes gleamed. At the door, he turned and touched a finger to the brim of his hat. She could only see him in silhouette against the light. 'Dan is a good man, Zoe,' he said, as if it were an afterthought. 'He stayed. Let him in.'

She was about to reply, but the door had clicked softly shut behind him. Somewhere in the corridor a nurse switched on the lights – rather later than usual, it seemed to her – and all the room's shadows were chased away by the bright glare.

25

'You'll be going home soon, my lovely.' Nurse Andreou bustled about arranging the latest of Dan's flowers in a glass on the bedside cabinet. 'I'm going to miss you. And your husband – he's charmed the pants off everyone. Look at these gorgeous roses.'

'I don't think I've been much company,' Zoe said. They had taken her off the ventilator now but she spent most of her time pretending to be asleep, in order to avoid having to talk to Dan.

'Nonsense. Dr Chaudhry's very pleased with you. He wants to sort you out with a mood stabiliser, and obviously that requires special care because of your condition—'

'My *condition?*' Zoe shuffled herself up the bed. 'You mean, my lungs?'

The nurse turned pale under her careful make-up. 'Oh. Me and my – wait there – I'll get the doctor.'

Dr Chaudhry arrived with his usual harassed expression. He ushered the nurse out before closing the door behind him.

'I understand Nurse Andreou has been indiscreet.' He stood by the bed, rapidly clicking his ballpoint pen in and out with his thumb, as he did when he was preoccupied. 'I was going to leave it a little longer, but we may as well discuss it now, before your husband comes back. Mrs Bergman, you're in the early stages of pregnancy. As far as I can tell there have been no adverse effects from your recent trauma. You're under-weight, but we're working on that.'

Zoe blinked at him. 'That's not possible.'

'In what sense?'

'I haven't – it only happened once. And he didn't – he pulled out.'

He gave a faint smile. 'I think you're old enough to know that's hardly a failsafe method of contraception.'

'But I had my period a couple of days before, the first one in months. It only lasted a day or so, but I thought—'

'Sperm can live for up to five days, as I'm sure you know. You must have had an early ovulation. That's especially likely if your cycle has been erratic.'

'I'm nearly forty-three. I *can't* be. It must be a mistake.'

'No mistake, I assure you.'

'Does Dan know?' Her eyes widened with panic; she struggled to sit up.

'I haven't said anything to your husband yet. But it is pressing, because the pregnancy will affect what medication I can prescribe for the depression, and that will have a bearing on when you're ready to be discharged.'

'Don't tell him. You can't – it's not for you to decide.'

He set his mouth and glanced at the door, giving the impression, as he often did, that his mind had already moved on to his next patient. 'Mrs Bergman, I realise this is sensitive, but I understand from your husband that you had been living apart before this – occurred. That's why I haven't mentioned it to him – in case there's a question of – well, of course, I wanted to let you know first. As I say, it's very early days, so you're in plenty of time to take the appropriate steps if the pregnancy is not welcome news.'

'How long?' she asked.

'Almost four weeks. Conception must have happened shortly before your accident – would that be right?'

She lay back on the pillow and nodded. She thought of Edward; she closed her eyes and dredged up an image of his shy smile, the freckles over his nose, the way his hair fell into his eyes when he looked at her from beneath his fringe, but the details were fading. She thought of that last, frantic tussle in the kitchen, the way he had pushed her up against the sink, his touching apologies afterwards for the ferocity of desire that had overtaken him.

She slid a hand under the sheet and laid it flat on her belly. The whole thing seemed impossible. She tried to picture his parents, wondering where they might be now, as they tried to contain their wordless grief. She had known him so little, she reflected; she had never even asked if he had siblings. Had they lost their only son, as she had? She wondered how much they knew about Edward's death; how much they had been told about her. They would know he died saving a woman from the sea, but would they have heard the rumours?

She spread her fingers out over the warm skin of her concave stomach. Perhaps she should get in touch with them. Would they want to know, she wondered, that there was some part of him left? If they had a grandchild? Would it be crueller to tell them or to keep it from them? She could guess what they would think of her, a woman twice his age. They would blame her for his death.

And with that came the other, darker thought, the one she had tried to push away since Dr Chaudhry's announcement. *If.* Because there was not only her hectic encounter with Edward in the kitchen that day; there was also the night before. That waking dream of Tamhas and his experiments, the unreal shadow lover who had possessed her – that was the word – so thoroughly that she had felt every tremor in her muscles and bones. *If* . . . She could not allow herself to imagine that; she would go mad. It was impossible.

But it also seemed impossible that Charles should have survived the sea that night, and yet he was alive, though he had offered her no real explanation as to how. Every time she recalled his visit she was tempted to write it off as another hallucination, except that there in the drawer of her bedside cabinet was the silver cross he had pressed into her palm. His words came back to her with startling clarity, as if she could see them printed on a page: *Be brave*, he had said. *It's not over yet.* And he talked of Ailsa's child having a choice to turn to the light. *Remember that, when the time comes.* Had he *known*, then? Did he somehow know that she was carrying a seed of that dark island history away inside her?

She squeezed her eyes shut harder and felt the trickle of hot tears down the sides of her face, to her hairline. It was so easy to believe, when she talked to Charles, in a world beyond the visible; without him, all that crumbled away in the fluorescent glare of hospital lights, the bustle and the incessant electronic noises of machines, and everything that had seemed plausible on the island appeared absurd, like the memory of a lurid dream. What if Charles were no more than an old crank who had done too much ayahuasca, and she merely a grieving mother on psychiatric medication, thrown off balance by her own submerged longings?

And then there was Dan to think of. Charles was right; he was a good man, in his way. He had stayed with her, in spite of everything. But would he stay through *this*? Her fingers moved tentatively over her belly; she could hardly credit that anything could have sparked into life there, when she felt so scoured and empty. Perhaps it would be best if she never had to tell him.

When she opened her eyes, Dr Chaudhry had gone. She opened the drawer beside her bed and took out Ailsa's pendant, turning it between her fingers, until the door slammed open and Dan loped through, all broad shoulders and long limbs, flinging himself into the chair with a stream of bright chatter, holding out a bag of Starbucks brownies he knew she wouldn't touch. She bunched the necklace in her fist beneath the blanket and watched him with a pang as he carried on talking, oblivious, through a mouthful of cake. She did not trust herself to speak. It was only now, looking at him, that she began to understand what she stood to lose. Whichever choice she made, it seemed, would rob her of something irreplaceable.

26

'I've been offered a job with the Seattle office,' Dan said, as the seatbelt sign was switched off and all around them the other passengers began to stir and stretch, craning to look for the drinks trolley. 'Less money, but fewer hours. Think about it, will you? I thought it might be a good opportunity.'

'For what? For you to hang out more with Lauren Thing?'

'Jesus, Zo.' He pulled her head to his shoulder and laughed, but there was exhaustion in it. 'Lauren Carrera is married. To a woman named Melissa. We've had this conversation before.'

'Well, I can't see how that would put you off.' She turned to face him and he caught her grin; he ruffled her hair with his knuckles. The beard suited him, she thought; it lent him an air of maturity.

'I thought it would be an opportunity for us. To start over. New city. Leave the old house behind. It's time, don't you think?' When she didn't reply, he withdrew his arm. 'I boxed up Caleb's things while you were away. I couldn't stand to see them any more – it wasn't healthy, Zo. Leaving his room like that, as if he was coming back, all his toys. I thought I was helping you by agreeing, but I realised it was doing the opposite.'

386

'You didn't throw them out?' she asked, in a small voice.

'Of course not. I put them in the attic. I thought we could find a good home for them. The kids' hospital, maybe.'

'Not Mr Bear?' The threat of tears swelled in her throat. She had bought Mr Bear for Caleb while she was pregnant, before they even knew he was Caleb. Dan had not liked the idea of buying toys for the baby before it was born, so she had had to hide it; he had been superstitious about that. Perhaps he had been proved right.

'Hell, no. Mr Bear stays with us.' Dan squeezed her thigh. She pressed her forehead into his shoulder; the plane tilted smoothly into a turn, still rising. 'It doesn't mean we forget him, Zo. But we can't pretend he's coming back. We have to . . . ' He took a breath. 'You know. Live in the present.'

'You sound like Dr Schlesinger.'

'Actually, you'll laugh, but I had a couple sessions with her while you were away. She talks a lot of sense. Where's that trolley?' He lifted himself in his seat, trying to wave down the cabin crew. 'So, will you think about it? Seattle?'

'I'll think about it.' She leaned back against the plush headrest. Dan had managed to get them upgraded to Business somehow; she guessed he had sweet-talked them with tales of his invalid wife. He was good at that, she remembered.

'I found your sketchbook when I was packing up that house,' he said after a while. 'I've got to tell you, there was some interesting stuff in there.'

'That was private,' she said, looking out of the window.

'No shit. It was like some kind of Victorian fetish porn. Never seen you draw things like that before. I'm not saying I didn't like it – just, naturally, I wondered where you got the inspiration.'

'I don't know. It was experimental.' She turned to him in alarm. 'You didn't bring it?'

'I put it in your case. I wasn't sure if it was part of a project, or—'

'Burn it.'

'What?'

'When we get home, I want you to burn it. Don't open it again, I don't want to see it. You shouldn't have brought it.'

'OK, hon, whatever you say.' He stroked her hand with a soothing motion. 'I wasn't to know. Anyway, what's this necklace you've started wearing? You've drawn a woman wearing one exactly like it in the book.'

Her fingers strayed to the silver cross at her throat. 'It's from the island. It was a gift.'

'Oh, yeah? From one of your Scottish lovers, eh?' He nudged her with his elbow and grinned, though there was an edge to it. She managed a weak smile in return.

'From a friend. It's an antique. It carries a lot of the island's history.'

'I don't like it,' he said, with unexpected force. 'I'm not sure I want you carrying the island's history around with you. Burn it along with the pictures, I say. Sooner we can forget that place, the better.'

'The cross is supposed to bring courage,' she said quietly.

'Well, God knows we could all use a bit of that. Right now I'm going for the Dutch kind. Hi!' he said to the smiling quiffed young man who drew up beside their seats. 'Jack Daniel's, on ice. Make it a double. Anything for you, honey?'

She shook her head.

'She'll have some water. Are you OK?' he asked, when the drinks had been served. 'You're very white.'

'I'm a little nauseous, that's all.'

'Uh-huh.' He popped the cap of his miniature bottle with satisfaction. 'Probably those new meds. Dr Chaudhry says you'll be better on those, once you get used to them, and we can get them at home too, if they're working. I liked him, didn't you? Seemed like a good guy.' He leaned forward and began pressing buttons on the screen, scrolling through the movie menu. 'New start, baby,' he said, clapping a hand on her thigh in what she supposed was an encouraging gesture, the way you might slap a horse, but his attention was already fixed on the flickering images in front of him.

She turned away to the window and peered out into the darkening sky. Below them was nothing but cloud; she would not even be able to watch the lights of the coastline receding beneath her. She folded a protective arm around her belly. Before long she would have no choice but to tell Dan that there could be no forgetting her time on the island. Whatever had waited there for her had drawn her in, threaded her into its story, and would follow them to their new life. She carried its history inside her. She would explain all this to him, soon, when the time was right.